Door Into Light

Sequel to *House of Shadows*

Rachel Neumeier

DEDICATION

For all the readers who told me *House of Shadows* didn't feel like the end. You were right.

CONTENTS

-1-

Three weeks before the spring solstice, one week after the door to Kalches had first appeared in this whimsical, unpredictable, willful house where he had lived for the past month and more, Taudde stood before that door, his hand on the knob, recruiting his nerve to open it.

The door to Kalches, land of music and sorcery and the high winds that both cut like knives and sang like harps, stood in the long hallway of the house, between two high, narrow windows. Brilliant sunlight blazed through the nearer of the two; silver moonlight glimmered through the other. Between day and dark stood this door: solid, weathered, and ordinary, exactly as though it was a normal door and had always waited there for a hand to fling it wide. Though it did not match any other door in the house, somehow it did not look out of place. Its frame had been hewn roughly out of granite. The door itself was of common pine, the wood neither stained nor painted nor carved with any decorative figures nor even planed entirely smooth. When Taudde opened that door . . . when he opened it, he knew exactly the wind, fragrant with pine forests and the cold, clean scent of lingering winter, that would skirl out of the distant mountains and into this house.

He did not mean to step through the door, not yet. But this afternoon, weather permitting, he would finally step from this house into Kalches, crossing all the intervening miles in an instant.

He was not looking forward to that at all. Or he was, of course, in a way. He had been so long away; no matter how bitterly he would miss Lonne and the sea, he couldn't help but anticipate his return to the stark, cold country that was his home. But his homecoming would certainly be . . . fraught. Taudde did not at all relish the thought of facing his grandfather and explaining everything that had happened. Or, really, anything that had happened.

Still, he dared not leave his return too late. Three weeks was little enough time.

He had asked leave from the prince of Lirionne to step through that door and into Kalches. Tepres had granted it, of course, exactly as he had promised. At noon today, Taudde would formally ask leave from the king of Lirionne himself, Geriodde Nerenne ken Seriantes. The king would also grant it. Taudde had very little doubt of that. Then he would open this door for the third time, and step through, from the early summer of Lonne, the Pearl of the West, into the lingering stark winter of the Kalchesene mountains.

With Leilis, so that was something, at least; no matter how little Taudde expected to enjoy his own interview with his grandfather, he *did* expect to enjoy witnessing the meeting between that stiff old man and Seathrift of Cloisonné House, which was the name Leilis went by when she put on the robes and manners of a keiso. He wanted to watch the old man try the edge of his tongue against her wit and unshakable composure. She would render his grandfather absolutely speechless, which was not something many people could do, but Taudde had no doubt she would do it. He looked forward to that very much.

But though he was resolved to go through, he thought he had better see how the weather lay on the other side of this door. This door opened into the mountains above the town of Kedres, not into the town itself, and storms were common in those mountains as winter turned to early spring. If the weather looked too difficult, well, that would be reason enough to put off his homecoming at least another day.

"Well? Will you open it, or do you merely mean to admire it as it stands?" inquired a light, quick voice at his shoulder. It was a voice that, to Taudde, was unmistakably underlain with an echo of the dragon's voice. When ordinary men called Prince Tepres the Dragon's heir, they were generally thinking merely of the king, the infamous Dragon of Lirionne. But ordinary men did not know of the true dragon beneath the mountain, and ordinary men did not possess Taudde's trained ear.

Karah, Moonflower of Cloisonné House, the newest and youngest keiso in all of Lonne, stood beside the prince, her fingers twined with his. Though she had come to this house this

morning ostensibly to visit her younger sister, Taudde's student
Nemienne, the romance between Prince Tepres and the beautiful
young keiso was a very, very open secret throughout Lonne.
Karah was far too honest to hide her feelings for the prince, and
as his father did not disapprove, Prince Tepres also openly
acknowledged his infatuation with her. Everyone looked forward
to an eventual flower wedding. This gave the city a charming,
pretty subject for speculation and gossip and helped take
everyone's mind off the coming solstice. Taudde was perfectly
certain the king had thought of that, and would not have been
surprised to discover that Prince Tepres was deliberately making
certain public gestures of favor for the same reason.

Jeres Geliadde, the prince's companion and bodyguard,
stood behind them both. Nemienne hovered to one side, most of
her attention on the door. She had long since accepted her
sister's romance with the prince and wasn't much concerned
with that; she was much more interested in doors and windows
and the whims of the house. And in Kalches. Taudde had not yet
decided whether he would permit her to accompany him to his
home. He was almost certain it would be safe enough for her to
come, but . . . he wasn't entirely certain. None of them could be
entirely certain about anything of the kind until the solstice came
and went and did not give way to a summer of iron and blood
and fire.

Prince Tepres said drily, "If you are not inclined to open it,
Taudde, I might lay my hand to it."

Jeres Geliadde cleared his throat.

"Or, then, perhaps not," the prince conceded, tilting a straw-
pale eyebrow at Jeres. He did not touch the door, but half turned
to give his bodyguard an ironic look. The prince's thin, arrogant
mouth seemed made for irony. He bent that look on Taudde.
"Someone needs to, however."

Taudde eyed Prince Tepres with resignation.

"Of course my father will give you leave to go, Taudde.
Surely you don't doubt it."

Taudde steadied himself with an effort of will. "No. I don't
doubt your father's . . . generosity."

"Your own grandfather's, then?" the prince asked, more
gently than was his habit.

3

A sudden hammering on the door interrupted Taudde's attempt to frame an acceptable answer.

It wasn't the door to Kalches; that would have been *far* beyond merely startling. This was merely the ordinary door that simply opened out onto the Lane of Shadows. Men did come to that door from time to time: mages who came to study bardic sorcery or the occasional tradesman daring enough to seek custom among the mages who lived along this lane. Prince Tepres, of course, or one or another of the young men who were his companions. Now and again, on a few memorable occasions, the king himself.

None of them had a knock quite of this sort. There was a disconcerting urgency to it.

Prince Tepres, quirking a pale eyebrow at the intrusion, stepped forward to answer that hammering. It was not his place to do so, but he might have meant to reprimand whomever was there for so rude a summons. Certainly whoever pounded roughly on the door would be embarrassed to find he had disturbed not a mere foreigner but the Dragon's own heir.

Taudde, moved by an alarm he did not entirely understand, said sharply, "Wait!" just as the prince reached the door.

The prince, startled, turned his head, to look back at Taudde.

Jeres Geliadde, responding perhaps to the alarm in Taudde's voice, thrust himself past Karah and Nemienne and strode suddenly forward, his hand dropping to the hilt of his sword.

The prince's hand fell on the latch. The latch dropped and turned under the pressure of that touch.

The door slammed open.

For a heartbeat, that was all. There were men there, poised on the weathered gray stone of the porch, a crowd of men: a few in the black of the King's Own and a handful in the flat red and gray of the army; two men in the black and white robes of mages, and, most fraught of all, three men wearing robes embroidered at cuffs and collar with the saffron-gold that no one in Lonne but those of royal blood had any right to wear. The one in the forefront was a man nearing middle years, heavyset and hard-featured, powerful and angry. The man a step behind was younger and more elegant, with a narrow mouth and small chin;

his angular eyes cold with bitter triumph. The third was a younger man, well back, surrounded by soldiers.

Taudde had never met the left-hand princes of Lirionne, but he knew at once who they must be: the youngest must be Prince Geradde, of whom he knew nothing but the name. The cold, elegant man must be Prince Telis, whom the folk of Lonne called Sa-Telis, the serpent, even to his face. He had a serpent's look to him: a cold look. He was said to be mage-gifted and clever and dangerous to cross.

And the one in front had to be Prince Sehonnes, eldest of the king's sons, but keiso-born and thus not his father's heir.

Not the king's heir so long as Prince Tepres lived.

Taudde's flute, recently carved of driftwood he had gathered himself from the broken shore below the Laodd, was in his hand. It had come there as automatically as Jeres Geliadde had drawn his own sword. But it was not the same as his old flute, which Taudde missed suddenly and acutely.

But for a long, reverberating moment, no one moved or spoke. Jeres would have leaped forward; he had his hand on his prince's arm, ready to snatch him back from danger. But Prince Tepres had flung up a hand to check him and by that seemed to check them all, so the moment drew out, tension singing in the air until it became all but audible.

Prince Sehonnes, too, held up his hand. He, as Tepres, might have meant to restrain his men. But there was something else in the gesture. Something ostentatious, something that was meant for display: *Look at me*, like a vain boy showing off a new and expensive bauble to his friends.

Prince Tepres was staring at Sehonnes, at his hand . . . at the ring he wore: a heavy iron ring in the shape of a dragon, with twin rubies for eyes. Their father's ring. The ring of the Dragon of Lirionne. Tepres had paled. His thin mouth set hard and stern, and he put his shoulders back and stood very straight. He looked, in that moment, very like his father.

"Brother," said Prince Sehonnes, grimly, and Sa-Telis added, sharp and urgent, "I want the sorcerer alive!"

Tepres tried to swing the door closed. The heavy gauntleted hand of one of the soldiers caught it, a booted foot came down to brace it open, a sword went up . . . Jeres jerked his prince back and caught that descending blade with his own shorter sword, closing with the other man to counteract the soldier's advantage of reach, shoving the man back out onto the porch with his weight and the sheer force of his will. But Jeres was only one man, and the door was still open.

Tepres, unarmed, reached after a sword he did not have.

Taudde lifted his flute, meaning to get those men off his porch and sweep the left-hand princes after them—perhaps he would fling them all into the dark under the mountain; he thought he could and was frightened and angry enough to try. But the mages blocked him, Sa-Telis stepping to the side to get a clear view of Taudde. Of course the mage-prince and his allies had known Taudde would be here. Both those mages had actually studied with him—he recognized them now—they knew very little sorcery and pretended to scorn what little they knew, but they knew him a little, and they had plainly come prepared to counter his sorcery.

And Taudde, who had devoted considerable thought during the past winter to ways in which a bardic sorcerer might avoid being caught in a magecrafted net of silence, found himself, in the moment in which it mattered, unprepared to meet them. He had more or less trusted the Dragon of Lirionne; *he* had not expected the door of this house to open onto enemies and sudden battle.

So he was not quick enough to answer the attack when the mageworking set itself against him, binding him into silence so that his flute uttered no sound, so that his shout of frustration fell into silence and was utterly lost. Taudde found himself unable to unravel that mageworking as fast and as powerfully as the two mages set it.

Out on the porch men struggled, but Taudde, caught by a web of magecrafted silence, could not hear them. Jeres had killed one man. Another of his attackers, slashed across the belly, folded slowly down over his terrible wound. The man's mouth was open, but if he was screaming, Taudde could not hear him, either. Prince Sehonnes' mouth was open as well, but he seemed to be shouting rather than screaming. He was pressing straight forward through the melee, toward Prince Tepres. One soldier had gotten around Jeres—there were too many men, far too many, they were getting in each other's way, but that wouldn't last and anyone could see how this particular battle must end.

Tepres, unarmed save for a short belt knife, gestured urgently for Karah and Nemienne to get back and himself stepped forward to face his attackers. Nemienne was trying to pull her sister away, but Karah was clearly refusing to go without Tepres—the girl wasn't actually wrong, the prince absolutely could not be allowed to sacrifice himself—Taudde started forward, meaning to grab the prince's arm and haul him bodily back farther into the house, which after all was not an ordinary house—there was no need, even now, for heroic last stands, but with the silence on him he could not even *say* so.

Jeres Geliadde faced two more armed men, but another man, behind him, kicked him behind the knee, and Jeres collapsed to one knee. The man drew back his sword for a killing thrust . . . and Jeres, his face blank, lunged upward and sideways and whirled his sword around in a short, vicious arc. Prince Sehonnes' hand leaped away from his arm, seemingly of its own accord, blood spraying across the gray stone. The left-hand prince staggered, his expression one of disbelief and anger rather than pain. At the same time, the man behind Jeres completed his thrust, and Jeres, his body fully extended in his own smooth attack, could not even attempt to counter that blow. He did not counter it, and the sword slid into him, stabbing from back to front so that several inches of the blade emerged from his chest.

Despite that terrible blow, Jeres, in a smooth continuation of his own movements, as though stepping through the choreographed movements of a dance, caught Sehonnes' amputated hand as it descended and flung it with deadly accuracy past half a dozen startled soldiers and through the door of the house. Where Prince Tepres, as though the move had been practiced in advance, put up his own hand and caught it.

For a moment that seemed frozen in time, everyone stopped. Prince Sehonnes, face twisted, clutched at his maimed arm. Even the serpent-prince hesitated, his dark eyes narrowed, to all appearances unmoved, but his attention momentarily fixed on his stricken brother.

Taudde, feeling as though he had been somehow caught in a play, was seized now by a wild desire to laugh. He seized

Tepres' arm in a hard grip and pulled him, resist though he would, back down the hall, sweeping the girls with them, and the pause shattered. In perfect silence their enemies came after them, rushing forward—too many and too well armed and nothing to laugh at, so that Prince Tepres yielded at last and backed up willingly, shoving Karah behind him, but it was impossible, anyone could see they would not be able to get clear. The soldiers rushed forward, and in that instant, without thought, Taudde seized the knob he found ready under his hand, flung open the door, and snatched Prince Tepres and Karah sideways out of the house and out of Lonne entirely, into sudden dazzling cold. The mage-prince strode forward, his mouth open in an inaudible shout, but Taudde slammed the door shut between them, staggering with the force of that motion and with footing gone suddenly uncertain.

Prince Tepres, staggering also, jerked himself free of Taudde's grip, shoved Karah away toward safety, and whirled back toward the door to face his brothers, lifting Sehonnes' amputated hand as though he might fling it at their faces in a macabre gesture of defiance.

Only the door was not there. Where it should have stood was only brilliant light pouring down a steep knife-edged ridge and into the empty gulf beyond, light glittering off an equally steep cliff rising on the other side: light and naked stone, empty air and blowing snow, here in the heights where snow would linger all through the short northern summer.

Tepres straightened, slowly. In one hand he still held the grotesque trophy his bodyguard had thrown to him, but not, now, as though he were aware of it. Tipping his head back, he stared up at the sharp peaks above them. Karah, who had stumbled into the snow beside the path, scrambled urgently to her feet, forgetful of keiso dignity, and then stopped as well, struck by the shock of cold and the stunning view. She turned slowly in a circle, peering in astonishment down from the heights. Far below, a road curved around a shoulder of the mountain where they stood. Taudde, too, glanced down, though he already knew where they were. The jagged pattern of these mountains were familiar, though less so from this angle. He knew exactly where they were: high on the side of Kerre Irelle, greatest of the mountains that loomed above the town of Kedres. He could follow in his mind's eye the curve of this road down and down and farther down, toward the green valley and distant town still invisible below.

"Of course you would seize upon this door, of all doors in that house," Prince Tepres said at last. "Of course you would. And . . . where is the door now?" His tone was commendably neutral.

Taudde cleared his throat, glancing up the bare slant of gray stone. The wind drove tiny particles of snow into their faces, stinging. In Lonne, the warmth of summer had already come. Below, in the valley, he knew spring flowers would be blooming. But nothing at all occupied these heights but stone and snow, singing winds and glittering light.

"Of course," Tepres said once more, following his glance. Straightening, he faced Taudde straight on, as though they were adversaries. His voice was still neutral, but undertones of wariness and grim suspicion lay beneath the neutrality.

Taudde could not even blame him. "If I hadn't closed it, they could have come through after us," he pointed out, a shade too quickly. He heard the defensiveness in his own voice. He *felt* defensive, embarrassed, as though he were at fault. He said sharply, "We had to get out of their reach—beyond the reach of their mageworking as well as their blades—that, first of all."

"Yes, of course," Tepres said politely. The prince didn't say, *There were other doors in that hall,* though that was true. He didn't say, *Any of them would have been better than this, for me,* though that was without question true.

He didn't have to say anything of the sort. Taudde knew it perfectly well. He started to say something else, justification or excuse; it was perfectly true that he had not had time to *choose* which door to open, though he could not blame Prince Tepres for his mistrust.

Karah broke the moment. "Where's *Nemienne?*" she asked, sharp and desperate, and both Taudde and Prince Tepres broke off to stare at her and then, in growing horror, at the ice-glazed stone around them.

Nemienne was not there. Only the three of them, in all these empty heights.

"My half-brothers—" Prince Tepres began, and then halted.

He had started to say *My brothers have no reason to harm her*, Taudde guessed. But they all knew that was not true. Because the girl was Taudde's own student, and had been for months, and if Prince Sehonnes forgot that or forgave it, Sa-Telis surely would not. "The left-hand princes were focused on Prince Tepres," he said quickly. "And on me. Not on Nemienne. She will have gained the safety of another door, I'm certain. She could see and open any door in that hallway—they were only steps away."

This was plausible. It might even be true. They could not know, and had no way to find out, but it *could* be true. Karah drew a breath and pressed a hand over her mouth, and Tepres went to her. She blinked hard and her gaze fell to the grisly hand he still held. "Your father . . ."

Tepres looked down, too, and his mouth tightened against, Taudde suspected, an exclamation of disgust. Moving with quick, decisive precision, the young prince stripped his father's iron ring from his brother's bloody hand and then, in uncontrollable revulsion, hurled the hand away away as hard as he could, so hard that he staggered and might have fallen save that Karah took his arm and steadied him.

The prince's breath came hard. He stared after the vanished hand as though he might actually be able to see it—no. As though that horrid token of battle was not after all what he saw. He held his father's dragon ring clenched in his left hand, but he took Karah's hand with his right and she did not pull away.

"We cannot know what has happened," Tepres said. "Not to my father nor your sister. Nemienne was not in their grasp when we fled, and they will not take time to pursue her now. Above all, it is a disaster for my half-brothers to lose me to Kalches." Then he faced Taudde and added, with an edge to his voice, "To be sure, it is a disaster for me as well."

Taudde didn't move. "Prince Tepres, we are here through no intent of mine. But other chances might have been worse. If we had fled under the mountain, they might have followed, and then what? Would you have led Sa-Telis and his mages beneath the mountain? Risked your own death there in the dark of the dragon's cavern? Your brothers—"

"Half-brothers," the prince said sharply. "*Half*-brothers. Sehonnes—Telis, one is hardly surprised by *his* treachery, but even Geradde—even Geradde was with them—" he broke off, pressing a hand against his mouth. Karah laid a tentative hand on his arm, and he did not jerk away, but straightened his shoulders, lowered his hand, and said in a hard tone, "Jeres knew *exactly* what he was doing when he struck Sehonnes. Did you see him? Did you see what he did?"

"He knew he couldn't evade the blow. He chose deliberately to do as he did. I am sorry for his death, and your loss."

Tepres laughed, a sharp, bitter sound, reminding Taudde that this young prince was not unacquainted with death and loss. The prince began to speak, but stopped. Then he said at last, "I will hope for the opportunity to tell the tale of his courage and loyalty. We can only wonder which other men will show such quality in the coming days." He glanced again to the empty air where the door should have stood. "You cannot bring back the door?"

Taudde, too, glanced up the mountain. But then he shook his head. "I think it was, in a very real sense, never here. Not from this side."

Tepres nodded, unsurprised. But he said, "If not a door, then perhaps—"

"I'm sorry, Prince Tepres. I'm not a legendary mage, to set a thousand invisible doors into a house when I build it. Or even one, into the stone of this mountain."

"Will you tell me your bardic sorcery cannot fling a road through the air itself between my mountains and yours? Or that you do not have the skill or the strength to do it?"

Taudde paused. Prince Tepres, after all, had *seen* Taudde wield sorcery as a tool and a weapon. With both skill and strength, and under the most dire circumstances. He said at last, "There was a great deal of power loose that night, you will recall. You will recall . . . afterward, it was not the same."

Tepres seemed only half convinced, but he said only, "If your bardic sorcery cannot open a proper door, then I must trust you to protect and guard Karah while I take the long road home." He looked, in that moment, sufficiently determined to try.

Taudde waited a moment, out of respect for that brave declaration. Karah glanced from one of them to the other, but said nothing; he was certain she already understood that what the prince proposed was impossible. Finally he nodded toward the road that curved across the face of the mountain. "That road leads to Kedres. You're in the heart of Kalches, and it's a hard road through these mountains even in fair summer weather— harder still in this season, when sudden killing storms can come out of any clear sky. But suppose you lived to reach Teleddes, and then Pinenne, and took a riverboat down the Kemsennes and so came back at last to Lonne: what do you suppose you would find waiting for you there?"

The prince met Taudde's eyes steadily, but said nothing.

Taudde said softly, "Even if I could make a sorcerous door, set it into the air, open it across hundreds of miles . . . should I send you back to Lonne? Would you even be wise to go back, if a door opened for you? That is your father's ring in your hand, is it not? Who rules in Lonne, now? Who now is the Dragon of Lirionne?"

Tepres glanced down at his clenched fist. After a moment, slowly, as though it took physical effort, he opened his hand. The iron ring lay there, his father's dragon ring, the twin rubies of its eyes like sparks of fire in the brilliant sunlight of the high mountains.

Closing his hand again without answering, Tepres thrust the ring into his belt pouch. His hands were shaking, but that might have been the cold.

"And in less than a month, the solstice will break the Treaty," Taudde went on, remorseless because he had no choice. "I swore an oath to you and to your father. But the solstice will free me from that, too. And here we are, the two of us, your father's son and my grandfather's grandson." Taudde paused once more. Then he said, "Prince Tepres, I must ask that you release me from my oath."

Karah flinched, but Tepres did not. He had clearly known already that this request must come. He said, an edge of bitterness underlying the steady calm of his voice, "Of course I free you of it, Prince Chontas Taudde ser Omientes ken Lariodde. After all, I would not wish you to be forced to *break* your oath."

Taudde bowed his head in acknowledgment and sincere gratitude. "We will go down to my grandfather's house. No one will offer Karah insult or offense; I promise you that." He hesitated, looking at the pale, set face of the Dragon's heir, because he could not promise as much for Tepres. Who, from his air of hard-edged arrogance, knew that perfectly well. Taudde said instead, layering his voice with undertones of sincerity and determination, "However events play out, Prince Tepres, I will ask you to believe that I am still your friend."

Tepres did not answer. But he did not, at least, throw that carefully proffered gesture back in Taudde's face. That was a greater generosity than Taudde had really expected.

He said, "It is a day and a night from this place to—"

"Taudde," said Karah. "Are the storms in this season truly so dangerous?" She was not looking at him, but past him, out and up at the stark stone and the sky. Her voice came out small and clear, but the undertones were all of growing fear.

Taudde stopped, and turned, following her gaze, up and up, to the storm that was rolling down from the heights.

Even as he watched, the storm cloaked the farthest mountains, Kerre Ires and Kerre Gaur, in a pewter-hard dusk struck through with lances of lightning. It was still distant, the thunder had not yet reached them, but Taudde thought he felt it in his bones. Streamers of cloud were already shredding around the high peaks, and below the clouds, not the whirling white blizzards of winter but, far worse, the freezing rains of spring, glazing all that they touched in deadly ice.

Tepres raised an expressive eyebrow.

Taudde played them through the storm.

He played warmth and quiet air out of his flute . . . a simple little melody, at first, a melody almost any bard in Kalches could have woven, not even real sorcery, not as Kalchesene bardic sorcerers used the term. But he layered a harmony beneath the melodic line as the storm came down on them, bending the cutting winds and icy rain aside so that they walked in a space of quiet air. Even a simple harmony took sorcery, with his simple flute. He wished he had twin-pipes. Or an ekonne horn. Or, most of all, another sorcerer to help him.

Ice glazed the road, so that they could not go quickly. He might have pulled warmth out of the stone to melt the ice, if he had had the attention and strength to spare. Nemienne could have done it, if he had not lost her; her skill was unpredictable and fit peculiarly into the world, but she could have called the warmth of remembered summer into the stone of the roadway.

Taudde had been afraid for her because he had left her behind; but now he feared his carelessness might have doomed them all. But he could not even take time to curse himself for losing Nemienne. Listening to the heartbeat of the storm, he scattered a handful of notes around and through his main harmony, sending lightning to strike behind and beside them, closer than he liked, barely far enough away. Karah, directly in front of him, flinched and gasped. Taudde might have, too, if he had been able to spare the breath to gasp.

So far as Taudde could tell, Tepres did not even twitch. His concentration was that entire. He was in front, finding their way along the icy road, seeking always the step where one might set a hand against the cliff to their left, where if one's foot slipped, there was enough space to catch one's balance. The drop to their right was sheer, the freezing rain slashing down into emptiness; if they had come near to the gentler slopes, they could not see well enough to know it.

Karah came behind Tepres, so he might catch her if she slipped. Sometimes she did slip; sometimes they all did, but Karah's delicate slippers had never been meant for anything but the polished floors of civilized life and were already tattered. Tepres had wanted to give her his boots, but her feet were too small and the road was too steep and icy for the girl to wear boots that did not fit. She insisted her slippers would do. They would have to, for the storm, strong as it was, would get worse. Taudde dared not let them stop on this most exposed and steepest part of the road; he knew he would not have the strength to protect them until the storm was past and the skies cleared. If his attention failed even for a moment . . . if he did not hear the lightning in the storm before it struck, or if he lost the strength to turn aside the icy rain . . . he flinched from such thoughts, but doubt crept back in as the storm strengthened.

A day and a night to Kedres, if there had been no storm. But not so far to descend from the heights to the roots of the mountains. There, where the stone folded and turned and made little sheltered places, they might find a safe place to wait. But Taudde, disoriented by the violence of the storm, pouring his attention into sending the cutting winds and icy rain whirling around rather than across the tiny bubble of quiet air he had made, could not guess now how much farther they must go or how he would find the strength to get them there.

He could hardly imagine what his grandfather would say if, after everything that had happened, he let himself and his companions die in a spring storm hardly an hour's walk from the valley's shelter.

There would be farms below, nestled down in protected places at the foot of Kerre Irelle. It could not be so very far now to the nearest of those. An hour's walk. Less. He could play the three of them through the storm that far. If they could only get down to an easier part of the road, Tepres would be able to carry Karah, if her slippers were worn through.

Ice and stone, the cutting wind and freezing rain . . . Taudde played warmth and quiet air. Lightning leaped through the storm, brilliant and deadly, and he sent it aside. And again. Thunder rumbled slowly and then crashed, and Karah slipped. In the still air that surrounded them, Prince Tepres heard her gasp, and turned, and caught her. And slipped himself, twisting to cushion her fall, taking the impact on his hip, both of them skidding in exactly the worst direction. Karah caught at the rocks at the edge of the road, but her fingers could not close on the icy stone and the precipice lay only an arm's length farther—

Taudde played a heavy series of notes, setting them in empty air like stones across a dashing stream. On these notes, Tepres caught himself, his boot hard against solidity where there should have been nothing but the precipice. He didn't make a sound, but twisted around and half threw Karah back toward the safe—safer—part of the road and then began, very carefully, to try to crawl after her.

Then lightning struck, and struck again, far too close, and Taudde found himself on his hands and knees, dazed, his flute nowhere he could find it, icy rain coming down across him with a cold so brutal that in that first moment he couldn't even whistle through chilled lips. Taudde almost wanted to laugh it was so ridiculous, but it was infuriating and terrifying, too. At last, at last he had returned to Kalches, he'd brought Prince Tepres and Karah here to *save* them, and now, if he couldn't recover fast enough, the mountain and the storm could kill them all and no one of his family would even know he had come home.

2

Nemienne was lost.

When Karah and Taudde and Prince Tepres had hurled themselves through the door into Kalches, Nemienne had tried to follow them. But it had been impossible. All those other men had been in her way, and then Taudde had slammed the door shut anyway and even if she might have opened it—she thought she might—she knew she daren't let the prince's enemies through that door.

So she had gone the other way, three more steps down the hall and hurled herself against the plain door, the black one, the one that led into the dark caverns beneath the mountains. Beneath Kerre Maraddras, maybe Kerre Taum as well. And it had opened for her, as it had before.

She had stepped from this darkness into Cloisonné House before. Once, she had stepped out of this darkness straight into the house where all her other sisters lived. That was what she had had in mind when she fled through that door. But some of *them* had come through the black door after her. She knew they had. She hadn't gotten the door closed again fast enough, or else one of the mages among those men had known how to find and open it. She had seen the mage-lights gowing coldly behind her.

So she had just run, without thinking about where she was going. She had been terrified that those mages might come after her, and so she had just run as fast as she could, with no thought but *away*.

Now she still hurried through the dark beneath Kerre Maraddras, along a narrow passage within the vastness of the mountain, where rippling curtains of stone closed in from both sides and the slightest sound echoed. She was nearly certain she was nowhere near the dragon's chamber, and nearly certain that was a good thing. She did not want to lead mages to the dragon, but almost as important, she didn't dare rouse the dragon herself, either. Because who could guess what it might do, this time? This time, it might decide to bring down the mountains after all and destroy Lonne and all the ephemeral works of men.

That was what it had said last time. *The ephemeral works of men.* Only last time, the king had persuaded it not to. And Nemienne herself might have helped a little bit. Now the king might be dead and Prince Tepres was probably in Kalches, and so was Taudde, and Nemienne definitely did not want to find herself facing the dragon alone.

Someone was behind her. She thought she could hear him, more often now than earlier: the cautious sound of someone wearing boots trying to walk quietly, an occasional scrape of metal against stone when her pursuer stumbled. Sometimes she thought he was far behind her and sometimes she thought he was quite near, but no matter how she hurried, she didn't seem able to get away from him.

At first she had hoped she might simply be peopling the dark with imaginary terrors. But she was almost sure now that her pursuer was real. She thought it was only one man, but the sounds behind her echoed strangely so that she could not be sure. She never glimpsed magelight when she looked over her shoulder, so she hoped at least her pursuer was not a mage. But she wouldn't be able to get away from a soldier, either, if he caught her. She thought probably he was a soldier. If she opened a door out of the dark, maybe she could get away from him. Except that she was afraid if she did, he might come through it after her.

And she was afraid that any door she opened here in the dark would lead her straight home. She was afraid and cold and alone; she wanted warmth and her sisters, so how could she open any other door? She was afraid that no matter what door she might try to open out of the dark, she would only be able to open that one. And then what if the man behind her rushed through after her, bringing danger to all her sisters?

So she didn't dare try to step out of the dark into light. And she didn't know what else to do.

Nemienne lifted her hands and sent pale light—it was not quite light, in fact, but one could more or less see by it—spreading out ahead of her, looking for a way to get out of the narrow passage in which she had found herself trapped. Any path she could take that might confuse her pursuer. Leave him baffled in the dark, make him give up and go away, leave her *alone*, so that she escape the dark and go *home*.

And then what? She had no idea. No idea at all. If those had been the left-hand princes—she was sure they had—and if they had killed their father, and if Tepres was trapped in Kalches with Taudde, who was Kalchesene himself . . . how was *she* supposed to know what to do?

She thought the sounds behind her were getting closer. Maybe. It was hard to tell, but she thought so. The cavern floor here was nearly level, and the way was narrow, so anyone behind her could almost run. So could she—she *was*—but if it came to that, any man would be able to run faster than she could.

It was horrible. Like the kind of dream where no matter how you tried you couldn't go fast enough, and when you looked over your shoulder, there was nothing there, only there *was*. Exactly like that.

She wondered if other men had made it through the other door, the one that led to Kalches. She wondered if Prince Tepres and Karah were also being pursued by mages or soldiers.

At least they would have each other. And Taudde, who was a very powerful sorcerer. But his first loyalty was to his grandfather in Kalches. She didn't *know* what he would do, now, even if none of the prince's enemies had come through that door after them.

Except Taudde would surely protect Karah. Surely no one would hurt Karah.

She wished she could be sure no one would hurt *her*. She had been so certain she could get away. She wasn't so certain of that now.Whoever that was behind her, he was *determined*. There should be something she could do, only she simply didn't know how to do very much magic. She could call light into the dark. Not ordinary light, no, but this pale radiance that was *like* light. But that only meant her pursuers would be able to see where she went. So she looked and looked for a different way to go, a way that would let her duck away and let the dark crash down and hide her.

Only this part of the caverns didn't seem to *have* any

tangled paths. It was all a straight tunnel through the dark, here in this part of the caverns. And she was more and more sure that the steps behind her were getting closer.

She should be able to *do* something. Especially if it was just a soldier behind her. Mage Ankennes could have done all kinds of things, horrible things maybe, but things that would have *worked*. He could have shattered stone, brought half this narrow passageway crashing down on anyone behind him. Or he could have laid a barrier between himself and any pursuer, a barrier that no one could cross without his bones turning to fire. But he hadn't taught her any of those things before he died.

Taudde could have done things, too, with his little flute or just with his voice. He could probably have walked right through the stone, or stepped one, two, three and on the third step come out of the caverns to stand on the shore, with the waves sending a lacework of froth against his boots. Or he could have played three notes sharp as knives and left his pursuer bleeding on the stone. Bardic sorcery was good for things like that.

But Nemienne had learned hardly any bardic sorcery, yet. She didn't know how to do anything at all that would help.

She hid, in the end, when she was sure her pursuer was going to catch up to her. She tucked herself down against the cold curtains of stone and sent a darting pale luminance on ahead, to lead the man on and away. Once he was past, she could creep back the way she had come, very quietly, feeling her way through the heavy darkness. Then when it was safe, she could think of other kinds of light. She could remember the homey warmth of a fire in the hearth and the welcoming glow of lantern light, and then she could follow those memories home and leave her pursuer blundering in the dark until one of his friends came after him.

That was what she meant to happen. But it didn't work that way. Because the man following her did not blunder on past. Nemienne thought he would, at first. Certainly he should have. He came into sight only a moment after she had hidden. It was just one man after all, one man by himself, so that was better than it might have been. He didn't see her—he wasn't a mage, to create his own light, and he didn't have a torch or lantern; not even a candle. So that was good, too. Nemienne knelt very still against the wall, and the man didn't see her. He was striding along fast, peering urgently ahead, chasing the light she had sent away. She could hear him breathing: short, sharp breaths, like a man who has been hurrying for a long time and does not dare stop. She held her own breath.

That was her mistake. She realized that later. She had been breathing a lot like that herself, almost panting, and then she held her breath, and even in his urgent hurry, somehow the man heard or felt the difference. He checked and swung around, and even in the dark that was barely illuminated at all by the glimmer of her retreating not-quite-light, Nemienne could see how his hand went to the long knife sheathed at his belt.

She darted away, back the way they'd both come. That was her second mistake. That one, she recognized almost at once, because of course there was nowhere to go in this narrow passageway, and she had no hope of outrunning him. She didn't outrun him. He caught her before she'd gone twenty steps, grabbing her arm and dragging her around. She hit his wrist hard, twisting to get away, to make him let go, and he *did* let go, but he also grabbed her other arm, so she shoved at him and bit his hand, and he hissed under his breath, a sharp, pained sound. She almost did get away then, but he hung on after all, grabbing a fistful of her hair to keep her from biting him again and using his weight to pin her against the damp stone.

Nemienne struggled, but it was hopeless. He had both her wrists trapped in one large hand, now, and he still had a firm grip on her hair—she tried to jerk free, tears springing to her eyes because of the pain, but that was hopeless, too. She tried to kick him, but he was too close, and he had his hip turned so she couldn't use her knee, either. But even though she fought him and fought to get away, he didn't hit her or shout at her—she noticed that even at the time—or threaten her with the knife. He must not even have *drawn* his knife; it certainly wasn't in either of his hands.

She said, a quick, gasping plea, "Let me *go!*"

That was stupid, because of course he wasn't going to, but actually he did let go of her hair, though not her wrists. He said, "Hush, hush, easy," firmly and soothingly, the way one might speak to a frightened horse or dog.

Nemienne stared at him, in the almost-light she had called up again almost without realizing it. She didn't mind him saying 'Hush' to her like that; it was a lot better than him hitting her. He didn't look, now that she came to see him properly, like he wanted to hit her. She thought perhaps if she pretended to give up, maybe she would be able to get away from him even now.

Now that she looked at him, she could see that he was a young man. Younger than she had expected, not so very much older than she was. She thought he must have been with all those other men who had attacked Tepres; she was almost sure she had seen him with them, but he didn't look . . . angry, or scary. He wasn't wearing the flat red of a soldier, but the black of the King's Own Guard, except that the collar and cuffs of his overrobe were stiff with pale green embroidery. From that, she guessed he must be someone important, or at least the son of someone important. A lot of the King's Own guardsmen were the left-hand sons of important men.

The young man didn't have a sword, only the long dagger sheathed at his belt—indeed, he hadn't drawn it. She still didn't think he looked angry, even though he had been chasing her for so long and even though she had bitten his hand. He looked intense and relieved, as though catching her was the most important thing he had ever done. That made her heart sink; she could see that it would be very difficult to get away from him.

His eyes were set wide and rather slanted in his sharp-boned face, his mouth was small, his chin narrow. His breath was coming as hard and fast as Nemienne's, and an unexpected tremor had become perceptible in the hand that gripped her wrists. He was exhausted, Nemienne realized. He looked just as exhausted as she felt. She wondered how long she had been hurrying through the caverns, how long he had been chasing her through the dark. It seemed like a long time. She felt somehow that it might be very late at night, much later than she had guessed until this moment, as though she had been running through the caverns for hours and hours. Perhaps for days. Her captor certainly looked exhausted enough to have been chasing her for hours and hours, or for days.

The young man's hair, long and straight, had been braided back but was coming loose; it was some pale shade, greenish in the not-quite-light Nemienne had made. He brushed it back abruptly and sank down to sit on his heels. He pulled her down with him, but not roughly. More as though he suddenly lacked the strength to keep his feet, but was determined not to risk her making a sudden break for freedom. Nemienne tried, gently, to pull free of his grip—gently enough that she hoped he would believe she did not mean to leap up and away if he let her go. He gave her a look and let go of one of her wrists, but kept the other one in a firm grip.

"You are Nemienne, daughter of the stone merchant Geranes Lihadde," he told her. His voice was a bit ragged at the moment. But it was a nice voice. It was the kind of voice, Nemienne thought, that a dog or a horse would like. He was looking at her carefully, as though she might turn abruptly into someone else. He went on, "You were apprentice to Mage Ankennes; then you were a student of the Kalchesene prince. The Kalchesene got away, did you see? Through a different door. Did you know he took Tepres away with him? Do you know where he took him?" He paused, and then asked, his tone gaining intensity, "Did he take him to Kalches?"

Nemienne stared at him, surprised he would say so much— surprised, too, that he would say *Tepres* like that, with such easy familiarity. Maybe that was the way men in the King's Own spoke of the princes. Maybe this man had been one of Prince Tepres' own personal guards, a friend as well as a guard. That would make sense. But if so, he had betrayed him. Maybe he had looked at Prince Tepres with just this kind of earnest expression and then betrayed him. That would be horrible.

"It *was* Kalches, then," the young man said, apparently taking her silence for assent. A different note had come into his voice—a kind of frustration that was almost despair. His hair had fallen into his face again. He swept it back impatiently and demanded, "Did you mean to go with them? Could you follow them now? *Could* you do such a thing—open that door? Even Telis could not, but if you were the Kalchesene's student, perhaps *you* could open it and step through to follow in my brother's footsteps."

"Your brother?" Nemienne repeated blankly. His *brother*? She knew now who he looked like, and why he had looked to her, in the first instant she saw him, like the son of someone important. She said, "You're *Prince Geradde*. You don't—you don't look like Prince Tepres, much." But he did, she thought now, look a little like his father. She could see the king in him, now that she knew to look for the resemblance.

Prince Geradde's mouth crooked at this: not quite a smile, not quite amused. "You didn't know me."

Nemienne shook her head, still staring at him. She didn't know why she should be surprised. Of course all the left-hand princes had moved together to bring down their father and their right-hand brother. Well, probably not Meiredde, but the rest of them, why not?

"Well," said the prince. "I knew *you*. But perhaps that was the simpler task. There can surely be few girls who would have been in Ankennes' house, and fewer still who would run through that black door when frightened. I trust you will be able to find a way to return to Lonne from this place?" His swift glance and minimal gesture took in not only the narrow passageway where they both sat, but by implication all the caverns below Kerre Maraddras, perhaps below all these mountains. Nemienne thought for the first time that she could see a resemblance between this young man and Prince Tepres—a resemblance in that minimal gesture, and in the ironic edge to his tone.

Nemienne did not know whether she should say *Yes, of course* or *No, I'm lost*. She was perfectly certain she should not admit that the only place she was *certain* she could find from this place was her own home—her sisters' home. That she could probably summon light, or the memory of light, and step directly from this dark into the long gallery where her sisters slept. She said instead, cautiously, "I don't think I would be able to open the door into Kalches. I'm not Kalchesene, and I hardly know any sorcery." She tried to stop there, but couldn't help but ask, "Will you try to make me open it? Are you going to take me to Prince Sehonnes? What will he do if I can't—if I can't open it?"

"Sehonnes?" said Prince Geradde. He leaned his head back against the folds of stone behind him and laughed, his voice cracking with exhaustion. "Take you to Sehonnes," he said again at last. "Hardly."

24

3

Taudde did not find his flute. But Karah put it into his hand, and closed his numb fingers around it.

At first, Taudde was shaking too hard to play it. But he would be ashamed to die with his flute in his hand and not at his lips. He dashed freezing rain out of his eyes and looked for Tepres—couldn't see him, and then did, flat at the edge of the cliff, unable to retreat across the icy stone from the edge of the sheer drop.

For a terrible moment, Taudde did not know what to do. He could help Tepres—or turn the rain and wind—or listen for lightning—or play warmth into the air and stone, but he could not do all of those things at once, and so much of his strength had already poured itself out into the cold and he could not seem catch his breath.

But he lifted his flute and began, with painful effort, to set notes like the rungs of a ladder, one after another, for Tepres to haul himself along, out of immediate peril. Although the cold alone would kill them all if Taudde could not get them off this mountain, and never mind the lightning—

Then the rain began to turn aside. It wasn't Taudde's doing. It was someone else. The strong, warm voice of a reed-throated wooden flute, its tones almost familiar, turned the rain and gentled and softened the air, and a sharp darting of silver-edged notes, precisely timed and harmonious, sent lightning striking above and below but never close to the road.

Another bardic sorcerer had come. Two others at least, wooden flute and silver, Taudde knew them before he saw them, dimly, through the rain that dashed down between. Whoever they were, they clearly had the strength and experience to rescue careless travelers from a spring storm, and in that confidence he let his grim effort go at last.

Taudde did not quite lose consciousness. But nor, for a little while, was he clearly aware of where they went, nor in whose company. It seemed to him he blinked once or twice and then opened his eyes to a gravel path running beside a brook, flowing full now with the rain. Then he blinked again and found himself staring at a wooden gate, with beyond that a sprawling house, all gray stone below and silvery pine shingle above, so that it might have been carved out of the mountain by the rain. There was a familiar harp-and-star carved in relief above the door of the house. Only when he saw that did Taudde realize what house this was. He said to the woman walking next to him, astounded yet in another way not surprised at all, "Aunt Ines!"

"Taudde, my dear," answered his aunt, lowering her wooden flute. "I would say you are well come, save that one hardly sees how you are come at all, out in the weather and so ill-prepared for it!" Sweeping off her cloak of oiled wool, his aunt shook off the wet and turned to open the gate, while her companion with the silver flute kept off the rain with a quick and lively melody.

"Bring that girl into the warmth!" said Aunt Ines, not to Taudde but to Prince Tepres, who was now indeed carrying Karah. Aunt Ines went swiftly ahead of them, around the corner of the house to throw open the kitchen door, then stood back to allow Tepres to go in ahead of her. The prince slanted one unreadable glance at Taudde, obeying the woman's gesture without a word.

In Lonne, the kitchen entrance was for servants, but in Kalches no one ever came through the parlor door, certainly not in bad weather. No one cared if water or mud dripped on the slate floor of the kitchen. They were certainly bringing a sufficiency of water and mud with them now, despite all that sorcery could do.

"Ah!" said another woman, stout and matronly, coming forward to help Karah to a bench and chafe her hands. "Poor child! She's half frozen. What strange clothing—pretty, I'm sure, but not what I'd choose for a stroll in the freezing rain high on the mountain's shoulder." She added to Aunt Ines, "You were right about seeing sorcery at work on the road above, then."

"Irelle saw it," said Aunt Ines, and turned to smile at the girl with the silver flute who came last into the house.

"I saw the rain falling sideways, and lightning striking everywhere but where it wished to strike," Irelle said coolly. She tossed her wool cloak onto a peg by the door and thrust her flute through her belt, accepting a warm towel from the other woman.

"A *silver* flute?" Taudde said to her. "You must have a strong and beautiful gift, cousin."

Irelle was the oldest child of Aunt Ines and Uncle Heronn and thus Heronn's heir. Taudde remembered her as sharp of wits and tongue even as a girl, with something of her father's serious air and even more of her mother's aptitude for sorcery. That had obviously blossomed in the past years, which was just as well as she was second in line for the throne of Kalches. He wondered if he should warn Tepres that Irelle was, in Kalchesene terms, a princess of very nearly his own rank. Though of course, Tepres should guess as much, from the sorcery if not from Taudde's saying *aunt* and *cousin*.

Irelle had been a child when Taudde had left Kalches, but her hair was up now, not loose over her shoulders as he remembered it, and he could see that she had passed on her wooden beads to some younger girl, replacing them with the delicate jewelry of copper and silver wire that was proper for a woman grown. With her hair up, he could see how much she resembled Aunt Ines, with wide-set eyes and a high forehead and strong bones. She was not particularly pretty, but if she took after Ines, then in twenty more years, or forty, she would still look strong-willed and striking.

Her mouth had crooked at his compliment. She said, still coolly, "Not yet so strong as yours, cousin. At least, I could not step in a heartbeat from the heart of Lirionne into the heart of Kalches, as from your clothing I gather you did, nor bring friends along with me for the journey. I will say, you might have put more thought into the moment and manner of your arrival."

"I would have greatly preferred a chance to put any thought at all into the moment and manner of my arrival," Taudde said fervently.

"Like that, was it?" said Aunt Ines. "Sit down, Taudde, and let Merissa see to the girl's feet. There's soup, I'm sure. Will you make your friends known to me and tell me your tale?"

Taudde hesitated. "Better not, just yet, perhaps. Grandfather had better hear it first. I meant to go straight there," he added ruefully, sinking down on a bench by the fire. "I admit, I didn't anticipate a spring storm. An hour to recover ourselves in the warmth would be welcome."

"And it's like that," said his aunt, unsurprised. Her shrewd gaze took in first Karah, pale and bedraggled, smiling with all her natural charm at Merissa as the woman set down a bowl of soup; and then Prince Tepres, standing stiff and young and arrogant beside Karah's bench, foreign from the jet-and-ruby clip that held back his dripping pale hair to his boots, which despite their hard use still glittered with gold and purple embroidery. He was as out of place in this hall as though a hawk had come into a dovecote.

"Well, an hour should be neither here nor there, I am sure," said Aunt Ines in a decidedly bland tone. "Irelle and I will go up to the house with you, of course."

"Aunt, I would be most grateful," Taudde assured her.

Aunt Ines nodded graciously. "Heronn is up at the house tonight in any case, so that's simpler than tracking everyone down separately, I suppose."

As her daughter drew a breath to comment or object or agree, she added smoothly, "Irelle, my dear, perhaps you might make yourself useful and play us all a bit less damp. Such a nuisance to steam wet things by the fire, and then likely you still find yourself clammy around the edges hours later."

Irelle paused, raised her eyebrows at her mother, then shrugged and pulled her flute out of her belt. It was not a girl's simple cord belt, Taudde saw, but a belt of dyed leather, indigo and gold, with a loop on one side for the flute and a twisted cord on the other that was probably meant to hold a set of pipes or a finger harp in its case. So she must be a serious instrumentalist, for her age. He wondered if his cousin had made her flute herself, as was the custom for students of sorcery. It was a complicated instrument, with all the fittings to multiply its notes and extend its range. He already knew from its tone that it was well made.

Few enough women worked with metal. Girls who wished to become instrumentalists or bardic sorcerers generally worked with wood and bone and horn. Metalwork was usually something left to the men. He suspected that if Irelle had wished to learn metalwork, she would simply have gone straight to . . . who was the best metalworking instrumentalist in Kedres? Uncle Tames? Taudde didn't doubt she had made him teach her.

If Irelle could play them less damp, as Aunt Ines had asked, then her sorcery possessed subtlety as well as strength. And Aunt Ines wished him to know that. That was something to remember, as well.

Soup and dry clothing and an hour to rest made an enormous difference, not only for Taudde but clearly for Prince Tepres and Karah as well. Even their boots were dry. Karah had brushed out her hair, braided it and tucked the ends out of sight somehow; not ordinarily a keiso style, but not Kalchesene either; and somehow she had made friends with Merissa, who brought her a pair of new slippers that might not be as delicate and beautiful as they made such things in Lonne, but nevertheless did not look too out of place with her overrobe and jeweled pins. Prince Tepres had not spoken a word to anyone, save for a murmur of thanks here and there as appropriate, but even his manner had become a trifle less stiff.

The storm still blew; the rain still came down, but here in the valley the winds came with less force and the rain was not as cold. Even the thunder was muted, lightning now stalking the farther mountains beyond Kedres; and the sun slid free beyond the low clouds in the west, layering all the world in a dusky lavender twilight. The very air seemed softer, and smelled of wet earth and growing things.

In Lonne, even in the heart of the city, wealthy men owned fancy equipages, often stabling their horses some distance from their townhouses. Taudde had done that himself; his man Benne had chosen carriage and horses and stable, and driven the equipage when Taudde had called for it. Taudde had not had a moment to think of his servants; of Nala, the woman who kept his house for him, and most of all of Benne, whom he had promised to bring to Kalches when he returned. A promise broken; that was ill-luck for a sorcerer. Nala had been out of the house, but Benne had been somewhere about. Taudde did not even know if the man still lived.

One more thing he did not know; one more hostage held by fate. He could do nothing about any of that now. Nor had he leisure to fret as he might; he had plenty to concern himself with here.

In Kedres, very few men owned fancy carriages, for Kedres was a good deal smaller than Lonne, and grain for horses more costly. But those who traveled frequently between the outlying homes and the heart of Kedres often owned a pony cart, as well as a sledge for winter. The ponies were small, shaggy beasts, mostly sorrel or gray, hardly more than hip high, but strong and easy to keep. And, more to the point at the moment, sure footed as cats on icy roads. Aunt Ines' pony cart had a canopy that could be put up against wind and rain, and though it was not meant to carry more than one or two people, the ponies made nothing of the weight of three women. Taudde put the hood of his new oiled cloak up over his head, glad of the softening of the storm, and Prince Tepres did the same, and they walked beside the pony cart.

They came to the first outlying houses of Kedres just as full dark fell across the town. Lanterns shone everywhere now. At the edge of town were the homes of merchants and tradesmen and minor gentry, the former distinguishable because merchant families nearly always lived above their shops, so that merchants' homes usually displayed carved wooden signs declaring their business. The wealthy lived farther in, closer to the king's house, though compared to Lonne no one in Kedres would likely count as truly wealthy.

All the buildings in Kedres were of stone, homes and shops and roads and walls, until one could imagine the town had not been built by men, but had been carved full-formed out of the mountains by the wind. The walls, low and usually without gates, were not meant to protect anything other than privacy. They only provided support for espaliered apples and defined the edges of the occasional tiny private garden, bursting in this season with the early flowers of spring, the small, hardy bulbs that bowed down in a storm and then raised their flowers again when the storm was past. Kedres did not need strong walls. The mountains themselves were the wall that protected the heart of

Kalches, and so thoroughly that not even Taliente Neredde ken Seriantes, Tepres' great-great-grandfather, the first and most aggressive of the Seriantes Dragons, had ever attempted to conquer the lands here.

In Lonne, magecrafted street lamps burned all night, drowning the light of stars and moon. There were no such extravagant lamps here. The people of Kedres had neither the wealth nor the magecraft to make such things. Their lanterns were ordinary, of porcelain or milky glass or even, in poorer homes, heavily waxed paper ensorcelled to hold a memory of moonlight. But even through closed shutters, the lantern-glow provided enough light for a pair of late travelers to find their way through the streets.

Taudde observed Prince Tepres as they entered Kedres. The Dragon's heir glanced from one side of the narrow street to the other, from the windows outlined with lantern-light to the faint reflection of that light from the cobbles and the damp stone of the low houses. Taudde closed his teeth on a defensive comment about the people of Kalches not wishing to block the sight of the stars with magical lamps. It was true, but he knew how poor and backward this town must seem to the Dragon's heir. Lonne was the wealthiest of cities in the wealthiest of countries, the Pearl of the West, and Kalches was the poorest of lands and had no cities at all. Kedres itself, a fraction the size of Lonne, was the largest of its towns.

Taudde had not liked Lonne's street lamps, nor its crowding, nor its sumptuary laws, nor its arrogant nobles, nor the elliptical deference with which the people of Lonne handled all their formal business. He had not expected, returning at last to Kedres, to feel embarrassed by his home's relative poverty. He had not expected to find himself defensive of its pride. Though Tepres made no comment at all, Taudde could not help but see Kedres through the eyes of the Dragon's heir. This exasperated him, but it was true and he could not pretend otherwise.

They came to Taudde's grandfather's house in the dark, unable to see anything of it but its many lantern-lit windows shining back to the star-flecked sky. Even so, it was evident that this was a low, sprawling house, in no way like any palace of Lirionne and still less like the fortress of the Laodd, built above

Lonne by Tepres' father's father. Taudde did not have to see the house in daylight to know how it stood, its dimensions, the feel of the courtyard flagstones underfoot, the fire-lit warmth within.

The central part of the house, built during the height of Kalchesene strength and therefore with considerable attention to beauty, was two stories high and fronted with smooth pillars. The polished stone of that part of the house glowed faintly with reflected lantern-light, and the occasional night-black stones scattered through the gray glittered like glass.

The westernmost wing of the house, constructed two generations later to suit an entirely different aesthetic, was long and low, all of pine and imported oak rather than native stone. And to the north, the other, larger, wing of the house had evidently been guided during its construction by no aesthetic sense at all. It sprawled in a cluttered-seeming series of haphazardly-connected structures, never more than one story high except for a single crooked tower that thrust up, a narrow afterthought, from the most remote corner.

The house was not set off from the town—indeed, Taudde knew, the northern wing of the house wandered away into the nearest quarter of the town, its farthest courtyard belonging half to a public square where, in the summer, an open-air market appeared. For a prince of Lirionne, it must be hard to imagine this rambling, informal structure could possibly be the house of the Kalchesene king. When Aunt Ines drew up the pony cart before its door, Prince Tepres gazed at the building for a long moment, expressionless.

There was no wall, nor gates, nor guards. There were glass panes in the windows, though most of them also had wooden shutters over the glass to keep out the cold. Yet even through the closed shutters, Taudde could hear faint voices and music—the resonant voices of big floor harps interwoven with the sharp metallic notes of a hammerharp, and behind the stringed instruments the crisp, clear rhythm of a set of palm drums, and then over that the sweet voices of pipes and, barely audible, a single delicate silver flute. He tilted his head, picking out the instrumentalists by ear . . . he knew that flute, and he was equally certain he recognized that hand on the drums.

Prince Tepres glanced sidelong at Taudde, his pale

eyebrows rising, saying nothing at all.

"It really is the king's house," Taudde said. "And, from the music, my grandfather is indeed in residence." He turned to hand his aunt and cousin out of the cart. Tepres did the same for Karah and then turned, not letting go of her hand at once. At last he glanced once more at Taudde. Who, after all, had no choice now; no more than the Dragon's heir had any choice in what would happen now. Taudde tilted his head to the side and held out a hand toward the house in a gesture half of invitation and half of command.

The king of Kalches, Chontas Berente ser Omientes ken Lariodde, had ruled for a long time. Long enough to see one Seriantes Dragon and then another press the borders between their two countries, long enough to see Kalches halved and the majority of his people forced either out of their homes in the northeast, or else to accept overlords appointed from the ranks of Lirionne's nobility by the Seriantes kings. Kalches had lost one war and then another, and then a third, each defeat more disastrous than the one before, until at last had come the field of Brenedde, and the defeat and death of Taudde's father, Chontas Gaurente ken Lariodde, prince of Kalches, son of Chontas Berente.

And after that, the forced Treaty of Brenedde, by which Kalches ceded to Lirionne all the lands west of Teleddes and east of Anharadde and swore besides fifteen years of peace. Those fifteen years would end at the coming solstice . . . and everyone knew there would once again be war. Because no king of Kalches could possibly allow Lirionne to hold permanently the lands it had taken, so near the heart of Kalches.

And now Taudde—Chontas Taudde ser Omientes ken Lariodde—had brought to the heart of Kalches, more or less accidentally, the only legitimate Seriantes heir.

Aunt Ines had guessed something. Perhaps Irelle had guessed something else. But Taudde suspected that neither of them had realized the full truth. How could they? It was like something from a tale, but less plausible. He met his aunt's eyes for a long moment, gave Karah a smile that he hoped was reassuring—she looked very young, her eyes wide and quiet, absorbing everything. He murmured to her, "Do not fear," and gave Prince Tepres a small nod as well, *Do not fear for her.* Impossible as that injunction must be, they both nodded back, Karah nervously and the prince with a short decisive jerk of his head that said as clearly as though he had spoken the words aloud, *You had better be right.*

Taudde thought he could guarantee at least so much. He hoped he could. He led the way along the covered gallery toward the wide front porch.

King Berente ser Omientes seldom kept formal state, less often still while in his own house, and least frequently of all after dusk, which Kalchesene custom declared ended the day—one point of similarity, at least, between Kalches and Lirionne. But from the voices and music within, Taudde guessed it must have been a day for petitions and arguments, and that the day must have run long. That alone would have drawn his grandfather's temper short. Not that even the most expansive mood engendered by the most pleasant of days would likely divert the king's attention on the occasion of Taudde's long-delayed return.

Taudde took a deep breath. Then, with a single phrase from his flute, he quieted the ensorcelled horns that stood on either side of the door to warn of any enemy's arrival. He heard his aunt's indrawn breath, and knew that she had certainly guessed part of the truth from this, if she hadn't before. But that was well enough, now. It might even be better so. He led the way again, past the horns and through the main door of the house, and past two bored men-at-arms who did not look up from their game of rods and dice, and down the long and oddly-angled hallway that brought them at last to the wide dining hall where servants were just bringing dishes and platters to the table. The men and women of the king's household were still mostly on their feet, some meandering in the general direction of the table, some chatting with the occupants of the instrumentalists' gallery, and still others persistently circling about the king, who was waving his hand impatiently for them all to go away.

Taudde's grandfather was standing to one side, frowning, speaking with an earnest man who tried to press a scroll into his hands. The king refused the scroll with a gesture of sharp irritation and the petitioner, earnest as he might be, did not try to press it on him again.

King Berente was a stern old man with a quick, acute glance, a mouth that gave away nothing, and a scathing turn of phrase when someone annoyed him. Or, to be sure, when one of his grandsons behaved like a fool and got himself into trouble. He had not exactly approved Taudde's little venture to Lirionne. In fact, he had directly commanded Taudde to stay out of Lirionne. A command which Taudde had defied. With results that were, at least . . . unexpected.

Nor was this exactly the manner in which Taudde had intended to return.

His grandfather had not yet noticed his arrival, however. The king unclasped his heavy cloak and handed it to a hovering servant, then stripped off and handed to a different servant all his nine rings of office. He still wore the crown of thick gold wire set with amber and obsidian and wickedly heavy Kalchesene granite. His own sense of the fitness of things forced him to wear that crown while conducting the formal business of the court or hearing even the least of petitions, but he always put it away at the closing of the day. He would be annoyed all over again if Taudde forced him to take that crown up again after he had put it aside.

So Taudde did not wait, or try to press through the bustling room. He whistled instead, a light, dancing melody that slipped delicately by the attention of almost everyone in the hall but caused his grandfather's head to snap around as though Taudde had shouted his name.

Taudde's appearance, unexpected as it must have been, did not count as a formal event of court business. Berente ser Omientes glowered at his grandson. But he would not have hesitated to put his crown aside if Taudde had been alone. What prevented him, as Taudde knew very well, was the presence of Prince Tepres, who had put off his muffling cloak now and stood revealed in all his foreign elegance. He held his shoulders straight and his hands at his sides, and his head was tilted at an arrogant angle, as though he saw nothing that impressed him. He had taken a step away from Karah, who was as clearly foreign, but who looked young and beautiful and harmless. Even with neither sword nor knife nor any weapon, Prince Tepres looked anything but harmless, and if no one but Taudde heard the dragon's heartbeat behind the young prince's, it was only because they did not know how to listen.

Silence spread gradually out from the motionless king, first to those closest to him as they realized something had caught his eye and tried to follow his gaze through the crowded room, then to people farther away who realized something interesting might be taking place, and then farther still, until the whole huge hall was filled with silent men and women who turned, stared, and then eased aside to leave a clear pathway between Taudde and his grandfather.

Taudde did not ordinarily mind drawing public attention. Given the current circumstances, he might have been better pleased by a little discretion. Though . . . there were advantages, too, to facing his grandfather under the eyes of half the town. Aunt Ines was somewhere behind them, not far; that might be an advantage as well. He hoped it would prove so.

He took a deep breath, glanced sideways at Prince Tepres, gave the prince a small jerk of his head to tell him to follow, and strode forward.

"Taudde," said King Berente. "And hardly before time." He was not glaring, yet. Quite. He looked Taudde up and down with grim deliberation, then glanced at Prince Tepres. "And who is this?"

His grandfather looked older than Taudde remembered. The man Taudde remembered had seemed ageless. But now, seeing his grandfather again after these years away . . . the king's sharp gaze was unchanged. But the king seemed not only old, Taudde thought, but grim and weary. Though he still stood as straight as a young man, his face had acquired the thin, pared-down quality of age. His hands, once clever with harp or flute, had also thinned with age, and Taudde could see in them the faint tremble that afflicted some of the elderly. Most noticeable of all, his hair and close-trimmed beard were pure white, where Taudde remembered both as grizzled silver. The past years had been hard for the king of Kalches. Of course. Taudde had known it must be. But he had not felt the guilt for his own absence strike home until he saw the marks of weariness and age on his grandfather.

Taudde cleared his throat. He said formally and clearly, "Sir, allow me to make known to you Prince Tepres Nemedde ken Seriantes, son and heir of Geriodde Nerenne ken Seriantes, king of Lirionne."

You could have heard a single harp note, anywhere in that hall. It would have stood out like a lightning stroke in the dark.

King Berente stared not at the Dragon's heir, but at Taudde. He said, his expressive bard's voice layered with query and the beginnings of anger, "You have broken the Treaty." It was not a question, but neither was it quite a statement.

Taudde drew breath to deny the accusation, but then hesitated, because in a way it was true—well, it was actually *perfectly* true, though not in the way his grandfather surmised—but Prince Tepres cut across his hesitation.

"Prince Chontas Taudde ser Omientes ken Lariodde opened a door for me into your country in order to save my life," declared the prince. His light, cool, haughty voice was like a drawn weapon in the silence of the hall. "Thus marking the second time your grandson has preserved my life against the machinations of my enemies, and so acted to preserve the terms of the Treaty. You, of course, may now break the Treaty of Brenedde with your own hand, if that please you, O King. I have no recourse to prevent you. But I ask you to be gracious to my companion, the keiso Moonflower, who was by chance caught up in my misfortune. She is no rightful object for Kalchesene vengeance."

King Berente gazed at him for a long, long moment. Then he studied Karah, who knelt gracefully in the manner of the keiso, bowed her head and said absolutely nothing. Finally, turning to the man at his shoulder, he said, his expressive voice for once absolutely flat, "Toma. The tower—"

"No," said Taudde, and met his grandfather's incredulous stare. He raised his voice and said, for everyone to hear, "I owe the prince of Lirionne a debt. I ask my grandfather to show Prince Tepres generosity now on my behalf." There was a ripple of near-silent reaction through the crowd. Taudde pretended not to notice it. He waited, holding his grandfather's gaze.

The king said, without expression, "Naturally a man to

whom my grandson owes a debt is due a certain generosity from me. And what lodging shall I offer the girl? I'm quite certain you have a recommendation there as well."

"There is no need to set a close guard on a keiso. Let her lodge with my Aunt Ines."

"Out of the—"

"The child will do very well with me, Berente," said Aunt Ines, with her most gracious manner but with the undertones of her voice filled with conviction. "I can only be delighted at the opportunity to meet one of the famous keiso of Lonne."

There was a very slight stir, immediately hushed. Taudde hoped fervently neither Karah nor Tepres knew what the Kalchesene people thought of the keiso of Lonne. But Uncle Heronn, stepping forward from the gathering, cleared his throat and declared, "I'm sure my wife's judgment is, as always, impeccable."

"Do you think so?" said King Berente without looking at him. "Toma. The Kinsana Suite for the Dragon's heir. The girl can, for the moment at least, lodge with Heronn and Ines."

Toma Piriodde came out of the crowd. He was as thin as the king and as old, but he appeared as tough and lean as an old wolf and almost as likely to tear out your throat. His hand rested on the hilt of the narrow-bladed sword at his belt, though he did not draw it. He gave Taudde an expressionless glance, Karah an untrusting stare and Prince Tepres a cool look. He said coldly, "If his eminence the prince of Lirionne will be pleased to come with me." His free hand twitched to the side, indicating the direction.

Prince Tepres did not glance at Taudde, nor even at Karah. He gave Toma a short nod and strode the way the man had indicated, with a haughty air that suggested he was the one leading the way. His boot heels rang like drumbeats upon the stone of the floor.

Neither Taudde nor his grandfather moved or spoke until both men had departed.

King Berente glowered at Ines, but didn't actually say, *I will speak to you about this later.* Aunt Ines only smiled politely, and after a moment, the king said to Karah, "You had better get up, girl."

Karah rose as gracefully as she had knelt and lifted her head to look the king in the face. She did not seem afraid, though whether that was keiso training or her trusting nature, Taudde couldn't have guessed. She said in her soft, gentle voice, "Thank you, O King."

"Far too early for *that*," snapped the king. He added to Taudde, "Come with me." Then he turned his back, and stalked stiffly toward the door that led to his private apartment within the house.

Taudde cast a speaking look at his aunt, nodded apologetically to Uncle Heronn, who had after all had no warning at all of any of this, and followed his grandfather.

Taudde had thought, of course, about how to tell the tale. He had thought about it all during the course of the winter and then thought about it a great deal harder during the walk through the town to this house. He was, after all, a bardic sorcerer. He was not unaccustomed to weaving tales.

But when his grandfather turned at last into a plain, small room well away from the crowded halls of the house, sank into a straight-backed wooden chair, and fixed Taudde with a profoundly skeptical expression, Taudde found he did not know what to say. He stood before his grandfather and king, his shoulders straight and his hands clasped before him, feeling much like an impudent boy called sharply to account for some outrageous provocation. He wanted to take his flute out, turn it over in his fingers, soothe himself with the feel of its smooth wood. Except that would be like shouting his discomfort aloud. He stood still.

King Berente fixed Taudde with a censorious glower. "Disobedient, foolish, rash, overconfident—I'm sure I'm leaving out half of what I should say. *Far* too certain of yourself, *far* too determined to get your own way, no matter the cost to me or to Kalches." The old man brought his hands down to rest on the arms of his chair and leaned forward, his voice not rising in volume, but gaining intensity. "Self-indulgent, childish, stubborn, impatient—of all my sons and grandsons, you have always been the least governable. Too much power too young made you arrogant, and far too ready to dismiss the opinions of those wiser than you. Taudde, is there any reason in the world I should be anything but disappointed and disgusted with your behavior, both five years ago and today and at every point in between?"

This was about what Taudde had expected. Except even more blistering. He was profoundly grateful his grandfather had at least been merciful enough to deliver this scathing tongue-lashing in private. He said soberly, "No, sir. I deserve all of that, though I hope you may not utterly disapprove *everything* I've done, once you hear the tale."

"You think there's anything I could possibly approve, in any honest accounting?"

"I hope so, sir, though I fear there's a good deal that will disappoint and disgust you."

His grandfather leaned back in the chair. After a moment, he said, "Very well, Taudde. You had better tell me the tale, and then we'll see. Begin with the worst and go on from there."

Taudde cleared his throat. Then he said, as briefly and plainly as he could, "You said I would be a fool to go to Lonne, and you were right. I was discovered, as you warned me I would be. Not by the king of Lirionne, or at least not at first. By those who conspired against him." Taudde took a deep breath, bracing himself, and said, "Despite the Treaty, I allowed myself to be used as a weapon against the Dragon and his heir. Briefly. But for almost too long." He met his grandfather's eyes. "You have every reason to be disappointed and disgusted by my behavior, sir, though almost at once I saw I was wrong and did everything in my power to make it right."

King Berente tapped his hand lightly on the arm of his chair, frowning. "Well, if you learned some measure of humility in Lonne, at least that's one useful outcome of your sojourn there. Go on."

Taudde doubted very much that was all his grandfather meant to say on the subject. But at least he had got out the worst part. His grandfather had been right to make him start with that. He was certainly glad enough to move on. He said, "One of the conspirators merely desired political advantage, I believe. But the other was a mage whose goal was to destroy—sir, you may not know of the dragon that sleeps in the caverns beneath the mountains of Lonne—"

The king raised one white eyebrow, but did not interrupt.

"But there is a dragon there. Or a creature *like* a dragon, but not at all like one of our mountain drakes." Taudde tried to sketch his meaning in the air, wishing he could set the dragon of Lonne into music so that he could show his grandfather what he meant. He would need more than a simple flute for that. He would need . . . roaring drums, the kind called thunder drums, perhaps. And deep-throated ekonne horns, the enormous bass horns that were taller than a man. Even then he knew he would not be able to capture a fraction of what he had seen and felt in the caverns below the mountain of Kerre Maraddras.

"Not like a mountain drake. Like a sea-dragon, then?" King Berente sounded patient, which meant, Taudde knew, that he was actually suppressing quite powerful impatience.

"No . . ." Taudde tried to gather his thoughts. "More like the tide. Like the heartbeat of the ocean. Extraordinarily powerful."

"Indeed. An extraordinarily powerful dragon, like the tide."

Taudde could see that he should have arranged for thunder drums and ekonne horns. He spread his hands. "I know how it sounds. But why do you think Taliente Seriantes originally chose to establish his capital there between the mountains and the sea? The harbors are far better farther south. But he heard the heartbeat of the dragon, and somehow he bound himself and his line to it. We all know what came of that—"

"I much doubt that Taliente Neredde ken Seriantes required any great magic to tune his heart to a dragon's heart," King Berente said drily. "He was born so, I imagine."

Taudde did not argue. He said, "In any case, sir, the mage meant to slay the dragon while it slept, thus pulling down the Seriantes line. Instead, it woke. It might have destroyed us all." This was true, though Taudde was in fact leaving out almost everything. He honestly did not know how to describe that desperate struggle beneath the mountain. He did not know how to explain what Mage Ankennes had wanted him to do, or what Taudde had done instead, or what had come of it. He said instead, "In the end, I killed the mage. I might have gained the dragon's goodwill by that. I don't know. It isn't—it isn't an ordinary creature. I—we—I would not want to see war between

Kalches and Lirionne while that dragon is wakeful. Believe me that we cannot begin to guess what it might do. We would have no hope of stopping it from doing anything."

King Berente made an uninterpretable sound.

"You didn't see it," Taudde said sharply. "You weren't there. You may question my judgment in many matters, sir, but surely not in sorcery. I tell you, that creature could have destroyed all of Lonne. For a time, it seemed it might. You may say that would be well enough, but what after that? I much doubt so powerful a creature would have gone tamely back to sleep after pulling all the mountains of Lonne down into the sea."

"Indeed. And then?" inquired the king, his tone more and more dangerously neutral. "I gather you saved the life of this prince of Lirionne? From this . . . creature that was like a dragon?"

"From the mage. It seemed the right course to take. At the time. Sir. Only . . ." Taudde hesitated. Then he said baldly, "The king of Lirionne himself came to that place beneath the mountain. He took me captive. His soundless prison is—" *indescribable* "—just as you warned me. Yet I . . ." he hesitated again, then went on, "I proved to have gained at least some measure of King Geriodde's goodwill. Or at least the goodwill of his son. Who is my friend, sir, though you will not likely credit it."

That eyebrow again. "Your *friend*, is he?" His tone was gruff, but not as heavy with censure as Taudde might have expected. The undertones of the king's voice were masked and hard to read. "Are you lovers?" he demanded abruptly. "You and that young Seriantes Dragon?"

Taudde jerked his head up in outrage. "No!"

His grandfather gave him a keen look. "Shocked you, did I? Why? You're certainly willing to bite in his defense—ah. There's a *woman*. You don't want to be taken for anyone's lover but hers. Fool boy, you've fallen for a woman of Lonne."

King Berente had always been quick. Taudde, trying to look as though he were at his ease, met his grandfather's eyes and made no attempt to deny it.

"That girl you brought with you? The keiso? One does hear stories about the keiso of Lonne, though I'd have thought you poured yourself too much into your precious sorcery to think of even those flower women. Well?"

"A keiso," Taudde admitted. "Not that girl." He didn't want to admit the Dragon's heir was in love with Karah, so he said instead, "The woman I mean is not so young, not so innocent, not so trusting. But clever. Wise . . ."

"Would I approve of her?" his grandfather demanded.

"If you met her, I think you would. I had intended to bring her to meet you, in fact. But events got a little away from me."

"Events. Indeed. I would not object to meeting this woman, if circumstances eventually permit. But for now you had better describe these events that got away from you."

"Yes, sir. Prince Tepres was visiting me when a coup occurred." Taudde was aware even as he said this that it did not sound very likely. He forged ahead anyway, since there was nothing else to do. "There was an attempt, at least. One of the prince's half-brothers, perhaps all of his half-brothers. You will know how in Lonne they recognize their bastard sons without shame, which perhaps is not wise, for it was these half-brothers who struck at Prince Tepres and drove us—drove me—to open a door into the heights above Kedres, bringing the Dragon's heir with me, though we have no idea what might have happened to the Dragon himself." Taudde stopped, watching his grandfather's face. He could very well anticipate an explosion, just at this point. He was fairly certain he could see one coming.

He was not wrong.

"So you brought the *heir of the Dragon* to Kalches, and to my house! You snatched him away from the hands of his enemies and put him into my hands, and now you tell me he's your *friend* and ask me to be generous to him! A coup in Lonne, the heir of the Dragon flung at my feet, the Dragon himself possibly dead or deposed, and you hand all this to me with the solstice barely three weeks away!"

Taudde said quietly, "Though you may question my judgment, I can only hope you will not question my intentions. Though I have earned your displeasure, I swear I have not earned your distrust."

The king sat back slowly, his fierce gaze still fixed on Taudde's face. But he said after a moment, almost gently, "Well, boy. I believe that, at least." Then he leaned forward again and added sharply, "If you'd obeyed me to begin with, *none* of this would have happened!"

Taudde bowed his head. "You are entirely correct, sir, and I apologize most humbly for my stupidity." He didn't say, *Other things would have happened, everything would be different, everything might be worse.* That might be true, he thought probably it *was* true, but obviously it would not be remotely helpful to say anything of the kind. He said instead, "But once a note is set free from the flute, it cannot be recalled."

"True. That is true." King Berente leaned back once more, setting aside anger with a clear, precise, practiced effort. "So, boy. Tell me what I should do with your friend Prince Tepres Nemedde ken Seriantes. Even if the Dragon of Lirionne lives, I gather you would not like to see me hold his son until the solstice and then begin sending him back to his father in small pieces."

"I would like to take him your assurance that you will do no such thing. I would be glad to go between you and the Seriantes Dragon—"

"No," said the king, with finality. "I am not prepared to offer assurances. If there has been an attempted coup in Lonne, well, let us see what comes of that. We shall wait, we shall all wait, to see what word arrives by way of more ordinary channels. We should not be required to wait very long," he added, at Taudde's slight movement of protest. *"This* news will fly across miles and mountains."

Taudde knew this was true. Any spy, and in fact any number of ordinary men who were not usually spies, would expect to earn great rewards for carrying the earliest word, or the most accurate word or the most up-to-the-moment word, of the events unfolding in Lonne. There would no doubt be a parade of hopeful informants over the next week or so. No doubt his grandfather's decision was wise and sensible and practical and kingly. But, though Taudde might have learned something approaching humility over the course of the past winter, he had most assuredly not learned to like *waiting.*

He said, since his grandfather was plainly waiting for it, "Yes, sir. I will be grateful for any small measure of generosity you find yourself able to grant to Prince Tepres. Whatever you decide to do, I will obey you."

"That's good to know," his grandfather said drily. "As you currently have no apartment within the house, and as the tower is, by your request, unoccupied, *you* may occupy it."

Taudde jerked his head up in surprise, and found his grandfather watching him narrowly.

He had expected a painful interview. But he had not expected this. But he could not say he had earned anything better. With a painful effort, he bowed his head again. "Yes, sir."

"Good." King Berente had been watching him narrowly. Now he leaned back in his chair once more. "You are, of course, a powerful sorcerer. Perhaps even the tower cannot hold you. But it *will* hold you, Taudde. From this moment until I give you leave, I forbid you to use any sorcery greater than required to light a candle or snuff one out. You may leave your flute with me." He held out his hand, regarding Taudde steadily.

Taudde hadn't expected that either. He took out his flute, slowly, turning it over in his fingers. It was not his first masterwork; that one had been lost in Lonne. Destroyed. He missed it still, but . . . he had carved this flute from driftwood, to suit his experience of the sea. He had gathered the wood himself from the shore below the great fortress of the Laodd, and carved a single blank from its heart. Then he had made his new flute from that blank, setting not one but two reeds in its throat. Other than the reeds, the instrument was very simple. It had no fittings of brass or silver. Its range was narrow, its notes turned to an ordinary descene scale. It might have been a child's toy, except for the soft doubling of its notes. But the wood from which he had carved it remembered the sea. Each note he sounded on this flute ran in and out like waves upon a shore.

Meeting his grandfather's uncompromising gaze, he set the flute in his hand.

There was perhaps the slightest softening of the king's stern mouth. "Good," he said. "Now I have a great deal to consider, it seems. You may inform Toma he is to escort you to the tower. Go."

It was not merely a command, clearly. It was a test. Taudde bowed his head again, briefly, turned on his heel, and went.

4

Leilis stood on the highest balcony of Cloisonné House, gazing out across the city as the sun, low above the sea, sent the last of its warm light across the opaque wash of the tide and laid a golden sheen across the slate rooftops and wide streets of Lonne. Above the city loomed the Laodd, its white walls glowing pale rose-gold in the light, its thousand windows glittering like jewels. Beside the Laodd, the great cataract of the Nijiadde River flung itself in infinite mad power down from the heights, shattering into spume at the base of the cliffs before rushing down to the sea. The rocks there, where the sea came against the shore below the Laodd, were jagged and black as charcoal.

They threw men down from the Laodd, sometimes. Not so very often. Perhaps half a dozen times that Leilis could remember. Men convicted of despicable crimes. They fell into the wild sea. Some of them, the sea cast back onto those jagged rocks, eventually. Others disappeared into the waves and the sea gave back not even the smallest finger bone.

Treason was a crime that could earn such a punishment. Though the king had spared his sons that death, when first two and then a third had been caught plotting treason and usurpation. Geriodde Nerenne ken Seriantes had simply ordered his treacherous sons beheaded, so they said. They said he had attended the executions. That he had watched the executioner's ax come down with no more expression than if he had been watching the tide come in.

Leilis believed that tale. She had met the king and she believed it. But she could not imagine it. She had no child of her own, but still . . . she could not imagine it.

Nor could she easily imagine that King Geriodde Nerenne ken Seriantes, whom men called the Dragon of Lirionne, might now meet the same fate as those three of his sons. Or perhaps already had. But she believed it was true. Rumor had run through the city, closely chased by fear. The round white lanterns of the candlelight district should have been lit to glowing life all along the river, in this gentle summer dusk. As the sunlight faded, the lanterns would echo the moon. In Lonne, poets made songs about the moon above and the lanterns below. Poetry and music and the silvery light of lanterns: that was the river at night.

But tonight the lanterns remained dark. The aika establishments did not hang out their paper lanterns, either: not the blue ones shaped like flowers nor the silver ones shaped like crescent moons. No flames burned within the elaborate candelabra that advertised the theaters; the restaurant porticos did not shimmer with lantern light. Tonight, the court and the city and the flower world alike kept close and kept quiet and waited for dawn. Only Leilis had put back the shutters of the highest banquet chamber and stepped out onto the balcony to listen to the night. And to think. And to worry, though she tried not to let that interfere with thinking.

From time to time the stillness of the evening was punctuated by distant shouting and the ringing crash of battle . . . on the other side of the river, for the most part. Not here, not close. Not yet.

She wondered whether King Geriodde's left-hand sons would ever have struck against their father if he had not first had their right-hand brothers put to death. It seemed unlikely. First because no left-hand son could possibly have stepped so close to the throne had Gerenes and Tivodd and Rette lived, and then because Sehonnes and Telis and even young Geradde must surely have become afraid of their father after their brothers' deaths. Of whether their father might someday suspect them of treason as well. Of what he might do then. And so the king might be said to have brought this night upon himself.

On the other hand . . . on the other hand, Leilis had to wonder as well just how strong the evidence against the right-hand sons had been, and just how difficult it would have been to create false evidence. Because there was no doubt that the left-hand sons had all stepped much closer to the throne as all but one of their right-hand half-brothers died. There was certainly no doubt that they—at least Sehonnes—now meant to take their father's throne by force if he could, the remaining right-hand prince notwithstanding. Perhaps Sehonnes merely seized an opportunity. But Leilis wondered whether he might have instead *made* that opportunity. They had never known the limits of Lord Miennes' conspiracy.

Either way, death was abroad this night. Stalking everyone: the king, his left-hand sons, his remaining legitimate son. The men who supported each. Some of those men would die. Possibly women, too. Especially, women who were known to be close supporters of one faction or another. And everyone knew that in all the candlelight district, there was no keiso more clearly or intimately linked to Prince Tepres than Moonflower of Cloisonné House.

If Prince Tepres were already captive or dead, then Cloisonné House was probably safe. If he had escaped, if he had fled into the city, if his ambitious, treacherous half-brothers searched for him . . . if that should be so, then in all the flower world, no House was more imperiled.

Leilis wondered whether she should feel ashamed to hope that, if the king had fallen, his heir had fallen with him. But she did hope for that.

Though she hoped much more fervently to hear instead that Geriodde Nerenne ken Seriantes had triumphed, and that it was the treacherous princes who would be cast down.

It was hard to know so little, and to know as well that whatever unfolded, she could do nothing to shape events. To know that when men drew their swords and slaughtered one another, women could do nothing but cower in silence and hope for kindness from the victors.

To the west, the sun slid slowly beneath the sea. In Lonne, shadows stretched out across the streets. Though the moon was neither high nor full, the magecrafted street lamps flickered alight, lending their greenish luminescence to the city streets. Above the city, the Laodd and the plunging cataract of the river and the granite heights still lay in a lingering glow. Leilis tilted her head back and stared up at the blank faces of the cliffs and the equally blank windows of the Laodd. She wondered what anyone gazing down from that height might see of the city where ordinary folk lived, or whether such a possible watcher would see nothing but the shadow of the Laodd.

"Leilis?" said a voice behind her.

Of course there were many girls and many women who lived in Cloisonné House, but Leilis knew every voice and every step. She said without turning, "Rue. You have had word from your younger sister, I hope? Has Moonflower returned to the House?"

"No," Rue said quietly. "I fear she has not."

Rue, as Moonflower's elder sister, was the younger keiso's teacher and guide to the flower world, more so even than Leilis. So Rue had approved Moonflower's visit to her sister Nemienne, and set the time when she must return. Only Moonflower had not returned.

Leilis inclined her head. "Taudde would not have left them alone together in his house. He will protect her." If he could, considering whom his other guest had been on this day. He had sent no word to Leilis, not in all these hours. But she did not say that aloud.

Leilis and Rue both knew precisely whom the girl had truly meant to meet when she so prettily asked leave to visit her sister. No one was less apt to deception than Moonflower. But there had seemed no harm in such a tiny bending of the rules. Until suddenly there had been great harm in it. If Moonflower had been near the Dragon's heir when the left-hand princes had moved against their father and his sole remaining right-hand heir . . . anything might have happened. When princes and mages battled, harm could so easily come to any near at hand. No matter how harmless and innocent.

All the keiso who had gone out on early errands during the afternoon had been returning quietly by ones and twos. Men clashed in the city, so women must slip through suddenly dangerous streets to seek such safety as could be found in their homes, or their Houses. One did not send anyone after those who were late in coming. That would only set more girls at risk. One merely waited, and hoped all the sisters and daughters of the House would return safely and soon. Almost all had returned. But not Moonflower.

Though, of course, whether Moonflower returned or not, the House offered merely an illusion of safety. That was one of the things Leilis had been thinking about. She said thoughtfully, "Everyone knows Prince Tepres has been courting Moonflower of Cloisonné House, but who knows that Moonflower is really Karah, daughter of Geranes Lihadde?"

Rue lifted her hands in a helpless gesture. "I know it. You know it. Mother knows it, and Terah, and anyone who cares to slip into Mother's rooms and read her ledgers."

"Yes," Leilis said, "Of course, ledger entries can be altered. I have been thinking that perhaps it might be as well to suggest to Mother that she alter that one."

"Oh, yes!" exclaimed Rue. "Of course! Will she do that?"

Leilis glanced at the other keiso. She was younger than Rue, and had been a keiso for a much shorter time, but somehow she felt much older and more experienced. But then, Rue had always been absorbed by her art nearly to the exclusion of everything else. Leilis said calmly, "I will alter the entry myself if necessary. But I will not be surprised if Mother has already done it. The flowers of Lonne bend beneath every storm, but when the storm passes, we are still here."

Rue looked a little bit relieved. She began to say something else, but she was interrupted by the rattle of a carriage in the shadowed street below. Its wheels had been wrapped in cloth, and the hooves of the horses that drew it had been likewise muffled, and it came along the dim street in the dark, with no lantern lit to warn passers-by out of its way. Rue caught her breath and stared at Leilis.

Leilis made herself smile the reserved, imperturbable smile of a keiso. She said in her calmest tone, "Whoever that may be, Mother will undoubtedly send for me. I think we shall not wait for her summons."

"Yes," Rue said. She was leaning forward, tense, wanting to run through the banquet chamber and down the stairs.

"Slowly," murmured Leilis. "Slowly." She gave Rue a chiding glance because the other keiso was too old to behave like a heedless girl. Then, of course, she had to set a decorous pace herself, partly because keiso did not dash madly through hallways and partly to give herself time to try to imagine who might have come to Cloisonné House, muffled and hidden and yet by carriage, which, however dulled the sound of the wheels, was hardly the way to go secretly through the streets. It seemed an odd choice.

The carriage had gone around to the back of the House, though the alley there was almost too narrow to allow it passage. There was no doubt at all, now, that it was coming to Cloisonné House, nowhere else. A cluster of women and girls, keiso and deisa and servants, had gathered in the kitchens and in the back hallways of the House, peering over one another's shoulders to see who might have come.

Mother came down the hall one way just as Leilis led Rue down the stairs from the other direction. Mother and Leilis gave the clutter of women and girls an identical long look and those at the rear began a disappointed withdrawal.

"Out," said Mother firmly. "Go to your rooms, all of you. Do you think this is a play? Do you hear music to signal the start of the hero's dance? You keiso, are you foolish girls, coming to gape when you don't know whether this is a dog come for shelter or a wolf come for blood? You should know *far* better! Out of sight and out of harm's way, everyone to her room! Terah, see to it!"

Terah, a retired keiso and Mother's close advisor, began to shoo the women and girls firmly back into the house. Most of the keiso, embarrassed because they knew perfectly well that Mother was right, went without protest.

"Go up to the balconies and watch for Moonflower," Leilis said quietly to Rue, touching the other keiso on the hand. "Be ready to keep her from the door. Who knows who might be watching? You know how girls sneak in and out—if you see her, bring her in that way."

Rue's brows drew together worriedly, but she nodded and slipped away.

At nearly that same moment, a hard knock fell on the door that led into the kitchen from the back alleyway. Mother, who had been turning to speak to Leilis, stood still. They both stood silent, motionless, staring at that door for what seemed like a long time, though it could not have been more than a few seconds.

Then Mother herself stepped forward, walked the length of the kitchens, drew back the bar and opened the door.

51

Narienneh, Mother of Cloisonné House, though growing elderly, still owned all the grace and elegance of the keiso. She was fine boned but not fragile, stately though not overly tall, and clad in exquisite keiso robes, pale blue and dark, colors washing into one another from one shoulder to the opposite hem. Her white hair was braided into a circlet around her head. Her dark eyes, dusted with violet powder, held reserve and authority.

Leilis herself wore the elaborate keiso robes to which she had so recently gained the right. A lacework of ocean spume flung itself up around the hem of her slate-blue overrobe, and white gulls flew from knee to shoulder. She wore a gull of pearls and hematite in her dark hair, and three silver bangles on one wrist. Anyone who saw her would know at once she was a keiso. That was important. Beauty and grace and a keiso's name could be weapons in a woman's hand, if men came with edged steel. But even so, she did not know whether she could have unbarred the door and flung it wide with the calm resolution Narienneh displayed

Leilis did not know whom she expected. Her first thought had been Taudde, but of course that was stupid. But if it was not Taudde, it would more than likely be someone worse.

It was not, in fact, someone worse. Or it was, but not in the way Leilis had feared. It was Neriodd, the king's personal bodyguard. The lines around Neriodd's harsh mouth and deep-set eyes had deepened; blood stiffened the sleeves of his overrobe and streaked his face. Leilis had first met him only months earlier, in the midst of those difficult events beneath the mountain. Neriodd, not a young man, looked ten years older now than he had at that time.

The reason for the strain in Neriodd's face and the source of the blood on his robe was immediately obvious, for behind him came two men of the King's Own guard, and between them they carried King Geriodde Seriantes himself. Out in the alley came the low sound of the horses blowing and shifting their wrapped hooves, and then, hardly louder, a creaking and thumping as the muffled carriage moved away.

Ordinarily the man called the Dragon of Lirionne drew every eye. He was a tall man, with the same angular cheekbones and narrow, arched nose and thin mouth as his son Prince

Tepres. But where in the son those strong features merely seemed aristocratic and haughty, in Geriodde Seriantes they seemed severe and stark. Even cruel. Everyone knew the Dragon of Lirionne could be cruel. Not so many knew, as Leilis knew, that the king could also be generous when it suited him. That he could even be kind.

Though at the moment, he had clearly lost the capacity for either cruelty or kindness. The king was obviously badly injured. Someone had wound a black underrobe around the king's chest as a kind of rough bandage, but blood dripped from the cloth and spattered on the clean floor of the kitchen, vivid crimson and alarming. Blood ran from his hand or arm, too . . . yes; from his hand, Leilis saw. That was bandaged as well. From the shape of the bandage, she guessed that king was missing at least one or two fingers. He sagged between the men who carried him. Though his ice-gray eyes were slitted open, they held little awareness. The absence of the king's acute, ruthless intelligence was more disturbing than the blood.

Mother's gaze moved from the wounded king to Neriodd. "You brought him *here?*"

"Here he would come, and not elsewhere," said the bodyguard, sounding wearied nearly to death. "Seeking Tepres—he is not here? I gather not?" From his tone, he had not expected it, but had hoped he might be wrong.

"If *he* would come here seeking his son, who else might come?" murmured Leilis.

"Hush!" said Mother. But then she added, looking at Neriodd, "But of course that is quite true. Though we will assuredly do our utmost to protect him—naturally Cloisonné House supports the king against any usurper."

"Yes," said Neriodd, wearily. "I know he can't stay here."

"We shall think of another place to hide him," Leilis promised the King's Own guardsman. The beginning of an idea nudged at her thoughts. She asked, giving it time to come clear, "This was Sehonnes? Or was it Telis? Surely not Geradde." She was thinking again of what it might mean for Cloisonné House if either Prince Sehonnes or Prince Telis, the two elder of the left-hand princes, cast down their father and took power in Lonne and in Lirionne. When she met Mother's eyes, she knew the older woman's thoughts were running with hers.

"Sehonnes," Neriodd said curtly. "It was Sehonnes struck the blow, though one may well guess Telis was back there somewhere behind him, prodding him into it. Whether Geradde was involved, I do not know, but if I met him now, I wouldn't hand him a dagger to hold." He gestured to his men to lay the king down on the long kitchen table.

Leilis suspected Neriodd was right about Prince Telis orchestrating all these terrible events. Of all the left-hand princes, Telis was the subtle one. Cold-hearted, they said in the flower world: cold-hearted as a serpent. It was the flower world that had begun calling the second left-hand prince Sa-Telis: the serpent-prince.

All the flower world knew that Prince Meiredde did not care for anything but his ships and the sea; that young Prince Geradde loved the candlelight district better than the court; but that Sehonnes hated his keiso heritage and despised the whole flower world. Sometimes left-hand sons were like that. The flower world offered so little place for the sons of keiso, and many of those sons took nothing from their keiso heritage but resentment for their legitimate half-brothers. But no one claimed to know what Sa-Telis thought, for Prince Telis kept his thoughts behind opaque eyes.

"Let us not find any prince at our doorstep tonight!" said Narienneh. She studied the injured king and said to Leilis, "But do you think Terah will be able to deal with such injuries? Well, she must. Leilis—"

Leilis gracefully inclined her head and went to find Terah. The older woman had learned something of the healing arts as she grew older. Many keiso, particularly those who never accepted a keisonne, took up some valuable trade as they grew older and chose to leave the glamorous keiso life to younger women. Terah was not precisely a surgeon, nor even a fever-doctor, but she was the nearest to either Cloisonné House could supply. And Narienneh was right: they did not dare reach outside Cloisonné House to bring in a real healer.

The king's most severe wound was the terrible slash across his chest, where ribs had been not merely broken but laid bare.

Though if the sword had struck the king six inches lower it would have cut through his belly, and if that had happened, no one would have needed to worry afterward about his health. Besides that chest wound, the king's hand had been mutilated: the thumb and first two fingers of his left cut away. Leilis found it far too easy to picture the unarmed king lifting a naked hand in hopeless defense against a sword, the blade sweeping down, sheering through the flesh and bones of his hand and continuing on to slash against his chest. She flinched from that image, but it returned, persistently.

"His left, at least," Neriodd said grimly. "That's a mercy, if he lives," meaning that the king was right handed and would at least remain able with sword or reins or quill.

Neriodd himself had proven, unsurprisingly, to be quite a competent surgeon, at least as pertained to sword wounds. It was he who stitched up the slashed blood vessels and the layers of muscle, while Terah was merely called upon to assist. Leilis made certain no denizen of the House came or went while they worked, grateful to have reason to quit the kitchens, where Neriodd and Terah worked over the unconscious king. Neriodd's men stood unobtrusive guard before and behind the House, wary of Sehonnes sending men here simply on the chance of finding Prince Tepres. Or Sa-Telis, or even Geradde, if the youngest of the left-had princes was also involved. None of them knew now who else might be an enemy.

Narienneh, as Mother of Cloisonné House responsible for the safety of every woman and girl who belonged to the House, hid her anxiety behind keiso serenity as she moved from the front of the house to the keiso galleries, noted the quiet arrival of Featherreed, almost the last of the absent keiso to return to the House. Mother and Leilis each at a different time took a moment to step out on a balcony and listen to the intermittent and still-distant clamor of confusion and battle. Despite her calm façade, Leilis could see how worried Narienneh was.

In all that time, Moonflower did not make her way back to the House. Leilis glanced into the room the girl shared with Rue, just in case they had all somehow missed her return. No one was there save her silver kitten, now a leggy young cat, curled into a ball on her pillow. Moonglow at least did not seem disturbed.

She opened her leaf-green eyes, blinked at Leilis, and went back to sleep. Leilis gave her a little nod and closed the door as she left the room.

"The Kalchesene will have protected her. Or she may have fled to her other sisters' house," Mother murmured to Leilis when she returned and shook her head. "It might be better if she had."

"If she returns, I will send her there," Leilis agreed, trying not to think of the sorts of things that might have sent a helpless girl fleeing from Taudde's protection to her sisters' house. "In either case, let the rest of us forget she ever bore another name. Let Karah, daughter of Geranes Lihadde, return to her sisters' home if she can and will; and Moonflower of Cloisonné House vanish without leaving even a shadow."

"I have amended the ledgers. Moonflower was the daughter of a keiso. Cloisonné House has never taken in the daughter of anyone named Geranes Lihadde."

Leilis nodded, unsurprised, and they both moved quietly back into the kitchens to see whether the king yet survived.

The last stitch had been set, the clean wounds bandaged, the bloody towels put to soak. "The king still lives," Neriodd said to Narienneh, his voice gritty with weariness and strain. "And if he lives now, perhaps he will survive. Yet I fear he may be too badly wounded to endure a move to a more secure place."

"We shall set him in my room for the moment," Leilis said. "We may find it easier to move him gently from there to a more suitable and hidden place." She glanced at Mother.

Neriodd's expression lightened. "You have an idea? Don't tell me what place you have in mind." He was quite serious, Leilis saw. He went on, "But you must not take the king away from Lonne. He *is* king. If once he cedes control of Lonne to a usurper, that will be in doubt."

Leilis considered this a foolish and impractical consideration, but it made no difference to her idea. She inclined her head in gracious agreement.

"Good, then. Good. I can't stay," Neriodd muttered. He pushed himself up, straightening his shoulders with an obvious effort. "I mustn't stay with him. I have—there are things I must do. In his service. But you—"

From the back of the house, from the alley, there was a sudden clatter, a heavy thud as of a blow, the sound of an oath, and then fraught silence. Neriodd, naked sword in his hand, strode to the door and flung it wide.

Two of his people came in, a man held roughly between them. Their captive was massive, heavy-boned, clearly strong as an ox. He had a broad coarse-featured face and looked simple, even stupid. He looked like anyone's idea of the most common sort of thug. But he had no weapon, and between the two King's Own guardsmen, no chance to resist.

He was also very familiar to Leilis and not a thug at all. She said, startled, "Benne!" Drawing breath to explain, she turned to Neriodd.

But the king's bodyguard was already signaling his men to release their prisoner. He said, his tone grim, "Benne. You have news of your master?"

The big man, freed, straightened slowly. But he looked at Leilis, not at Neriodd. His thumb brushed a tiny decorative drum hanging from his belt, a drum made of a feather and a scrap of parchment. He said to Leilis, "He is not here, then." His mouth moved when he spoke. If one did not know the secret of his voice, the illusion was very good.

Leilis was accustomed to Benne and to the magical voice bardic sorcery had restored to him when he had none of his own. But she was not accustomed to the big man asking her for reassurance. Especially not—she said, her tone sharp, "Taudde is not safe at his house? And the others, his guests today, have you word?"

She should have known better than to trust that even Taudde could be safe on a day such as this. She should have known that no one in the entire city could possibly be safe. Not even a Kalchesene sorcerer living in a house built by mages, with its doors that led to strange places. Not if Sehonnes had his cold-eyed brother or any of the mages of Lonne to help him.

Benne glanced at Neriodd, registered at last the unconscious body of Geriodde Seriantes, covered with a blanket, laid out on the largest kitchen table. His eyes widened. His gaze flickered from the king back to Neriodd and back to Leilis. His thumb touched the little drum once more, and he said, careful even now to move his mouth with the words, "I went there. There had been fighting. Outside the house, and inside, in the hall. Jeres Geliadde was dead there, in the street. There was more blood than his. Blood inside the house, all along the hallway. On the walls, on the doors. Blood on the new door." He turned his broad, stupid-seeming face toward Neriodd. "That is a door to Kalches."

"Kalches!" Neriodd exclaimed. He had been leaning against the table where the king lay, one hand resting lightly on the king's wrist, undoubtedly for the reassurance of feeling Geriodde's pulse beating against his fingers. But now he straightened, incredulous. "Kalches!" he said again.

Benne nodded. "If my lord needed immediate refuge, what other door would offer retreat where neither soldier nor mage would dare follow? Maybe it flung itself open for him before he ever laid hand on it. But when I tried it, the door would not open for me. Maybe it would not open for anyone but my lord."

Every now and then, Benne let men see that he was not stupid at all. For a long moment, no one said anything. Then Leilis said coolly to Neriodd, "Taudde would protect Prince Tepres. Even from his own people." Then she asked Benne, "You did not see Moonflower there, or Nemienne? Well, it seems we may hope that they all found refuge in Kalches."

Neriodd gave her a profoundly skeptical look, plainly not trusting that the Dragon's heir would find any kind of welcome in Kalches, even with Taudde to speak for him.

Leilis could not blame him for worrying. She assured herself that *Taudde*, at least, would be safe among his own people. At least she could be confident of that.

Though she did not like to think of the blood on the door. Taudde might easily have returned to his own people, but wounded. Dying, perhaps. She tried to imagine how his grandfather, king of Kalches, would feel if his grandson staggered through a magecrafted door and fell dying in his own house. In company with the heir of the Dragon of Lirionne.

She said aloud, "We can do nothing for Prince Tepres or for Taudde, or the girls, if they are gone to Kalches. But we cannot be certain they fled through that door. Perhaps they fled through some other door, or merely deeper into the house. It is, after all, a house of magic. It might well be difficult for enemies to find them there."

Neriodd rubbed a hand across his face, leaving streaks of blood. "Or perhaps the left-hand princes took the lot of them. You're right; we don't know." He was still a moment, considering. "I may be able to find out whether the treacherous princes took them," he said at last. "That much, at least."

"And send us word?" said Mother.

"If I find your little keiso, if I can send you word of her fate, I will. Believe me, finding Prince Tepres is my very first and most urgent task. Or—" he hesitated, not quite glancing at the king. "My first task but one."

"Everyone will be searching for Prince Tepres, if he got away," said Benne, then pointed to the king and added, "But for *him*, even more."

"Yes," said Neriodd. "So merely waiting to see if men search will tell us nothing." He took a deep breath. "So yes, hide him away as you will and can, and then—"

Benne interrupted him. "There will be no way to hide him. So long as he has not been found, men will search, if they must look into every closet and cellar and attic in all of Lonne."

Neriodd stopped He did not attempt to refute Benne. The big man was too plainly correct. Neriodd looked weary to death, but he also looked at Leilis, obviously hoping she would have an answer for this.

Narienneh turned to look at Leilis. She, too, was beginning to look overwhelmed. Leilis knew exactly how she felt. She felt overwhelmed, too. She knew Benne was right. If the king wasn't found quickly, his treacherous sons would only search harder. She could almost hear even now the weight of yet another blow on the door, the brutal thud of boots on Cloisonné House's polished floors, the ring of swords, the ruthless threats and the terrified cries of the girls.

It must not happen. She could think of only one way to be sure it did not happen. She said smoothly, trying to sound confident, "The king must be found. Then his treacherous sons will cease searching, and we may hope they and theirs will go about the business of men and keep far away from the flower world." She looked at Neriodd. "The king must be found dead.

Then he may recover in peace."

There was a pause.

Neriodd said at last, "He would never accede to such a plan. It is the same as leaving Lonne. If he is thought dead, then Sehonnes will seize the throne uncontested. Once power is lost, it may well prove impossible to regain. No king would step aside and allow himself to be supplanted, even as a ruse. Certainly *he* will not."

"And yet," Leilis said drily, "I hear no protest from the king."

Everyone glanced involuntarily at the king, as though he might indeed sit up and protest. He did not move, of course. The bones of his face stood out in stark relief. Even unconscious, his thin mouth was set with pain. He looked . . . not dead. One could see the wounded chest rise slightly and fall again beneath the blankets they had thrown over him. But he did not look so very far from death, either.

Leilis said, "He must have warmth and quiet and gentle care. He cannot be carried far or roughly. If he is thought to be dead, everything is simpler. The exigencies of a later day can be addressed . . ." she held out a hand, palm up, in a slight, dismissive gesture. "Later."

"This is *Geriodde Seriantes,*" Narienneh said suddenly to Neriodd, whose mouth was turned down in doubt and disapproval. "Neriodd, my friend, I think you need not fear that the Dragon of Lirionne will fail to make himself recognized, however many months pass and however many of his wicked sons declare they have laid him in his tomb."

Neriodd, though he still frowned, now looked indecisive.

"I know where to find a body," Benne said. His deep voice rumbled like a drum in the quiet kitchen. "The dead-wagon by the quarry, where they throw the dead quarry workers. They throw them in the sea, but not every day. There are always the bodies of one or two or half a dozen dead men there, with no guard set and no one to see who might come and go."

"Well," Neriodd said after a moment, "And I know how such a body could be battered enough no one could tell whether it had been a quarry man or a king. And how to be sure that it is found." He was beginning to like the idea, Leilis could see. If only because he knew, as well as any of them, that any search for a living king would grow more intense with every day that passed. He was not stupid. He knew Leilis was right: that the only way to protect the king was to make his sons believe he was dead.

"So," said Benne. "If you can find a body with the right hair and general build . . ."

"Oh, we can. One way or another. The means you suggest would certainly be simplest." Neriodd rubbed his face, then ran a hand though his gray-streaked dark hair. The lines around his mouth deepened as he frowned. "That face . . . no one would mistake it, but cut the hand to match, cut the chest, then tie the body under a pier, let the waves bash it around for a day or two. After that there won't be enough left of the face to matter. We can leave the body on the rocks beneath the Laodd, make sure it's found before it washes off again . . ." he glanced distractedly around the room. "We can do this. I don't imagine *he* will approve, but as you say, he's not protesting. It's my decision and my responsibility. Right?"

"Sir," muttered one of his own men. "It's a good idea, sir, and I'll say so to *him*, and glad to do it, if he's just alive to hear me."

Neriodd clapped the man on the shoulder, looking fractionally less exhausted. "I won't ask you to say it, Beren. But thank you." He looked at Leilis. "And I thank you as well." He gave Narienneh a belated nod as well. "All of you, and your gracious House. Don't tell me where you hide him—don't tell anyone. Not until he's back on his feet. I . . . I will have a great deal to do before that, if he's to have a chance to take Lonne back." Neriodd glanced once more around the room, gazed for a long moment at his king, nodded to Leilis once more, and walked out without ceremony. His men followed him. Benne looked indecisive, but Leilis beckoned to him and he stayed where he was. Leilis and Narienneh and Benne all stayed still, by the unconscious king, listening to the sound of the men's boots retreating, and the muffled clatter of the carriage as they took it and themselves back into the dangerous, shadowed streets of the city.

Those here, of course, were in a different kind of danger.

Leilis looked at Narienneh. "The girls, the keiso—they'll all be frightened."

"Yes,"said the Mother of the House. "Yes, of course." She straightened her shoulders and touched her hair, braided elegantly up as always, not a strand out of place. Her face settled into an expression of gracious serenity. "I shall reassure the girls," she said calmly. "And inform them that no one is to trouble you tonight. I shall leave everything else to you."

Her voice trembled just perceptibly on the last words. Leilis pretended not to notice. "Of course, Mother," she murmured. She couldn't say, *Don't worry*. She said instead, "Benne will help me, I am sure. I shall take care of everything."

Which was a dangerous thing to say. But she really thought she had a plan. It would get the king to a place of safety where he could lie concealed and be well cared for until the other man's body could found in place of his. Her plan would protect both Cloisonné House and the king, and it would work.

She only wished she could protect Taudde. Well, and Prince Tepres. And Karah, and Nemienne. Wherever they were. Kalches—perhaps, or perhaps not. Together—perhaps, or perhaps not. She did not know; she had only surmise for comfort. It was a pale comfort. Particularly since she knew that if Taudde had taken Prince Tepres to Kalches, then Taudde was safe but the prince was not, and if the king of Kalches chose to take vengeance on Lirionne in the person of the prince . . . she thought of Taudde, torn between irreconcilable loyalties, and winced away from the thought. Should his grandfather choose such action, Taudde might not be safe after all.

But she was a keiso. And a keiso did not tremble or weep. The face Leilis turned toward Benne was as carefully serene as ever. "We shall carry the king up to my room," she told him. "First."

Leilis' room in Cloisonné House was small and odd-shaped, and the bed too narrow and not really long enough for the king. But the room offered far better privacy and comfort than the table in the kitchen. And, of course, Leilis' room in particular, as she knew and almost no one else, possessed one other advantage. Because if one knew the way, if one's heartbeat was tuned to the heartbeat of the dragon of Lonne, one might step from that room into the darkness below the mountain. Leilis had never done it, not alone. But she thought she might. She thought she could.

Stepping out of the darkness again, out into the place she wished to be . . . that was the part that worried Leilis.

5

Nemienne, sitting beside Prince Geradde in the dark, tried again to pull away from his grip, though she was unsurprised when he did not let her go. Giving up for the moment, she said, "Maybe you don't realize that I saw you there. I saw you with them. With—with Prince Sehonnes and Prince Telis and all those other men. I *saw* you. I know you're on their side."

"I was certainly there," Prince Geradde agreed without heat. "When my brothers came to me this morning, they made their expectations very clear. Well, Sehonnes made *his* expectations clear. He had our father's ring, after all. One always has to guess about Telis's intentions."

"They *made* you come with them?" Nemienne wondered if she dared believe this.

"It seemed wisest to accept my brothers' . . . sudden invitation, let us say. And then find, as quickly as possible, a way to get out from between them. Especially since . . . well, Sehonnes has a temper when he's balked; one hardly wishes to be near him now that he's . . . lost our father's ring."

Along with the hand he'd worn it on. Nemienne nodded, wincing.

"Yes, exactly. And I have never been on good terms with Telis. I don't doubt that his plans have a place for me. I don't want to find out what that place is. So when you flung open the black door, it seemed a practical solution. I certainly did not pursue you on behalf of my *brothers*. You may be quite confident of that."

Nemienne wished she could be confident of anything. She didn't say so. It probably wasn't polite to tell a prince you thought he might be lying.

Prince Geradde straightened his shoulders and looked at Nemienne directly. "Especially because I hope you will be able to open the other doors in that house. The door to Kalches in particular. I want Tepres *back*," he told her. Then he repeated, more quietly but with no less intensity. "I want him back. Do you think I want *Sehonnes* on the throne? Only it would be Telis, in the end, I expect—and that would be worse. No. I want Tepres back—and not in pieces, as the king of Kalches might decide to return him. Not," he added, more quietly as his intensity or courage or strength ebbed, "Not that I have the least idea how I will find him in Kalches, or get him away. But if you could open the door, it would be a start. Can you open that door? Will you?" A note of humor entered his voice and he leaned his head wearily back against the stone. "I warn you, I am prepared to sit here in the dark until you agree. Indeed, I will be quite pleased to sit still. It was a long chase you led me."

It had seemed long enough to her, too. Nemienne said nothing, not willing to admit to sympathy with this left-hand prince.

Her silence did not seem to offend him, though. The prince only lifted his head again and gave her an ironic look. "Don't you wish to find your Kalchesene master? Would it not trouble you to leave Tepres in the hands of Kalchesene sorcerers? I fear to wait too long. I fear the passing hours. Who knows what the king of Kalches may do with my brother while I scramble to find a way to go after him? Say you will help me! We will go together to Kalches and find some way to rescue Tepres. Perhaps you can persuade your master to help. I had thought him genuinely on good terms with my brother. Will you not try to persuade him?"

Nemienne studied Prince Geradde. His father had meant to avoid war with Kalches if he could. Taudde said so, and Leilis said so, too, so she was sure it was true. Prince Tepres had not wanted war, either. But she could not guess what Prince Geradde might want. Maybe he really did want to follow after his brother and rescue him from whatever fate the king of Kalches might have planned. Maybe he really did want to bring his brother back to Lonne and help him take his father's throne.

Or maybe he was lying to her. Every word he said might be a lie, and how would she know? Probably a sorcerer could tell whether he was lying. Or a mage. But she couldn't at all. He was right that she was worried about Taudde, and Prince Tepres, and she was particularly worried, though he didn't seem to have guessed this, about Karah.

She thought the door to Kalches might well open for her. But . . . take *him* there with her? She said firmly, "Very well. Let me go, then, and I will help you."

The look of irony deepened. "Let you go? And risk wandering in these caverns until I leave my bones to turn to stone in these blind passageways? No, I think not. You were difficult enough to catch the first time." His mouth crooked again. "I hardly know whether I would survive another such pursuit."

That certainly explained why he had kept after her, and *kept* after her and never, ever fallen behind enough for her to evade him. It had not occurred to Nemienne that her pursuer might be even more terrified of losing her than she was of being caught. She hadn't meant to be sorry for him, but . . . for him to be lost in the dark beneath the mountains might be worse than for her. If he had no way out . . . she didn't want to think of it.

But she said skeptically, "But how lost could a Seriantes prince be, here below Kerre Maraddras? Are these not your caverns? Isn't that your dragon—no, I know," she added, seeing his eyebrow rise. "But I mean, you're *all* similar things to the dragon, aren't you?" Or maybe it was just Prince Tepres, because he alone among the surviving princes was the heir. She tried to decide whether she could hear the dragon's heartbeat behind Prince Geradde's heartbeat; whether she could glimpse the dragon's long, elegant head behind the prince's sharp-boned features. She was not sure.

"I would hardly make any such claim," said the prince, his tone rather dry. "I feel thoroughly lost, I assure you. I do know of the dragon, after what happened with your Kalchesene master and Tepres. But I have never even seen it myself. My father forbade—" his voice caught and he stopped, perhaps struck anew by the fact of his father's death. Nemienne knew just how that felt. He said at last, in a different tone, "I am told it is not safe to trouble the dragon's rest. Even for a Seriantes. Perhaps especially for a Seriantes."

"Well . . ." Nemienne couldn't assure him it was safe. She knew it wasn't. She said, "But if you *did* want to go there, I could find the dragon's chamber, I think." She almost wanted him to agree, though the dragon terrified her. It was a different kind of terror than when she thought of the treacherous princes, or when she thought of what might happen to Prince Tepres and Karah in Kalches. And . . . she almost wanted to take Geradde to the dragon's chamber so that the dragon could show her his heart. She had liked what it had shown her of her own.

Though probably it would eat them both if they troubled its rest. Or do something worse. It wasn't *exactly* a dragon, after all. She thought it was . . . greater, than a dragon. Probably it wouldn't do something as trivial as merely eat someone. She said regretfully, "But you're right that it isn't safe. At all."

"Then perhaps another suggestion would do better."

Nemienne nodded and tried to think. She *was* sorry to lose the chance that the dragon might show her his heart. She began, "But even if—" but then she thought better of it and stopped.

"Even if you trusted me?" said Prince Geradde, with that ironic tilt of his mouth. "Difficult, perhaps, but it must not be impossible. Because if not this . . . if not this, I don't know what to do."

Nemienne *didn't* actually trust this left-hand prince, that was true. But she definitely understood that weary tone. That, she understood perfectly. She touched the prince's hand in sympathy. "I'll make the stone warm," she suggested. "We can both rest for a little while longer. Then maybe we can think of somewhere to go."

"Delay—"

"Will be less if we think now instead of rushing into action. Isn't that so?" He still held her left wrist in a firm grip, but she reached out with her right hand to touch the stone, and thought of warmth. Warmth. Not burning fire nor the powerful heat of an iron stove in the winter, but a gentle warmth, as sun-warmed stone would yield back to the dusk after a long summer's day.

The prince let out a slow breath, his shoulders relaxing a little.

"Tell me about your brothers," Nemienne suggested. "About Prince Telis. Why is he worse than Prince Sehonnes? Why is it so important to rescue Tepres? To you, I mean," she amended. "I know why that's important to me."

"*Is* it important to you? I should like to think so." Geradde studied her. Then, yielding, he leaned back against the now-warm stone.

Nemienne thought she might get away now if she tried. But now she wasn't sure she should try. She settled beside the prince instead and coaxed again, "Tell me about Prince Telis. And Prince Sehonnes, and everyone. What really happened? Do you know? No one—I don't think anyone really knows. Except—well, anyway. *Do* you know?"

"I have one or two surmises," Geradde said after a moment. "I don't trust Sehonnes to have told me the truth about what happened between him and our father—nor Telis to tell anyone the truth about anything." He sighed, and glanced around. "I don't suppose you can draw water as well as warmth from this stone?"

Nemienne was immediately thirsty. She said regretfully, "It isn't truly water here beneath the mountain. Just as it isn't truly light."

"Of course not," the prince said, his tone resigned. "Of course not."

Once Geradde mentioned water, though, Nemienne found she was very thirsty. *Prince* Geradde, but he was not as intimidating as Tepres and far, far less so than the king. So it was hard to remember.

It was also hard to worry about such things when she was so thirsty. Maybe she should try to find a way out of the caverns right now, after all.

Geradde said slowly, "We will leave these caverns. Will you agree to that much? We will go somewhere in the warmth and light, where the water is truly water, and then I will let you go—you will not be my prisoner and I won't be yours, and then we can talk more easily. Do you agree?"

Nemienne nodded cautiously.

"Good." Prince Geradde gave her a smile that looked as tentative as she felt. "I hope you'll be able to shorten the way we return. We must go carefully. I must confess that I do not know where to go. We dare not return to Ankennes' house—Telis may still be waiting there, or more likely one or another of his allies. Nearly all of the mages are his, I believe. Nor do we dare venture into the Laodd; Sehonnes will have secured it."

Nemienne thought immediately of her sisters' house. But she wouldn't take this charming left-hand prince there, no matter how smoothly and earnestly he asked for her help to rescue Tepres. She thought maybe she might believe him, she might believe everything he said—but she didn't dare risk all her sisters' lives merely on her feeling that she could trust him.

But Nemienne didn't know where else they could go, or how else to step out of the dark.

Might she risk taking him to Cloisonné House? She thought she could find the way, if she tried. Leilis would know what to think of Prince Geradde. Leilis would know all about this keiso-born prince, as she knew everything about everything in the flower world. But what if Prince Geradde proved as treacherous as his full brothers? Then he would find out all about Cloisonné House and Leilis, and then perhaps he would find out that Moonflower of Cloisonné House was really Nemienne's sister Karah. If he did, and turned out to be lying to her, whatever harm came, it would be Nemienne's fault.

But Leilis was clever. Surely he wouldn't find out anything that Leilis didn't want him to discover.

Nemienne could not decide.

She listened to the sound of water falling, drop by drop, from the high places of the caverns, and tried to think where else she might take them. A place that would be safe for her, that would betray no one, that would let her get away from Prince Geradde if she needed to—but a place that would be safe for the prince, too, if he had told her the truth about supporting Prince Tepres against his own full brothers. She did not know what to suggest

Then he said, a little hesitantly, "Perhaps my mother's kin in Maple Leaf House might shelter us for a little while. Would you agree to go there? I know proper girls seldom venture into the candlelight district . . ."

Nemienne stared at him. It made sense, though. Unlike Cloisonné House, the keiso of Maple Leaf House had no reason to fear the treacherous princes searching among them for Moonflower. She said, "Would they protect you from your brothers? You are all equally Skyblue's sons . . ."

Prince Geradde said flatly, without hesitation, "Sehonnes hates the flower world, and no one trusts Telis. They would not betray me to either of my brothers."

This sounded true. And once she was at Maple Leaf House, she could surely slip away and make her way to Cloisonné House. Nemienne nodded. "Very well!" she said "I'll find the way out of the dark, but I don't know how to step directly into Maple Leaf House. But . . ." Not her sister's house, but somewhere in the light. "Somewhere in the light. Somewhere along the shore," she said aloud, and thought he nodded, though she wasn't certain. She listened to the distant sound of the falling drops of water. The sound echoed the rhythm of the waves, somehow. Or perhaps that was the silence, which came between the falling drops in almost a similar way as when the waves came against the shore

Those waves ran against the broken rocks beneath the Laodd, where the ever-present thunder of Nijiadde Falls, dimmed by distance, formed a background to the rhythm of the ocean. She almost thought that even here she could hear the thunder of the Falls and the wash of the waves, like a rushing in her ears.

Taudde had liked to go down to that part of the shore. He said the sea sounded different below the Laodd. More like itself, more filled with magic. Nemienne hadn't known what he meant, but she thought she might understand that better now. Because beneath the rushing thunder of Nijiadde Falls and the sound of waves running against stone and the reverberation of falling drops of water, she found herself listening to the heartbeat of the dragon.

Or maybe that was Prince Geradde after all. Maybe every Seriantes prince, whether born on the right or the left, had a heartbeat that echoed the heartbeat of the dragon. Mage Ankennes had believed them all corrupted by its power and influence. At least they might all be tied to it, somehow.

Even though she had been standing still for a long time, Geradde did not speak or try to hurry her. He waited patiently. She *did* think she liked him—or she believed she would, if the situation weren't so dire and he weren't a prince. But she was grateful that he gave her all the time she needed to tune her own heartbeat to the heartbeat of the dragon, and then to the darkness, and then to the memory of the waves running against the cliffs— to the memory of light that struck across the running sea, and the dark shining stone below the Laodd.

At last she laid her hand over Geradde's, where he still gripped her wrist, and stepped blindly forward into the dark, drawing Prince Geradde after her . . .

. . . and her foot came down, but not where she had expected.

It was like stepping onto a stair that wasn't there. It jarred Nemienne's bones from her ankle all the way up her spine and sent her staggering, flinging out a hand for balance, and someone caught her, not Prince Geradde—he was gone, suddenly—but there was a hard grip on her shoulder, close by the base of her neck. It hurt. Nemienne tried to wrench away from that hold, but whoever held her only tightened his grip and shook her until she gasped in pain. She felt she couldn't breathe. Her ears roared.

And she was blind. There was light: the wrong kind of light, brilliant and glittering, nothing like the subtle, pale glow she had summoned into the caverns. Nemienne blinked hard against tears, trying to see. Prince Geradde was shouting—no, that wasn't his voice; someone *else* was shouting. Beyond the roaring in her ears, she could hear the sound of a struggle and then Geradde cried out too, wordlessly, sounding frightened as well as furious. His voice was thin, here, lost in the air and the pounding roar that still filled Nemienne's ears. Guilt shook Nemienne as much as terror and shock, because she hadn't *meant* to fling Prince Geradde straight into the hands of his enemies. They were plainly enemies, and this time she couldn't even bite the man who had caught her. He held her too hard for that, and too expertly.

She blinked and tried to shake her head, but she couldn't even do that. But she blinked again, fiercely, and the dazzle resolved at last, though the roaring lingered.

She did not know where they were. Not in the caverns any longer, but not on the shore below the Laodd where she had meant to take them. Somewhere she didn't know at all. They stood in a single great room, vast enough to hold two of

Cloisonné House without crowding. On three sides, the oddly uneven walls were stark and sheer and white, softened by neither tapestries nor wooden screens; the fourth wall was simply *missing*, so that they looked straight out into the sky. The sky was fiercely brilliant, but it was bitterly cold, as though no warmth ever came here.

Prince Geradde stood, not far away, pinioned between two older men, both in gray and brown, the colors of servants—but they did not look like servants. They looked like thugs, like the kind of men who set on honest people in smaller streets, when the hour was late and they thought they could get away with it. She could not turn her head well enough to see the man who held her, but she guessed he would have the same look. Of course, Taudde's man, Benne, looked like that, too, but she doubted any of these men was like Benne, who was clever and kind and careful of his strength.

Besides the thugs, there were two others: a man and a woman in the black and white robes of mages. The man held a long pale stick, though it looked too thin and fragile to be a weapon; and the woman held an irregular ivory sphere in both hands. Both mages had backed away from the struggle and were only now coming forward again, cautiously.

But one other man had not backed away at all. This was the one who drew the eye, once Nemienne had a chance to notice him.

He was older than Prince Geradde, older than Taudde, but not *old*—probably only in his third decade. He wore black and slate-gray, but the embroidery on the collar of his overrobe was saffron-gold, so Nemienne knew immediately who he must be. Everyone knew it was Prince Telis who had friends among the mages of Lonne.

She looked at him carefully, trying not to be obvious about it. Prince Telis was elegant, with angular eyes and a narrow mouth and a pointed chin. He looked very much like Prince Geradde, in fact, and a little bit like their father. But she could see neither Prince Geradde's kindness in his face, nor the king's stark, ruthless patience.

"Geradde," he said now. "*You* weren't the one I thought to capture in this net! But how extremely opportune, after you so inconveniently slipped away." His voice was just a little breathless, so Nemienne thought it might have been difficult for him to interfere with her magic and bring them both here. Wherever "here" was.

Prince Geradde stood very still between the men who held him, his head up and his eyes brilliant with anger—too proud to struggle uselessly, Nemienne saw, and also too proud to bend his neck before his older brother. She could see now that his eyes were gray; not as dark as Prince Tepres' nor as pale an ice-gray as the king's, but a shade in between, like pewter or the flat sea beneath the winter sky. Prince Telis had blue eyes rather than gray, an unusual color in Lonne, and his hair was dark. He looked like his mother, who had had those eyes and that fine straight hair, dark as the night sky. Nemienne knew that because her little sister Liaska had a painted miniature of Skyblue of Maple Leaf House. Everyone who collected miniatures of keiso had that one.

"I was almost certain I'd find you before you could run back to Sehonnes and grovel for protection," added Prince Telis. "Not that Sehonnes could protect you. You didn't matter until that fool let Tepres get away from him. Now . . ." He looked his younger brother up and down. "You'll do."

Nemienne wanted to say, *Wait,* who *was it who let Tepres get away?* But she didn't dare. Prince Telis was too frightening.

His voice was much like his full brother's: smooth and with an elegant turn on the vowels. But there was an impatient edge to his voice that Geradde's lacked, and something else, something worse than impatience. Nemienne wondered what Taudde might have heard in that voice, and wished suddenly that Taudde had found a chance, sometime before this, to hear Prince Telis speak. They called him Sa-Telis, didn't they, in the flower world especially. Maybe Taudde would have heard treason and treachery behind that smooth voice. She thought she could hear those things now. But it would hardly take a Kalchesene bardic sorcerer to hear treachery in Prince Telis' voice *now*.

Then she wondered what Taudde might have heard in Prince Geradde's voice. Nothing, maybe, if Geradde would not speak. He did not answer his brother at all, but only stood still, his shoulders level and his back straight, his gaze on Prince

Telis' face. Nemienne could see he expected nothing good from his brother. It was so strange, brothers who hated one another. She tried to imagine Ananda or Enelle or any of her sisters looking at her the way Prince Telis looked at his younger brother, with those hard eyes and that tight mouth. He looked at him as though he thought he was an enemy to be punished, or perhaps a rival to be crushed. Nemienne could not even begin to imagine that kind of expression on any of her sisters' faces.

Then Prince Telis turned away from his brother and looked at Nemienne, and that was worse. He didn't look at her as though she was an enemy. She couldn't think how to describe how he looked at her. There was no hatred in it, nor resentment, nor dislike. She thought he didn't see her as a person at all. She thought he looked at her as he would look at an object he meant to use. She stared back at him, mute with dismay.

"How convenient that the snare I set for the girl caught you as well, brother," Prince Telis said over his shoulder to Geradde. "Pity it didn't close around the keiso as well. Still, this will certainly do."

Geradde still wouldn't answer, but his silence didn't seem to disturb Prince Telis. Telis turned expectantly to the two mages, who had drawn forward now that the threat of violence seemed past. "What say you?" he asked them, with a nod toward Nemienne. "Neither mage nor bard nor enchantress, just as we'd been told. But don't you think there is an echo of all of that in her? As well as an echo of the dragon. The dragon is almost as strong in her as in my brother. You hear it, of course."

The woman mage, so addressed, came a step forward to peer with interest at Nemienne. She said, "Indeed, eminence, clearly the girl has learned to listen to the heart of darkness. A dangerous aptitude. But she should do well."

Do well at what, Nemienne wondered. Or *for* what. She almost asked, only then she saw that the lumpy ivory sphere the woman held in her hands was actually a skull, polished clean and smooth by time, but intact. The horror of that shocked her silent. She only made a small sound, a pained little huff that escaped before she could stop it, and looked quickly at the other mage, the one holding the pale stick. She knew the stick must be a bone before she even looked. It was: something smooth and long, with a knob on both ends. She thought it might be an arm bone, or maybe one of the bones from someone's leg. It was horrible. The way the man held it was the worst part: casually, as though it was in fact no more than the stick she had first thought it. She wanted to step back, but the man who held her didn't let her move.

"Do well for what?" Geradde asked. Nemienne glanced at him in surprise that he would ask that for her, and then kept looking at him because she couldn't bear to look at the mages. Geradde's tone was cool, ironic, a little amused. His manner was the manner of one who does not really care about the answer to the question he has asked. But somehow Nemienne felt better when she looked at him. As though he might be an ally. As though she might not be on her own. She was glad Geradde was there, which made no sense, but she couldn't help but be glad he was there so she wasn't alone.

She wondered if he felt better for her presence. If he thought of her as an ally, even though she had brought him out of the darkness below Kerre Maraddras only to cast him into his brother's hands. She wouldn't have blamed him for hating her, or at least for being furious with her. He would be right to be furious. If she had only thought to look, she might have been able to glimpse the edges of what had plainly been a magecrafted trap, waiting for her or for someone to step into it.

But Prince Geradde didn't seem to feel that way. Or at least he had tamped all his anger and fear down deep, where neither she nor his brother could see it. But even if he were angry and terrified underneath, he did not seem stunned, as Nemienne felt stunned and blank. He had even asked the question she had most needed to ask, when she was too frightened to ask it.

She knew now where they must be. She had tried to step out of the darkness onto the shore, but she knew that Prince Telis must have brought them instead to Kerre Taum. That they must be standing right in the King's Tomb, high above the Laodd, above even Nijiadde Falls. It was the great Falls that roared so, of course; it surrounded and engulfed every other sound, as though the light itself had been given voice.

She felt very cold. The darkness below Kerre Maraddras had not been nearly so cold as this. It seemed strange, to stand in this great brilliant outpouring of light and be so cold.

"For binding the dragon, of course," Prince Telis said impatiently to his brother. He didn't even glance at Nemienne, and she felt again how she wasn't really a person to him, but just a tool apt for a task he had in mind. All his attention was on Prince Geradde—at least he seemed to feel that his brother was a real person.

Or perhaps not, because then he went on, "The girl can wake it, if necessary. She's done it before. *You* can help me bind it. You'll look perfect on the throne. No one wants Sehonnes. Sehonnes the parricide! He'll deny it, of course, but who would believe him? Everyone is simply waiting for an alternative. It's not me they're waiting for, but men who would never hail me will nevertheless be ready to call *you* king, and never look into the shadows behind the throne. You will do well."

"Will I?" said Geradde, disdainfully.

But Nemienne understood what Prince Telis meant. Geradde didn't see it yet, but *she* did. She knew that Prince Telis meant to make his brother into a puppet by some kind of magecrafted binding, and since Geradde was a similar thing to the dragon, Prince Telis would work through him to make the dragon into a puppet, too. Or he planned something of the kind, at least. She could almost see how that might work. If he managed anything like that, it would be horrible. Only . . . she said, hardly aware she spoke out loud until she heard her own voice, sounding thin and worried, "You can't bind it, though, no matter what you do to Prince Geradde. Even Mage Ankennes never thought he could *bind* it—"

The man holding her shook her hard so that Nemienne bit her tongue and gasped in pain. "Quiet, girl," he snapped at her. His voice was just as she would have expected: malicious and self-satisfied. She was sure he would like her to protest again so that he could hurt her. She didn't dare say anything.

But she could see that Prince Telis wasn't going to listen to her at all, anyway. He said dismissively, already turning away, back to the mages and their bones, "Take them back into the tomb and keep them safe for me. The girl knows almost nothing of magecraft and no doubt less of sorcery, but keep in mind she does walk through walls and air and distance. Don't let go of her for an instant. Isonne, weave a binding for her—for both of them. I shall reinforce it shortly, and it will hold. We'll have no accidents now, when we're so close."

And then he just walked away, indifferent as a serpent. But Nemienne didn't doubt that he meant what he said about bindings, and about having no accidents. She found she couldn't imagine him making a mistake.

This time, she didn't see how either she or Prince Geradde were going to get away.

-6-

Leilis was almost certain her plan would work. The first part of it, at least: getting the king away from Cloisonné House. The second part, getting him to a place of relative safety where he could be cared for properly . . . that part, she was not quite so confident about.

She stood stroking Karah's kitten Moonglow, and said to Benne, "I would say the best chance is that this will work. The second chance is that we might simply lose ourselves in the dark and no one will ever find our bones, which would no doubt distress Neriodd, among others. Or, third, we might find that we have followed Karah, wherever she is, and if that proves to be Kalches, we will have delivered the king into the hands of his enemies. Or, if we wish to contemplate an even more exciting possibility, we might find ourselves speaking with the dragon below the mountains, and who knows what might come of that?"

Benne had wrapped the king up carefully, checked his pulse, and then lifted him as gently as possible in his arms. Since, so occupied, he could not touch the tiny drum at his belt, he had no voice. But the look he gave Leilis was eloquent.

"Yes," Leilis said. "I also wish Taudde were here." She stroked the kitten again. Moonglow purred drowsily.

Mother would change every House record that provided even a hint of Karah's real name. By dawn, everyone in the whole House would know that Moonflower of Cloisonné House had been born to a keiso mother, an obscure woman who had never been well known and had died young. Everyone would know that Moonflower's first name had been Tamiah but she never used it anymore, that she had never had any sisters other than the girls in the House. Before a single day passed, the whole flower world would know that tale. Probably they would all hold to that story. Leilis was confident that they would—as long as no one frightened them too much. And why would anybody doubt it? Everyone knew most of the keiso *were* born in the flower world.

Meanwhile, Leilis must see to it that if anyone came to search Cloisonné House for a young keiso named Moonflower, they did not find an injured king instead. She did not intend to sacrifice King Geriodde to protect Cloisonné House and the flower world. But she was willing to risk the possibilities she had just laid out for Benne.

His first loyalty was not to the king of Lirionne, either. She suspected that if he had been able to speak at this moment, he would still not have said a word.

No one should be looking for Karah yet. Leilis was certain no one could *possibly* be looking for her, yet. Sehonnes would have more important things to do this night than hunt down his right-hand brother's favored keiso, especially since she wasn't yet officially his keimiso, his flower wife. Sehonnes must surely still be struggling against the king's supporters, and possibly against his brother Prince Telis as well. Everyone in the flower world knew those two had never been friends. Perhaps now they had become open rivals. Leilis was certain she had plenty of time to take the king to safety and return.

As long as she could find her way through the dark.

If Taudde could not be here, then she wished Nemienne were with her. Karah's sister had always proven apt to find her way through the shadows that fell from the daylight world into the dark caverns beneath the mountains. All Leilis had was a Pinenne Cloud kitten and a heart that beat, so she had been told, in rhythm with the dragon of Lonne.

Benne, despite his silence, was a comforting presence. He was so solid and calm. He didn't look like he had ever been nervous about anything in his life. Leilis thought that if he had been a woman, he would have made a good keiso.

In her arms, Moonglow yawned and wiggled. Taking this as a suggestion that they should begin, Leilis knelt by the massive fireplace that dominated the narrow room and traced the narrow fissure in the hearthstone, the one that Nemienne had said was really the rune of traveling. Leilis did not have Nemienne's gifts, but she had her father's blood and a heartbeat that was, perhaps, tuned to the dragon's heartbeat. Shutting her eyes, she traced the spiky rune a second time. She tried to listen to her own heartbeat, but there was only silence. Save that, after a moment, she almost thought she heard within that silence the rhythm of the tides, and the silence at the heart of the mountain.

She opened her eyes. A kind of light that wasn't really light poured out of her hands and into the cracked stone, widening the jagged strokes of the rune. Light spilled into the fractures, and darkness spilled out of them, until darkness and light mingling and became the same.

Moonglow leaped out of her arms and, with a flick of her silver tail, disappeared into the light and the darkness.

Leilis laid her hand on Benne's arm, and led him into the darkness, following the kitten.

Pinenne Cloud cats could, of course, find their way through the dark. For a moment Leilis wondered what might have happened to Enkea, the cat that lived in Ankennes' house. And didn't the king himself have a Pinenne Cloud? She wouldn't have minded having an older, steadier animal with her for this experiment. But then, it was Karah's kitten who knew how to get from Cloisonné House to the house of her blood-sisters.

Or so Leilis hoped. It was, at least, a route by which she knew Nemienne had taken Karah—at least twice since the events of the past winter.

Then she set all such questions aside, fearing to lose sight of Moonglow if she allowed herself to become distracted. Around her, the darkness seemed to twist, turn itself inside out, and stretch out—and up—and out again. She gripped Benne's arm hard, not daring to think of losing him here.

She was not lost. She knew this dark. She heard the great heartbeat that thundered silently through this darkness. Her own heart beat in rhythm with it. Before her, Moonglow slipped through the dark in what seemed a light of her own, dark stripes showing through her silver-tipped fur as she moved. She knew where Leilis wished to go—or Leilis hoped she knew—or wherever she led them, let that be a place of warmth and safety! She wished again, fervently, for Taudde, or Nemienne, or even for Karah herself, whose kitten this was—Moonglow would surely never abandon Karah in the dark—

Ahead of her, the kitten suddenly sat down on her plump

rear and looked over her shoulder at Leilis, her leaf-green eyes glimmering now almost gold.

And the world swayed and steadied and narrowed, and bloomed with ordinary lantern light, and filled with the surprised clamor of a crowd of girls exclaiming at once, and they were no longer in Leilis' little room high up under the slanted roof of Cloisonné House, but in the warmth of the long gallery lined with the beds of Karah's sisters and illuminated with the light of eight lanterns, one hanging on a chain above each bed.

It was a good deal like the deisa's gallery in Cloisonné House, but warmer and a bit shabby and noisier and, at the moment, infinitely more welcome. Leilis swayed, feeling for a moment faint with relief, though she hoped she did not show how anxious she had been. She turned, looking for Benne.

He was there, just where he should be, at her elbow, with the king still cradled like a child in his powerful arms. Leilis let her breath out, tension running out of her, taking her strength with it so that she had to sit down suddenly on the bed. The big man stood stolidly, not looking at any of Nemienne's sisters, but gazing with tactful concentration at the fireplace that warmed the far end of the gallery.

"Forgive our intrusion," Leilis said to the girls in the gallery—there were only four here at the moment. Tana, she remembered, already taller than Karah and just beginning to get a woman's shape; Miande, sweetly pretty in an ordinary way; Jehenne was about eleven or ten, and of course the youngest one was Liaska. Leilis did not really *know* them as she knew all of the women and girls of Cloisonné House, but, curious to see the home that had produced Cloisonné House's newest keiso, she had made sure to visit this house and meet all of Karah's sisters. None of them was as pretty as Karah, none had her special charm, but any, in Leilis' opinion, would have been an asset to a keiso House. The youngest child in particular had a charm of her own—

"Leilis! Who's that man?" Liaska asked, in a high, excited voice, jumping on her bed to stare at Benne and then at the king. "Who's that *other* man? Is he sick? Is he *bleeding*? Oh! Did you bring him here to hide him from his enemies?" She sounded fascinated rather than fearful.

"Yes, in fact," Leilis told her. "He's . . . a friend of Karah's." In a way. If one could say so of the father of a woman's keisonne—intended keisonne, since Karah was not yet flower-wed to Prince Tepres. Perhaps that was stretching the term a little.

"Liaska, don't jump on the beds," Tana said firmly. "And put on an overrobe at once! What would Ananda say? Jehenne, go fetch Enelle! Leilis, *is* that man hurt? Is he—" but then her eyes widened and she stopped suddenly, and then said instead, almost a wail, "Oh! But why did you bring him *here*?"

Leilis patted Tana on the arm, approving of her quickness. "Because nobody could think of anyplace else to take him." She had to admit, now that she looked around at her prosaic surroundings and the wide-eyed clutter of girls, the solution seemed possibly less ideal than she had hoped. But she only added, "Could you help me push two of the beds together? These two, perhaps, nearest the fire. And maybe someone could go make tea?"

"Tea," said Miande, blinking. "Tea. Yes. I could make tea." She seemed grateful to have an ordinary, familiar task to do, and backed away toward the door, not taking her eyes off Benne and nearly colliding with Enelle, who had just flung open the door and hurried in.

"Leilis!" Enelle exclaimed. Then she looked at Benne and at the man he held in his arms, and fell silent. Enelle was not slow.

"If you'd help me shift these beds?" Leilis said to Tana, who hadn't yet moved to do so.

"That's—" said Enelle.

"Yes," said Leilis. "But hush."

"But—"

"Yes, I know, said Leilis. "But he came to Cloisonné House looking for his son, and we didn't know of any safe place in the flower world to hide him. It's perfectly safe—" or she hoped it was at least *nearly* safe. "There's no reason anyone would think to search for him here, and very soon no one will be looking for him anyway. Tana? Benne can't stand there and hold him all night."

Tana jumped and hurried to help Leilis move two of the beds so they were right beside each other, and quickly began to rearrange the linens and blankets.

"Ananda—" Enelle said, naming Karah's eldest sister.

"You had better let her know," Leilis agreed, beckoning to Benne. "You can put him down here, Benne. Ananda can persuade Petris to go along, can't she?" Petris was Ananda's husband. Leilis knew nothing about him at all, but at least nothing to his discredit. Karah had never said anything against him, but then Karah seldom spoke ill of anyone.

"Ananda can get Petris to do anything!" Liaska said, rolling her eyes and making a face. "But who's that man? You all know! I can tell! *I* don't know! It's not fair!"

The older girls all looked at one another. "Um . . ." said Tana.

"If we thought you could keep a secret, we could tell you," Enelle said, her tone very bland.

"I *can*. You *know* I can. Tana! Tell her!"

Tana's round, pretty face turned pink. She said to Enelle, "She can, if she wants to, you know."

Enelle lifted an eyebrow, an expression so much like an elder keiso to a younger that Leilis had to suppress a smile.

Then Benne stepped forward, his step heavy, and carefully laid the king down on the double-width bed, easing the linens and then the lamb's wool blanket up over his bandaged chest. Leilis moved quickly to check his heartbeat and make sure his maimed hand wasn't jostled. His color seemed better already. Save for the hollowness of the king's face, she might have believed him only asleep, and not injured near to death.

"They'll search everywhere for him!" Enelle said. "What if they find him here?"

Leilis gave her a soothing nod. "They're going to think he's dead. In another day, or maybe two, they're going to find his body. The sea's going to cast it up below the Laodd. All of this is *very* secret," she added to Liaska and the other younger girls.

Enelle stared at the unconscious king. She said grudgingly, "I suppose that might work."

"But—" Liaska began.

"Hush!" said Enelle. "You'll understand if you hush and think for half a moment!" Then she added to Leilis, "It's still a risk! Who else knows?"

"No one except Benne," Nemienne promised her. "Not even Mother—though she might guess if she thought about it. But no one knows but us. I brought him here because Karah's kitten could show me the way, and believe me, I am very glad to find myself here and nowhere else." Enelle nodded unhappily. She didn't look satisfied, but Miande came in just then, with Ananda behind her. Miande carried a tray on which were arranged a fat pot of tea and half a dozen small porcelain cups painted with indigo dragonflies. Ananda carried a plate of sticky cakes. The whole gallery seemed suddenly to be filled with the fragrance of the tea and the scent of honey and lavender.

"Miande told you? Did you explain to Petris?" Enelle asked Ananda.

"Miande told me something, yes, but I don't think I understand enough yet to explain anything to anybody," Ananda said, her tone resigned. "If you and Miande think this is a good idea, whatever it is—oh, Leilis, this is a surprise! I didn't realize you—" her gaze fell on the king, and she was abruptly silent.

Ananda was the oldest of the sisters, and what she thought mattered even more than what Enelle thought. Leilis watched her face, waiting.

Ananda absently brushed a strand of cider-colored hair back from her face. She glanced at Leilis, looked around the room, opened her mouth and closed it again, paused, took a breath and said, "Well."

"Leilis says everyone will think he's dead by tomorrow," Enelle said.

"Or the day after," Leilis murmured. "But that should do. There should be no reason for anyone to look for him here in the next day or two. No one could possibly have seen us bring him here, obviously. We are hiding Karah's birth name—I grant that is a risk, but almost no one in Lonne ever knew her history. I— there was nowhere else to bring him, nowhere we *could* bring him where there was no chance of his being seen, but I do think it should be safe." She tried to sound certain about this. She tried to *feel* certain about this.

"Oh!" Liaska cried suddenly, bouncing up and down on her bed. "He's the *king!* I should have *known!* Is he going to *die?*"

"Not with you girls here to look after him," rumbled Benne,

in his deep voice that sounded almost like an ordinary voice. "If
you will, little mistress." He turned his broad face to meet
Ananda's startled gaze. "I think it's not much risk. I do think not.
The king's men will be keeping everyone distracted. They will
lay one false trail tomorrow, and then another and a third, until
Sehonnes won't know up from down or front from back. Then
he'll be so glad to find a body, he won't look at it over-close."

"It was Sehonnes, then?" Ananda said faintly. "We've
heard—well, I'm not altogether certain what we've heard. A
hundred rumors are running loose tonight. There's been
shouting, now and again. In the distance," she added thankfully,
and crossed to the widened bed to gaze down at the stricken
king. She laid the back of her hand gently against his cheek, just
as though he were any ordinary man, then touched his throat.
"He's got no fever, yet. And his heartbeat seems strong enough.
Though a little fast . . . what happened to him? Oh, I see, his
poor hand! But that can't be all, or he wouldn't be . . ." She
folded back the bedding, traced the long bloodstained bandages,
and looked at Benne.

"A sword cut," the big man told her matter-of-factly.
"Shallow, mostly, but there're a couple broken ribs. He must've
nearly got out of the way, but it was a bad enough cut even so.
He's been dosed with goldenthread. That will keep him down for
a while. He'll want to be up on his feet the moment he opens his
eyes, I expect. You mustn't let him up. He won't be able. But I
doubt that'll stop him trying."

"Well . . ." said Ananda. She looked at Enelle. Enelle
opened her hands in a mute gesture of bafflement and cast her
gaze upward, silently turning the decision over to Ananda.

"We can't just put him out on the street like a stray cat!"
Tana said.

Ananda nodded. "I see that. I do see that. We can't, no."
She took a deep breath. "Well, let's build up the fire, then, and
Miande, you'd better boil some water and find the wound salve.
And the willow bark. And the goldenthread, in case we . . . in
case. Jehenne, perhaps you and Enelle could bring up the
butterfly screens from the parlor? It's hardly decent otherwise,"
she added, but absently. "I'll tell Petris . . . I'm not entirely
certain what I'll tell Petris. He never comes up here," she added.

"So perhaps he needn't . . . in case anybody should ask questions, you know. Petris would never betray us, but he isn't very good at pretending . . ."

"I'm *very* good at pretending!" declared Liaska. "If anybody asks questions, Ananda, you should let *me* answer them!"

Ananda smiled at her youngest sister. "I'm sure it won't be necessary, Liaska, but if it is, I'm sure you'd pretend splendidly." She turned to Leilis. "You can get safely back to Cloisonné House?"

Leilis certainly hoped she could. "Of course," she assured the other young woman.

"Of course," Ananda echoed. "And then . . . will you send Karah to us here? If it's safer for him in our house, surely it is much safer for her as well. And Nemienne—I wanted to go find her today, but I understand there has been trouble in the Lane of Shadows. Have you heard— ?" Ananda paused in mingled hope and dread.

"Ah," said Leilis, though she should have expected this. She also paused.

Enelle said tensely, "What? Just tell us!"

Leilis met the girl's eyes and then glanced around at all of them. "We don't know for certain—" *what's happened to your sisters* sounded too frightening "—exactly where either of your sisters is. Karah was visiting Nemienne when . . . there was trouble at the Lane of Shadows. We believe they may both have fled to Kalches with Taudde ken Lariodde."

"Kalches!" cried Liaska. "Why don't *I* get to go to Kalches?"

No one else said a word. Miande pressed a hand to her mouth. Jehenne gripped the sleeves of her overrobe and looked away. Enelle said, "But you don't *know* that's what happened?"

"We don't," Leilis admitted. "You may be confident Taudde will protect your sisters if he can. Or if they fled into Lonne, we will find them. The flower world has ways to protect our own, I promise you." She didn't promise that anyone could help the girls if the left-hand princes had already found them. There was no way to make such a promise. She guessed from their expressions that both Ananda and Enelle had thought of the possibility on their own. Neither of them put it into words, either.

Benne said, "It's true my lord will protect them if he can. But remember Nemienne's got a touch of magecraft and a touch of sorcery—and a touch of something else, too, to hear my lord speak of it—and she's a brave girl. She's not helpless, wherever she is."

There was a silence. No one wanted to point out the obvious truth that, wherever Karah was, *she* was helpless.

"They'll take care of him," Benne said, once they were out-of-doors and slipping though the shadowed and far too silent streets. He was carrying Moonglow beneath his overrobe, though Liaska in particular had wanted to keep the kitten. It had been out of the question, of course; Karah's Pinenne Cloud kitten was far too recognizable—more so than Karah herself, who could at least change her keiso robes for plain garb and vanish into the crowd of her sisters.

Benne's drum-voice muttered low, half to Leilis and half to himself, "He'll be safe there."

Leilis nodded. That didn't worry her—one of the few things in this terrible day that didn't. She had considered it possible, though not likely, that Karah's older sisters would refuse to take in the injured king. But she had no doubt at all that once they agreed to care for him, they would do so as devotedly as though they were his own daughters. At least until he regained his senses and frightened them. Even then, she suspected those girls were too level-headed to allow even so forceful a man as Geriodde Nerenne ken Seriantes to kill himself overspending his strength. She hoped she was right about that.

"It's a good plan," added Benne. "So long as the other part comes off. And so long as the girl isn't seen finding her way back home to those other girls."

He was avoiding names, though there was no one to hear them. Leilis approved. Benne looked so simple. Even though Leilis had known him for months, it was hard sometimes to remember that he was actually a clever man, and a subtle one. He was right, and she hadn't even thought of that possibility. She had been assuming, without ever putting the conviction into words, that Karah and Nemienne had indeed both fled into

Kalches, along with Taudde and Prince Tepres. If that weren't the case, if Karah were seen—as Moonflower—at her sisters' house, that could indeed precipitate disaster. There was nothing to be done about the possibility now. She murmured instead, "It will be nearly dawn before we're back. I fear we are all too likely to find one group of men on our doorstep at some time during the coming day, if not another. On the whole, I would prefer soldiers to mages. But what I truly do not wish is for anyone to come asking questions when I am not there." She wished they'd been able to go back to Cloisonné House the way they'd left it, a short step from light to dark and back into the light, but she wasn't Nemienne, to step into the dark from that cheerful gallery. To her eyes, that unshadowed gallery held no cracked stone or dark doorway that opened into the silence and the dark.

She tried not to think about what might happen if they were stopped in the streets by the wrong men, out here in the city where tonight any movement must invite the wrong kind of attention. She was not dressed as a keiso, and Benne might be taken for a common laborer, but far better not to have anyone ask questions at all. Especially as Moonglow was still tucked under Benne's robe.

Benne gave a short nod. "Not so very far now," he muttered. He knew this part of the city far better than Leilis, who knew nothing of Lonne once she ventured away from the candlelight district and the Paliente. Benne was leading the way through narrow alleys that she didn't know at all. She was utterly lost, and it was so dark she hardly dared take a step for fear of tripping over something unseen and raising a clatter that would summon attention from half a mile around. She was afraid there might be a lot to trip over; from the smell, she guessed that families who lived in this area simply threw their garbage into the alleys. And the sewage ditches along the sides of the alleys weren't covered over, which she discovered by very nearly falling into one. Benne caught her. She steadied herself on his arm and assured herself that he knew exactly where they were and precisely how to get from these alleys to Cloisonné House.

He did seem to. The dark plainly didn't bother him much. He walked fast. Leilis had no idea how he found his way, but he didn't pause often.

Silence crept through the streets, like the mist. Far away, someone shouted, a man's voice, angry or frightened, the words impossible to distinguish. It was hard to believe that everything had been so normal just a day earlier.

The alleys turned into broader avenues again, losing most of the rank smell of sewage and picking up instead the fragrance of the flowering trees planted along the fast-running river.

"The candlelight district," Benne muttered, unnecessarily. "This way." Now Leilis might have found her own way, but he led her by a circuitous route through the alleys that ran behind nearly every aika establishment and theatre and restaurant. Leilis approved. Once she glimpsed someone else hurrying alone from one shadow to the next, and once she saw a cat—not Pinenne Clouds, but an ordinary gray-striped cat—picking its graceful way along the top of a wall. Now and then she heard riders or the stamp of booted feet, but not too close. Except then Benne touched her urgently on the shoulder and suggested she stand still, tucking them both out of sight in a narrow doorway. A moment after he'd hidden them, a company of men rode by, down the wide avenue and around the corner, the hooves of their horses clattering urgently on the cobbles.

Leilis peered around Benne and wondered to whom those men thought they owed loyalty. Were they king's men, or did they belong to one or another of his treacherous sons? She still didn't understand how Sehonnes had persuaded proper soldiers into treachery. What in the wide world could he have offered men to make them turn on the king, especially now, on the very eve of the solstice, when everyone knew the solstice would bring war?

Which made her think of Kalches, and the missing Prince Tepres, and Karah and Nemienne, and most of all Taudde. She struggled to put aside both fear for them all and a surge of rage against the left-hand princes for putting so many people she cared about in such danger. Fury wasn't helpful. She had learned that, in her life. Fury was warming; it was far better than cold fear; but it was better still to keep one's thoughts clear. She shook her head. She had enough worries and dangers of her own without spending her time fretting over people she couldn't help and things she couldn't do anything about.

"Not far now," Benne muttered, once the mounted company had passed by.

Leilis nodded. She, too, now knew where they were. She could tell by the lingering odor of spices and fish that they were now crossing through the alley that ran behind the noodle-and-dumpling restaurant nearest Cloisonné House. They had actually come more than halfway through the candlelight district, and even yet it was not quite dawn. By sunrise, she would have shed her plain robes and become once more a keiso of Cloisonné House, ready to face the dangers of the coming day. She breathed a sigh of relief at the thought, almost feeling that she was already laying out her keiso robes and pouring warm water into a basin for a bath.

Though it *would* be nice to have the chance for a nap, first.

She stepped out from behind Benne, ready to hurry the last little distance, already thinking of how she could climb the trellis at the side of the House and slip through the balcony door on the second floor. The trellis looked too light to take even a little girl's weight, but actually it was reinforced so securely she was almost certain even Benne could come up that way. Girls had been sneaking in and out of the House by that means for years. Generations, probably. Certainly Narienneh had never tried to prevent all such girlish adventures, merely the ones that seemed over-likely to rebound too sharply on an otherwise promising girl. The Mother of Cloisonné House considered that deisa of spirit profited from the exercise, and believed that girls too foolish to bring off a successful escapade or two would never make successful keiso.

In practice, this meant that no one need be aware of Leilis' return, any more than they had known of her departure earlier in the evening. Save Rue, perhaps, or some other keiso who might yet be keeping watch for returning prodigals.

Leilis slipped around the corner of the restaurant, glanced back to be sure Benne was with her—he moved very quietly for such a big man. She checked both ways along the wide avenue that lay between the restaurant and Cloisonné House. There was no way to cross that street discreetly, but she could see nothing moving anywhere. With a nod for Benne, she hurried out of the shadows and into the earliest light of dawn.

Only before Leilis could slip around the corner and through the next alley and up the trellis, she heard the unexpected clatter of the mounted company returning—or another such company, perhaps—it made no difference. What mattered was that the company had come back so unexpectedly, moving at some speed, and that she and Benne had come too far from the shelter of the alleys to duck back out of sight. The first riders, wearing the flat red and gray of soldiers, were already around the corner and pointing, it seemed to Leilis, directly at her.

She took a step back, involuntary, because it was probably not a good idea to run—nothing could be more likely to draw pursuit—but nor did she dare stand and be recognized. This was a terrible place to be caught—the worst possible place; here directly outside of Cloisonné House. Whoever commanded those men, he would certainly know that Prince Tepres greatly favored Moonflower of Cloisonné House; he could hardly fail to discover that Leilis was also called Seathrift of Cloisonné House, and certainly he would ask himself—and her—why she should be out in the streets on this particular dawn.

Leilis traded a narrow look with Benne, who likewise must surely be recognized if he were taken up by anyone of sense, as a servant of the famous Kalchesene sorcerer.

Ahead of them, one of the men shouted. As though his shout was a signal, Leilis turned and darted back toward the alley. And, as she had known he would, Benne plunged the other way, across the open street, heading for a more distant alley that he was not likely to reach.

7

Karah had several times met Geriodde Nerenne ken Seriantes, the fourth Dragon of Lirionne. She had first encountered him under very difficult circumstances, when he had been saving his son's life, and incidentally hers as well. At the time, distracted by the *other* dragon and overwhelmed by all the terror and magic loose below the mountain, she had hardly understood who he was or what was happening.

She had met the king of Lirionne again shortly after that, but she had still been too confused and muddled to be properly afraid of him. She had mostly thought of him as Tepres' father, and had only realized later that she should have been afraid of the austere king with his frost-gray eyes and thin, severe mouth. By then it was too late, for she had already learned to trust him.

She did not trust the king of Kalches at all, and though she knew that he was Taudde's grandfather and that Taudde spoke of him fondly, she was already afraid of him before he said a word to her. He held too much that she loved in his hands: Prince Tepres foremost, of course, but also the hope of peace.

King Berente ken Lariodde of Kalches. She knew the king's full name, for everyone in Lonne knew the tale of how Chontas Berente ser Omientes ken Lariodde had surrendered to the Seriantes Dragon on the field of Brenedde, giving up half of Kalches in exchange for an end to the fighting and fifteen years of peace. She knew, as everyone knew in Lonne, that in mere weeks, at the solstice, when the fifteen years ended, King Berente would certainly resume the war.

She knew, as perhaps only a few of the folk of Lonne knew, that the Dragon of Lirionne had in recent years had his fill and more of death and grief, and would as soon have peace.

She thought King Berente would crush that hope in his hands.

King Berente ken Lariodde was an old man—older, Karah

thought, than Geriodde Nerenne ken Seriantes, who was not young. King Berente was not stooped, but age had deeply graven his face and thinned the flesh over the bones; age had stolen the color from his hair and the steadiness from his hands. His fingers trembled with the palsy of age when his hands were at rest.

But his eyes were unclouded, and his gaze was acute, and he looked at Karah as though he meant to . . . open her up, perhaps, and take out her heart and weigh it in his hand.

Karah had no doubt that Leilis could have changed the expression in the eyes of the king of Kalches. Any of the older keiso could have done it. Karah thought even she might have managed it herself, if she had only had her best keiso overrobe, with its great white moths and moonflowers, and a jeweled moth for her hair, and proper slippers, and powdered lapis dusted over her eyelids. Leilis and Rue were right that beauty could be made into a shield and a weapon. She felt now, for the first time in her life, how true that was and how much she needed a weapon and a shield. But she had nothing save her second-best overrobe and borrowed slippers.

Taudde's aunt, Lady Ines, stood to one side, with Irelle, and two men and another woman that Karah didn't know. That Lady Ines was present was almost a comfort, and not too great a surprise. She knew now—for Lady Ines had explained a little about who people were—that Ines' husband Heronn was actually Prince Heronn Lakadde ser Omientes ken Lariodde, King Berente's oldest son and heir; and so she guessed that the man standing nearest Lady Ines was most likely Prince Heronn. He was perhaps in his fourth or nearing his fifth decade, a sturdy man with a calm air that made Karah at once feel more at ease. The other man had a closed, scornful look that she didn't like, and the other woman scowled at Karah when she caught her eye; she tried not to look at either of them.

Irelle was the youngest person present, but Karah also knew now that Irelle was Prince Heronn's oldest daughter. In Lirionne, a daughter could not inherit her father's throne, but Karah thought in Kalches it must be otherwise. Why else permit a young woman Irelle's age to attend her grandfather's councils? She guessed Taudde's cousin must be only one or two years older than she was herself, though this was a little difficult to tell—the Kalchesene garments the women wore, clinging lightly on the upper parts of their bodies before falling straight from hip to floor, accented womanly curves and might, Karah thought, make it easy to misjudge a young woman's age by several years. Perhaps Irelle was actually her own age, or even younger.

Irelle's expression was neutral, now, in this company, but she had not been so careful earlier. Karah already admired Irelle, who was obviously a skilled sorceress and would never have needed to be carried down a mountain in a storm. But she was afraid Irelle disliked her. It was too bad, because she knew she was to stay in the household of Lady Ines. She wished very much that she might instead go to her own pallet in Rue's room in Cloisonné House, where she might feel safe and know she was among her keiso sisters.

But then she could not wish for Prince Tepres to be entirely by himself in this house, where even Taudde belonged and he did not. She did not hope to be allowed to see him, but at least he would know she was here also. Surely that would make him feel a little less alone?

She felt very much alone, just a this moment, even knowing Tepres was somewhere in this house.

It was at least true that Karah had of late become accustomed to the company of princes and lords. No keiso of Cloisonné House would be otherwise. A lord's keimiso, his flower wife, was expected to try to make a friend of his true wife. Karah had not belonged to the flower world for long, but she knew already that all keiso benefitted when wives and flower wives were not at odds. She had known, too, that Prince Tepres must soon marry for reasons of state, and had felt sorry for whatever lady he would be commanded to marry to suit the cold designs of political advantage. She had tried, tentatively, to imagine herself becoming a friend to such a lady. It had seemed like the greatest difficulty she was likely to face.

Now it seemed a simple task, hardly frightening at all.

She knelt before King Berente's chair as she would have knelt before her own king, with deliberate grace and lowered eyes, and waited for him to speak. She wanted to ask after Prince Tepres. She wished King Berente would promise her he would not harm him. She wanted to explain that Tepres hadn't come here to make trouble; that he, as his father, desired peace for the coming years; that his left-hand brothers were terrible men. Besides that, she wanted to ask where Taudde was, and why he wasn't here. She said nothing.

But when King Berente spoke, he took her by surprise. Because what he said, without preamble but in a surprisingly mild tone, was, "The dragon beneath the mountains of Lonne. Do you know of that? Tell me of it."

Karah did look up then. So many images and memories crowded onto her tongue that she could not speak. The dragon of Lonne; the dragon Tepres' great-great-grandfather had found in the darkness below Lonne and to which, as she had learned, he had bound his sons and his sons' sons. Karah's sister Nemienne had woken it. It had woken out of stone, in that place where the darkness was not real darkness and the light was not real light. She had never seen anything else so beautiful or so terrifying.

After that, not even stern old Kalchesene kings were frightening. So she said without a tremor, "Yes, O King, I was there. I don't remember everything clearly, but I remember the dragon. Mage Ankennes—" she hesitated, not sure how much Taudde must have already told his grandfather, not sure how much she should say herself.

"You needn't fear to bore me," said King Berente, still mildly. "Go right on and tell me the full story."

Karah nodded. Then she hesitated again. "It's hard to explain," she said apologetically. "I was—elsewhere, for part of it, and I never understood exactly why Mage Ankennes tried to—to kill Prince Tepres."

"I gather my grandson prevented him from doing so."

There was a little edge to that observation. Karah bowed her head. "He saved us both," she said simply. "No one else could have, not after what Mage Ankennes did. It was why my king spared him, I think. Or it was one reason." She thought it might be better not to speak very much of King Geriodde, however, and said instead, "But you wish to know about the dragon." She paused, this time for effect, and then continued more deliberately in the cadences of a storyteller.

"I saw a sea-dragon once. My father had taken us with him to Ankanne because he had business there, and the sea-dragon rose up from the deep sea right beside our ship, so near anyone might have reached out to touch it." She had herself reached out to do so, in fact, but she didn't mention that; this was a different story. She went on, "It was as beautiful as the sunlight on the waves. It might have been made by a jeweler's art, of gold and black enamel, of sapphire and citrine, if any jeweler could set his hand to so great a creation. It was as vast as the tide. I could not have measured its eyes with the span of my arms, and I am sure it might have crushed our ship if it had wished to. But it went back down into the deep sea and so we did not perish." She paused, pleased because even with that little bit of the story she had caught them so far that none of them interrupted.

Then she said, "The dragon below Lonne is to the sea-dragon as a sea-dragon is to a serpent sunning itself on a rock in your garden." That wasn't quite right, though, so she tried again, "It was not so much larger, for the sea dragon was very large. But it was . . . greater." That wasn't quite the word, and she amended herself: "It was *deeper*. If it had spread its wings, the shadow would have cast all of Lonne into the shade, but it would not have been ordinary shadow. It would have been the shadow of the darkness below the mountain, which is more than darkness." She paused.

Then she went on. "It was not so much more beautiful, for the sea dragon was very beautiful. But the dragon below Lonne has a beauty that is *deeper*. It is beautiful not as a creature is beautiful, but as a fire or a storm is beautiful. If it had spread its wings, perhaps instead of darkness they would have cast a shadow made of fire and light, and the first stroke of its wings would have brought down all the lightning of the world in that one moment. It might have done just that. It asked if we desired that it should bring down the mountains. Its voice was as the voice of an iron bell. But its voice was deeper than that. It was like the voice of the storm made into the tolling of a great bell." She paused, looking into the king's face, and added, "If that is the dragon your grandson Prince Taudde ser Omientes ken Lariodde described to you, then you have already heard the truth."

The king leaned back in his chair, frowning. He coughed and rubbed his chest absently, then shook his head, not quite disbelievingly, "This great dragon *spoke*. To *you*."

"Not to me," Karah said at once. "It spoke to my king, and to Mage Ankennes, and to my sister."

"Your *sister*," said the other man, the one with the sour expression.

Karah bowed her head a little more to hide that she did not like him. She explained obediently, "My little sister, Nemienne." And how Karah wished she knew where Nemienne was now, and whether she was all right! She wished she knew that her sister had made it back to their sisters' house and was safe with Ananda and Enelle and the little girls! Although wherever Nemienne was, she was surely safer than Karah herself.

She went on softly. "My sister was apprentice to Mage Ankennes. She woke the dragon after . . . after Ankennes betrayed us all. He meant to force your grandson Prince Taudde to do murder upon Prince Tepres Nemedde ken Seriantes. But Taudde saved him instead, and me, and then Nemienne woke the dragon out of stone and silence. And after that Ankennes . . . " she shivered, remembering. "He died," she said in a low tone. "The death he unleashed rebounded on him, and he died."

"And the dragon?" asked Prince Heronn.

His voice was pleasant, low and calm, but Karah looked at him in surprise. "It is still there, I suppose. Beneath the mountains, Kerre Maraddras and Kerre Taum. I never heard that it had gone, so I suppose it is still there. Perhaps it has wrapped itself in stone and sleeps again, or perhaps it is still awake. I would not know." She wondered if King Berente knew it was bound to the Seriantes line. She wondered if she should tell him. Would it be better for Tepres if the king of Kalches knew that or if he did not? But Taudde knew, anyway, so it could not matter what *she* said.

King Berente leaned forward in his chair again. "Could you lead a man into those caverns to find that dragon?"

Karah, entirely certain she didn't want to do anything of the kind, answered promptly, "I am sure I could not. Those are not natural caverns—or not wholly natural caverns. Least of all the part where the dragon lies. I don't think anyone could venture there safely, except for mages. And sorcerers, of course, I am sure," she added quickly. "But even if they did find the dragon, I don't think anyone, mage or sorcerer, could predict what it might do, or stop it doing as it wished." She took one beat longer to ask herself if she were sure she should go on. Then she added, feeling her heart speed, hoping she was right to speak and not keep silent, "Except perhaps someone of the Seriantes line, as they are bound to the dragon."

To her relief, the king only nodded impatiently, as though already familiar with this tidbit of history. So if he believed that and believed what she—and surely Taudde as well—had told him, then surely he must hesitate to rid himself of the Seriantes prince he held in his hand. Especially on the very eve of the solstice. Karah wondered if she dared ask what he intended to do with Prince Tepres. Perhaps he did not yet know himself. That seemed quite likely. But she was beginning to think he might not be so impatient and angry as he first seemed. She could feel herself becoming a little more at ease, perhaps because King Berente no longer seemed to dislike her as he had at first.

He asked abruptly, "You are a keiso? One of the—" he hesitated. "Flower girls of Lonne?" he said at last.

Reminded, Karah lowered her eyes demurely, and turned her foot a little to make her robes drop gracefully, as Rue had been at such pains to teach her. "The keiso of Lonne belong to the flower world, O King," she answered softly. "We take the names of flowers, yes, and sometimes we are called the flowers of Lonne. My keiso name is Moonflower, of Cloisonné House, which is the finest and most elegant keiso House in Lonne. My elder sister is named Rue, which is not a showy flower, but many of the dancers and instrumentalists prefer such names. Rue is very famous in Lonne for the beauty of her dancing."

"Her *dancing*," Irelle said, the first time she had spoken.

Karah looked at the other girl in surprise, not understanding her scornful tone. "Why, yes. Rue is the finest dancer in Lonne. I'm sure she will never take a keisonne, though I know Mother has had offers. She's the sort of keiso who is, as they say, wedded to her art. Rue told me herself she would make a very bad keimiso—that is a flower wife," she added, suddenly realizing that the Kalchesene girl might not know. "She says no matter how generous a keisonne might be, she would resent him for intruding on her time. I'm sure she is right; she is always in the studio. Half the time she would forget to eat if I didn't bring her supper." She paused, realizing that Irelle was now frowning, apparently in astonishment. Lady Ines was smiling, though; and so was Prince Heronn; a wry, friendly expression.

"But *you* are not a famous dancer, nor adverse to the company of men," commented Lady Ines. "Indeed, I believe I'm not mistaken in—" but then she broke off, turning sharply toward the king. "Berente, are you well?"

The king had been pressing the heel of one hand against his chest and frowning, his expression inward. But now he waved irritably at Lady Ines, dropped his hand to the arm of his chair and snapped, "Perfectly well, as always. Merely annoyed at the persistent efforts of the world to complicate every possible situation, also as always. Heronn! Have I made time to see the Dragon's heir tonight?"

"Yes, sir. In half an hour, now." But Prince Heronn was frowning at his father, and did not seem at all surprised when King Berente waved his hand again and declared, "Tomorrow will do. Arrange it at some convenient hour. I suppose I had better talk to that boy again, first—"

With a faint shock, Karah realized that by *that boy*, he meant Taudde.

"If you would prefer, I could—" began Prince Heronn.

"No, no! Though you had better attend, I suppose." The king's scowl deepened. "Out," he ordered generally. "I will see you all at breakfast. Or no, better, at noon! Out! Ines, take the girl with you and see she is properly settled."

"Of course," agreed Lady Ines, not reminding him that he had already given that order earlier. She dismissed her own daughter with a nod, but beckoned to Karah, who rose gratefully and moved to join her.

"*Is* the king well?" she asked in a low voice, uncertain once they were out in the corridor.

"Of course," Lady Ines said briskly. "Merely irritated with the world, as he is the first to acknowledge. He will be better now that Taudde has finally returned—or he would be, if Taudde hadn't insisted on bringing all these complications with him. Well, but I rather have the impression Taudde has learned a touch of humility in his various foreign adventures, which is all to the good and will please the king no end."

"I—King Berente was worried about Taudde?"

"My dear!" Lady Ines gave her a wry look. "Shouldn't he have been?"

Karah had to smile back, acknowledging the truth of this.

"And of course Taudde was always one of Berente's favorite grandchildren. Such a difficult boy. Not that it isn't hard on a boy to lose his father, but Taudde might have been better off with a little less sorcery and a little more sense. I do suspect he has improved, however." She added, "*You* are a sensible young woman, I think, but exhausted. I'm sure there are those worried for you, and not without cause, I admit, but I hope someday soon you will be able to tell them yourself that Kalchesene hospitality is no poor cousin even to the comforts of Lonne. Heronn and I have an apartment in this house, of course; fortunately with an extra room next to Irelle's—"

"Could I . . . would it be possible for me to see Prince Tepres? I'm sure he would wish to know of your kindness to me." Karah certainly wished to assure herself that he was being treated as kindly. Or at least, not cruelly. She clasped her hands together, giving Lady Ines a look of appeal.

The shrewd glance she got back made it clear that Lady Ines had not missed any of this. But the older woman only said kindly, "I fear not without Berente's approval, which I doubt he will give just yet. Perhaps tomorrow, or in a few days. I assure you, your prince will be well enough. The Kinsana Suite is a comfortable apartment and no dire dungeon."

Karah nodded, trying to be content with the hope that she might be allowed to see Prince Tepres tomorrow; trying to believe that King Berente would be sensible and kind and would listen to Taudde, who was one of his favorite grandsons. Trying to believe that in the end they would all be glad of the chance that had brought them through the door into Kalches.

8

The tower apartment in the king's house of Kedres was not precisely a prison.

No doubt, like any king, Berente ser Omientes ken Lariodde had been tempted from time to time to incarcerate a troublesome relative or political opponent for a few years. King Berente had a temper, and scant patience for certain kinds of foolishness. But in Kalches, where people were long accustomed to place the rule of law above the whims of kings, there was little tolerance for a king who indulged such whims. So the tower was not a *prison*.

But it was certainly under the king's eye.

The tower was not particularly tall. It was three stories, only one story taller than the main house. It had wide windows, so it didn't feel so terribly closed in. Taudde had opened them all to admit the early-summer breezes and the sweet fragrance of violets and pimchi and roses. Everyone in Kedres planted spring flowers, and so the whole town was filled with flowers during their short summer.

In Lonne, the roses had begun to bloom a full month earlier. They had reminded Taudde too much of spring—his own spring, spring in the mountains. He had found himself wishing to be in Kalches, watching the season turn in these mountains. He had wanted to bring Leilis here and introduce her to his grandfather and show her the beauty that was spring after a harsh northern winter.

Now he was here, and the spring had come at last, but he was alone. Despite the windows, the tower apartment was thoroughly and pointedly separate from the life of the house or the town. Taudde had never before realized how many different ways there were to be alone. He wondered whether it might be possible to capture all the forms of loneliness in music. Pipes might be better than a flute, for the minor keys that came into his mind. Or a kinsana, perhaps.

The highest level of the tower which contained the apartment, consisted of just one large room, divided merely with low couches, not with walls or even screens, so that one might take in the entire space at a glance. The couches were comfortable, however. So was the bed at the far side of the room. But that was practically the extent of the furnishings

Music was everywhere in the king's house, but there were no musical instruments in the tower; no kinsana or ekonne horn or set of pipes. Not so much as a finger harp or feather drum. This was not supposed to prevent a resident from working sorcery, as Taudde well knew. After all, a bardic sorcerer could whistle, or hum, or tap out a rhythm with a spoon. It was meant as punishment. Any resident of the tower apartment was meant to be contemplating the king's displeasure, not amusing himself by playing through his entire repertoire of kinsana solos.

After two full days and three nights in the tower, Taudde felt he grasped his grandfather's displeasure quite adequately. He was more than willing to receive a summons, little though he looked forward to a second and possibly even more uncomfortable interview when it came. Surely the moment word came of events in Lonne, his grandfather would send for him. He hoped for that as early as today.

Or if no word came, he hoped a summons might come anyway. Surely his grandfather had been considering his possible options, even before solid news came across the mountains from the south. Surely he would make time soon for a more complete account from Taudde.

Not that it was impossible to leave the tower. The apartment's single door wasn't locked. He could have walked through whenever he chose. On the other hand, the door was warded with the king's personal seal. King Berente always knew who came and went from the tower apartment. He would know at once if Taudde left it.

Unless he slipped the ward. Which, true, a gifted sorcerer might manage without the king being the wiser—not that Taudde would make any attempt to do so, naturally—but then he would find himself on the second level of the tower.

The second level was also a single room, its stairways up and down set across from each other so that one had to walk through the entire room to get from one to the other. Though it appeared empty to a casual glance, the wide space was actually filled with cobwebs of sorcery. Some of these were ancient and some so new they still glittered like morning dew on spider webs; some were entirely contained within the tower room and others flowed out the windows and stretched across the outside surface of the tower. They were so various, and spread out in so many different directions, that no matter how gifted a sorcerer might be, he would find it practically impossible to bypass every single strand.

Given specific leave to come or go—by the king himself, or by Uncle Heronn, or by Toma Piriodde, or by one or two others—a man might pass through those threads without disturbing them. Without leave, it was a different matter. The webs wouldn't stop a man from walking wherever he would, but each, if disturbed, would reverberate with tones of warning and warding that would cling most persistently to the one who had disturbed them. Even a sorcerer as gifted as Taudde would find, if he were to walk straight through that room and allow even one of those threads to cling to him, that every sorcerer in the entire house—in all of Kedres—would know just what he had done. Any sorcerer would be able to follow in his footsteps, and any of the more powerful sorcerers would be able to catch the end of a trailing thread, call his name, and require him to answer a call and come.

It was really a very clever bit of sorcery. Or a thousand overlapping bits of sorcery. Taudde had set a few of those webs in place himself. Everyone did. It was a standard teaching exercise for bardic sorcerers of a certain strength.

Below the level of cobwebs, the bottom level of the tower comprised Toma Piriodde's wardroom, from which his guardsmen came and went according to some arcane schedule that no doubt made sense to them. Not that the guardsmen would stop Taudde if he simply walked through the door and down the stairs, passed through the cobwebs of sorcery and strolled right through the wardroom and went on wherever he liked. But one or two men would certainly follow him if he did. Also, they would certainly inform their captain, who would not be amused if he were required to assign his men from some important duty merely to trail along behind Taudde.

Naturally, a gifted sorcerer who managed somehow to get past the cobwebs of the second level might evade the notice of even the most alert guardsmen. On the other hand, Toma Piriodde was no man anyone with sense would want for an enemy, and he had no humor at all when anyone used sorcery against his men—every one of whom was also carefully warded, and some of whom were sorcerers themselves.

In practice, if the king commanded one to retire to the tower apartment, it was generally wisest to simply remain there until his temper eased enough for him to set some more official punishment, which after a day or two of excruciating boredom would probably come as a relief.

Taudde had certainly been in far worse prisons. But he missed his flute.

And he was worried about Prince Tepres. Not so much about Karah—she might be anxious, she might have been fearful at first, but she was a charming girl, so plainly innocent of any ill intent that Taudde was fairly certain even his grandfather—even *Toma*, reliably suspicious of everything and everyone—would conclude she was exactly what she seemed: charming and innocent. Besides, he knew that Aunt Ines would take care of her.

But he was very worried about what other conclusions his grandfather might draw from recent events, or what possibilities he would see in the sudden unlooked-for arrival of the Dragon's heir in his very house.

Taudde was also angry, tired, frustrated, and impatient. It was a poor frame of mind for sorcery. It was an even worse frame of mind for sleep. Though the hour grew late and passed the hinge of night and became early, though the dawn began to streak the mountains to the east in silvery apricot on this third day of his confinement, he still paced from window to window through the chamber. The numerous low couches were an impediment for pacing, so that he was tempted to reduce them all to kindling and throw them out the windows. Except that his grandfather would not find any such indulgence in the least amusing.

He did not precisely blame his grandfather for ordering him

to the tower. He had not expected it, but he was acutely aware, around the edges of his anger, that in his grandfather's place, he would very likely have done the same. Or worse. There *was* a prison in Kedres, a small one, seldom used. It possessed cramped, chilly cells a good deal less pleasant than the tower apartment, and with far more serious restraints to one's departure than the threat of the king's displeasure.

Taudde knew, if he were honest with himself, that he had all but asked for the full measure of his grandfather's disapproval, and perhaps some measure of his distrust.

He was still angry, however. He struggled to put his anger far enough aside that he could think, or at least rest.

Surely his grandfather would soon send for him. He would ask for the full, detailed account of Taudde's sojourn in Lonne, and Taudde would tell him the whole tale. He would be very angry—Taudde winced at the thought—but he would understand that he must be careful of Lirionne; that the dragon resting below Lonne was nothing to hazard; that now it was wakeful, Geriodde Seriantes was equally disinclined to risk disturbing it; that the solstice need not—could not be permitted—to turn to a summer of blood and iron. That there was a chance, now, to forge a gentler turning of the year—so long as no bloody-handed usurper was allowed to take the throne of Lirionne.

If not his grandfather, surely Taudde would be allowed to speak with Uncle Heronn. It might be even worse if he must lay out the more shameful parts of the tale to his uncle, but—

There was a sharp knock on the door, and Aunt Ines came in. She gave Taudde a brief, warm smile and a nod.

Taudde restrained himself from saying *At last!* He said instead, trying to keep his tone polite, "News from Lirionne?"

"You've been impatient, I know, but actually the messenger made very good time. The poor man is exhausted, but I'm sure Berente will reward his effort." His aunt looked him up and down. "*You* look rather worn yourself. You had no need to worry, you know. The girl you brought along is not at all what I might have expected. Really, she is quite delightful. Heronn and I both think so, though I fear Irelle has rather avoided her company."

Taudde inclined his head in gratitude. "For her sake, I was

glad you stepped forward, Aunt. Karah . . . if the keiso were an orchestra, she would be a flute solo. Not like Irelle's flute. A silver flute is heart-stoppingly pure. There are keiso like that, but Moonflower is another sort. She is more like a wooden flute. An alto flute, I think, with a comfortable range and a warm tone. Ah, you're smiling, Aunt! You agree with me."

"I do. And she is so plainly in love with the Dragon's son, which rather speaks well for him, I feel. As does your defense of him, of course."

"And . . . is *he* well?"

"His position is difficult, to be sure, but no one has troubled your friend, Taudde. You can't have expected any such trouble after you . . . nudged your grandfather to treat the young man as a guest. That was well done, by the way. It's always best to start off politely, I feel, as it's so difficult to recover a man's good opinion after offending against his dignity."

Taudde nodded, reassured. "I'm glad you approve, Aunt Ines. I . . ." he paused.

"My dear?" Aunt Ines said kindly.

Taudde asked, not certain he wished to hear the answer, but unable to stop himself, "Do you remember my father? You weren't actually much at Kedres so many years ago, surely, and you can't possibly have been at Brenedde . . . "

Aunt Ines turned a grave look on him. She did not seem to find this abrupt change of topic at all surprising, but she also did not answer at once. But at length she said, "It's true I seldom left my own estate in those years, because of the children. And your father was seldom at home, because of the war. But before such things ruled our lives, when we were all young and Heronn was courting me and Gaurente was courting your mother, our paths crossed often enough." She paused.

Then she said gently, "I don't believe Gaurente would have been displeased by his son making a friend of the Dragon's son. Given all that had come before. Gaurente had a temper—you have that from him as well as your mother. But he wasn't one to cling to a grudge till it withered to dry bone. I think he would have acknowledged Geriodde's generosity to you, and not likely have thrown it back in the Dragon's face. I think he would have recognized worth in Geriodde's son. And I think, Taudde, that he would have been glad to see you make up your own mind in such matters, rather than allow yourself to be blinded by anger at past wrongs."

Taudde closed his eyes for a moment. Despite his question, he hadn't quite expected his aunt to understand his heart so precisely. He should have remembered that she was also a sorcerer, and accustomed to listen beyond a man's words, to the truth contained in the undertones of his voice.

"Thank you, Aunt," he said, inadequately, and went on at once, in a much brisker tone, "Shall we go down?" He touched his belt where his flute should have been, set his teeth against the sharp always-surprising fact of its absence, and gestured politely for his aunt to proceed him out the door.

The man who had finally brought reliable news of the Lirionne coup's success, or probable success, or at least partial success, was a Kalchesene spy. A clever and observant man who had posed, Taudde gathered, as the factor of a merchant house based neither in Lirionne nor in Kalches, but in Miskiannes. It was, in fact, a role similar to the one Taudde himself had played not so long ago.

The merchant houses of Miskiannes had, of course, officially no opinion concerning any political matter involving Lirionne or Kalches. Miskiannes could afford neutrality, protected as it was from Seriantes aggression by its wealth, and by the rugged distance that lay between the two lands, and most of all by the narrow, mountainous, enchanted realm of Enescedd that lay between itself and Lirionne. But Miskiannes was a land that prospered best in times of peace, when all trade routes were open and safe and goods could flow easily back and forth between lands far inland and the sea. And because everyone else prospered from that trade as well, representatives of Miskiannes' merchant houses were always welcome in the Pearl of the West, as they were welcome in the heart of Kalches. And so both the Seriantes Dragon and the King of Kalches pretended that they did not know that some of those representatives must in fact be men spying on behalf of their enemy.

The spy had first taken his time in Lonne, gathered reliable information from reputable sources, with supporting details and specific names and careful attention to separating rumor and speculation from known facts. Therefore, when he reported the death of the Dragon of Lirionne, tension between the left-hand princes, and sporadic violence throughout the city of Lonne and the surrounding countryside, Taudde knew it was all most likely true. He knew for certain, of course, that Prince Tepres had mysteriously vanished from Lonne. But it was interesting to hear that the truth was circulating among the many rumors concerning Tepres' disappearance. One or more of the men with the left-hand princes must have told his friends what had happened. In fact, now that he thought of it, Taudde was a little surprised that Sehonnes had not yet sent a representative inquiring about the fate of his legitimate brother.

Or perhaps he had, and the king had not seen fit to inform his out-of-favor grandson. That seemed very possible, too, once Taudde thought of it. He wondered if he dared ask.

King Berente received the spy's report in the crowded warmth of his private library, which actually contained few books. Some of the books that were supposed to be in the library were histories and some were concerned with the making of instruments or with other crafts, but a good many were long, convoluted romances. These tended to wander. People borrowed them, especially when the weather turned cold; or the king himself took them away to his private chambers and his grandchildren found them there and carried them away to read, so all through the winter books turned up in odd places. In the spring, the servants gradually found them all and put them back on the shelves, but even this close to the solstice probably no more than half of King Berente's collection had been gathered up.

So the library held few books. But it was a large room, with enough tables for the king and his advisors to spread out papers and maps, and with a fireplace at each end to drive out the chill of the mountain nights. And the room had the sort of heavy, formal look King Berente liked: all dark carved wood and formal brass fittings, a floor harp set in one corner, and all along one wall a single vast painting of the stark mountains.

At the moment, the king occupied a massive carved chair placed directly beneath that painting. This was where he sat when he wished to make it clear that he was acting as the king and not merely as Berente ser Omientes. He had made that doubly clear today by wearing the heavy Kalchesene crown and a mantle of mink trimmed with ermine. This show wasn't for the spy's benefit, Taudde was certain. He suspected the king would send for Tepres after hearing the spy's report. Taudde would have liked to be able to guess his grandfather's thoughts, but could not even read the tones of the old man's voice.

Uncle Heronn stood to one side of the king's chair, reading over his shoulder. He was a steady, intelligent man of fifty or so; he handled a great deal of the day-to-day business of ruling Kalches, and he did so with unflappable calm. Aunt Ines stood close beside Heronn. She collected each paper as the king finished with it, glanced over it with every now and then a slight lift of an eyebrow, and passed it to Irelle—and if Taudde had needed any further sign that his little cousin had become someone to take careful account of in his grandfather's court, *that* would have made it clear. Though the room was crowded with uncles and cousins, no one else was reading those notes.

King Berente glanced up. "So," he said. "The body of Geriodde Seriantes, cast up by the sea on the beach below Lonne's fortress. The body had been identified by Prince Sehonnes himself, you say."

"Would Sehonnes recognize his father's body, do you think?" Uncle Heronn asked, glancing shrewdly from under his brows at the spy. "You write here that the body was much battered, that the face was badly damaged."

"Yes, sir," agreed the man, leaning forward a little and making a small gesture for the Heronn to turn the page. "Yes, that's so, but if you look there, you'll see the servants who took care of the body, who washed it and redressed it for the funeral, they recognized it—him—as the Dragon. His own servants, sir, as had served the king for many years. They were talking about it to the other servants, you see there, that's all there in my report, sir."

"I do see. You have been very thorough." King Berente flipped through the next few pages of the report, frowning. "Sehonnes had not yet declared when you left Lonne, I see. You say here that he has gained the support of at least some part of the army, but you believe Telis is preferred by the mages and perhaps the merchants of Lonne?"

"Yes, sire," agreed the spy. "But the common folk, they don't like Telis. Call him Sa-Telis, the serpent, like in the old stories. They don't trust him. Say he's got too much of the dragon in him."

"You'd think that would be a compliment, in Lirionne," Irelle said. Not hesitating, Taudde noted. She met their grandfather's bristling glance with aplomb. "Well, wouldn't you?"

The spy shrugged. "Well, lady, I wouldn't claim to know just what they mean by the phrase. But they don't sound like a compliment when they say it."

The king glanced at Taudde, but Taudde had to admit he did not know. "I can't remember hearing much one way or another of Prince Telis, sir, and I never met him. Until that last moment, of course. I see now that I should have wondered when the mage-prince, of all men, avoided me so assiduously." He hesitated. Then he added, "I, too, would have thought that a phrase like that would be a compliment in Lonne. But they wouldn't call him Sa-Telis if they meant it so. Or I don't believe so."

The spy nodded, waited a beat to make certain Taudde had nothing else to contribute, and added, "Sehonnes, now, he says Telis is the one who struck down their father and he only stepped in because he'd no choice, with the Dragon dead and the legitimate prince vanished away. Most people I talked to believe Sehonnes."

"You don't, then," observed Irelle.

The man shrugged. "Who's to say who did what? Sehonnes hasn't made any move to arrest his brother, not yet. Why not, if Sa-Telis is guilty?"

The king tapped his fingers on the arm of his chair, considering this question. "One might imagine possibilities. He daren't, because his brother has too many partisans or holds damaging information. Or because Sehonnes depends on his support."

"Sehonnes and Telis came together to attack Prince Tepres," Taudde put in quietly.

His grandfather pinned him with a hard stare. "Did they? Together?"

Now that he thought of it, Taudde wasn't certain. "They were both *there*. So was the other left-hand prince, the younger one—Geradde is his name. But whether they all came there together, I don't know. Telis might have come after *me*, and simply crossed paths with his brothers. It was Sehonnes who seemed in the forefront, Sehonnes who had claimed the Dragon's ring." He opened a hand. "It was a confused and violent moment, and I was mostly trying to get out of it. I'm not sure, sir."

King Berente grunted and flicked a finger for the spy to go on.

"Well, sire, you see there—no, another page on—the other fighting men, the ones they call the King's Own Guard, at the time I left Lonne, they mostly hadn't stood up for one prince or another, not yet. Waiting for the right-hand heir to come out of hiding and declare, is my guess. The youngest bastard prince, he might have been with the others when Prince Taudde saw him, sire, but he's fallen out of sight since, so I hear. If the Guard doesn't trust the other two, I would wonder if maybe they might not be hiding him themselves, waiting for a better moment to let him step up. That last is just my guess, though."

"Well, well," the king muttered. "The elite guard, disaffected and not inclined to bend the knee to Sehonnes. We might do something there, especially if the bastard sons are indeed quarreling. Or if they're not, maybe we can encourage them to start, eh? More than once in the long span of the years, such a struggle has been decided by a palace guard. Possession of the rightful heir might offer a sensitive place to set the tip of a lever. A little push at the right time and place, and who knows if the old Dragon's guard might be persuaded to turn against both Sehonnes and Telis. That might be useful." He turned another page.

Taudde set his teeth and said absolutely nothing.

"Yes, sire," the spy said earnestly. "There're all kinds of other rumors; one for every man, woman, and child in Lonne, I don't doubt. I didn't dare take the time to untangle them all, but you hear one thing after another about all those bastard princes—not so much about Meiredde—"

The king snorted.

"Yes, sire. No one thinks he'll bring his ship into harbor till it's all done and past and wrapped up with a little bow. He's not one to join a wrestling match, Meiredde, or that's what they think there in Lonne. Now, that young one, Geradde, he might run for the sea and join Meiredde. That's another guess of mine, if he's not tucked in with the King's Own. He's not counted ambitious, see, and getting right out of it would make sense if he's not up to the weight of his brothers."

King Berente made a wordless sound that might have expressed agreement or merely acknowledgement. He shuffled through the last few pages of the report and then said curtly, "Toma, bring the young Seriantes prince to me."

Taudde straightened away from the wall and moved forward a pace. "I'll go. I'll bring him, sir."

Almost at once he became aware that everyone had turned to look at him. He could hardly have failed to know it. His cousins Penad and Lamanes, both much involved with the Kalchesene military and neither with a note of music or sorcery in his blood, glanced at Taudde and then at each other, carefully expressionless. Uncle Heronn gave Taudde a long, thoughtful look. Irelle raised her eyebrows. Aunt Ines gave Taudde a small nod, though whether of approval or acknowledgement or something else was not clear to him.

King Berente, frowning, began to speak.

Taudde could hear the refusal in his grandfather's voice before the king had finished even his first word. He protested sharply, "How would you wish a son of yours treated in like circumstances?"

There was a deadly little pause. Cousin Penad straightened in outrage, opening his mouth, but Uncle Heronn checked him with a look. Even after three days back in Kedres, hovering on the edges of his grandfather's court, Taudde had not decided what role Penad actually played now in this house and the court. A year ago, Uncle Heronn had unquestionably been the man most in touch with the day-to-day business of the court, and Penad had worked closely with him. Uncle Heronn's role did not seem to have changed—it would have astonished Taudde if it had—but it seemed to him that Penad had shifted away from assisting with Uncle Heronn's prosaic duties and toward a far greater concern with matters touching on military preparedness and plans to regain the lands lost to Seriantes aggression—and, Taudde gathered, Penad strongly preferred plans that included punishing that aggression.

Taudde had once been rather inclined toward that preference himself. He still believed that Kalches needed to reclaim her lost territory. But for the rest, he was much less certain. He met his grandfather's eyes and said, "I don't mean to defy you—"

"No, of course not," King Berente said drily. "You mean to rebuke me."

The silence in the room deepened, as from simply not speaking, everyone in the gathering went to holding his or her breath. Taudde felt his face heat. He could see perfectly well that this was true. "I beg your pardon."

"I should hope so." The king paused. Then he lifted one eyebrow and added, "It is, however, true that I would prefer a son of mine to be dealt with gently. Go, Taudde, and bring the young Seriantes prince here to me."

Thoroughly startled, Taudde could only stare at his grandfather for a moment. He was aware, nevertheless, that Irelle's expression was carefully neutral, his cousin Penad was scowling, and Lamanes looked both amused and offended. Uncle Heronn only exchanged a glance with his wife, gave a little nod, and began once more to shuffle through the stack of papers the spy had brought.

Taudde's grandfather was not generally given to whims. Nevertheless, Taudde moved rather hastily toward the door, not willing to risk the king changing his mind a second time. Only once he had slipped through into the hall and shut the door behind him did it occur to him how earnestly he had tried to compel his grandfather to give him the privilege of informing a son of the death of his father.

For a moment he wished he could change his mind and let someone else carry this news to Prince Tepres.

The Kinsana Suite comprised eight handsome rooms in the western wing of the king's house. Heavy draperies over the windows and thick rugs on the floor kept out the chill; every room had its own fireplace, with carved chairs with velvet cushions drawn up close to the hearths.

One stepped first into a formal reception room, with tapestries on the walls—scenes of forests and mountains, which was the custom in Kedres. Then there was a music room to the right, where an extraordinarily handsome kinsana occupied pride of place, and a sitting room to the left. After that a short hall led to a small private kitchen, a formally appointed dining chamber, and finally a small but beautifully appointed bathing room with a bedroom on either side. It was the sort of suite appropriate for guests of the highest rank and had not, so far as Taudde was aware, ever before housed a prisoner in some danger of being sent back to his home in small pieces.

There were, of course, soldiers posted outside the door. Less visible but more closely attentive was the constant ripple of sorcery through the suite. Taudde perceived this as a half-heard harmony, as though the faintest breeze was passing across the strings of the kinsana. One of the soldiers on duty would always, of course, be a reasonably skilled bardic sorcerer, thus ensuring that their Seriantes prisoner could not possibly slip the attention of his jailers.

Taudde gave the soldiers outside the door a brief nod, stepped between them, and rapped gently on the door.

After the briefest pause, Prince Tepres opened it. Though his pale hair was caught back with a heavy silver ring in the manner of Lonne, he wore a fine blue Kalchesene shirt and black trousers rather than the elaborate robes of his home. His long black Kalchesene coat had a double row of brass buttons down the front and more buttons on the flaring cuffs, and was embroidered across the shoulders and down the front in indigo and sky-blue. Kalches had no such sumptuary laws as Lirionne, but even so, anyone could see that that so fine and expensive a coat could only be worn by a man of rank. Though with his aristocratic features and the arrogant set of his mouth, Prince Tepres might have made a laborer's rough clothing look royal.

The prince did not seem surprised to see Taudde, but only inclined his head in haughty recognition and stepped back in implicit invitation.

Taudde came a step or two into the reception hall and shut the door.

Immediately the prince's haughty manner eased. He gave Taudde a thin smile and a very small bow. "Taudde. Prince Chontas Taudde. I am glad to see you. I wish to beg your pardon, if you will allow me, for the three days you once spent in silence and solitude in the Laodd, before my father came to hear your account."

This wasn't the greeting Taudde had expected. His surprise must have shown, because Prince Tepres went on at once, "I swore I would say that to you as soon as I saw you again. I had not realized until now what those days must have been like for you. I am, as I say, glad to see you."

"Forgive me that I did not come earlier. I was not permitted. My grandfather has not . . . that is, I believe he has not yet . . ." Taudde paused, unable to think of any graceful way to finish that sentence. He began again, "But you look well, eminence. I gather you have not been much troubled."

"Troubled? No. I might believe I had been forgotten entirely, save for the guards, who come on duty and then depart, and the servants who bring food and clothing. They do not, however, speak to me. Not even the lowest servant will answer me when I speak to him. Though they do respond to simple requests, for which I am grateful." The prince's tone was light and wry. He moved a step back and turned, waving Taudde past him into the apartment. "This is a comfortable prison. Is Karah well? I have assumed she must be treated at least as kindly as I. Less strictly held, I hope."

"My aunt has her in charge. There could be no better place for her."

Prince Tepres inclined his head, accepting this. "You relieve my mind. I confess, I had not realized how difficult silence and solitude can be as one's only companions. One becomes inclined to take council of one's fears, I think."

"Yes . . ." Taudde thought of Jeres Geliadde, the prince's long-time companion, dead in the street in front of Ankennes' house. He said, inadequately, "I'm sorry."

"For what? But I am grateful that your grandfather has lifted the ban." Prince Tepres studied Taudde. His dark eyes narrowed under his fine, straw-pale brows. "I see I had better ask what has prompted this sudden liberality." After another moment, when Taudde did not answer, the prince's manner took on a new reserve. He said formally, "Prince Chontas Taudde, will you make known to me the thing you have come here to say?"

Taudde hesitated, then moved, more or less reflexively, toward the music room. He needed that—the comfort of being surrounded by beautiful things that were also tools of both music and sorcery. The kinsana for which the suite was named drew the eye, but nine different harps were displayed on the floor or on shelves along one wall, and three sets of feather-drums were arranged along the opposite wall. Taudde walked across the room before turning, resting his hand on the back of the largest harp. He did not quite look at Prince Tepres, who had followed his lead to this room and stood now near the door, his arms crossed over his chest and his head to one side, regarding Taudde with shuttered attentiveness.

Taudde said flatly, "We have received word from Lonne." He gave Tepres time to understand, to begin to guess what that news must entail. Then he said, "We have received word that your father is dead, and that your brother Sehonnes has declared he will take the throne of Lirionne."

Tepres' reaction was not dramatic. But he turned quietly away, moving to stand at the window, his hands flat on the sill, gazing out. Taudde was fairly certain he saw nothing of the town outside, nothing of the wintry mountains that rose in the near distance to close off the horizon. Without turning, Tepres asked, his voice steady, "Is it certain, then?"

Taudde said gently, "We might doubt Sehonnes' word. But it seems beyond dispute that a man's body was cast up on the shale beaches above Lonne where, we are told, the tides do carry . . . things the sea relinquishes."

It was very much like picking your way from one uncertain stone to the next across a treacherous river, Taudde thought. There was no way to bring such news kindly. But he tried. He kept his tone nearly expressionless, but layered with subtle sympathy beneath the overt neutrality. "The body was . . . much battered, we are told. But the servants who had charge of preparing the body for the funeral declared it was truly your father's body. I am sorry. But there seems little doubt."

Tepres nodded. He had not moved throughout this difficult recital. He did not turn now, but put a hand up to his face.

"I am sorry," Taudde said again.

"You hated him," Tepres said. His voice had thickened. "You had reason. I know that. Sometimes I think I—" but he cut that thought off short.

Taudde said gently, "Your father was a hard man. Ruthless with himself, and with everyone else. But there is no doubt he loved you. I am sorry for your loss."

Both of the prince's hands closed hard on the windowsill, and he bowed his head.

"I believe, when the solstice had come, your father would have tried to find a way through the summer. A way other than blood and iron. I think I had learned not to hate him. Your half-brothers I do not trust at all. So you see, I am truly sorry for your father's death."

Tepres nodded. He took a deep, shuddering breath, rubbed his hand hard across his face, and turned at last. "And the city? Is there fighting? Sehonnes has declared, you say. I imagine some part of the army supports him, but I can't imagine my father's own guard . . . well. What other factions have emerged? Are there men still in Lonne who might be loyal to my father if he— if he had lived?"

And who might be loyal to me? he did not ask, but Taudde heard that question clearly. "That is not . . . entirely clear. There is some fighting, but we believe there has not been much violence in the wider city. We do not know what may be happening within the Laodd itself. We believe that perhaps some may prefer Telis to Sehonnes—most of the mages, certainly; some of the townsfolk, possibly. We know your brother Meiredde remains out at sea. No one expects him to set foot in Lonne until everything is settled one way or another."

Tepres nodded at this, unsurprised. "Geradde?"

"No one has heard much of him, I think."

Tepres bowed his head. "I always liked Geradde. I hope my other brothers have done him no harm. I could believe Sehonnes might have him killed, to forestall him making accusations of conspiracy and murder and treason. My father's people might support Geradde despite his youth, if—" If Tepres himself was dead, but he cut that thought off and did not put it into words. He said instead, "And he and Telis have always disliked each other." Taudde nodded again. "We don't know yet whether . . . whether your father's death will bring his partisans to retire—"

"The people will never support Sehonnes!" Tepres said fiercely, his head coming up, his voice echoing with undertones of fury and pride. "A king who is a traitor and a parricide as well as born on the left? Lonne will never accept Sehonnes!" He stopped, then went on more moderately, "But people might accept Geradde, if it came to that. Young he may be, but if men believe Sehonnes and Telis conspired to murder our father, while Geradde is innocent of that blood . . . and, of course, all of Lonne may well believe there is no right-born Seriantes prince left alive in all the world."

After a moment, Taudde said, "Perhaps they may learn otherwise."

"Yes. Perhaps." Tepres paused again. "Of course your grandfather is considering how he may respond to this news."

"He sent me to bring you to him." Taudde hesitated, then added, "I think he may intend to inform not only Kalches but also Lirionne that he holds you in his hand."

Prince Tepres considered this. "Yes," he said at last. "To stiffen my father's partisans against Sehonnes, you mean? Is that what your grandfather intends?"

"Something of the sort, perhaps."

"One perceives the potential use he might make of such a strategy." Tepres paused again. At last he added, "Whatever he intends, I am grateful to him for sending you to bear this word to me. That was a kindness."

Taudde did not know how to answer this. He said, "If you wish to take a little time . . . "

"No." Prince Tepres glanced once around the music room, perhaps trying to steady himself. There could be little here to reassure a Seriantes prince, in this place where every detail must be a forceful reminder of where he was: in what kingdom and in whose house. The prince took a breath. Then he said again, "No. Delay would help nothing. I will come now."

King Berente had not moved from his chair in the library. He supported his chin against the back of one hand and gazed at the air, at nothing. Thinking, or perhaps brooding. The corners of his mouth were turned down, never a sign of good temper.

The spy himself had gone, but Uncle Heronn had moved off to one side, found another chair, and was now examining the details of the man's report with careful attention. Aunt Ines was perched on the arm of Uncle Heronn's chair, one hand on her husband's shoulder, reading the report along with him. Irelle was seated to one side, evidently lost in thought.

Penad and Lamanes had retired to the far end of the room, where they were arguing, low-voiced, with three more of Taudde's endless number of cousins. Uncle Manaskes, Penad's father, stood by the door at that end of the room, frowning, his thumbs hooked in his belt, listening with half an ear to the argument, but most of his attention appeared to be on the king. Toma leaned against the wall near the king's chair, lean and forbidding, arms crossed over his chest, glowering impartially upon them all.

But the moment Prince Tepres stepped into the room, all attention focused on him. The young men turned to stare like so many wolves measuring a stag they had brought to bay. There was less hostility and more assessment in the glance that Irelle and another of the female cousins, Tarina, turned toward the prince of Lirionne. Uncle Manaskes' frown deepened. Uncle Heronn laid the spy's report aside, and Aunt Ines straightened and folded her hands demurely together, giving Tepres a swift, measuring glance and Taudde a small, warm smile. Toma's glower did not change, but he dropped one hand to rest on the hilt of his sword. And King Berente set his hands on the arms of his chair and turned his forceful glare on both Prince Tepres and Taudde.

Prince Tepres ignored everyone but King Berente. He met the king's eyes without a tremor—Taudde suspected that living with his own father had been good training for such moments. Tepres walked without hesitation straight across the room, his back straight and his shoulders level, stopping a pace or two before the king's chair. After the faintest pause, he inclined his head haughtily. Despite his Kalchesene dress, he looked at that moment every inch a prince of Lirionne and the Dragon's heir. Taudde half heard the powerful rhythm of the dragon's heartbeat in the stillness that had fallen across the room.

Then Tepres said, coolly, "I thank you, King Chontas Berente ser Omientes ken Lariodde, for your hospitality over these past days. I believe I am tolerably well acquainted with the news from Lirionne that has come across the mountains and to your ear. What would you have of me?"

King Berente's hooded gaze shifted to Taudde for the barest instant, then returned to Prince Tepres. "I am considering, Prince Tepres, what use I may best make of the Dragon's heir, given these interesting circumstances."

Without so much as blinking, Tepres answered, "Forgive me, King Berente, that I, your guest and prisoner, must correct you. But I believe you are acting under a misapprehension, o king. I am not the Dragon's heir."

Without looking, he drew from his coat pocket a small object. A ring, Taudde saw. It was his father's ring, of course. Of course it was. The tiny rubies of the dragon's eyes caught the light, flaring up like twin sparks of crimson fire as Tepres held up the ring.

Still without looking down, without for an instant looking away from King Berente's heavy stare, Tepres slid the ring onto the first finger of his left hand. He lifted his hand, then, to display the iron ring to all. "I am not the Dragon's heir. As my father has been foully murdered, as my father's body lies now beneath stone and surrounded by stone, as I have no brother before me, as there is no other legitimate claimant . . . *I* am the Dragon of Lirionne. And now," Tepres said, with no faintest flinching in his manner or in the undertones of his voice, "now, King Berente, let us discuss all the matters that lie between us and all the matters that lie between our two countries."

There was a long pause. Everyone, of course, had seen that coming—but only from the moment Tepres had lifted up the ring. Before that moment, not even Taudde had guessed what the young prince of Lirionne intended to do. Yet Tepres must have thought of this possibility at once, Taudde realized now; from the very moment his man Jeres Geliadde had flung Sehonnes' grisly hand with its royal burden across the intervening struggle and Tepres had caught it. Tepres' thoughts must have turned to this strategy even while they struggled through the bitter storm that had scoured the mountain road above Kedres. Taudde was only surprised that he had not himself guessed then the path Tepres' thoughts had taken.

Penad looked angry, Taudde saw, glancing swiftly around, but his father, Uncle Manaskes, had put an urgent, warning hand on his arm. Uncle Heronn had a speculative look in his narrowed eyes. Aunt Ines, curiously, seemed pleased. Tarina had her head bent toward Irelle's, whispering to her urgently. Irelle was frowning, but to Taudde she seemed thoughtful rather than offended. Toma's expression, of course, hadn't changed at all.

Taudde's grandfather propped one elbow on an arm of his chair, leaned his chin on the back of his hand, and regarded Tepres with narrow-eyed intensity. "A broad claim," he said mildly, "for a man in your position, Tepres Nemedde ken Seriantes." He gave Tepres no title at all, Taudde noticed. The naked name seemed to hang in the air among them all.

"It is not a claim," said Tepres, his tone cold and purposeful. "It is the clear truth."

"Yet a throne generally belongs to the man who is position to take it. Or hold it. Bastard or no, it is your brother Sehonnes who is in Lonne. While you are . . . " King Berente gave a little wave of one hand. "Here."

Tepres didn't flinch. "My half-brother Sehonnes is not a bastard," he said, his tone perfectly level. "But it is true he was born on the left. That is not an insupportable obstacle. Now and again, left-hand sons do inherit position and power and property from their fathers, when right-born sons are lacking. However, Sehonnes must be widely known as a parricide, or at least suspected of having colluded in that worst of crimes. All men must suspect it. No one will trust him. Who could?" His eyes flickered just briefly to the sheaf of papers lying on the table by Uncle Heronn. Then he returned his steady gaze to King Berente's face. "Sehonnes will find that Lonne—and beyond the city, Lirionne entire—has little taste for any left-hand Seriantes prince who lays a bloody knife on the throne. Certainly my left-hand brother will find the Dragon's throne precarious, once it becomes known that the true Dragon, preserved against

121

treachery by the swift action of powerful allies, reaches out to claim his inheritance."

Tepres again lifted and turned his hand so that the rubies set into the iron ring glittered and flashed. "So," he said softly, "I think we have many things to discuss, King Chontas Berente ser Omientes ken Lariodde. Old treaties, and the possibility of new treaties. Borders both long settled and recently disputed. The perils of having a bloody-handed and ambitious parricide as King of Lirionne, contrasted with the value of gaining an honorable ally."

"An honorable ally!" muttered Penad, but under his breath, so that only a man with Taudde's gifts and training was likely to have heard him. King Berente, who had both, sent a sharp glance his way, promising a blistering reprimand for any further boldness. Penad lowered his eyes, scowling.

"An ally, is it?" King Berente said to Tepres. Taudde listened carefully to the undertones of his grandfather's voice, but heard nothing overt; neither anger nor outrage nor even surprise. The king's voice was not perfectly neutral, but it was very hard to read. "Borders and treaties, do you say? You wish Kalches to recognize you as King of Lirionne? Then make me an offer, Tepres Nemedde ken Seriantes of Lirionne. Make Kalches an offer, and perhaps we shall indeed have matters to discuss."

Tepres gave a small, acknowledging nod. "I see no need for long debate, King Berente of Kalches. The matter seems simple enough to me. Fifteen years ago, my father took into his hand the town of Anharadde and all the lands east of that town and west of the mountains. Now let my father's son restore those lands to Kalches. Let the border be re-drawn from Anharadde through Thibarr Pass and so to Teleddes. All these lands between the mountains and the sea Lirionne will return to Kalches. And for so little: for the loan of a hundred Kalchesene swords, perhaps. I think it should hardly prove difficult to win my father's partisans to my cause. They have no cause to love Sehonnes—"

"You think we will trade Kalchesene lives for the cause of the *Dragon's* get?" Penad snapped. "For *Anharadde*, is it, and *Thibarr Pass!* Is it Thibarr Pass you will barter for your very *life?* And what of *Brenedde?*"

If Tepres had ever argued with Taudde over the proper

disposition of the border, Taudde could have made certain the younger man understood how high Kalchesene tempers still rode over Brenedde. But Prince Tepres had been too polite to broach so difficult a topic with Taudde, and now that Taudde saw he should have raised the issue himself, it was too late.

And since Tepres did not understand, he only flicked a scornful glance at Penad and said haughtily to King Berente, "It is a generous offer, o king. It is a proposal that sets back into Kalchesene hands valuable lands, which you well know Kalches could not reclaim by force of arms. I am quite certain you will hear no similar offer from Sehonnes."

King Berente tilted his head to one side. "And the far west? Sarodde, where my cousins once ruled, until your great-great-grandfather cast down the houses of my kindred? Getodd, there by the bay where the mountains run into the sea? The lands south of Anharadde? Brenedde, cupped like a jewel in the bowl of the mountains, where the river runs swift from the frozen heights? Nothing of these will you offer, for your life and your crown? For I think you have little hope of keeping the one or claiming the other, young Dragon," he added, still in that mild tone, "save by my generosity. Will you declare you have any just claim on Kalchesene generosity?"

Taudde cleared his throat, a discreet little sound that nevertheless compelled attention. He said smoothly, "Perhaps we may, however, agree *in principle*, sir, that borders may be re-drawn by peaceful agreement rather than by force of arms; and that the Dragon of Lirionne may more easily engage in such an agreement if he retains full possession of both his life and his crown. If the solstice comes and goes without any such agreement, I fear we shall find—"

"The sea taught you cowardice as the refrain to its song, we know!" sneered Penad.

Taudde didn't look at his cousin. He knew the color had come up into his face. If he answered that at all, he would say too much. He was aware that his grandfather must find Penad's outbursts useful, or he would have silenced him himself. Penad didn't matter; it was his grandfather Taudde needed to persuade. So he kept his attention on the king and didn't so much as glance at Penad. He said quietly, layering conviction beneath every word, "In Lonne, they do not fear the coming solstice or the ending of the Treaty of Brenedde, though they know Kalches will rise up against Lirionne. They don't fear that, because they are certain of their own strength. They know that Lirionne will crush Kalches in the field because—"

"They will learn better!" declared Penad. "Forget these councils of caution and cowardice! No, let us send *half* this Dragon's whelp to Sehonnes, and the other half to Telis. Let the Dragon's bastard sons have *proof* this one is dead, and then let them quarrel over the bloody throne! If all of Lirionne rises against them in revulsion for their crimes, that will be best of all! We shall *take* all our lands back, and more besides. *Then* let them take Kalches lightly!"

Taudde took a grim hold of his temper. But Tepres, finally and comprehensively losing his, asked contemptuously, "Do you also expect the wolf to tremble at the yapping of little dogs?"

Penad shook off the restraining hand of a horrified cousin, evaded his father's alarmed grab, and hit Tepres. It was a fast, powerful blow, and Tepres, taken absolutely by surprise, had no possible chance to evade or block it. He staggered backward, arms flailing; caught after his balance, failed to reclaim it, and fell, slowly and spectacularly, pulling over a table and flinging an ornamental lamp to smash against the nearest wall.

Taudde whistled a fast series of minor tones that rose fast and fell sharply and cut through the air like knives. Penad cried out breathlessly and staggered, his hands flying to his mouth.

King Berente came to his feet, his ice-blue eyes brilliant with fury. *"Enough!"* He did not shout; he was too angry to shout. Though his voice was not loud, it filled the room with power.

Taudde, his hands trembling with fury and shock, stepped back. Tepres, plainly stunned, began to make vague movements to get to his feet. Penad, now rather pale, coughed and rubbed his lips. He coughed again and dabbed his mouth with his sleeve, coming away with specks of blood on the cloth. He glared at Taudde, but said nothing—unable to speak, just at the moment. His father had stepped to his side and now gripped Penad's arm, looking both furious and dismayed.

Most of the cousins hovered near the door as though

wishing they could flee, but did not dare to move. Uncle Heronn was on his feet, his expression grim; Aunt Ines stood silent, one hand over her mouth, a set of slender reed-throated pipes in her other hand. Irelle held her silver flute like a weapon, or perhaps like a shield. She did not appear alarmed—nor shocked. She wasn't looking at Penad, though she might have been a moment before. She was gazing at Taudde, her expression thoughtful. Toma had straightened, but he had not otherwise moved; his mouth was crooked with something that might have been suppressed humor.

King Berente said icily, "Taudde, how dare you use sorcery against your own cousin in this house? Penad, if you have the manners of a untrained hound, little wonder if guests should observe the fact! Tepres Nemedde ken Seriantes, I apologize most profoundly. Can you stand? Did my mannerless puppy of a grandson break your jaw?"

Tepres ignored the hand Toma, stepping over to him, offered. He got slowly to his feet, bracing himself on the wall and then on the back of the heavy chair that stood nearest. His breathing was quick and shallow, and he kept his face turned away—no doubt perilously near losing the composure he had held so hard and so long. He made no answer, perhaps not trusting his voice if he should try to speak.

"Out!" commanded the king, rounding on Penad. "Manaskes, keep your son out of my way, or I shan't answer for him. Go! Out, all of you lot!" With a furious wave at the clutter of cousins and uncles. As they nearly all fled, all but Heronn and Ines and Irelle, he snapped, "Toma!"

"My king?" Toma answered smoothly, his eyes glinting.

"Escort the Seriantes Dragon to his apartment! You will have no need to speak to him, but if you do, be polite! See that a physician attends him, if necessary!"

"Of course, my king," murmured the guard captain, without the trace of a smile. "Eminence?" He stepped back, indicating the door.

Tepres turned. His composure had not broken, but there was a brittleness to his hard-held calm, a revealing tension in the set of his jaw, which was already discoloring with a bruise. When he spoke, his voice had gone hard and smooth as glass. "King

Chontas Berente ser Omientes ken Lariodde, I assure you I am perfectly well. I hope I may look forward to a civilized conversation with you at your future convenience." He put no emphasis at all on that *civilized*. Taudde knew everyone still in the room heard that missing emphasis. He saw, because he was watching her now, the corner of Irelle's mouth turn up. But Tepres did not look at any of them. He merely added, still with that brittle calm, "I shall hope that moment is not too long delayed, O King."

"I assure you of it!" snapped King Berente.

Tepres inclined his head with exact courtesy and turned toward the door. He did not so much as glance at Taudde, far less acknowledge Toma, who opened the door for him and then stood aside for him to go out first. When he walked out, he did not look back.

"Taudde!" said King Berente, once Toma had closed the door quietly behind him.

Taudde flinched, turned, and bowed. "I beg your pardon."

"You are an intemperate *fool,* boy! Penad was thoroughly and *solely* at fault, save for *your* taking the *Dragon's* part against *your own cousin*—" he stopped, uncharacteristically, in mid-tirade.

"Sir, I—" Taudde began, and halted, alarmed by the look on his grandfather's face—the way his grandfather pressed his hand against his chest—"

"Berente!" said Ines, bending urgently over the old king, her pipes in her hand. She lifted them to her mouth, but gave her husband an urgent glance before she set them to her lips. "Heronn—"

"Yes, play!" Heronn answered, already half out the door. "I'll bring the physician." He was gone.

"Grandfather—" Taudde began, caught between rushing forward in concern and backing away in horror.

"Stay out of it!" Irelle ordered him. She was kneeling at the stricken king's feet, chafing his hands. "Go back to the tower, Taudde! Half the cousins will be saying *you* brought this on—at least have the kindness to keep out of the way, and with luck we can have everyone believe you were out of this room before he collapsed and not after."

Taudde stared at his cousin, amazed at the cold calculation of her words set over the terrible grief in the undertones of her voice.

"Irelle is right," Aunt Ines said, though more kindly. "Go, Taudde. To the tower, nowhere else, make no mistakes now! I promise you, I will bring you word as soon as I am able."

Taudde started to say something but found all his words choking him in an agony of confusion and anxiety and anger. In the end, he only bowed his head to his aunt and fled, thoughts and emotions alike in a roil, half unable to believe that anything could ever put an end to Berente Lariodde's fierce vitality and half terrified at what the king's death might mean for Kalches; relieved that at least Uncle Heronn and Aunt Ines were ready to take up the burden of guiding Kalches through the fraught summer but wholly dismayed at the thought that his grandfather might actually *die* and the last moments between them be left filled with anger and disapprobation.

9

Two days and almost dawn of a third. Two full days and almost another night since Leilis had brought—*him*.

Enelle was deeply afraid, for they had heard nothing from Leilis since, and neither Nemienne nor Karah had made her way to them here, and no one knew what new disasters might befall the city while princes whom no one trusted struggled for power.

Prince Sehonnes had taken a body from the sea and declared it his father's. None of them had commented when Miande had brought that news home from the market. Sehonnes had claimed throne-right and declared he would crown himself on the solstice, and no one had reason to doubt he would, unless Prince Telis fought him for the throne. Prince Telis had disappeared, but so had nearly all the mages of Lonne and no one thought they had retired from public view because they had all suddenly decided to write long scholarly books about magic. No one knew where Prince Geradde was, either; in the market, people were murmuring that Sa-Telis might have done away with him. Prince Meiredde might swing the balance to one of his brothers or another, but everyone knew he would hold his ships out at sea and not come in to the docks until everything had settled.

What everyone hoped was that Prince Tepres might yet live, and might reappear. Some people said that Sehonnes had tried to kill him, and some said that Telis had tried to save him from the Kalchesene bardic sorcerer, but everyone knew that the sorcerer had snatched Prince Tepres away to Kalches. There were a thousand different opinions about what might happen to him there, but so far as Enelle knew, all of Lonne was furious with Kalches and with the Kalchesene sorcerer, yet at the same time suspected Prince Tepres might be better even in Kalches than in the hands of his brothers. Enelle wasn't quite certain how one person could believe both in the appalling perfidy of the sorcerer and in Tepres' greater safety with him than with Sehonnes, but it seemed plenty of people managed.

Enelle, at least, knew the sorcerer wasn't appallingly perfidious. Nemienne had said so, and Nemienne might be distractible and vague about everyday matters, but she could hardly be wrong about Prince Taudde ken Lariodde of Kalches. Not after everything that had happened earlier in the year. Karah said the sorcerer and Prince Tepres were *friends*, and though she generally liked everyone, she was not likely to be wrong, either.

Enelle only hoped Tepres *and* Karah *and* Nemienne were *all* safe, with the sorcerer or otherwise. Mostly she just wished it were over and everything were back the way it should be.

But of course she knew what hardly anyone else in Lonne could know: that the struggle for the throne of Lonne could not actually be *over* until King Geriodde had either died or recovered enough to take it back for himself.

Enelle had been the one looking after the king, mostly— Enelle and Tana and Miande and Jehenne, taking it in turns. Liaska was not allowed into the gallery, for fear she should wake or tire the king, though nothing in all this time seemed really to rouse him to full awareness. Liaska's bed had been moved to the room where Ananda and Petris slept, which pleased no one, but they all hoped it would be for only a little while.

Tana and Jehenne were asleep now at the far end of the gallery. Tana was exhausted, from worry—they all were—and she had sat by the king for the early hours of the night. Then Jehenne had taken the second watch, and Miande the third. Then Miande had gone down to the kitchen. These days she made gentle rice gruels and broths for the injured king as well as ordinary food for the rest of them. So it was only Enelle here by the king now at dawn.

Ananda had been helping too, a little, but she and Petris officially knew nothing at all. They stayed carefully clear of the gallery where the younger girls, and now the injured king, slept. Petris in particular never asked after the king, in case anyone came asking questions or wishing to search the house. Petris seemed so simple and trustworthy; no one would suspect him of harboring dangerous secrets, surely. And the little girls were prepared to hide the king beneath blankets and pretend Enelle was the one who was ill, if they had to.

Enelle felt she should be able to look deathly, if anyone actually insisted on inspecting the gallery. At least, she certainly felt worried nearly to death.

The king, too, looked deathly. Despite all the girls could do, his wounds had taken fever. Miande made poultices along with rice gruel. Enelle sometimes thought they were working to bring the fever down and sometimes thought they were not.

The king had lost weight every day; sometimes it seemed every hour. And he had already been thin. His bones stood out starkly beneath his skin. He looked old and fragile. Enelle remembered her father's death. That had been sudden and terrible. In some ways, this slow wasting of flesh and strength was worse. Though one could struggle against it, one could see the end written in the king's flesh.

Ananda had begun to say that they should bring in a surgeon or a fever-doctor. She said they would have no need to say who the sick man was, that the king looked nothing like himself now that he was so ill. Enelle thought anyone who saw the king would have to be very stupid not to realize exactly who he was. But she also thought that if they went on as they were, he would probably die. She was beginning to agree that they would have no choice but to find a fever-doctor and hope he could be trusted.

At least the weather held warm and quiet. For wound-fever, one wanted warmth. Enelle turned from building up the fire, and paused in blank surprise.

A cat was standing on the bed beside the king's head. Not a bony stray that had come in through the window—besides, the shutters were closed. This was a big cat, broad and powerful, seeming entirely black to Enelle's first startled glance. But when he moved, ripples of white showed through from his undercoat, and when he looked up at her, one of his eyes was green and the other gold. The gold eye glowed with the light of the fire. The green eye was shadowed.

Enelle knew this cat. She had never seen him, but he was utterly unmistakable. Karah had described him to her sisters. She had been explaining how much prettier her kitten was than the king's own cat, how Moonglow had teased the old cat and made him jump to the king's shoulder, how he had made a show of ignoring her.

Because this was the king's own Pinenne Cloud cat, Dark Of The Moon. It could be none other.

There was no way the cat could have found the king, or made his way through closed doors and shutters fastened against the night air, except he was here. Nemienne, who lived with one, had said that about Pinenne Cloud cats—that they could find their way anywhere, that they were allied with some kinds of magic and some kinds of dragons. But Enelle had not really believed it, or guessed what that might mean. But here he was, Dark Of The Moon, kneading the pillows and purring.

"I don't know," Enelle said to the cat "He's very sick. You must be careful of him."

The powerful black cat did not seem concerned at the sound of her voice. He only curled himself into the space between the king's shoulder and chin, slitted his eyes, and began to purr.

The king opened his eyes and shifted a little, his breath catching. Enelle stared. Then she moved quietly to his side and put her hand gently on his arm, and he stilled and, after a moment, sank back and closed his eyes again. Dark Of The Moon purred more loudly.

Feeling hopeful for the first time in days, Enelle woke Tana and Jehenne—it *was* dawn. "If you would ask Miande to send up gruel and tea," she said to Jehenne.

Jehenne nodded, tentatively stroking Dark Of The Moon. With no hitch in his purring, the cat slitted his odd-colored eyes and bumped his broad head against her hand, and she smiled in delight. "He *will* get better now," she said, with a confidence Enelle hoped was justified. "Can we get a kitten?"

"Maybe in a little while," Tana said hastily, with a glance at Enelle's face. She added hopefully, "At least he doesn't seem any worse. Do you think his fever's breaking? I'll get more wood for the fire." She took Jehenne's hand and the two girls ran out, talking excitedly.

Enelle knelt down by the king's bed. She wanted to *make* the king awaken by the sheer force of her will. She wanted him to awaken with all the intelligence and resolve and ruthless strength of will it would take, to tear all the world apart to the bare stones, if necessary, until he found his son and her sisters.

The cat stopped purring, and for an instant, Enelle's heart seemed nearly to stop. But then she saw that the king's eyes were open again. Dark Of The Moon untucked himself and sat bolt upright, peering at his face, his whiskers canted forward. The king's eyes were blank at first, but with a fierce awareness coming into them as Enelle watched. She had not quite realized what the king's contained intensity might be like. She certainly realized it now.

The king moved a hand to push himself up—his wounded hand—and his jaw set.

Without thinking, Enelle shifted forward and touched his shoulder, a light touch, only to let him know he was not alone. "Geriodde," she said quietly. "You are safe. You are among friends. You are well, or you will be well."

The king's eyes moved to meet hers when she spoke. When she fell silent, he turned his head slowly from side to side, inspecting the small part of the gallery he could see: the cat, the chimney to one side, the high, narrow ceiling, the unlit lamps, the screen that granted him a measure of privacy and contained the warmth of the fire. At last he looked back at Enelle. His lips parted, and he drew breath, but the sound he made was a husky, wordless mutter. His brows drew together.

"I'm Karah's sister. Enelle," Enelle explained. "You are at my house. My sisters and I have been taking care of you, but you will be better now." Tana was at the door with tea, her eyes wide with excitement; Enelle took the tray and sent her sister away with a jerk of her head, afraid to tire the king with too much company all at once.

She could see the king *would* sit up, or try, whatever she said, so she helped him with that first, quickly borrowing pillows from other beds to prop him up a little. Then the pot of tea, sweet with expensive honey and fragrant with warming spices—she had to lift Dark Of The Night to the other side of the bed for that. The cup was plain, not the delicate painted porcelain that would fit a king. But it was also small enough a man without strength in his hands might hold it, and deep enough to make it hard to spill.

She put the cup in the king's hand—it shook; plainly he could barely muster the strength to lift his hand at all. Enelle had to steady the cup so he could lift it to his cracked lips.

He sipped the tea. One sip. Another. A third. Enelle steadied the cup as it trembled, carefully matter-of-fact. He was weak; he would get stronger; while he needed someone to steady his cup, she would do that. There was no reason for a man to fret himself about such temporary weakness. That was what she tried to say with her manner, as she took the cup out of his fingers before he could drop it.

"Moonflower," he said to her. His voice was husky, but not thin. He sounded stronger than she had expected. He sounded . . . contained. Hard. Impervious. His brows drew together. "You are her sister. Her natural sister, not keiso."

"Yes," Enelle agreed, with a wry twist of her mouth at the thought anyone might even for a moment mistake *her* for a keiso. "She is the beautiful one. I'm the practical one."

"Practical," murmured the king. "Good." Then he added, which she had not expected, "Enelle. Daughter of Geranes Lihadde. This is your father's house? Your sisters', now," he amended, with precision. "And yet, even though you are the practical one, you feel this is safe?"

For a moment, Enelle was too surprised to answer. Then she was not surprised at all. Of course he would know all about her. Of course her father's name would come easily to his tongue. Probably he knew all her sisters' names, right down to Liaska. And naturally he would think right away about what it meant that he was here. Or at least, because he thought of that, she need worry . . . at least a little less.

She said, "We think no one guesses you are here. No one could have seen you brought to this house, not the way you came. No one has come to search. We have not heard they are searching anywhere. This is three days since—since it happened. This is the dawn of the third day."

The king's expression did not change, but his eyes closed, and opened. He said, "Does Sehonnes hold Lonne?" And, seeing the answer in her face, he went on, "Yes. Then why does he not search? What is happening in the city? What of—" his voice checked, just perceptibly. Then he asked steadily, "What of my other sons?"

Enelle touched his hand. "It is not so bad as it might be. Lonne is quiet. There is trouble, of course there is, but it is quiet trouble, we think in the Laodd and not so much in the city. Tepres—" she faltered and then went on, "Tepres is safe. Taudde . . . Taudde got him away. My sisters, too—Karah and Nemienne. So they are all safe." She hoped she sounded like she believed this last. She wanted to believe it. She met the king's eyes guilelessly, as though she were reassuring one of the little girls.

"Taudde ser Omientes ken Lariodde," murmured the king. His thin mouth, so like his son's, tightened.

"Karah trusts him," Enelle reminded him. "*You* have trusted him."

"Yes. True." The line of his mouth relaxed a little. Enelle put the still-warm cup into his hand, gently insistent that he drink. He did, impatiently, then put the cup aside with a hand that was noticeably steadier. He said, his tone sharper this time, "Neriodd brought me here? Was Dark with me then?"

"Dark—Dark Of The Moon just . . . appeared this morning. I don't know how he found you, or got in. It was Leilis who brought you to us. Of Cloisonné House." Enelle gestured vaguely off to the west, meaning to indicate the candlelight district. "Neriodd brought you to her, I think, and she brought you here to us because—because she knew she could bring you here without any risk of anyone seeing."

"Leilis," murmured the king. "The sorcerer's . . . friend."

"Yes," said Enelle, who had rather gained the idea from both Karah and Nemienne that this was true.

"I see." The king was silent for a moment. Then he said decisively, "I must speak to someone who knows what has been happening in Lonne and in the Laodd. This quiet you say has lingered in the city makes no sense. The keiso will know." A kind of chilly humor came into his eyes and he added, "Leilis will assuredly know, I have no doubt. And she may know—" he stopped. Then he commanded, with no humor at all, "Bring Leilis here to me."

"Yes," Enelle agreed, though she hadn't the least idea whether it would be safe to send a message to Cloisonné House. She would think of a way. She would probably have to go herself.

She did not say this to the king. She said instead, "I will

find Leilis, if you will take a little broth and bread, and then rest again. I will send my sister Miande with broth, but you must not frighten her, eminence. You must allow her to serve you, and then you must rest."

He said, "Indeed." Then he said, "Now you do not call me by name."

She had done that. She hoped he wasn't offended. She said, "I thought . . . a wounded man waking, ill from fever in a strange house, might wish a friend to call him by name."

He did not answer for a moment. But then the corner of his mouth turned up. He said, "You are the practical one?" But he leaned his head back against the pillows and closed his eyes without explaining what he meant by that. Some of the tension had gone out of his face.

Enelle stood up, grateful he had not asked more about his sons or about the Kalchesene sorcerer. "I'll send Miande."

The king nodded slightly, without lifting his head or opening his eyes. "Bring me Leilis. And I need Neriodd. My enemies—" but he stopped, perhaps thinking of enemies and sons, and how, even if he defeated this treachery from Sehonnes and Telis, that would be *five* sons dead by his own hand.

Enelle could not even imagine such a terrible thing. She would have understood if that thought had brought him to despair. She said quietly, "You will take Lonne back into your own hand, eminence, and you will cast down all your enemies. And what you will do then will be by your own choice."

"Yes. As it has always been," answered Geriodde Nerenne ken Seriantes, the Dragon of Lirionne. He opened his eyes and gazed at Enelle, the lines around his mouth deepening with bitter humor. She thought she could see at last a hint of the dragon Nemienne said was linked to the Seriantes line. Enelle hadn't understood that. She thought she understood it better now.

She wished Nemienne were here now. She wished she knew what had happened to her, and Karah, and whether they had escaped their enemies.

She wished she knew how to safely send a message to Leilis, or a way to go herself through the city without drawing the notice of anyone who might be watching Cloisonné House.

Enelle slipped away before the king could glimpse the fears

crowding behind her eyes. She was the practical one. She would figure it out, and she would do it right, and no one watching for surreptitious movement in the city or spying on Cloisonné House would notice a thing.

-10-

It was hardly dawn on the third day following the coup when two dozen men in the flat red and dark gray of soldiers appeared at the door of Cloisonné House. Leilis was only surprised it had taken so long for them to arrive. They looked at her with blank professionalism when she opened the door— Leilis was careful to be at hand for any fraught arrival, these days. She was only too grateful she *was* at hand, for if Benne hadn't led the soldiers away from her as they returned two days ago from Karah's sisters' house, they might have taken her then, and who knew what they might have learned from her? But Leilis had had two full days to hide all the important secrets of Cloisonné House; to arrange for the entire flower world to forget certain things if the wrong men came asking questions. Though she was not confident of her own safety when she opened the door upon those soldiers, she *was* confident that the secrets she had hidden would not be revealed merely through some careless oversight.

She did wish very much that she knew what had happened to Benne. Not merely for his own sake. She was coldly aware that he, too, had owned those secrets. He was clever and experienced, and she was certain he knew how to disappear into the streets of Lonne, and he had had Karah's kitten with him, so for all she knew he had stepped into one shadow and out of another a dozen miles away. And besides all that, she suspected any enemy would find it uniquely difficult to force Benne to reveal any secrets he wished to hold. But for all that, she wished she knew for certain where he had gone and that he had not been taken up by the hand of some enemy.

There was a mage with the soldiers, too. His presence worried Leilis far more than that of the soldiers. He looked her up and down with obvious contempt and dislike. Mage Ankennes' treachery had been revealed and thwarted earlier in the year, and she had played a small role in his downfall. She feared this mage knew that, and recognized her, and hated her for what she had done.

Beyond Cloisonné House, the candlelight district and the city lay still in the gray dawn. This was not merely the early hour. It was because, though the king's body had been found—or so Leilis hoped people still believed—nothing had yet been clearly settled in the Laodd or the court or the city. All through Lonne and beyond, men must be maneuvering—but quietly, quietly; hardly anything was yet happening in the light of the open day. Everyone knew Prince Tepres was missing, but though a great many disparate rumors concerned the fate of the right-hand prince, very few people believed he was dead. Nevertheless, Sehonnes had proclaimed that he would take the throne and the crown and the title on the very day of the solstice. Perhaps men were waiting for that. Perhaps the king's man, Neriodd, was waiting for that, or for something. She herself feared it might be unwise to let these unsettled days stretch out, but she must hope Neriodd knew what he was about.

Now here were these men: two dozen soldiers, commanding in Sehonnes' name that Cloisonné House open its doors. And the mage. Perhaps Sehonnes and Sa-Telis were working together after all. Perhaps they always had been. The possibility did not ease her fear. Especially not if Sehonnes—or could it be Sa-Telis?—had decided at last to take the keiso called Moonflower into his hand as a hostage against the possible return of his right-hand brother.

She feared also that someone might know, or have guessed, that Nemienne was the sister of Karah-called-Moonflower. That implied that the mages might also know the paternity of the two girls. If they knew that, they would know just where else to look for them: in their father's house, where their six sisters still lived. The house where now the king was hidden. There could not be a greater disaster.

She reminded herself that everyone in Lonne, nearly, believed that King Geriodde was dead. Even if the king's enemies sought Karah and Nemienne at their sisters' house, they would have no reason to search that house closely. Enelle was a clever girl. She surely had a plan to protect the king if necessary.

Unless someone else gave away the secret. And hardly anyone knew it. Except, of course, herself.

Her face placid, Leilis bowed her head to the officer at the head of the small company of her enemies.

The keiso were in their rooms, the deisa in their gallery, the servants out of sight in their part of the House. Mother was also in her private rooms, carefully out of sight, though she was so practiced in elegant dissimulation that Leilis was not afraid she would give away any secrets. But Leilis hoped to avoid having anyone at all save herself speak to these soldiers or this worrisome mage.

She wore her slate-blue overrobe with its ocean spray and its white gulls. She stood with her head slightly bowed and her hands clasped together before her. Her whole attitude was quiet and yielding. In her mind, ocean waves rose and rolled before the wind. The waters of the ocean yielded before every blow. But its power was without limit. Men might rise up and go to war, ships might burn and founder, but after all the violence passed, the ocean was still there, untouchable as the sky.

Sometimes Leilis thought the women of the candlelight district should take their names from the sea rather than from flowers.

She said softly to the officer at the forefront of the company, "I am Seathrift." The name, so recently hers, felt like a lie in her mouth. But it was hers; her name, now; the name of the little white flower that bloomed where the tide ran, all along the inhospitable stony beaches of Lonne. It was not a showy flower, but pretty in its unassuming way, and tenacious despites its apparent delicacy. She bowed her head a little lower so that her neck curved gracefully, and murmured, "How may Cloisonné House serve Prince Sehonnes, estimable captain?"

"Moonflower, of Cloisonné House," the captain said bluntly, without preamble. "She is here, or she had better be. His eminence Prince Sehonnes commands her to appear before him, or he will have close questions for this House if she does not." The officer's manner was brusque, but Leilis saw the lines fatigue had carved around his eyes and his mouth and knew these days of treachery and murder, the uncertainty and ambiguity about who had betrayed whom, the tension of the approaching solstice, must all be weighing on this man. She guessed that he might still be struggling to make sense of his own place in the overturned order of Lonne. Leilis could have sympathized with both the weariness and the uncertainty, except she did not forgive the man for choosing the wrong prince to follow.

Opening her hands softly in a graceful gesture of obedience and regret, she murmured, "I am sorry, estimable captain, but the young keiso you seek is not within the House. She had gone out on that night, most unfortunately on that particular night, into the streets of the candlelight district for the evening, as keiso do, and I fear some mischance must have befallen her in the confusion, for she did not return. We are all most concerned."

The officer had been looking past her at the dim reaches and stairways of the House, but at this little speech, he turned a disconcertingly shrewd gaze upon Leilis. "Indeed," he said, his tone tiredly skeptical.

Leilis lowered her eyes in graceful deference and murmured, "Cloisonné House would be glad if you would search through the city for Moonflower, and return her to us safely if she is found." She wanted to say, *Surely all men know that the keiso Moonflower fled into Kalches with her sister and the bardic sorcerer and your rightful prince.* She did not say any such thing, but noted that evidently powerful men were *not* certain that was how it had all happened; that someone important doubted who had gone where and who might yet be hidden somewhere in Lonne. On the whole, that seemed regrettable. She would prefer to be certain all four of the missing were indeed in Kalches than to remain uncertain. And she would certainly prefer in particular that no one search in Lonne for Karah.

"An unfortunate night for Cloisonné House, mislaying so famous a young keiso," observed the captain.

"Indeed, that was a troubled and difficult night for all the city," Leilis agreed. She met the captain's eyes with grave sincerity and went on softly, "We do not wish to impede you in your duty. You are welcome to search through Cloisonné House; through every room and hall and gallery and attic. But you will not find the one you seek, for she is not here. If you must search, I will ask you and your men to be kind as you make your way through this House. We are only defenseless women and girls."

The officer gave Leilis a weary half smile that suggested he was aware that her sincerity was a mask, but that he wasn't inclined to challenge her on that account. "We will search—" he began.

The mage standing behind him said abruptly, "The woman is lying."

The captain closed his eyes, briefly. Then he opened them, turned his head, and asked, his voice flat, "What did you expect, Mage Karende? And what difference does it make? We must still search the House, and when we don't find the keiso, as I expect we won't, we must still report that failure."

The mage's jaw tightened. He was a slender young man with narrow shoulders and a thin mouth and a supercilious tilt to his head. He looked at Leilis with a frightening intensity of dislike in his eyes.

Since there was nothing else she could do, Leilis said softly, "But I am telling you the truth. Moonflower is not here. Cloisonné House does not know where our lost keiso may be, nor what has become of her."

"So *you* say—" began the mage.

The captain said bluntly, "Oh, I expect that much's true enough, for what it's worth. The girl would hardly have stayed here, even if she's still in the city after all." He turned toward his men, probably to issue the order to search.

"When we leave, this woman comes with us, whether we find the other or not," the mage said abruptly. "Let her tell Prince Telis she does not know where to find the keiso." When the captain stared at him, he shrugged, sharp and disdainful. "She comes with us," he repeated sharply.

The captain only gave the resigned nod of a man serving under the orders of a superior he dislikes. He said, mildly enough, "She may be required to answer any questions Prince Sehonnes may have, first."

The mage shrugged disdainfully, but did not argue.

Leilis also said nothing. Keiso never argued with men lest they appear ill-tempered; they did not protest any male whim, lest they seem nervous or untrusting. Keiso learned other ways to tilt circumstance in the direction it should go. Leilis had never had much opportunity to deploy the weapons of the keiso. But she knew very well what those weapons were.

The search of the House was cursory, since the captain was already certain that Moonflower was not hiding here and blandly dismissed Mage Karende's urgings to search aggressively just to be sure. His dislike of the mage was hardly hidden behind studied civility. Leilis, who stayed at the captain's side throughout, with a soldier constantly attending her to make sure she did not stray, considered what use she might make of that evident antagonism.

The search was conducted with quiet courtesy, which almost made Leilis think better of the captain, if he had not shifted his obedience so very quickly to an usurper. But he was polite to her during the search. He waited courteously as she explained to Mother that she must go to the Laodd and as she soothed Narienneh's nervous protests—not that Mother allowed herself to *seem* nervous, or to protest overtly. Only Leilis knew Narienneh well enough to see the depth of Mother's fear behind her serene manner.

"As you must venture through Lonne and into the Laodd, perhaps you may locate our missing girls," she told Leilis. "Or any of the women of the flower world who may need succor." She turned, her manner regal, to the officer. "Cloisonné House is not alone in missing some of our daughters, captain. No doubt they are sheltering where they may, for storms are not kind to flowers. Should your search locate any of our girls, I hope you will see they are returned safely to us. In this difficult time, Cloisonné House will shelter any woman in need."

The officer murmured something polite in return. And he continued to be everything that was courteous all during the long walk from Cloisonné House, across the Niarre River and through the width of the Paliante and the King's District and at last up the long curving road that led to the gates of the Laodd. He set a gentle pace that whole way, and asked her twice if he should have his men commandeer a conveyance for her. Leilis, who was using the delay afforded by that long walk to think, declined gracefully, murmuring that she was glad to walk and would not wish to put anyone to such trouble.

But they reached the Laodd at last, and Leilis still did not know precisely what she should do, far less what she might get a chance to do. Nor had she yet been able to guess Mage Karende's intentions, nor did she see any way to ascertain what the mage might know or guess save by allowing him or his prince to question her, which seemed a very bad idea. Though she did not yet know quite how she might escape such questioning. The Laodd was not an easy fortress from which to come or go; only the one road led from the city to its broad doors, and it was a high, narrow road that left anyone who set foot on it entirely exposed to anyone who might watch or guard it. And the soldiers continued alert, however polite.

Leilis had entered the Laodd before, twice. But not as a prisoner. Or . . . not *precisely* as a prisoner, though in fact neither of those earlier visits had been precisely comfortable, either. But she certainly had not entered the Laodd as the prisoner of a mage she distrusted and feared.

Now, as they crossed the last little span of the high road, she found she was afraid of everything. She was afraid of Mage Karende and of the prince he served. She was afraid of Sehonnes and his ambition. Most of all she was afraid of the events that were rushing out of her control. She was more afraid with every step she took. She could give away far too much; she could give away everything, and she had no defense save for her keiso training. This did not seem a very adequate weapon, under the circumstances.

The Laodd rose up above Lonne, dauntingly blank and impersonal, its sheer walls gleaming, its thousand glass windows opaque in the early light. As one approached the fortress, the vast, violent cataract of nearby Nijiadde Falls drowned sound and sense with its thunder, as though giving voice to the power housed in the Laodd itself. Spray filled the air above the lake where the falls broke, and mist drifted, cold against Leilis' face, as she walked, surrounded by enemies, toward the Laodd's wide doors.

Usually men stood before those doors; soldiers, their presence meant to underscore the Laodd's power and authority. Today the road was empty. The absence of the soldiers might have made the Laodd seem more open or welcoming. Today, that absence was like a warning.

Inside the Laodd, even with the doors standing open, the thunder of Nijiadde Falls, though still audible, became muted. Thought and speech became possible once more. Leilis did not find this entirely welcome, for she could not think, and there was nothing that she wished to say and far too much that she did not. Normally soldiers stood watches here within the Laodd as well. Today the great vaulted entry hall was empty both of soldiers and of the functionaries who usually determined whether visitors had proper appointments and directed them to appropriate offices. No doubt, Leilis thought, many men were coming and going from the Laodd about all manner of business, but few wished their coming and going to be marked. And no doubt the princes and all their various supporters and opponents had better use for soldiers than to leave them standing ordinary watches in the great hall. Today, anyone who came to the Laodd might enter freely, but must find his own way through the fortress, and had no way of knowing what he might encounter.

Mage Karende gestured sharply to the right, where a wide corridor led away from the great vaulted entry hall. "Hold her there," he ordered the officer. "I will inform Prince Telis that I have brought her here—and Prince Sehonnes, of course!" To Leilis that last was plainly an afterthought, a sop to the officer and his men. From the captain's tight jaw, Leilis thought he had heard it the same way.

Mage Karende went on, "I expect—"

Hurrying footsteps interrupted him, and another mage, this one a sharp-featured woman of middle years, came out into the great entry hall from one of the farther corridors. Seeing Mage Karende, this woman lifted her hand in a swift, imperative gesture that he should wait, and came quickly to meet him.

"You are here at last!" she said, once she was near enough to speak without shouting. She completely ignored the soldiers, but gave Leilis a swift, dismissive glance and then spoke only to Mage Karende. "We needed you yesterday—or the night before—or the day before that! And here you have been wasting your time assisting these—" she sniffed—"soldiers."

"I was *told*—" began Mage Karende, sounding offended.

"Yes, of course, I know! But we needn't after all trouble

with searching among the keiso, though of course your efforts are to be commended, I am sure," said the woman, making it clear that she did not really think so. "Prince Telis summons you. He summons us all."

"Ah! Our prince is ready at last?" interrupted Mage Karende, with frightening eagerness.

The captain did not visibly react to any of this, but he was certainly listening. So was Leilis. She tried to make herself relax, to show nothing but a calm keiso mask to the world.

But the woman jerked her head in impatient negation. "No! Well, yes, nearly! We have his—the other one, you know. We need you at once, in case—"

"Of course, enough!" snapped Mage Karende, stopping her before she could say anything more. He turned to the captain. "Hold this woman in the nearest chamber. Or, no—take her to the mages' gallery and turn her over to—to—Mage Rohorras, or Mage Isonne—"

"No, Isonne is working with the prince," said the woman mage. "No matter that *some* of us may have twice the experience working with—" but the woman cut that off herself, with a sharp, annoyed glance at the soldiers. She added only, "No, Isonne is busy."

Mage Karende made an exasperated gesture, looking harassed. "Of course." He turned to the officer. "Very well, captain, put this woman someplace safe and keep her till I or Prince Telis have time to send for her!" He hurried away, the other mage at his side, their soft-soled boots nearly silent on the stone tiles of the floor.

The captain gazed after the two mages, his expression utterly neutral.

Leilis tried to think. So Prince Telis was *nearly ready*. That was probably not good, though she had no idea what he might be nearly ready to do. But who was "the other one?" *We have his— the other one.* Could the serpent-prince's pet mage *possibly* have meant to say *We have his brother?* Had Sa-Telis gotten his hands on Prince Tepres after all, and they had been wrong all along about Taudde taking him to Kalches? She longed to know for certain; enough of terrifying guesses scattering across her thoughts!

She knew so little, and could ask nothing. But perhaps she could learn from the questions others asked her. Or perhaps— Leilis slanted a glance up at the captain's blank expression— perhaps a man worried by all these disasters might be inclined to speak more freely, once there was no one to hear him but his own men and a single harmless keiso.

Leilis said softly, gazing up through her lashes at the captain, "This is so alarming. The days have become so frightening."

The captain swiveled to stare at her.

Leilis bowed her head meekly. "We of the flower world have been entirely bewildered by these recent alarms and events. Word of violence and terror comes to us through the air and the dark. But it cannot be true that Prince Sehonnes has become a murderer and usurper and parricide, for surely no loyal soldiers of Lonne would obey such a man—"

"That was *Telis*," the captain snapped.

"Indeed, it must be so," Leilis murmured. "I am glad to be made aware of your confidence regarding these terrible events."

"It *was* Telis," the captain insisted. "Sehonnes—I mean, *Prince* Sehonnes—knew nothing about his brother's plans until it was too late. Tepres got himself ensorcelled by that cursed Kalchesene, and here we are, the king dead and the heir stolen away, but we must have order, and who would *you* rather see on the throne, eh?"

Leilis bowed her head a little more deeply. "Of course, you are right," she agreed softly. "But, forgive me, captain. I am only a woman, accustomed to the small matters of the flower world. So I do not understand why Prince Sehonnes should set his men beneath the hand of a mage who plainly answers to Prince Telis. But of course you understand all these greater affairs."

"I know!" said the captain. He truly did not sound happy. He went on in a quieter, grimmer tone, "It will be better when Sehonnes recovers enough to take the throne and the crown and the title. That will be soon, surely." He stopped abruptly, perhaps remembering that he spoke to a woman he did not know, and a prisoner besides, and that all his men were listening.

"Sehonnes has been injured? Badly?" That was something Leilis had not known, and she hesitated, trying to work out how that might affect everything else.

"Nothing that threatens his life," the captain said gruffly. "Nothing that will stop him taking the throne. And better him than Telis, even if—" but he stopped there, without completing that statement.

Leilis studied the officer covertly from beneath lowered lashes. She wished she knew what he had intended to say, there at the end. Better Sehonnes than Telis, *even if* Sehonnes is lying about who struck down the king? Better Sehonnes than Telis, *even if* Sehonnes will not repudiate his murderous brother? However the captain had meant to finish that sentence, she was more and more certain that he was not at all pleased to be forced into a position where he must support *either* of those two princes. She tried to think exactly how she might weave this officer's doubts and anger, and his sense of outraged honor, into a weapon that would let her cut herself free of the net that had trapped her. And murmured, "I recall you mentioned that Prince Sehonnes intended to ask close questions of Cloisonné House, if our sister Moonflower could not be found. But naturally you must obey Mage Karende's order to wait for him or for Prince Telis."

"Yes," said the captain gruffly. "I mean . . . yes. Still . . ." he cast a glance of dislike the way the mages had gone. "Yes. Come along," he said abruptly, plainly coming to a decision. "As you say, I am sure Prince Sehonnes will wish to speak with any woman of Cloisonné House, and as Prince Telis plainly does not have time for you now, there is no reason to delay." He moved a hand as though he might touch Leilis' arm, but then did not, only indicating with a short gesture that she should proceed deeper into the Laodd. Not, she noticed, the way the mages had gone. Quite another way, in fact.

"Sir—" muttered one of the other soldiers, not precisely in protest, if Leilis was any judge. "I must remind you, we were to obey Mage Karende . . ."

"I know!" snapped the captain. "But if Telis wants this keiso, I say let him apply to Sehonnes for her—and explain plainly what he wants her for. If Sehonnes won't put a leash on his brother, let's find that out, eh? And if he will, I say, let's give *Telis* a chance to find that out."

"Sir," said the man, sounding much better satisfied, and there were little glances and nods through the whole company. Leilis thoroughly approved this idea, too. She did not actually *know* that it would prove simpler to get away from Sehonnes than from Telis and his mages. But she knew that if someone were going to question her, she did not want it to be a mage. Far less a mage who already suspected her of something, even if he apparently did not know exactly what he suspected her of.

Besides . . . she might learn something herself, from a prince who thought little of keiso.

Prince Sehonnes was a heavy man, broad, with wide-set eyes and strong features and powerful shoulders. He shared very little with his father, beyond a certain cast to his features. But even less did he favor his beautiful and famous mother. She had been a keiso of Maple Leaf House before Geriodde Nerenne ken Seriantes had taken her as his keimiso, his flower wife. Her fine-boned elegance had set the standard for beauty for all the keiso of Lonne for a generation. Prince Sehonnes had inherited nothing from her save her midnight hair and, Leilis thought, studying him, perhaps her mouth and something of her chin, for his jaw seemed too softly rounded for his heavy-boned face.

In general, Prince Sehonnes was said to resemble no one more than his great-great-grandfather: Taliente Neredde ken Seriantes, whose enemies had called him the Dragon of Lirionne—the first to claim that title. Taliente Neredde ken Seriantes, who had undoubtedly known about the *other* dragon, when he turned Lonne from a pretty coastal town into an elegant and powerful city. Who had built the fortress of the Laodd above the city proper, and whose ambition had more than doubled Lirionne's size in his lifetime and whose son and grandson had held hard to the great kingdom he had built and expanded its borders still farther. Taliente Neredde ken Seriantes, whose heart, Leilis knew, had come to echo the heartbeat of the dragon that lay in the heart of darkness beneath Kerre Maraddras. King Taliente Seriantes, whose bones were laid now in the great tomb of Kerre Taum, within stone and under sky.

That was the ancestor Prince Sehonnes called to mind.

But his heavy features were drawn now with suffering. His

mouth was tight, his gaze hard and fixed with endurance. His right arm was in a sling, and—this was immediately, horrifying obvious—his right hand was missing. *Injured*, the officer had said. And, *Nothing that will stop him taking the throne.* That might be so, but no one had to explain to Leilis that many men would hesitate to acclaim so badly maimed a prince, especially one they already feared or disliked or mistrusted. Especially one widely believed to be a parricide and an usurper.

That was Telis, the captain had declared. He had spoken as though he knew, and maybe it was true. But no one who already disliked Sehonnes would believe it—and even those who hated Telis would always believe that Sehonnes must have been at least complicit. Leilis certainly believed that. She believed, from the officer's very lack of expression, that whatever he had said, the officer suspected that, too.

Prince Sehonnes had set up his household in a part of the Laodd that Leilis had never seen. Perhaps he was avoiding any place which his father had frequented; perhaps the long, stark room to which the officer had brought Leilis was one Sehonnes had always favored. This room might suit a man who wished to seem soldierly and plain, for no rugs adorned the tiled floor, no cloth hangings or tapestries softened the walls, no ornate carving decorated the backs or legs of the chairs. There were four chairs, all drawn up near the wide hearth at one end of the room, though only Prince Sehonnes was seated in one: there were half a dozen court nobles present, but all of them were on their feet.

Leilis knew one of the older noblemen: Minarras Perenne ken Saradd, a quiet, sober man of advancing years who had a great admiration for the art of dance and had long cherished Rue's company, though he had never sought her or any keiso as a flower wife. Minarras Saradd recognized her, too, and his expression, already closed, became remote and cold. But she could not tell whether this was because he disapproved of her, or because he disapproved of her presence here, and if the latter, for her sake or for some other reason. But she marked him as a possible ally anyway, because he admired Rue and because neither Rue nor any other keiso had ever complained of him.

The fireplace was huge and the fire laid in it commensurate, but even that fire could not dispel the chill in the room, for all the shutters were open to the light and the air. Despite the chill, Prince Sehonnes was perspiring. Fevered, Leilis guessed, and wished he would die of it. But she knew he would not. The very best of the healing arts would be instantly available should Sehonnes begin to fail. But she could see that pain and fever had put the prince into a foul temper.

"Well?" Prince Sehonnes demanded of the officer escorting Leilis. The officer had left his men outside the room, but he had escorted Leilis personally into Sehonnes' presence. Now he bowed as the prince raked her with an assessing, dismissive glace and added, sharply, "That is certainly not my brother's keiso."

Bowing her head and advancing one foot a little ahead of the other so that her robes would fall gracefully, Leilis concentrated on looking elegant and compliant. She watched Prince Sehonnes and the men with him carefully, but through her lashes, hiding her attention behind a mask of keiso poise. She saw Minarras Saradd lift an eyebrow. His mouth crooked just perceptibly. But it was too late, now, to adjust her attitude—and the nobleman did not seem inclined to comment on Leilis' meek air. At least, not yet.

"Eminence, no," said the captain, with a short bow. He spoke with far more formality now than when speaking to Karende or to Leilis. "This is another keiso of Cloisonné House, called Seathrift. A woman Mage Karende wished to have held for questioning when he is at leisure. Or held for Prince Telis to question. One gathers your eminent brother and his people are all much occupied about some other business just at the present." He did not actually say *Whatever business that might be, and do you even know?* But Leilis heard his meaning as clearly as though he had spoken those very words. She rather thought, from his tightening mouth, that Prince Sehonnes heard that, too.

The captain went on, without expression, "So I am to hold this woman someplace she will be safe. So I brought her here, eminence, because what place could be safer?"

"Indeed," said Prince Sehonnes.

In that moment, the prince's voice was very like his father's. Leilis did not allow her fear to show in her face or her manner, but moved swiftly to establish the direction of this interview before anyone else—the prince himself or any of the men here with him—could do so. She glided forward a step and sank down to kneeling, on one knee, gracefully, curving her shoulders and arching her foot to make her robes drape just so. "Eminence," she murmured, and went on immediately, without waiting for permission to speak, "We of Cloisonné House are afraid, for our sister Moonflower is missing from our House and without our care. Who can say, in these troubled days when all certainties tremble, whose hand might have plucked our sister from the flower world? And so we are afraid, and appeal to you for protection."

There was a pause. And if any man in this room did not realize what accusation Leilis had just made, and against whom, that man was not Prince Sehonnes.

The prince leaned back in his chair, studying Leilis narrowly. Though he must still be in a great deal of pain, his attention was sharp and clear. He was not a stupid man, by all reports. He surely resented and distrusted his brother. But all the flower world knew that he resented his own left-hand birth as well, and disliked all keiso. He said abruptly, "You believe my brother has already gathered your sister into his hand? Yet Karende evidently seeks her still. My brother's people search for her everywhere, I am told. This is not the first I have heard of it."

"Indeed, it does appear so," Leilis agreed softly. "It is true no one would have cause to seek a woman he already held in his hand."

There was another pause. No one said, *Appearances can be deceptive.* No one had to say it. No one had to say, *If your brother seeks to deceive you in such a matter, it can surely be for no good purpose.*

Prince Sehonnes said eventually, "There are many who might conceal this specific woman, however. From any who seek her. Certainly from me as well as from Telis. For a multitude of reasons."

This was, of course, a counter-accusation, for all that the prince's tone was flat. Leilis bowed her head a little more deeply and answered, "One bloom may disappear within a garden, eminence, and who should discover it among the multitude? But all know that the garden as a whole thrives only in the shadow of the generous and attentive gardener."

Sehonnes leaned forward, winced as the movement dragged at his mutilated arm, and leaned back again. He said, his voice tight and grim, "*I* am attentive."

"Of course, eminence," Leilis murmured.

"It is true," Minarras Perenne ken Saradd, put in, his voice low and grave, "that the girl in question is only a young keiso, hardly old enough to have changed her robes. And yet the mages of Lonne cannot find her?"

Prince Sehonnes leaned back, gripping the arm of his chair with his good hand and shifting his mutilated arm carefully within its sling. His mouth was tight, his gaze angry. Leilis lowered her eyes to the floor and stayed very still.

"One little flower might hide anywhere," growled Sehonnes at last. "The entire candlelight district is filled with places a girl could hide. Even from Telis. But not from me. Or I will break the whole district. Beginning with the keiso Houses. I doubt I shall need to make more than one demonstration. They claim to be sisters, those women, but when the scythe comes down, they care for one another no more than a field of flowers cares for one flower."

Leilis suppressed a shiver.

"Indeed, eminence," said Minarras Saradd, still quiet and serious. "Shall I see to this matter for you?"

Sehonnes gave him a hard glance. "You?" he said harshly. "No. I will send someone who was born on the left. Someone who knows better than to be seduced by pretty manners and clever speeches."

Minarras Saradd flushed, and then paled. He said, his tone stiff, "I think I am little swayed by pretty manners, eminence. But just as you wish." He stepped back, not even glancing at Leilis. She felt the forcefulness with which the old man did not look at her, and would have pitied him except she did not know why he was in this room at all except to accommodate himself to Prince Sehonnes.

"Take the woman aside and hold her," Sehonnes said to the officer, who still stood beside and a little behind Leilis. "You, yourself. I hold you responsible for her. And when my brother comes for her . . . bring him to me. I will see him, is that clear? If he sends one of his people, you may say that you are not to release this woman to anyone but my brother. And when he comes, then I will see him. That very moment, no matter the hour." He glanced dismissively at Leilis. "And her as well."

"Eminence," the captain acknowledged, and waited for Leilis to get to her feet and come with him.

"So that is the prince you choose to serve," Leilis said, once she and the captain were out of that room and there was no one to overhear but the captain's own men. She kept her tone grave and polite, but the sideways glance she gave him was profoundly skeptical. *I will break the whole candlelight district*, Sehonnes had said. That had been unusually clear and direct, and such a threat was not likely to be much to the taste of any ordinary man of Lonne.

And there could surely be only one reason, only one, for either left-hand prince to seek so assiduously for Moonflower of Cloisonné House. Prince Sehonnes had not said, *I will pluck this one flower so that I may use her as a weapon against my right-hand brother.* But he had hardly needed to *say* it. What other reason could he possibly have to seek his brother's favored keiso?

Which meant Prince Sehonnes, at least, believed Tepres was still alive. And *someone* had cut off Sehonnes' hand. Leilis felt her heart lift, despite the situation.

"Better Sehonnes than Telis," the captain answered as he had before, but more grimly. He rubbed his face with a hard hand, as though trying to scrub away doubts.

"Indeed, indeed. Of course you are perfectly right," agreed Leilis, smoothly enough to imply she did not agree at all. She glanced at him again. She could not mistake his tone. She was almost certain she did not mistake it.

Here, now, before Prince Telis found time for her and she found herself faced with worse than these impatient, worried soldiers, was perhaps her best—perhaps her only remaining—chance to win herself free. And she had, still, no weapons to put to the task but the gentle weapons of the keiso. Steeling herself for the risk, she met the officer's eyes and said, "But how confusing all these terrible events seem, to those who know nothing save rumor and surmise! Prince Sehonnes seems so harsh. Those of us in the flower world are not even certain that our king was truly struck down; perhaps it is possible he yet lives. One hears one rumor and then another and how is one to know what is true? Perhaps, estimable captain, *you* know with certainty that the true king is dead?"

The captain's gaze had sharpened through this little speech. He glanced at the closed door to the room they had just left. "Unfortunately it seems impossible our king should live." But then he glanced one way and the other down the corridor, took Leilis abruptly by the arm, beckoned his men to follow with a curt gesture, and led her quickly down the corridor.

Leilis made no protest, and the captain took her only a little distance before flinging open the door to a reception chamber. The chamber was not large, and it was almost ostentatiously plain; the sort of place a petitioner of little account might wait until someone of the Laodd staff might have time to inquire as to his business. This morning, unsurprisingly, the room was empty.

It did not entirely surprise Leilis when the captain led her into this chamber, signaling for his men to wait—and incidentally to guard the room against any possible intrusion. He closed the door behind them, let her go and glared hard at her. He crossed his arms over his chest, his whole attitude one of impatience and close-held anger, without the least trace of the blank stolidity with which he had met Mage Karende.

"Of course the king is dead!" he snapped at her. "Let's be plain, woman! There was a body found, you must have heard! His *own servants* swear it was his body—"

"Of course they would be deeply grieved for the king to whom they were long loyal," murmured Leilis.

There was a pause.

"I thought of that," the captain said at last, in a much different tone. "I don't know who else might have thought of it." He gave her a hard look. "Do you *know*, woman? Or is this a tale? If I find you've lied to me, you with your pretty keiso manners, if you've lied to me in *this*—" he stopped, his breath coming hard.

Leilis took a firm grip on her nerves. She said far more directly, "That was not the king's body, though it was made to seem so. The king lives, and he is safe—for the moment. This is the truth, captain. I know this; I, personally, for I have seen him. He was injured, but he will not die of those wounds; there is no reason he should die at all unless he meets further treachery. His man Neriodd brought him to Cloisonné House, but as you have seen, he is not hidden there now. But I know where he is." She paused. Then she asked, "Do you wish Prince Telis to question me? Do you wish Prince Sehonnes to ask me many close questions? Perhaps to ask me, eventually, what I know of the king?"

For some moments, the captain did not answer, but only continued to regard Leilis in silence. His hand rested on the hilt of his sword, and Leilis realized that he might think of more than one way to make sure she was never questioned. She folded her hands together and gazed at him with an attitude of grave trust, and he swore suddenly and took his hand from his sword. Leilis did not permit herself even an inward smile, lest it show in her eyes. She only waited.

"And Prince Tepres?" demanded the captain at last. "Do you know aught of him as well? There are rumors everywhere that cursed Kalchesene took him! Does the flower world know the truth of that tale?"

Leilis lifted her hands in a gesture of courteous bafflement. "The flower world knows nothing, estimable captain. The flowers only listen to the wind, which carries many confused tales. But we both know he must live. Even if the bardic sorcerer took him, that was a man trusted by the king himself."

The officer made a wordless sound of doubt and suspicion.

She tried not to let herself think of Taudde, of how torn he must be, of the terrible position he must now occupy if he had been forced to take Tepres with him to Kalches and his grandfather's court. She tried not to let any of her personal fears show in her eyes, but met the captain's gaze guilelessly and added, "Anyway, it is quite plain that wherever Prince Tepres may be, Sehonnes and Telis still fear him. Why else would they seek Moonflower of Cloisonné House? Would you wish either of them to find her?"

For a space, they regarded one another in silence: the grizzled officer in his soldier's flat red and dull gray, and the young keiso in gull-swept robes. Leilis had no weapons at all. But the captain had laid his down, too, now. Or very nearly.

"Yes," said the captain at last. "I mean, no." He grimaced and rubbed his face once more, plainly thinking. Plainly he did not much care for his thoughts. At last he looked up again, gave Leilis a hard glare, and declared, "You must not return to Cloisonné House. There is no safety for you there. Do you have somewhere else you can go? Perhaps even to Prince Tepres—or to the king?"

"One or the other," agreed Leilis. "That is my whole desire, now. Later—who knows, captain? Perhaps later I will find other things to desire." She added softly, "The moment I am free of the Laodd, I will disappear. I assure you, I will not be seen by any man's eyes, save as I choose to be seen fleeing Lonne, that all men may know I have not sought shelter anywhere in the flower world."

"That would be best, if you can arrange it," agreed the captain. He looked her up and down, but with cautious approval rather than doubt.

"I can," Leilis promised him. "I will."

"Good." The captain's eyes met hers, and he hesitated. Then he said, his tone hard, "If you are telling me the truth, woman, then if you should happen to have the chance . . . you may tell King Geriodde that Rehoras Temedd of the Fifth Division, and his men, will be waiting to see the rightful king's banner raised again."

"If I should see the king," Leilis promised, "I will assuredly remember your name, estimable captain. Or if I should see Prince Tepres, the same. Either will be glad to know that some of their officers are still loyal."

"Most of us," the captain said grimly. "*Most* of us. Sehonnes says one thing, Telis another, Prince Geradde is missing entirely, no one knows where the heir may be save perhaps hidden away by Kalchesene sorcery—you may well say the king trusted that sorcerer, but should he have, eh?"

Leilis bowed her head politely.

"So, well, a man must choose whom to follow, even when every choice is wrong. But who wouldn't welcome a right choice in all this disaster? *Most* of us would welcome a call from the rightful king. Tell him that, if you see him!"

"If I see him, I will be glad to tell him so."

The captain gave her a grim nod, then stalked to the chamber door, jerked it open and glared out.

Leilis stepped to his side and glanced out, too. The corridor was, at the moment, deserted save for the captain's men. She could not guess how long this would last; she did not know even the everyday patterns of life within the Laodd and could not guess how these terrible events would affect everything. But if she went quickly . . . if she met no one, or no one who knew who she was, or that Mage Karende had wanted her held . . . she stepped cautiously out into the corridor. Captain Rehoras Temedd followed, scowling around at his curious, worried men with wordless impatience and a curt wave of his hand. Whatever his men read from his expression, they looked carefully away from Leilis and eased out of her path, showing no sign of intending to argue with their captain or call out to Prince Sehonnes or do anything at all to hinder her flight.

The captain took her arm and led her quickly through the crowd of his men, who folded up around and behind them and followed. Their boot heels rang on the wide stone tiles of the corridor. There was no way for more than twenty soldiers to go quietly through the Laodd, but there was no way for them to look sneaky or guileful, either. Leilis supposed that anyone who saw them, and her in their midst, would only think they had all be ordered to escort her. Though half a company seemed an over-large escort for one harmless keiso. But what else would people think, after all?

Then she thought of one man who would not be fooled by any official appearance. She missed a step, and met the captain's eyes when he looked down at her. She said, "Prince Sehonnes knows what orders he gave you."

But after a moment he answered, "Don't concern yourself, woman. I much doubt he even knows my name—and there's ways, even so."

"He will discover your name," Leilis answered softly. "And he will remember he made you responsible for me."

"Sir?" said one of the soldiers to the captain, reproachfully.

"There's ways, I said," Captain Rehoras Temedd told both

of them. Despite the circumstances, his eyes glinted suddenly with amusement as he met his man's eyes. But he only gave Leilis a little nod, then lifted a hand to indicate the great hall and, still far across the hall's expanse, the open doors that led to the road and the city. The voice of Nijiadde Falls was perceptible even from here: a steady low thunder that Leilis felt in her bones rather than heard.

There was no one in the great hall—or no one who mattered. A servant, ducking away through another door; a handful of soldiers who acknowledged Rehoras Temedd's company as they passed. No one to stop or question them. Leilis could hardly believe her retreat from the Laodd was going to be so easy.

Then the sound of hurrying footsteps made her hesitate, not exactly irresolute but definitely uncertain. These were not boots, those quiet steps—but they certainly were not court ladies; not today, not here. The soldiers looked toward their captain. Captain Rehoras Temedd grimaced, turning toward the sound, but what he muttered, his voice low, was "Ah, there. As I said, there's ways to manage."

Leilis did not understand what he meant, but she was not surprised to see a pair of mages coming toward them. She could not stop herself from glancing quickly at the captain.

He was not looking at her, but at certain of his men, holding each man's gaze for only an instant. His hand was not, Leilis saw, on the hilt of his sword, but his thumb was hooked through his belt just in front of the sword's hilt. His expression was studiously blank.

"This is Mage Karende's woman?" the foremost of the two mages demanded abruptly as they came up, with no pretense of courtesy. He was an older man, not as old as Captain Rehoras but certainly not young. His hair, dark but shot through with gray, was clubbed back at the nape of his neck; his features were sharply carved and aristocratic; his manner was decisive.

His companion was a woman, younger than he but perhaps not by so very many years; plain, but plain in a compellingly elegant way. Leilis thought that if she had been a keiso, she would not have troubled to seek a keisonne and a flower marriage, but would have mastered some art and in that way acquired wealth and standing. It occurred to her for the first time that magecraft could be said to be an art, and that this woman was probably a master of that art, and dangerous.

Captain Rehoras, looking extremely stolid and exactly as though he had never dreamed of taking Karende's keiso to Prince Sehonnes, far less setting her free again afterward, made a small gesture that was like a salute, but did not actually answer. But the first mage looked Leilis up and down and nodded in curt satisfaction. "I see it is. Yes. Yes, I see why Karende thought her best brought in. You, you are a keiso, I see. What is your name?"

"My lord mage," Leilis murmured, offering him a graceful and docile courtesy. "I am called Seathrift, my lord mage."

"Seathrift, indeed!" snapped the woman mage. "And what is your *real* name, girl?"

Leilis, casting around for a safer option than the truth, began to give the birth name of an obscure keiso who had died years before without ever achieving prominence in the flower world. But she had only begun to form the word when Captain Rehoras made a small gesture. This one was not any kind of salute, and not meant to be seen by anyone but his men. It was only the turn of his hand. Leilis noticed the movement only because of the training that taught keiso that every turn of the hand must be graceful, that even the lift of a single finger might carry meaning. But even she did not expect the sudden violence that followed that signal, and neither mage had time even to realize that the soldiers had moved before they fell, the woman a heartbeat after the man.

Leilis, shocked despite herself, stepped hastily back from the spreading blood while the soldiers cleaned their knives—not one of them had even drawn a sword—and resheathed them. None of them appeared surprised, though despite their decisive speed, Leilis didn't see how they could have anticipated their captain's silent signal. She certainly hadn't. But the men actually had a satisfied air.

"Prince Telis thinks we're dogs, to take orders from any man who snaps his fingers," Captain Rehoras told her, his tone grim. "And his mages, never liked 'em, always plotting, and not to anybody's good but their own, look at that Ankennes. Prince Sehonnes at least has more sense than to think they're his men. It won't surprise him to hear they tried to take you by force, despite my orders, and his. And they got you away from me, I guess, by magecraft. He'll be angry, right enough—but not with me. You've got a place to go, girl, then go to it quick, before that Karende wonders why his people haven't yet brought you to him."

Leilis kept her eyes on the officer's face and firmly away from the . . . bodies. "Yes," she said. Trying to catch herself up, she took a deep breath, and regretted it immediately. She wanted to creep away home to Cloisonné House and hide in her own room. No: she wanted to run to Ankennes' house and through the door that opened to Kalches and find Taudde and hide with *him*. Soon, soon. If she was lucky and clever and kept *hold* of herself. She blinked hard, lifted her chin, twitched her keiso robes to drape just so, met Captain Rehoras' eyes and said firmly, "Indeed, that would seem the wisest course. I thank you, captain. And," she glanced around, "all your men."

"Dark days," the soldier said, the one who had spoken once or twice before. "All this confusion. Terrible." He was cleaning the blood from his knife, slowly and thoroughly.

Leilis inclined her head with automatic grace. And once more, to Captain Rehoras Temedd. She wondered what kind of further evidence he would arrange, to blame things on the mages and cast suspicion on Prince Telis. She was glad he would do that, but she hoped the captain was right about what Prince Sehonnes would believe and suspect and do. *She* would not have wanted to try to fool Sehonnes again. He was too angry, and angry princes were dangerous.

But she slipped out without another word and hastened toward the great doors, standing open and unguarded. Several of the soldiers glanced at their captain, but he only made a curt, wordless gesture, and they stepped out of her way and let her past.

-11-

Taudde's cousin Penad did not knock, but simply flung open the door to the tower apartment and strode in without waiting for permission. Taudde, who had been waiting *all day* in a wearing tension of nerves and confusion and anger and shame for Aunt Ines to follow after him—as she had *promised*, and where *was* she?—was for the first moment too much taken aback to prevent Penad from coming in. And then it was too late.

Not just Penad, either, but Penad's brother Mienas, and a whole handful of other cousins: big, thick-witted Davoedd and his even bigger brother Toronn; Taudde remembered those two as the sort that would follow anyone who seemed decisive and promised excitement. Also Lamanes—that was not a surprise— and behind Lamanes, at the tail of the group—and this *was* a surprise to Taudde—came Heronn's son Geras, looking a bit young and uncertain and out of place in this company. Taudde suspected, cynically, that Penad had gotten Geras involved mainly to provide cover for the rest of them if Heronn found them out, and wondered if Penad might regret it later. He could hardly imagine Geras holding his tongue about anything as rough as he suspected the rest of them intended this to be.

In all, and discounting Geras, it was a very nice collection of all the cousins Taudde least wanted to see.

Taudde had reached automatically after his flute, but that was not, of course, in its accustomed pocket. He closed his empty hand into a fist. Though he was not without resources, he was uncertain of his ability to throw all six of his cousins bodily out of his apartment single-handedly. Mienas had a set of twin-pipes in his hand, and Geras had a flute through his belt—silver, like his sister's. And Taudde was very far from willing to embarrass himself by screaming for the guardsmen below—who had in any case clearly allowed this intrusion.

So Taudde drew himself up, crossed his arms, and did his

best to look unimpressed. "Penad," he said. "Did your father send you?"

"You think anyone had to *send* us?" Penad retorted, and then Lamanes stepped past him and declared proudly, "Uncle Manaskes has *important* things to see to—more important than *you!*"

Lamanes was not usually the sort to put himself forward, or he had not been that sort a few years ago. But young men did change. Taudde remembered Lamanes as a tall, awkward youngster, rising twenty but looking younger. Now he was a man grown, with shoulders to match his height, and Taudde suddenly suspected that he had been misled by memory and expectation when he had taken that hot-blooded fool *Penad* for a leader among the young men. Lamanes was certainly not hesitating to put himself forward now; he had shoved his way to the forefront of this clutter of cousins, and Penad seemed perfectly willing to take a supportive place at his shoulder.

"Grandfather's *collapsed,* and it's *your fault,*" snapped Lamanes, not hesitating at all. He stepped forward, jabbing a finger at Taudde's chest. "I thought Uncle Heronn had enough pride to know better, but now *he's* actually talking to that young Dragon! A prisoner would have been fine, a hostage would have been fine, but there the little Seriantes is, with that dragon ring and his silk-smooth promise to let us buy *our own* lands back from him with *our* blood and effort! So generous, and then there he'll be, another Seriantes Dragon, and what do you think his smooth promises will be worth *then?*"

Taudde would have laughed in Lamanes' face, unwise as that might have been under the circumstances, except he was afraid his cousin might actually be right about whose fault their grandfather's collapse might have been. He would hardly admit guilt to this idiot cousin of his, but the doubt thoroughly quelled his first scornful response. Still, he tilted his head and said judiciously, "Actually, you know, the Seriantes Dragons always *have* kept their promises. We just have never wanted them to, until now."

"Shut *up!*" snapped Mienas, from behind Lamanes, and Penad said angrily, "We're not interested in anything *you* have to say, except if you're ready to admit you've become a Seriantes dog and turned against your own people, we'll hear *that*."

"And you *will* admit it," Lamanes declared grimly. "Not just to us here, but to Uncle Heronn, and Uncle Manaskes, too, in front of the whole household! *Then* let's see who cares to listen to that Seriantes prince's lies!" He stepped forward once more, waving at his followers. "Davoedd, Toronn, hold him—"

Taudde tapped his fingertips on his belt, but Lamanes stamped his foot and clapped to confuse the rhythm, and Mienas lifted his pipes warningly, and Taudde, not only partially disarmed but out of practice for children's contests, hesitated to take the definitive measures he might have exerted against deadly enemies. He hesitated a heartbeat too long. Davoedd's hands closed on his arms, shoving him back against the nearest wall. It was outrageous. Taudde drew breath to whistle, but Penad hit him then, a hard blow to the gut that drove out his breath and doubled him over. "Geras!" Lamanes snapped. "Hit him!"

Which explained how Lamanes meant to keep Geras from confessing any of this to his father. Involving Geras in this business was insupportable, and Taudde was not going to permit it, but he couldn't get his breath, not yet. He gave Geras a hard look to keep him out of it—the boy did not, at least, seem very eager to take his turn.

"Geras!" Lamanes ordered again, and hit Taudde himself to keep him quiet and stop him concentrating.

Taudde was beginning to be willing to use quite rough measures, but now it wasn't as easy to manage it. Possibly it had been a mistake to let Lamanes get this far. There was still no sound from the wardroom below—perhaps the second level masked the sounds, and after all they had closed the door, but Taudde suspected, grimly, that the guardsmen knew perfectly well what was going on and simply didn't care to stop it. Toma Piriodde almost certainly would not approve, but Toma would be with the king—if the king were still alive—the thought was too great a distraction; Taudde couldn't catch his breath or gather his concentration. He tried to shake off the cousins holding him, glaring at Lamanes.

"Gag him, quick," Mienas said urgently. "He's a *lot* better than me—"

"Doesn't take a gag to shut up a coward," Lamanes snapped. "He makes one sound, we'll beat him bloody, and he knows it. Don't you, you coward, you *traitor*. Always strutting, weren't you, and now you're trailing after that puffed-up Seriantes dragonling like a lapdog." He held one clenched fist up to Taudde's face. "You may have forgotten your own father, dead on Brenedde Field, but *we*—"

Taudde, furious but not quite beyond thought, whistled five sharp descending notes that snapped through the air like arrows. Lamanes staggered back a step, gagging on blood. Then Davoedd hit him again and he lost the breath to do more.

"I told you!" said Mienas. "*Gag* him!"

"I think we'd better stop," Geras put in, catching Davoedd's arm. "Lamanes, that's enough, we'd better not—"

Lamanes spat blood, glaring so ferociously at the boy that Geras actually took a step back. Brushing past Geras, Penad seized Taudde hard by the throat, plainly ready to choke him rather than let him make another sound. "And we *will* gag this traitor," he said furiously. "Mienas, get me a cloth—"

"Now, what could possibly be going on, here?" inquired Irelle from the doorway, where she had suddenly appeared as though by sorcery. She gazed thoughtfully at each young man in turn. Judging just from her expression and her voice, she did not seem unduly alarmed or disturbed or impressed, but she was pale, and her hair was untidy. And her silver flute was in her hand.

Under his sister's regard, Geras flushed, then went white, then flushed again. He looked anywhere but at Taudde. Mienas took a step back, opening and closing his mouth in confusion. Davoedd and Toronn both let go of Taudde, who immediately knocked Penad's hand away from his throat, coughing and breathing deeply. Though he could hardly imagine Irelle would need any help handling this, he also seized the chance to snatch the twin-pipes away from Mienas, who only backed away another step, ducking his head in confused apology.

Penad, staring at Irelle, began, stumbling over his words, "You—I—you're supposed to be—"

Lamanes grabbed Penad's arm, shaking his head. Livid with rage, he tried to speak, but his tongue and mouth were too swollen and he spat more blood. He started toward Taudde, but Geras stepped into his path, raising his chin stubbornly.

Irelle merely raised her eyebrows. "I wonder," she said thoughtfully to Lamanes, "whether you might someday be able to lead men into necessary danger, as well as boys into ridiculous and disgraceful . . . pranks. I suppose it's a bit early to say."

Lamanes appeared near apoplexy. He spat again and *did* speak, almost a shout, but his torn mouth made it impossible to understand what he was trying to say. He glared furiously from Irelle to Taudde and shook a finger at Penad, who began, rather weakly, "This wasn't a *prank*. We thought—"

"Yes?" said Irelle, with the faintest tinge of astonishment and the slightest lift of her eyebrows. Taudde made a note of her exact tone, though he doubted he would ever be able to deliver so thorough a reprimand with one word and a single lift of the brows. That took natural talent. She'd certainly brought Penad to a dead halt. Penad turned to Lamanes in helpless confusion, but, Taudde was pleased to see, Lamanes still could not manage to make himself understood. Taudde regretted not having done such a thorough job on Penad earlier, thus possibly heading off the whole lot of cousins before they'd gotten started.

Mienas had been looking in alarm from Lamanes to Penad. Now he turned to Irelle. "If you—it's not—" he burst out. "You don't understand!"

"I don't?" said Irelle, with exactly the same quelling note of astonishment. "Well, Mienas, since my understanding is lacking, you had better explain yourself to someone more mindful of all these complicated matters. Toma Piriodde, for example. I doubt he'll be pleased to be summoned away from our grandfather's side for . . . this, but I'm sure he will *understand* what you were about when you spun your song for his men. Or perhaps *Grandfather's* understanding would be most acute."

There was a short, stiff pause.

Then Penad said, the undertones of his voice suggesting baffled anger and a tinge of relief, "*Grandfather* sent you up here?"

Irelle gave him a look. "What did you think? I came directly from his side. I'm sure he will be so pleased by your willingness to . . . contribute, during this difficult time."

Penad looked at Lamanes, who shook his head furiously and started to step forward. But this time both Davoedd and Mienas moved to stop him. Mienas put a quick hand on Lamanes arm. "If *Grandfather's* awake—" he said. Lamanes shook off his hand, turned on his heel, and stalked for the door, his boot heels slamming down with angry force on the wooden floor.

Penad said to Irelle, this time in a quieter voice, "We'll go. For now." He glared at Taudde and his voice dropped even lower, taking on a vicious edge. "But you may be sure *my* father won't be taken in by a quick-tongued arrogant Seriantes prince! *Grandfather* wouldn't be listening to him at all if he were in his right mind—you've taken advantage of him, that's what you've done, and for what, to win the favor of the Seriantes dragonling? *Your* father would be ashamed to see you rolling over on your belly for that Seriantes princeling in the hope he'll—"

Taudde, white with rage, lifted the twin-pipes he'd taken from Mienas to his mouth.

Irelle said, "Taudde!" sharply. All the undertones of her voice were layered with anger and—could it be *fear?* Even in his rage, Taudde hesitated. Penad had shut his mouth with a snap and backed away now, toward the door, and all the cousins— except for Geras, who stood miserably still under his sister's angry glance—slunk away after him. At last. Taudde was shaking, but he was willing to let them go now that Irelle had checked the killing edge of his temper.

"There," said Irelle, stepping over to shut the door behind Davoedd, who was the last out. "That's a start, and we'd better give them time to get clear away from the tower, but we must be quick. They'll find out what's happened soon enough—Penad and Lamanes must be thoroughly confused. Idiots, both of them, but if they'd been thinking with their heads instead of their male parts, I'd never have gotten them out of here." She took a breath, giving Taudde an odd look.

Before she could explain what she meant, Geras muttered, glancing up and then down at the floor again, painfully ashamed, "I'm sorry, Taudde. I knew Lamanes was wrong almost at once, only then I didn't know what to *do*—"

"Next time, think of something!" Irelle said, rolling her eyes. "Honestly, Geras! If I thought you were as ox-brained as

Davoedd or Toronn, I would be less ashamed."

Geras ducked his head.

Taudde took a breath, and another, trying to breathe out his anger and breathe in calmness. He managed a reasonably composed, "He did try to make them stop." He gave the boy a small nod, all he could manage. Penad's words about his father rang in his mind like the refrain of a particularly vicious song.

"He should have done more than *try*," Irelle said tartly. "Honestly, sometimes I wonder." She gave her brother an exasperated look, at which he flushed more deeply. But she added, to Taudde this time, "But it's a very good thing you shut Lamanes' mouth for him. He didn't believe me for a minute, so we haven't a great deal of time. The problem is all the cobwebs. Lamanes got a token for his little gang of thugs, so Geras is all right, and Toma slipped *me* one, so I'm fine, but we really can't have *you* wrapped up in a thousand threads of sorcery, Taudde. That wouldn't do at all."

Taudde tried, rather blankly, to unravel this, but Geras, jerking his head up, demanded, "You were *lying* about Grandfather? I thought—"

Taudde cut in, "She was lying?" He swiveled back to Irelle. "You were lying? Is he—"

"Not gone, but not conscious," she said sharply. "It's *worse* than him dying, because if he were *dead*, Father would be king and everyone would know it!" She stopped, pressing a hand across her mouth for a second. Then she dropped her arm to her side, glanced at her brother, looked directly at Taudde, and went on, clipped and impatient, "Father said he would take up all this about borders and treaties with the young Seriantes you'd so conveniently brought us, Uncle Manaskes said he was a fool, everyone got into the argument, and I don't know how it would've come out, but practically everyone was on Uncle Manaskes' side. *Then* we got a messenger from the bastard Seriantes prince, the oldest one, Sehonnes, offering Brenedde and Anharadde for proof of his brother's death—"

Taudde caught a breath.

"Exactly, and Uncle Manaskes said we should send back the young Dragon's right hand as a token that we're willing to bargain and demand everything west all the way to Sarodde for his head. He said Sehonnes must be willing to give almost anything to be rid of his brother without getting his own hands bloody. Manaskes has a lot of support, and my father—if he were clearly king, it would be different—" She broke off, swallowing.

Steady, sensible Uncle Heronn, who had always been content to stay back in Grandfather's shadow and handle all the quiet details of the day-to-day rule. Heronn, who let King Berente do the shouting and wasn't accustomed to raising his own voice. Taudde could see exactly how a loud, furious man like Uncle Manaskes, utterly convinced of his own righteousness, could have forced a confrontation that Heronn, in the face of the king's confusing incapacity and of fifteen years of Kalchesene anger over Brenedde, simply could not win. He snapped, "Do they not *realize* that Sehonnes already *has* blood on his hands? That he's an oathbreaker and a parricide? Do they think he's afraid of Kalches? Sehonnes will agree to any bargain Uncle Manaskes demands and break any treaty he makes—"

"I'm sure he will," Irelle interrupted him. "But—"

"For once, we have a chance to see an honorable young Seriantes who is *well* disposed toward Kalches take the Dragon throne—and we would rather see a parricide seize power instead? That is *madness*."

"Taudde! An entire generation of young men has *lived* for the solstice for fifteen years. Believing our people will welcome your gentler Seriantes king—*that* is madness, if you like!"

She was right. But Taudde said stubbornly, "Aside from making bargains with treacherous parricides, the *greater* madness is rousing the dragon of Lonne. Above all else, we do not want that dragon turning its attention toward Kalches!"

"Yes, your dragon—"

"Not *mine*," Taudde snapped. "Quite real, I assure you, and quite another thing from the ordinary dragons we dismiss so easily. This is not a mountain drake, to content itself with an occasional lamb!"

"I—and my mother and father—believe you may be right. Which is why I'm concerned about the *cobwebs*, Taudde, can we please concentrate on the important detail that you are going to be traceable by every sorcerer in Kalches the moment you leave this tower? You're the finest bardic sorcerer of our generation, Mother says, so *think* of something and we will get out of here, get your *friend* tucked somewhere a little less visible, and avoid the risk of anybody taking precipitous action!"

Taudde stared at her. The cobwebs. Yes. They were a problem. He looked down at the pipes in his hand, turned them over thoughtfully. Rather a good set of pipes, though he doubted Mienas was up to making a truly excellent instrument. He wished for his own flute, with its hint of the rolling tide in every note. Though he couldn't see how to do as Irelle suggested no matter whether he had the use of Mienas' pipes or his own flute or every instrument in the entire house. Those webs of sorcery had been woven precisely with bardic sorcerers in mind . . .

"You might find this useful," Irelle suggested, producing his flute from some hidden pocket in her skirts and holding it out with a slight and forgivable flourish.

Taudde stared at her.

"Well, it wasn't doing anybody any good just lying there by Grandfather's bed. Go on, take it."

Without a word, Taudde tossed the pipes aside and took his flute. It felt comfortable in his hand, the wood smooth and warm, the stops familiar to his fingertips.

"You can have my token, too," Geras said. And then, earnestly, as they both stared at him, "No, it'll work. It's— Lamanes got them from the wardroom, they're just single-use nonspecific tokens, the kind the guardsmen use when they need to come up here. Taudde can use mine, and I can stay here to keep the alarms from going out along the threads." He hesitated, ducking his head. "You were right, Irelle, when you implied Lamanes lied to Toma's men. He did. He told them he had signed permission from Father to take you out of the tower, and that a dozen of Taudde's allies from Lonne were here in Kedres and Toma wanted all his people to report to the guard station at the bottom of the hill so they could deal with them without panicking the whole town, and he showed them the written order for that, too. Except I could hear in his voice he was lying. It must have been Uncle Manaskes who wrote it out for him, to clear the wardroom." He glanced at Taudde, shamefaced. "After I realized Lamanes was lying, I knew what he must really have in mind, but I couldn't think how to get away from them, and I didn't know if my father could do anything even if I warned him, and besides, I didn't think Lamanes could be planning anything—anything *too* rough, not with me along—"

"Bringing you along is exactly why he thought he could get away with it," Taudde pointed out, exasperated.

"I figured that out when he told me to hit you," Geras admitted. He met Taudde's eyes. "I'd have done it, if I had to, to get them to stop. Once Lamanes thought he had me on his side, they'd have taken you out of here, to Uncle Manaskes, I guess. Then I could have gotten away and—and gone to find Mother, I suppose. Which would have been really brave of me, I know," he added. "You don't need to say it."

After a moment, Taudde said, "Going straight to Aunt Ines was very likely the best you could have done, under the circumstances. I do prefer the current plan, however. Just so long as you're willing to stay here yourself and take the blame for my disappearance. You do realize Uncle Manaskes will know exactly what you've done."

Geras shrugged with assumed nonchalance. "He can complain of me to my father, if he likes."

Irelle said briskly, "I was assuming Taudde would have to think of something subtle and brilliant, but this is better. Fast, efficient, direct, simple—it *is* a good idea, Geras, so perhaps it was just as well after all that you got swept up in all this, but it does leave you facing the storm." She gave her brother a stern look. "Do *not* let Uncle Manaskes bully you. Think of what *Mother* would say if he tried it with her."

The boy lifted his chin. "I'll think of what *you* would say. If you need a place to stay out of sight for a bit, the maple taps tapered off several days ago and the sugar team will have left the shack by now. It'll still be warm enough, I expect, and no one will be there"

"Another good suggestion," Irelle agreed, with an approving little nod. Geras flushed, but he was pleased, too, and he gave Taudde his wardroom token without hesitation.

Then Irelle said briskly to Taudde, "Quick, now," and headed for the door.

The two guardsmen were still at their posts by the door of the Kinsana Suite, which was undoubtedly a good sign since there was no need to guard an empty apartment; but they did present an obstacle. One man, from the brass flute tucked in his belt, was clearly a bardic sorcerer. And neither Taudde nor Irelle had so much as a letter from Uncle Manaskes with a forged signature.

"I don't suppose you can simply tell them that Grandfather is awake and demanding their presence," murmured Taudde. Irelle gave him a look.

Taudde smiled, not very nicely. "I'll hold them. It won't be subtle, but in this case I think we might prefer something fast, efficient, direct, and simple."

"That does sound ideal," his cousin agreed blandly. "They'll be warded."

"It won't matter. But we don't know that Tepres is alone. For all we know, Uncle Manaskes is already in there with another dozen guards, making ready to cut off his hand and box it up in salt—"

"In the Kinsana Suite? Never. Uncle Manaskes would never risk getting blood all over those rugs and curtains."

Taudde grinned, and let his flute fall into his hand.

At his first rippling phrase, the two guardsmen stepped apart from each other so that a single attack couldn't take them both at once. The man with the brass flute grabbed for his instrument; the other reached for his sword—it would have wire wrapped around the hilt to turn aside the inimical magic of an enemy, Taudde knew. He had set that sort of sorcery into quite a few swords himself, when he'd been learning his craft.

Toma Piriodde made sure his men had good equipment and good training and a suspicious outlook on the world, though evidently not suspicious enough to guard them against Uncle Manaskes' lies. Or maybe these men simply agreed with Manaskes and were willing to pretend they thought his orders were legitimate. Maybe they even *did* think his orders were legitimate; Taudde didn't care. Both men were indeed warded against sorcery—against exactly the sort of sorcery Taudde was using. But Taudde was right, too: it didn't matter. All the great bardic sorcerers were Kalchesene, and not a few were members of the king's own family. Bardic sorcerers were presumed to be loyal to their king and their country, and nothing that protected those two guardsmen was meant to turn aside sorcery of the strength and depth Taudde could bring to bear.

Around those men, he laid down the age of the mountains that surrounded Kedres, and the immobility of stone, and the crystalline stillness of midwinter nights. He layered one phrase above another, softly, softly—this was music meant not to carry through the house, but only to those two guardsmen. They were caught. He held them. They would not even know it, until he let them go and they thawed again into mobility and life.

Then they would know what had been done to them, and who had done it. But now that Taudde had finally allowed his temper to slip into action, he found he was far too angry to care. He spun stillness like ice around the guardsmen, one and the other and nowhere else, so that Irelle could simply step between them to lay her hand on the doorknob. The door wasn't locked. If not for the guardsmen, the Kinsana Suite would not be a prison, but an apartment for honored guests. So Irelle simply stepped past the guardsmen, turned the knob and opened the door.

And, without a word or any apparent flicker of surprise, Toma Piriodde stepped out to face her.

-12-

Late on the afternoon of the third day after Leilis had brought King Geriodde Seriantes to shelter in the house of the daughters of Geranes Lihadde, when she decided it was impossible to put it off any longer, Enelle finally told the king that he was dead.

Though still weak, the king had become clear in his mind. He knew what he wanted. And what he wanted was reliable information about what had been happening in the city, when all they had to offer were the thousand rumors that ran through the market; and Leilis, who was missing; and Neriodd, whom they did not know how to contact and who might not even know where the king lay. Someone had to tell King Geriodde so. Someone had to tell him he was dead. Someone had to tell him everything.

Enelle *had* explained about Leilis, but not everything. She had told him that she'd gone herself to Cloisonné House and had discovered that Leilis had disappeared. That in itself wasn't so frightening, because if anyone in the city had reason to slip out of sight, it was Leilis. She hadn't told him that Leilis had been taken away by soldiers and had not returned to Cloisonné House. *That* news didn't seem likely to let an injured man rest, and there was nothing they could do about it.

She hadn't mentioned how frightened she had been that someone might see her visiting Cloisonné House and wonder why, or how very careful she had tried to be. She had gone to the market first and made herself look like a fishmonger's girl, then tried her luck selling fish—which the household could ill afford—at half a dozen keiso Houses and aika establishments before daring to make her way to Cloisonné House. And then she had only found out about the soldiers taking Leilis, so the whole return journey had been even worse, because who knew who might have been asking Leilis questions or what she might have been forced to tell them? Enelle had been absolutely terrified the whole long way back that she might find soldiers had come there before her, and the king and all her sisters were gone. Nothing of the kind had happened, but she hadn't felt safe since. And she had already been frightened enough.

At first, the king's weakness had made him sleep a great deal, so it was possible to delay a little, and offer gentle excuses, then add a dusting of powdered goldenthread to his tea and let him sleep again. But every time he woke, he was more demanding, and it was plain to them all that this tactic had come to the end of its usefulness.

No one else dared explain the king's own death to him. The right choice would have been Karah, because no one could stay angry at Karah for more than a minute and anyway everyone knew the king's son loved her, so the king himself surely had to be kind to her. But of course Karah wasn't here.

Ananda had barely spoken with the king, and it certainly wasn't fair to put the duty on any of the little girls. That left Enelle, who tried not to feel that somehow she was always the one getting stuck with the really unpleasant duties.

And the solstice was approaching; that, too. No wonder the king was impatient. The days crept past, carrying that fraught date nearer and nearer, until the whole city seemed to hold its breath in expectation of it, and of disaster. The Treaty of Brenedde would end on the solstice, and if it were true that Prince Tepres was in Kalches . . . Enelle didn't want to think of what that might mean for him. And even if that weren't so, Sehonnes would claim the throne on the solstice, and everything would crash down around them.

Or maybe the sense of rushing disaster was all Enelle's. She rubbed her forehead hard. She was certain Geriodde would want to declare himself immediately when she told him the truth. He wasn't well enough, but she already knew that wouldn't stop him from trying. Yet he mustn't try to face his sons or take back his throne until he was more able. She must persuade him of that.

So in the afternoon, when she and Ananda and Tana all agreed they truly couldn't put it off any longer, she finally went to explain to him that he was dead.

Wounded and weak as he might yet be, Geriodde Nerenne ken Seriantes was impatient enough. Illness did not suit him. It wasn't that he cursed or threw things or otherwise showed evidence of temper. To everyone's relief, the king of Lirionne had proved not to be the sort of man who would shout at the girls who nursed him. Particularly not at the little girls. He was even kind to them, and by now Tana and Miande and Jehenne had quite lost their fear of him—Liaska, of course, had never been afraid of him in the first place.

The little girls all called him *Geriodde* now, quite familiarly, as though he were an uncle. They never said *Eminence* nor seemed to remember that he was the king.

Nor had the king rebuked them, even after he had begun to recover his lucidity and his strength. Enelle suspected he liked to have the little girls worry over his comfort, and make sure his fire was always built up and his tea hot and his pillows scented with fresh spring flowers. Who wouldn't want those things when he was ill and weak? And Geriodde Seriantes had never had daughters of his own. She knew it must hurt him to think of his sons.

Jehenne was with the king now. She had been playing a game of tiles with him. It was a good choice for a man who tended too much toward grim melancholy, for it was a game that required careful thought and planning. From the number of mountain and sea tiles lined up along the edges of the board, the king had been winning, but not by as much as he had probably expected. Jehenne was clever at games, the best of all of them even though she was the youngest but one. And, of course, Jehenne was less distracted by broader concerns.

But the cold, contained look the king gave Enelle when she came in made it clear he did not think of her as a little girl to be protected or indulged. He was angry already, she saw, and probably thinking of all the grim work waiting for him, and the consequences of winning and losing more than a game. And she had not even explained anything to him yet.

Dark Of The Moon was curled beside Geriodde, half his body stretched across the king's lap. The cat was staring at the game board with every appearance of close attention. Dark was a big, heavy cat and looked bigger still because of his broad head and heavy shoulders and luxuriant coat, but his weight did not seem to bother Geriodde. Surely that was a sign that the king was mending.

The tip of the cat's nearly-black tail curled lazily up and down, and he reached out with one foot to tap one of the tiles. Jehenne laughed and rescued the tile, but the king, though he stroked the cat absently, did not smile.

"Jehenne," Enelle said to her sister, "would you please go down to the kitchen and see if Miande needs you to get anything from the market for her before supper?"

Then, trying to think how to begin, she tidied away the game board and the tiles, collecting a few tiles that Dark had knocked to the floor. She added a little wood to the fire, and poured tea into a cup from the pot warming on the heath. She was delaying, really, she knew. She still did not know quite what to tell the king, or how.

"I do not care for tea," he told her when she turned back toward him at last. "I am awash with tea. What is it that you are gathering yourself to tell me? Has news come at last? From Neriodd—or is Neriodd dead? You must tell me if you have heard such news. Have you heard aught of Kasenne? Or Toviodde? Or is it—" His tone tightened. "My son? Is Tepres dead? Is *that* the news you do not want to tell me?"

Enelle didn't know half those names, but here she held up a hand. "It's you," she said, and went on quickly before he could quite decide what she meant by this, "You are dead, Geriodde, and before you shout at me, you should know that it was Neriodd's idea." She called the king by name quite deliberately, because she wanted him to think of himself as a man first and only then as a king. A man could acknowledge weakness where a king must not. Or she hoped it might be so.

She also didn't actually remember exactly who had suggested first that the king should die. It might have been Neriodd or Leilis or someone else. But she doubted it made much difference, now. She said firmly, "It was Neriodd's idea, and it was a good one, because if your enemies had searched for you, they would have found you, so it was important that they believe they needn't search—"

"Indeed," the king said, coldly, and would probably have

said a great deal more—she could see it in the sudden chill in his eyes and the set of his mouth. Pain and fever and grief had pared the flesh from already stark bones, leaving him thin and old. But his ruthless strength had not failed. Enelle could not believe it would.

She came back to his side and, disregarding Dark, who was not very tolerant of anyone near him, knelt beside the bed. She took the king's bandaged hand in both of hers, and said gently, "You could not even sit up or speak your own name, Geriodde. If they had found you, they would have found us, as well. Then who would have protected us? Or Lonne? Sehonnes would have killed you. Then half the city would have risen against him, but who would have led your supporters?"

"And so *this* was Neriodd's idea," the king said, his tone flat.

"Yes," said Enelle, firmly, because it sounded better than *I think it might have been.* "And you know Neriodd is wise and clever and wants only what is best for you and for Lirionne." Not that she had ever met the king's personal guard herself, but she hoped it was true. She went on, "Now, listen, and I will tell you what we know, which I will tell you first is not enough, and then you will think what would be best for you to do. You know already that we believe Taudde took Tepres away with him. Now I will tell you that we think he took him—"

"To Kalches. Of course." This did not appear to surprise the king at all, though his good hand closed hard on the blankets. He said harshly, "That, I had guessed. Where else would that Kalchesene sorcerer take my son? From what other place would my son not return? If he were anywhere in Lonne, he would have made himself known long since—" he cut this off, grimly, his mouth thinning with the hard effort of control.

Though that last part had been a little confused, Enelle had followed it without difficulty. She said gently, "So we must trust Taudde. He took Karah and Nemienne with him, too, we think, so you see my sisters and I wish very much to trust him." She touched the king's shoulder. He had straightened, and she silently urged him to lean back again and rest. He allowed her to coax him back, though the muscles of his shoulders were still hard with anger.

She went on, "Nemienne trusted him, I know. This comforts me—"

"Sehonnes will already have begun to bargain with Berente Lariodde for Tepres' death. He would not hesitate, though I doubt he would want it known. Or not yet; not until Lonne is accustomed to his rule. But whatever he promises the King of Kalches, he will begin the war in order to force Lirionne to unify behind him. Berente Lariodde is not a fool. He will realize this. He will be thinking of how best he may use Tepres against his brother." Geriodde stopped and drew a careful breath, then added, "That may protect Tepres . . . a little."

"When you have taken back your rightful place, you can demand an accounting from King Berente. You can demand he return your son and my sisters, and he will have to do it." Enelle tried to sound confident about this, though actually she feared that perhaps the King of Kalches would be pleased to have a useful hostage in his hand and not so eager to give Prince Tepres up. She didn't say so. Instead, she said, "Besides, we must remember that Taudde is a Kalchesene prince as well as a bardic sorcerer. He will make sure it comes out all right." She believed that. She thought she did. She tried to *sound* as though she did.

"Berente ken Lariodde lost a son to my hand at the field of Brenedde," the king said flatly. "And now he has my son in his hands. Who knows what he will do? He has no reason to be kind to my son, far less to me."

Enelle hadn't thought of it quite that way. She would have been happier if the king hadn't pointed it out. But she said stubbornly, "He won't wish to give you cause to hate him, or to raze Kalches instead of conquering it. *I* think that Berente ken Lariodde will bargain with Sehonnes if he must, and meet him in battle if he must, but he would surely prefer to bargain with a king whose word he could trust. Surely he would even prefer to *war* against a man whose word he knows he may trust. As he knows he can trust yours."

Geriodde's mouth tightened. "Is that what you think?"

"You have met him and I have not," Enelle admitted. "But I remember that he *is* Taudde's grandfather. That comforts me. Does it not comfort you?"

Geriodde did not disagree out loud. He merely asked,

"What has Sehonnes said out loud for men to hear? *Has* he claimed my throne?"

"Not yet. He says he will do so on the solstice, so you see, there is a little time remaining."

"A little time, indeed." The king made a sharp movement, frustrated and angry. Dark Of The Moon, offended, leaped down from the bed and stalked away to sit on the hearth. The king ignored him. His eyes narrowed with pain, and his mouth flattened, but he made no sound.

Enelle laid a hand on his arm, gently, to suggest a restraint she could not enforce. She said, "We heard yesterday that Sehonnes has commanded his people to arrest Telis. He has proclaimed anathema against him. The charge is parricide."

King Geriodde made a contemptuous sound. "I suppose some will want to believe it, in order to believe the hand he sets on my throne does not leave bloody fingerprints."

"I think everyone will see those fingerprints, no matter what Sehonnes says."

"They should. His hands run with blood. It spatters everything he touches."

Enelle nodded. "Telis has vanished, so we've heard—he disappeared when Sehonnes declared him anathema."

"Did he? One wonders what he may be about. He certainly does not fear Sehonnes, though he must realize he hasn't the support to force my people to accept him as their king." He considered. "What of Geradde? What rumors concern the youngest of my left-hand sons?"

Enelle shook her head. "We listen, but we've heard nothing of Geradde. But we haven't heard of his death, either, and why would anyone conceal it? Nor has Sehonnes said anything against him. We think perhaps he has hidden himself. But we don't know."

The king said, grim and low, "I don't like to think of Geradde's position now. If he lives. The boy isn't stupid, but he has too strong a sense of honor. If he's hidden in Lonne, Geradde won't let Sehonnes' claim pass. But the boy hasn't the ruthlessness nor the patience nor the political sense to build himself a strong alliance. He'll challenge Sehonnes during the coronation, and Sehonnes will kill him. Or if not, there's Telis.

Telis never liked Geradde, nor Geradde, Telis." He fell silent, his eyes narrowed.

Enelle began to say something, she hardly knew what—it was terrible, what the king said about his sons; it was horrible to think of having sons that hated one another, even tried to *kill* one another. But the king said first, "And nothing yet from Neriodd?"

Enelle opened her hands. "Leilis brought you here. We think Neriodd probably doesn't know where you are."

"Ah." He was silent for a long moment. Then he met Enelle's eyes and said grimly, "I don't wish to place you or your sisters in peril. But I *must* contact Neriodd. Or if he is dead, there are others. But I *cannot* . . . step back among the living, until I have prepared the ground."

Enelle nodded immediately, glad he wasn't going to try to leap to his feet this moment and stride in person straight back to the Laodd. Among other reasons, she didn't think she would be strong enough to catch him when he collapsed. "If you have letters to write, you may dictate them to Jehenne. If you have messages to send, my sisters or I will take them."

"This *will* put you all in peril," snapped the king.

"Yes," Enelle agreed. "But you haven't anyone else to send. Besides, none of us is safe *now*. No one in Lonne is safe."

That was how Enelle found herself making her way through the city, once more hidden behind the manner and dress of a fishmonger's girl. Even in these frightening days, people had to eat. People *were* out in the streets and the markets, now. They had no choice: water must be drawn from cisterns and wells, steamed buns and noodles and chickens and fish must be sold or purchased. The ordinary business of life must continue, if quietly and cautiously. Even so, some of the marketers sent their children carrying wares to the doors of their customers who feared to go out and could pay for deliveries. A plain robe and a large basket filled with fish made a reasonable excuse for a girl to be out on the streets of Lonne—though getting lost would not help Enelle's disguise.

Along with the fish and the king's instructions, Enelle also had Liaska with her. That part, she hadn't intended. But Liaska had found out that Enelle was going to slip quietly out into the city on a secret and important errand, and she had simply been unable to resist the urge to join in. Enelle hadn't known her littlest sister was behind her until it was far too late to send the child back. This frightened her. On the other hand, no one could possibly suspect that Liaska was anything but an outrageous brat of a child. Even when she tried to be good, Liaska skipped and danced and made up rhymes and talked to everyone she passed, from a fruitseller arranging plums in ruby pyramids to a girl selling noodles in broth to an old man who needed help carrying a pair of chickens he had just purchased. So in a way, Liaska was a better disguise than any other. She was so abundantly herself, and so plainly not trying to sneak through the streets.

Enelle wished she were so fearless herself. She didn't like living in fear, she decided. It was definitely time for Geriodde Nerenne ken Seriantes to take back his own throne. Though she was sorry he must act against his own sons, again. That must take the heart out of a man, surely, to have one son after another become an enemy.

Though it was much easier to believe that the king's older sons had betrayed him, after what Sehonnes had done.

At least Prince Tepres was still loyal. She would not consider the possibility that anything had, or would, happen to Tepres. Taudde would never allow his grandfather to harm Tepres. Or Karah, or Nemienne, though the Kalchesene king wouldn't have any reason to want to harm them. She was certain King Geriodde would bargain to get her sisters back, too. She knew he would, so her sisters at least must be safe—

"Enelle!" Liaska said suddenly. "Look! Pimchi!"

Pimchi were flowers that grew in damp gutters and beneath stone walls—in any nook that held a little moist soil and was sheltered from the sun. The crinkled leaves were held low to the ground, but the flowers were lifted one at a time on delicate stems as long as a woman's hand. The petals, fine and fragile, were a pale pink that looked far too pure a color to grow in a city gutter. Liaska loved pimchi, but this time she meant that the little flowers were sometimes also called pink ladies or hinge-of-the-year or, most commonly of all, solstice flowers, because they so reliably bloomed at that time. People picked the flowers and put them in tiny clear glass vases and gave them to their friends, with wishes for good luck for the coming year.

This year, Enelle thought there simply couldn't be enough pimchi in Lonne. "Pick just one," she reminded her little sister. "More might harm the plant and turn away the luck."

"I know!" declared Liaska, offended that Enelle thought she needed a reminder. She collected the central flower, pinching the stem carefully at the base, and offered it to Enelle. "Put it in my hair!" she demanded.

Enelle tucked the flower behind her little sister's ear. This was even a good moment for little touches like flowers, because they were almost at their destination. They had only to slip through the outermost streets of the King's District until they came to the servant's alley that ran behind the fifth house along the Lane of Sea Dragons. The king had described the house very carefully, though he hadn't known its appearance from the rear alley. No gilded sea dragons reared up on pedestals to mark the entrance to one alley over another, so the most difficult part was making absolutely certain they had found the right house. There was a wrought iron fence, but the gate wasn't locked—the king had said it wouldn't be. "Everyone will desire discretion," the king had said. "No one will be calling at the *front* of the house. But watching at the servant's doors for anyone who might come and go? Assuredly so."

He had been right.

"You remember our story if the—if *his* friend isn't here, or if some else is listening, or if anything else goes wrong?" she whispered to Liaska, stumbling because it was awkward not to use names.

"Of course!" Liaska said, offended.

Enelle bit her lip. If the king's friend was *not* here, if this was even the wrong house, then story or no, both of them might be in danger. But there was no way through but forward. So when she tapped on the kitchen door, she rapped quietly but firmly. And when a man opened the door—just halfway, and from the way he was standing, she guessed his foot was braced behind the door in case he wanted to close it again—she stood straight, held up the basket, and said, "The fish you ordered, sir," in a clear voice, and then added much more quietly and as firmly as possible, "And a message you *will* want to hear." She had her other hand on Liaska's shoulder, just in case she had to push her little sister back and tell her to run, but her sister stood straight, too, and smiled brightly, radiating her delight in meeting someone new.

The man's eyes narrowed slightly. After a short pause, he stepped back, opening the door without asking anything. These days, questions and answers belonged behind closed doors. So Enelle didn't speak, but only stepped within—she thought too late that maybe she should have made Liaska stay outside in the alley, but then that wouldn't be safe, either, if anyone saw her and wondered.

The man glanced both ways along the alley, and then came back in and closed and barred the door. In all of this, he didn't say a word.

The man was obviously a soldier or guardsman, though he was dressed like a servant. Enelle doubted he could fool anyone. He stood as solidly as though he were made of stone, his shoulders squared and his arms crossed over his chest. Enelle thought he had opened the door very quickly, as though he had been waiting for someone to arrive. She wondered just how many people had been coming and going from this house in the past days, and on what business. Or whose.

There were other people in the kitchen, but they really were servants—one woman had been plucking chickens and another filleting fish, and a girl was standing by a pot with a long wooden spoon in her hand. The kitchen smelled of hot oil and simmering broth. All of the women were staring at Enelle now— and at Liaska. It was hard to guess whether they were more surprised by the sudden appearance of unordered fish or of a child.

Enelle studied the man for moment longer. He was not young, but not very old; not handsome nor very ugly; not small nor extremely large. This was the kind of man the king had described: unmemorable but solid. He *did* look solid. Reliable. She hoped he was. He was not carrying a sword, no doubt because he was dressed as a servant. But she would have been amazed if he did not have a knife tucked away somewhere. He still did not speak, but only tilted his head, waiting. She said quietly, "A message for the gracious lord Minarras Perenne ken Saradd. Or for a man of his, a specific man, whose name you might tell me."

The man's eyebrows rose. "From whom does this message come?"

Enelle glanced at the servants and didn't answer. Liaska, thankfully, was being very quiet and cooperative, though she was rather inclined to peer about, as though certain something very interesting must be hidden in this kitchen. A sword, tucked out of sight somewhere in easy reach of the man, would not have surprised Enelle a bit.

The man said abruptly, "If the name you want is Namir Karonnis, I am he."

Enelle let her breath out in relief. She thought she believed him. But she said, still quietly, "I must ask your pardon for my confusion. I was told Namir Karonnis was of the King's Own."

The King's Own guardsmen did not wear undyed cloth. They wore black. But this man did not seem offended at Enelle's question. Nor did he offer any kind of explanation or excuse for the way he was dressed. He merely said, "I am."

That unadorned statement also made her believe him. Enelle looked into his face again for a moment. She had known she would have to take risks—this risk in particular. There was no way to avoid it.

She took a ring out of a hidden pocket in her sleeve, proffering it on the palm of her hand. It was a very plain ring: hematite, completely smooth and unmarked. It was not a ring that would be valued for its *beauty*. The king had worn it on the little finger of his uninjured hand. He had said it was a ring meant to give away—but not to just anyone. Rings like this one had meaning to the King's Own Guard. That was what they were for.

The man did not touch the ring. He studied it for a moment, just as it lay. Then he studied Enelle for a longer moment. "Is that yours?"

"I was given it," Enelle said, as she had been told to say. "By one who had the right to give it. From his own hand."

The man—indeed he *was* Namir Karonnis, she was more and more confident—took the ring and held it up, looking carefully at the inside of the band and then turning it over and looking at it again. Then, to Enelle's relief, he gave it back to her. He said, "This way," and gestured toward the interior door that led out of the kitchens and into the rest of the house.

He did not lead them far. Just to a quiet parlor near the kitchens, without windows or other doors. He had a sword in his hand now, sheathed, so she had been right about him having one hidden near the kitchen door. But he set this aside on a low table and then leaned his hip on the nearest couch, a heavy piece of furniture that did not shift at his weight. He did not invite them to sit nor offer them tea, which was almost a relief, because refusing would have been unbelievably rude, but Enelle was too nervous to sit down or sip tea. He only said, his tone curt but not hostile, "Enough evasions, girl. There aren't many men who could have given you such a ring. Who gave it to you and told you to show it to me?"

Enelle took a quick breath. After these past days of careful silence and secrecy, bringing herself to answer that question was more difficult than she had expected. She found herself glancing at Liaska. Then it occurred to her that she *did* want her sister's opinion, and that this was a reason to be glad Liaska had followed her. Her youngest sister liked everyone and made friends with everyone, but maybe because of that she always seemed to have an acute feel for what people were actually *like*.

Liaska, seeing her sideways glance, bounced slightly. She said confidently, "You can tell him. He doesn't trust you, but he *wants* to."

Enelle hoped she was right—that the king had been right to send her here—that this was what she should do and that nothing terrible would happen because she answered that question. She said, "Geriodde Nerenne ken Seriantes gave that ring to me from his own hand. He said the King's Own would know it."

There was a small silence. Namir Karonnis was now standing absolutely still, ashen with shock. He had not been particularly expressive before, but now his gaze had gone quite blank. Where his hand a moment ago had rested easily on the back of the couch where he leaned, now the knuckles were white with the force of his grip. He said slowly, "He is alive? Is this true?"

"He was ill, but he didn't die, and he's better now," Liaska explained cheerfully. She seemed completely at ease. "We took care of him. He can beat me at tiles, but Jehenne can sometimes beat him—"

"Hush!" Enelle told her.

"He . . . was ill?"

"Wounded, and the wounds took fever, but he's better now. But he's—he isn't—he's been very difficult," Enelle admitted. "I don't think he's strong enough yet to move, but he is impatient. But he *is* better, truly. Thus he sent me to you." She looked at the man, a little doubtfully. "He trusts your lord, he says."

"So he should," said Namir Karonnis, with a grim little nod. "He thought Neriodd might have spoken to him already. He hasn't been here?"

The grim look deepened. "Not yet. That does trouble me. My lord might not have been the first, but nor would Neriodd have left him to the last. Were you to contact Neriodd through me? I can put out word here and there, but if Neriodd is dead . . . what is the king's message?" He added, when she hesitated, "I give you my word that if by our will or effort we can serve Geriodde Seriantes, we will."

Enelle took a deep breath. She had memorized it exactly. She said, "This is the king's message: The day before the solstice, he will move to set down Sehonnes and take back his throne. He desires all loyal men to be ready. He believes Lord Minarras Perenne ken Saradd is loyal and trusts him to know how best to use his strength. Neriodd should have been preparing the ground. The king wishes your lord to be aware of this, if he does not yet know."

Another grim nod.

"Neriodd knew the king was alive when he left him, but he doesn't know where he is. Nor did we have a way to send back and forth. If Neriodd returns to this house, you may tell him that the king—"

Namir Karonnis held up a hand in a sharp warning. "Don't tell me where he is!"

"No," Enelle agreed. "But if Neriodd needs to get word to the king, you can put flowers in the window—a window that can be seen from the alley. Pimchee," she added on impulse.

"Someone will look for that sign. But if nothing goes wrong, I am to say, you may tell Neriodd to expect the king to move on that day. One day before the solstice. It is short notice, I know. But he thought that best." Then she asked, "Do you expect . . . trouble?"

"One can never be certain," Namir said darkly. "There has already *been* trouble, or Neriodd would have moved before this—if he lives. It's as well he didn't know where the king lies. If he does come, or if anything happens that the king *must* know about, I will put pimchee in the window with my own hands." He considered her for a moment, then glanced at Liaska. Then he said to Enelle. "I would send a man with you when you go, but you won't want that."

Enelle nodded. "No, though I thank you for the thought."

"Brave girl."

This startled Enelle, who was not used to thinking of herself as *brave*. She said after a moment, "We all do what we have to do, these days." Then, on that thought, she added, "I am to say one thing more: that what the king most desires is to take back his throne without spilling quantities of blood. His intention is to pardon those who bowed their heads to Sehonnes, where he can. This, too, you are to tell your lord. He said that this could not concern Lord Minarras. But he said to say it."

There was a pause. Then Namir said evenly, "You may assure the king that my lord would not have hesitated on that account. Though my lord will no doubt agree that this is a wise policy. I will inform him. We will be sure that the king's word on that matter is broadly distributed, at the right moment."

Enelle nodded. "That's all the king said." She took a deep breath and added, "But *I* will say this: Whatever the king said about spilling quantities of blood, it would be best for everyone if there is just a little fighting. Just enough that Sehonnes does not live through it."

Namir's eyebrows rose.

"Any man's heart might break," Enelle said firmly. "It's not right for a man to put his own sons to death."

The man said only, "I think you are right. And Telis?"

"If he betrayed the king," Enelle said ruthlessly, "then, yes, it would be best if he did not see the sun rise on the solstice."

"If any of the king's sons is innocent of treachery, it isn't Telis," the man agreed. "That word also I shall pass to my lord. I know he will agree."

Enelle nodded. "Soon . . . soon, I hope all this may be *over*."

"I much doubt whether it will be over for years," Namir said. "However, we may surely hope that the days soon brighten. Now, what else may we do for you? If I can't send a man with you . . . let me give you money, at least. Hard cash has disappeared from the streets, I know; in troubled times, no one is willing to spend anything but script. That makes hard cash useful in case you must bribe someone. Or buy more fish."

Enelle nearly laughed. "A very practical suggestion. Thank you."

"I'll carry it," Liaska volunteered eagerly. "We can buy sweets on the way home, can't we? Say we can! Geriodde would like cakes, wouldn't he?"

This time Enelle did laugh, partly at Namir's expression when her little sister called the king by his name so casually. Namir had called her brave. She wasn't, but Liaska's cheerfulness helped. She wished they were home already, passing around cakes and telling everyone how well their errand had gone. She knew she would be afraid until they were home. Or until the king's authority once more extended through Lonne. Or really, until she knew Karah and Taudde and Nemienne and Leilis and Prince Tepres and *everyone* was safe.

She also knew Namir Karonnis was correct. She was going to feel echoes of everything that had happened for years. They all were.

Nothing at all was over yet. But she had hope that soon they would all be past the worst. She gave Namir a firm nod and a smile that she hoped was confident.

-13-

The road that led down from the Laodd to the city stretched out before Leilis, the sheer cliff to one side and on the other, the plunge to the churning lake below Nijiadde Falls. For a moment, though there was nothing but danger behind her in the Laodd, Leilis could not bear to set her foot on that exposed and vulnerable road.

Scattered men approached the Laodd or strode away toward the city, one on horseback and all, from their hurried pace, distracted and worried. Leilis told herself firmly that none of them would have either time or inclination to stop a single keiso walking openly from the Laodd down toward the city; and why should they? They would not know that Mage Karende had ordered her held and questioned; that Prince Sehonnes had also wanted her held. They would not know that a captain of the Fifth Division had let her go despite all those orders.

On the other hand, every single man who passed her would remember her. Leilis might not be one of the truly famous keiso, one of the women whose names was celebrated in poetry and song not only throughout Lonne but throughout all of Lirionne, whose image appeared on miniatures for girls to collect and dream over and who were remembered for many years after they retired from public view. But she was very obviously a keiso. Tomorrow, every man who saw her would say to anyone who asked, *Yes, a beautiful keiso with gulls on her overrobe, yes, I saw her, storm-gray eyes and a jeweled gull in her dark hair.*

The moment Leilis stepped off the road into the streets of the King's District and had a chance to slip into a tradesman's alley and out of the public eye, she took off her far-too-recognizable overrobe and turned it inside out. On the inside, the slate-blue robe was lined with plain slate-colored fabric. The fabric was still expensive, the stitching still fine, but now the robe's color was similar to the dull grays and browns worn by servants. Now it should with luck be nothing that would make anyone think of a glamorous keiso. She took the hematite-and-pearl gull out of her hair and hid it in an inner pocket, then shook down her hair and knotted it up again in a simple servant's style. That was how long it took the keiso to disappear and the servant to reappear in her place: hardly a moment. Hardly any time at all.

It was not far through the King's District to the Paliente directly below. Leilis told herself this, because it seemed like a long way. She did not know the King's District well; she did not know the best ways through the twisting alleys that gave tradesmen and servants a way to come and go out of sight of their betters. Yet she did not dare walk openly down the deserted streets. She could not entirely avoid the risk of watching eyes, but she went quietly and by a circuitous route, and she bowed her head and effaced herself on the rare occasions she could not avoid meeting someone. So it took her half the morning to make her slow and careful way across the width of the King's District and into the Paliante.

There, she could at last breathe in cautious relief. The Paliante was familiar to many keiso, for all the best Houses patronized shops in the Paliante and the rest wished they could afford to. Certainly Cloisonné House knew which shops sold the finest perfumes and jewels, the most elegant musical instruments and carved wooden screens and ornaments, all the oddments that lent a note of elegance and grace to any establishment.

Many of the lesser nobility owned townhouses in the Paliante—and so did many of the city's most celebrated artists, including many keiso of independent means, though sumptuary laws ensured that these homes were never so large nor so elaborate as those of the nobly-born. But every home in the Paliante, no matter how small, was faced with delicately carved stone or expensive imported brick of ivory or pale gold or pink, and every courtyard was guarded by intricate wrought-iron work twisted into the shapes of animals or trees or ships or whatever fanciful form appealed to the eye of the owner.

Silvermist, one of the influential keiso of her generation and even more influential following her retirement from the public view, lived in a small townhouse at the edge of the Paliante, close to the Niarre River, which separated the Paliante from the

Keiso Houses, aika establishments, fine restaurants, and theaters of the candlelight district. Silvermist knew everything and everyone and heard every rumor that ran through the avenues of the candlelight district—and every rumor made its way to the candlelight district eventually. Servants and street venders and shopkeepers, aika and actors and the keiso of every House passed on scraps of news and rumors and gossip to Silvermist, because she would talk to anyone and was simply the kind of woman everyone trusted.

Silvermist's townhouse was a narrow, two-story structure of ivory brick, with a delicate hip-high fence of wrought iron dividing its tiny stone-paved courtyard from the street and from the courtyards of its neighbors. Silver-leaved ivy tumbling over from its small balcony, and two great pots of glazed pottery, each almost as tall as Leilis, stood on either side of the gate, each containing a little smooth-barked tree with graceful upright branches. The trees were silvermist trees, with clouds of tiny white flowers like puffs of steam in late summer. Everything was elegant and tasteful and subdued, as befit a long-retired keiso of means.

Leilis, who had made her way to Silvermist's townhouse through the narrow alleys that provided a way for tradesmen and servants to come and go unobtrusively behind the private dwellings of the Paliante, stepped carefully past the ash heap and tapped on the kitchen door. When the door did not open at once, she tapped again. She could toss pebbles up against the shuttered windows if necessary, but that would be an overfamiliarity from a stranger. She knew Silvermist, not only as everyone knew her, but because Silvermist had once belonged to Cloisonné House and a keiso never lost her connection to her House. But the woman had accepted a keisonne and become first his flower wife and then independent before Leilis had even been born.

Silvermist herself opened the door before Leilis had to resort to pebbles. By that, Leilis guessed that stray keiso or deisa might not be unexpected. Of course Leilis would not be the only woman in the flower world who might come to Silvermist for help. She would not even be very much surprised to find other missing keiso, caught out by events, here before her.

Nor did Silvermist herself seem very much surprised to find

Leilis on her kitchen step. She welcomed her with a small lift of her hand, stepping back to invite her to enter. "There is trouble at Cloisonné House?" Silvermist asked, her voice low but with a beautiful timbre, for she was still noted as a poet and a musician. "You, or Narienneh, have need of some assistance?"

"Mother does not know I am here," Leilis told her.

Silvermist inclined her head gravely, still unsurprised. "Nor do you wish Narienneh to know? For her protection and the protection of the House, I imagine. I see. Very well, Leilis, come in and tell me what you know and what you need."

Silvermist had dark hair shot through with generous strands of white, braided now with narrow blue-gray ribbons and tucked into an elaborate knot. She wore the restrained overrobe of an independent keiso, a soft blue-gray dappled with pearl-gray from hem to hip. Her two daughters, Bellflower and Chelone, had settled near her, but they were not here. Each of them would have sought shelter with her own keisonne—Bellflower's keisonne was actually noble, and Chelone's more wealthy than most; both men could well protect their households and would certainly enfold their flower wives within that protection.

"A difficult time," Silvermist commented, pouring two tall cups of steaming wine from a pot on the stove. She dismissed a servant with a wave of her hand and showed Leilis to a warm, private nook off the kitchen. "And most likely everything will become still worse before the affairs of the great are settled." Her tone was just a little dry.

Leilis nodded. "You will know that Sehonnes is favored by many of the soldiers, Telis by most or all of the mages. Young Geradde is perhaps in hiding; Tepres, as you will also know, is missing; so for this moment the contest appears to be between Sehonnes and Telis. But perhaps many people, low court and high and common, might resume their loyalty to Geriodde himself if the king were found to be yet alive."

Silvermist gave her a long, thoughtful look. "Am I to understand that might occur?"

"Ah," murmured Leilis. "Well, one never knows, does one? Though possibly he has been wounded. Perhaps that is why he has not yet declared himself. Still, I would not be surprised to find that he lives to reclaim his throne—if neither Sehonnes nor

Telis nor any of their more dedicated followers discover him at the wrong moment." She added, "I think perhaps it might be better if no one at all discovers the king until he is ready to declare himself—if he does indeed still live."

"I see." Silvermist was silent for some moments. She swirled the spiced wine slowly in her cup, her eyes on the dark liquid, thinking. She was an acute woman. She undoubtedly guessed that Leilis knew exactly where the king was. Glancing up at last, she murmured, "I have heard several rumors. I have not heard that the king lives, however. I think it would be better if I do not hear that particular rumor—at least, not yet. But perhaps some of the other tales running through the city might interest you, for all they often contradict one another." At Leilis' gesture of polite assent, she went on, "I have heard that Sehonnes and Tepres fought, and that Sehonnes is now missing a hand but Tepres is missing entirely. Some think he must be dead; others declare he has hidden himself until he can gather enough support to return. I have also heard that Sehonnes fought his father and that this is how Sehonnes lost his hand, but that Sehonnes killed both his father and then Tepres. I have also heard that Telis is the one who struck down the king, but that Sehonnes took the ring from Telis because he is the elder, but Telis cut off his hand and threw the ring into the sea and that is why neither of them wears it." She glanced upward at Leilis through her lashes.

"So many rumors," Leilis said. "It is true that Sehonnes has lost his hand. I have seen this for myself."

"*Have* you."

"Under awkward circumstances, which I should like to avoid in the future, if possible. It is, I must say, rather a . . . fraught injury. I can well imagine men wonder. I gather the ring is definitely missing? I can tell you that Sehonnes does not wear it on his other hand, but surely he would not permit Telis to wear it?"

"Perhaps not. Perhaps Sehonnes has killed him. Telis has not been seen for at least a day, perhaps longer. But if he is alive, who knows what he might eventually do, or declare?"

"Indeed." Leilis was silent for a moment. Then she said, "I can tell you with assurance that if the king reappears, at least some of the soldiers who currently support Sehonnes would turn against him at once."

"Ah." Silvermist sounded pleased. "That is worth knowing. You had that directly? That is what I am to understand?"

Leilis was certain it could only help the king to have Silvermist know so much, though perhaps not more. She said firmly, "Yes. I also have reason to believe many of the soldiers who now profess loyalty to Sehonnes will prefer Tepres, if he were to appear. One suspects—though this I do not know—that they might also prefer even young Geradde, who at least has no bloody knife in his hands." Leilis held her cup in both hands, appreciating the warmth while she thought about what to say. At last she murmured, "I cannot return to Cloisonné House. I am likely pursued. You will have guessed as much."

Silvermist inclined her head. "Or you would hardly have come to me, child."

"Yes. I must leave Lonne entirely. I know where I wish to go. But to go that way, I must get into the house that used to belong to Mage Ankennes. But I think that house must be watched, even warded by magecraft. I don't know how I would get into that house." She met Silvermist's eyes, raising her own brows inquiringly.

"I see. Yes," said Silvermist thoughtfully. "Yes, I have heard that there are many different ways out of that house, if one knows the way to open the less . . . ordinary doors. And yes, I believe there are men there, though I am not entirely certain whose men they may be—"

"At least some mages are there, I think."

"Such difficult times," murmured Silvermist. "One can hardly be surprised, given it is *that* house. Still, I think I know precisely who can help you, Leilis. Nor need you have the least concern about this person's loyalties. Only tell him the rumor you brought me, and he will certainly wish to help you."

"You know everyone," Leilis said warmly. "I never doubted you would know just where I should go."

"Of course," said Silvermist complacently. "It is not even very far. I will send a little note with you to be sure he opens his door to you, but I imagine he would know you anyway. Would you care for another cup of wine?"

Left-hand relationships wove a complex web through Lonne. Important men, men of wealth and rank, those born high in court or those who rose high by their own merit—all those men had wives and sons, but many of them also had flower wives and left-hand sons. If an aika had a child, its father would most likely not acknowledge it, and so aika had ways to prevent the bearing of most such children. But custom more forceful than law required a man to acknowledge his keiso-born sons and support them to enter either court or a reputable trade. So keiso Houses maintained half-seen connections to men who moved freely between the flower world and the broader world. Leilis knew of some of those connections and some of those men. Silvermist knew them all, knew them not merely by repute but with a familiarity that opened every door, not only for herself but for any woman supported by her name and her signature on a hastily written note.

Leilis had known, but had forgotten, that Gerenes Brenededd, who owned a shop in the Paliante, was actually the king's own cousin. A distant left-hand cousin, but always acknowledged by the king. Gerenes Brenededd did not widely advertise the fact, being, Silvermist said, too proud to request favors that he did not in any case need. He was older than the king, well-established in his life, wealthy in a small way. He had married long ago, a woman of the candlelight district, though not a keiso. The woman had died years ago, but he had not remarried. He had no recognized children—nor any he had refused to recognize, so far as Silvermist was aware.

Perhaps Geriodde Nerenne ken Seriantes had appreciated a connection with a man who had never needed or requested royal favors or preferment, for though there was no close relationship—the king never tending toward close relationships in any case—he was known to be on cordial, perhaps even familiar terms with Gerenes Brenededd.

Gerenes' shop was one that sold expensive trifles and oddments, some imported from distant lands and some made here or there in Lirionne and some, including some of the best, made by Gerenes Brenededd himself. Painted bowls and blown glass, delicate lamps of porcelain or sea-ivory, sculptures of rare woods or bronze or brass or stone, small glass bottles containing perfumed oils, small musical instruments, delicate chimes—anything small and beautiful and well-made, those were the items offered in this shop. As well as the shop, Gerenes owned a small but beautiful and expensive house across the Niarre River, at the edge of the candlelight district.

"He could be at his home," Silvermist had told Leilis, and described exactly where the house lay and how to recognize it. But she also said, "Few of the shops in the Paliante yet dare open, as you know, and so their proprietors have barred their doors. But I think Gerenes is likely to be at his shop. He has a little workroom there. He will be very much troubled by all these recent events, and I think he will wish to find work that busies his hands and quiets his heart. And . . . he is too proud a man to hide himself out of view. There are those who will think of him, you know, Leilis. One way or another. But I think he is still there. I have not heard he has yet met with . . . any difficulty. Not even Sehonnes may move quite as he pleases—and Telis must be twice cautious, given the tales that already fly through the city."

Leilis saw at once the pride Silvermist had mentioned, though Gerenes Brenededd opened the door himself rather than sending a servant to do it. He flung the door open, in fact, with a sharp movement that suggested more than a little irritation with whomever had dared tap on his door.

Gerenes Brenededd was an elderly man, though he carried his years well. She thought she would have guessed his keiso heritage from his straight back and the way he held his head and his shoulders, but perhaps he had learned that elegance from his father's family—the sons of the powerful learned many of the same lessons taught the children of the flower world. He wore the plain colors prescribed in Lonne for any tradesman, no matter how wealthy, but even if Leilis had not known he was the king's second cousin, she would have guessed from the fine cloth and perfect workmanship that he must have some such connection. Or she might have guessed simply from the assurance of his manner.

Gerenes' frown was quick and sharp, his glance acute. But the expression in his eyes was not mere annoyance or disapproval. It was rage. He masked the intensity of his fury behind a show of mere temper, but not so well as a keiso; Leilis knew she did not mistake what she saw.

She was glad of it. He *should* be angry, this cousin of the king, this proud man who had all his life been on cordial terms with Geriodde Nerenne ken Seriantes and had never asked him for anything.

When he saw her, some of the rage shifted to puzzlement. He glanced at her face and assessed her plain robes—Leilis had begged servant's clothing from Silvermist, bundling her beautiful keiso robes into a satchel—and then at her face again. His glance was sharp, wary, assessing, uncomfortably perceptive.

"Keiso," he said first, despite her plain robes. And then, glancing at the letter she handed him, "Ah. Silvermist sends you to me, does she? Leilis, isn't it, of Cloisonné House." There was no doubt in his voice, and he stepped back with alacrity to let her enter.

He held, she saw, a very small, beautiful knife in his left hand, hidden out of sight until she came in. Its blade was only the length of a woman's finger and its hilt—sea ivory, she thought—was set with tiny sapphires. But it looked very sharp. She understood then that he had not expected a distressed keiso to come to his door, but that an armed soldier—or more than one, perhaps—would not have surprised him.

"An exercise in futility, of course," Gerenes Brenededd said, following her glance down toward the knife. "Yet I find I would not willingly bow my head to either Sehonnes or Telis— whichever might be the first to think of me. Probably Telis. Sehonnes thinks mostly of soldiers and the guard. Though I understand he has begun to demand a show of support from certain of the nobles of the court, and can I be far behind?" He made the knife vanish, so deftly that she was not precisely certain where he had put it. A hidden pocket in the sleeve of his robe, perhaps. Then he stepped past her to glance each way down the wide avenue before closing the door again, and locking it with a magecrafted seal as well as a prosaic bolt.

Leilis began to hope he might indeed be able to help her. Although—she asked, as she obeyed his gesture to step deeper into the shop, "Should they think of you, then? Sehonnes, or Telis?"

His swift glance was sardonic, and for the first time Leilis glimpsed a resemblance between this man and the Dragon of Lirionne. But he only said, lightly and smoothly, "One or the other will assuredly think of all of the king's better-known connections in the coming days. Though perhaps, if we are fortunate, not today. Now, what service may I have the pleasure of providing for Silvermist? Or does she offer to do me a service? Information, perhaps? I must admit I would welcome any solid information to support the edifices of fancy I have been constructing in my abundant leisure."

He laid a light hand on her arm, guiding her through close-set shelves and racks toward the back of the shop. A window there might have admitted sunlight to the workspace, but its shutters were closed and barred. A lamp glowed instead, casting its homey light across pieces of wood and horn, copper and silver wire, tweezers and something like a miniature chisel.

"The service is for me. I need to get into Mage Ankennes' house," Leilis said plainly. "Past anyone watching there. We believe there will be someone there, watching. I cannot stay in Lonne. There are things I know that it is better no one else find out. So if I must leave the city, then I will go through the door into Kalches and find Prince Tepres, if as we hope he is there. If he is a prisoner . . . or a guest of the King of Kalches . . ." Leilis hesitated. Then she went on, almost to herself, "Probably if he is there, he is a prisoner. Yet perhaps someone of Lonne, someone who is neither royal nor important nor an enemy . . . someone who stood as witness to . . . all that happened within the shadow of Kerre Maraddras. Someone like that might persuade Chontas Berente ser Omientes ken Lariodde to let him go. Besides, I . . ." she hesitated again.

Gerenes Brenededd looked at her with an expression that was impersonal and curious, yet somehow not without sympathy. "The Kalchesene bardic sorcerer, the Lariodde prince. It was he who removed your . . . curse. Was it not?"

"Yes," said Leilis. She met his gaze with cool dignity, grateful for the years of practice that let her do so. "Chontas Taudde ser Omientes ken Lariodde, grandson of the King of

Kalches. If, as we believe, he took our prince through that house and into Kalches, he will have given him into his grandfather's hands. But he will have protected him as well." She knew both these things were true as surely as though she had stood at Taudde's elbow over the past days. "But as he is Prince Tepres' friend, I am sure his position may be difficult." Was it arrogant, to think she might be able to smooth out some of those difficulties, if she could only find him?

"To be sure," Gerenes Brenededd said, his tone very dry. "You believe this Kalchesene bardic sorcerer indeed stands in friendship to Tepres? Yes; there is no need for dramatic protestations; so Geriodde also insists." He paused and corrected himself bleakly, "Insisted." Then he said, "Very well, then, you may take this with you." He reached, apparently without looking, to pluck a set of twin-pipes from a shelf.

The pipes were made of sea-ivory and horn and bone, bound with silver wire and with copper. There were six pipes in the set, in three pairs. The shortest of the pipes was no longer than Leilis' smallest finger and the longest perhaps twice that long. The longest pipe was inlaid, along its outside edge, with abalone and mother-of-pearl. The pipes were beautiful, but Leilis had no idea why Gerenes Brenededd was giving them to her. She looked at him inquiringly.

The man's lips curved, not in humor so much as irony. He said coolly, "Any keiso should have an instrument suited to her skill and her circumstances, and if you find a use for these, you may play them. But these pipes are actually a gift for your Kalchesene prince. A reminder, you might say, of the debt he owes to Geriodde Nerenne ken Seriantes, and to his son. And to me. These pipes are well made, if I may say so. There is no sorcery in them, but there is a touch of magecraft: if they are played properly, they will silence all other sound until they are themselves silenced." He paused, his cool gaze on Leilis' face. Then he added, "Who knows whether a bardic sorcerer might find such an instrument useful? But you may tell your Lariodde prince that if he should find a use for them in the service of his friendship to Tepres, I would count his debt to me well paid."

Leilis bowed her head. She could see that Geriodde Nerenne ken Seriantes had indeed told his cousin a great deal of the truth about everything that had happened earlier in the year. She said, "If I can, I will give him your words." Then she slipped the pipes away, safe in an inner pocket of her overrobe.

Gerenes rose, and held out his hand. "And as the pipes are for the Kalchesene prince, allow me to offer you another gift that perhaps you may find useful, under a rather different set of circumstances."

Leilis saw that he was holding out the tiny sapphire-set knife. She had not seen him take it from its hiding place, but it lay in his hand like a toy. It certainly was not a toy.

"The sheath," Gerenes said, and pushed up the sleeve of his overrobe to show her. There was no hidden pocket after all, but a slim wrist sheath, so small and carefully made that it would not show beneath even the most delicate fabrics. The king's cousin showed her how to place the sheath so that she need only flex her wrist to have the tiny knife slip into her hand.

"Practice, or you may cut yourself," he warned her. "It is very sharp, and strong for its size. But if you must use it, you must be bold. So small a knife can be used only from a very close distance."

"It's beautiful," Leilis assured him. "But plainly you have valued it. You shouldn't give it away; certainly not to me. I don't know how to use a knife." But she looked at it wistfully. She would feel safer with such a weapon, no matter how small and delicate it was—and it *was* beautiful. The workmanship was very fine, even aside from the sapphires.

Gerenes smiled at her, a small, deadly smile that glinted in his eyes. "It is not difficult to use a knife, I assure you. Slash across the throat." He gestured in illustration. "Or stab here, or here. Or if you are desperate, stab anywhere and run. It won't break, I promise you. It is from Erhlianne, where they know how to make such things. Besides, it's properly a lady's weapon, so better for you than for me. Take it, take it. It will make me fear for you less—and I have another that will do for me."

He made it impossible to argue. Leilis bowed graceful thanks and slid the knife into its sheath, then shook her sleeve into place to cover it. Though she lifted and turned her arm, there was no sign of the weapon once it was in place. "I'll fear for myself less, with this," she admitted. "Thank you."

"May you not require it—but if you do, may you use it boldly. Now, I will get you into Ankennes' house, and I will wish you fortune and speed," he told her. "Geriodde would certainly disdain both Sehonnes and Telis. He would assuredly wish to see Tepres on the throne. And so do I."

Leilis nodded. "Though we shall hope it need not come quite to that. Still, obviously, Prince Tepres must return from Kalches before the king reclaims his throne, because Tepres can be used as a threat against his brothers, but as a hostage against only his father."

Then she was aware of a sudden stillness in the way Gerenes Brenededd looked at her, and realized that of course he had not known until this moment that Geriodde Nerenne ken Seriantes was still alive.

He certainly knew it now. He cleared his throat. "I presume you are certain? Then I see," he went on quietly, "that we must certainly get you out of Lonne. As quickly as we may. More quickly than that. But—no, don't tell me. Only tell me this: he is well, and among allies who will support him?"

"He was injured," Leilis told him. She seemed to be telling everyone this, considering it was supposed to be a secret. But perhaps it was time this particular secret be opened up here and there. And she thought that Gerenes needed to know, and deserved to know. She said, "He will be well. He is among friends who will care for him. Neriodd acts for him now, but I am sure that soon he will begin to act for himself." She was a keiso. So she spoke as though she knew exactly what she was doing and meant to do, and had no doubts in all the world.

The king's cousin was standing very still, his gaze on her face. Probably he saw that she was not quite so certain as she wished to seem. He said, "Friends in the candlelight district cannot keep him safe."

"No one can keep him safe. He must re-establish his hold on the throne and the Laodd and the court, and on Lonne entire. But he is among people who will care for him until he is strong enough to do those things—and I believe it can only serve him if certain persons in Lonne expect him to reappear."

Gerenes Brenededd drew a slow breath. Then he gave her a swift, decisive nod. "Indeed. Well, you may be sure I will take care. I can think of one or two men who should know. And one or two women, perhaps, whom even Neriodd will not think to approach. Admirably conscientious, Neriodd, but better acquainted with the court and the King's District than certain other areas of Lonne. Well. Very well. And you shall go to Kalches, with my pipes."

"He will not have forgotten the debt he owes you," Leilis promised him.

There was a little pause. Then Gerenes gave her a curious little smile. He said formally, "I'm assuredly pleased to assist you. Quite pleased, under the . . . circumstances. And I believe I know how we might usefully approach your problem. Just let me gather one or two little items, and then we shall see if we may slip a little keiso through Ankennes's house of shadows, out of Lonne and into Kalches."

-14-

When Toma Piriodde appeared in the doorway of the Kinsana Suite, Irelle fell back a surprised step, half-heartedly lifting her flute. For the same startled instant, Taudde was also completely unable to adjust to Toma's sudden presence in the hallway. Then, catching a breath, he might have rewoven the sorcery in which he had captured the two guardsmen, but Toma leveled one stern finger at his chest and ordered, "Cease this immediately."

Despite himself, Taudde felt his sorcery stumble. He looked helplessly at Irelle, but she seemed as uncertain as he felt.

Taudde lowered his flute.

Both the guardsmen staggered, recovered, and reached after their weapons, but their captain coolly caught them each by an arm, halting them both instantly. He said flatly, "Unnecessary." Then he said to Irelle and Taudde, "Come." Then, turning on his heel, he went back into the Kinsana Suite.

The guards glowered murderously at Taudde, but the one with the flute tucked it back in his belt and the one with the sword shoved it back in its sheath. Then they both looked ostentatiously away, staring down the empty hallway, as much as to say to Taudde and Irelle, *You aren't even here.*

Taudde exchanged a speaking glance with Irelle and shrugged, leaving their next move up to her. She shrugged back, made a baffled gesture, turned, and followed Toma into the Kinsana Suite, leaving Taudde no obvious choice but to trail after her.

No one was in the reception room. But Tepres and Karah were both in the sitting room, along with Toma Piriodde. The guard captain was standing squarely in the center of the room, his arms folded across his chest, frowning. Karah, in a simple Kalchesene dress rather than her keiso robes, had been perched nervously on the least comfortable chair, but she leaped up when Taudde and Irelle came in. Tepres, also clad in the Kalchesene manner, had been standing beside her with his hand on the back of the chair. Nodding to Taudde, he said briefly, "Not before time."

"Ah—" Taudde began, and stopped, looking at Toma.

Irelle said accusingly, "You *knew* Lamanes and his lot were heading up to the tower. I *wondered* why all your men found Lamanes' tale so plausible."

Toma inclined his head to her. He said to Taudde, "You deserve to be left in the tower apartment for the rest of the year, if not for the rest of your life, you young idiot. But under the circumstances, it seemed tactically unwise to leave you there. Letting that pack of young fools up seemed the quickest way to provide you with a token. Other than simply handing you one personally, a solution which would have lacked elegance, as well as . . . plausible deniability. I prefer Lamanes rather than myself be required to explain your disappearance to Manaskes."

Taudde stared at him. He asked finally, "How is Grandfather?"

"Improving," Toma said coolly. "He is sometimes awake and occasionally lucid. However, just at the moment, I don't believe he would benefit from being forced to deal with the numerous idiocies of his various relatives. I therefore thought it best to ensure that certain idiocies cannot go too far, until your grandfather *is* strong enough to deal with them." He added to Irelle, "I did not anticipate your brother's involvement, however. That was unfortunate."

Irelle waved this away. "Not . . . necessarily, as it turned out."

"Ah? Well, if you and Geras found a way to add a certain finesse to this situation, then that was well done by you both and I'm sure your father will say so, eventually. At the moment, I think your father had better not be required to involve himself in all this foolery."

Irelle jerked her chin up. *"That's* why my father's not fighting Manaskes? To satisfy *your* tactical judgment?"

"Your father is fortunately wise enough not to require advice about such obvious matters," Toma stated, extremely bland. "Your father and I agree that when the king recovers, he might be annoyed to find hysteria within the family had constrained his options. To preserve these options, it seems tactically sensible to ensure that his Lirionnese guests are set safely out of the way. And you, of course," he added to Taudde. "You do excite a certain segment of your family." He gave Irelle a deep nod of the head, not quite a bow. "*You*, of course, as your father's daughter, may do precisely as you wish. But my advice is that for the moment you might do well to keep close company with your cousin and his . . . friends. No doubt you may pass the time in stimulating conversation."

Even Irelle took a moment to recover from this. Then she said in a more subdued tone, "We thought . . . the sugarers are out of the way, now . . ."

"The suggestion has merit," Toma said judiciously. "But I think we can do better."

To Taudde's astonishment, the guard captain brought them to his own personal apartment, directly next to the king's own suite. His men he sent back to stand outside the empty Kinsana Suite, after employing them to be sure the way between the two apartments was clear.

"They will say nothing to Manaskes, however much you and Taudde annoyed them," he said calmly when Irelle looked askance over her shoulder as the two guardsmen departed. "Your father would be another matter, but he will not ask. At least, not yet. Until he does, I am reasonably confident no one will look for you here."

Taudde was more than reasonably confident of that himself. He could not imagine anyone even entertaining a thought of searching for Kalchesene fugitives *here*. Though the sugarer's shack might almost have been more comfortable. The guard captain's apartment consisted of only two windowless rooms, neither large, and both indeed very plain. A narrow bed and a chest of drawers occupied the back room; a desk and a single chair the first; a tiny accommodation fortunately occupied a nook between the bedchamber and the office, equally plain, but at least supplied with running water.

There was very little else. There was a small fireplace in the bedchamber, but no fire was laid. There were no rugs on the floor nor draperies on the walls or around the bed; no ornamentation of any kind. There were no musical instruments, but a shelf above the desk held half a dozen bound ledgers.

"Don't look through those," Toma ordered, indicating the ledgers. "You may talk among yourselves, but quietly, if you please. Sound carries, and the king's bedchamber is just there." He nodded toward one wall. "I will lock the door. It is warded, as is this whole apartment, though not obviously so. Do not attempt to slip the lock by sorcery. If you must open the door, use the key." He gave this to Irelle and told her, "If your grandfather's condition changes, I will inform you." He paused. Then he glanced around at them all, unreadable as always and added, "If, while you are here, you are able to develop some proposal by which the king's life may be simplified, that might prove convenient." Then he nodded once, decisively, and left, closing the door quietly behind him. The lock clicked shut with a surprisingly definitive sound for so small a noise.

Taudde exchanged a glance with Irelle. She looked faintly stunned. He was sure he did, as well. He murmured to her, "Are *you* supposed to come up with some proposal to simplify our grandfather's life? Or was he talking to me?"

"Both of us, I suppose," Irelle said, a little blankly. She looked around, considered Tepres with a somewhat dubious expression, and added, "Or all of us."

"That is not a man I would wish as an enemy," Tepres commented.

"Oh, but he's so fond of the king," Karah said earnestly. "And so frightened for him. That's why he's so stern." She blinked at the universal astonishment this observation garnered and offered, "Though I'm sure it's true that the king is better," as though this was the part that had startled them all.

"Occasionally lucid!" muttered Irelle.

"How long do you think . . . ?" Taudde began, but let the question trail off because it was obvious no one could possibly guess.

Irelle shrugged, frowning. "I'm sure . . . I'm *sure* my father won't let Uncle Manaskes go too long or too far without checking him, no matter what happens with Grandfather. Or if he would, my mother won't! But however long it may be, I'm sure Toma is right. No one will ever think to look *here* for any of us, no matter how upset Uncle Manaskes gets." She looked around.

"Though it's true we may regret the captain's lack of amenities before very long." She opened a hand, not very enthusiastically inviting Karah to take the room's single chair. She herself folded up her skirts and sat down on the floor.

Then she said to Tepres, "And by what means would *you* choose to simplify my grandfather's life, eminence, given where we stand now, if the choice were solely yours? I wonder, should my grandfather or my father or someone do exactly as you wish and return you to your home, along with perhaps a hundred Kalchesene soldiers to support your claim against your brothers . . . what might you expect of your city and your country? What would your own people think of that? Surely they would be offended that you sought Kalchesene support for your claim?"

In Lonne, there would have been several minutes of polite circumlocution before anyone got around to the real topic. In Kalches, people were more plain-spoken, though Taudde thought this was rather direct even for Irelle. Tepres did not seem offended, however. He, too, sat down on the floor as though it had never occurred to him a couch might be preferable, thoughtfully clasping his hands around one drawn-up knee. Though he was dressed in the Kalchesene manner, Taudde saw that he was also wearing the dragon ring. He said slowly, "I hardly imagine that anyone, high court or low or common, has been pleased to see Sehonnes lay a bloody knife on the granite throne. But Sehonnes is, as least, seen as . . . predictable. There are those, especially of the low court, who value good order enough to accept a left-hand prince on the throne, if he has already established his claim and the alternative is civil war, and most particularly if he . . . plausibly denies that the knife was his. Therefore moving swiftly to prevent Sehonnes from establishing himself would be wise."

"If there should be an unavoidable delay?"

Tepres lifted a shoulder in a minimal shrug. "Should Sehonnes be *seen* to raise his hand against me, then public opinion will condemn him as faithless to his blood, even if he has already plausibly put the blame for my father's death into another's hand. Unless he has managed to put the knife into *my* hand."

"Would anyone believe that?" Taudde asked. It sounded

wildly implausible to him.

"If Sehonnes has already established himself, then some will *wish* to believe his lies and support his claim because that is simplest. This will be true largely for the low court and perhaps the common folk."

"Not the common people," Karah said firmly. "The common people don't like him." Everyone looked at her in surprise. She blushed, but she repeated, "It's true. Because of the way Prince Sehonnes treated his mother."

Irelle raised her eyebrows.

"It's true," Karah repeated earnestly. "I never paid attention when I was a girl, but I've heard all about it since I came into Cloisonné House. Everyone loved Skyblue of Maple Leaf House. Everyone who remembers her says she was always so generous and open-handed. They respected the queen, but everyone *knew* Skyblue. They say, what a shame Prince Sehonnes turned aside from the flower world and scorned her."

Taudde, amused at his cousin's expression, said, "It took me some time to get used to that sort of thing, too, but I'm sure Karah is right."

"She is perfectly correct," agreed Tepres. "My father's keimiso was very famous and well-loved."

"But—" said Irelle, and hesitated.

Tepres inclined his head. "My mother was a modest woman and not much in the public eye. When I was younger, she was better known, for Skyblue would invite her into one or another gathering. Later, of course, after my mother grew so ill, even that became impossible."

Irelle studied him. "Your half-brother's mother and your mother were . . . friends?"

"My mother admired Skyblue, and I believe Skyblue was fond of my mother." The undertones of Prince Tepres' voice expressed faint incredulity that anyone would expect otherwise, though he added, "Truly, it is not always so, but it is best when a man's wife and his flower wife are friendly with one another."

Irelle shook her head in disbelief, but only asked, "But Sehonnes, you say, scorned his own mother?"

"A keiso's sons do not always fill their hearts with bitterness against their father's right-hand sons. But Sehonnes blamed his mother because she was a keiso and thus gave him only such an inheritance as a left-hand son may have."

"Imagine that," murmured Irelle.

There was a slight pause. Then Prince Tepres said quietly, "It is a father's duty to see to it that his sons do not hate one another. My father . . . " But here he stopped. Karah reached out and laid her hand over his, and he bowed his head, unspeaking. Taudde looked away, not liking to intrude. Geriodde Nerenne ken Seriantes might be dead, but there were plainly some truths about his father that Tepres was still not willing to put into words. It occurred to Taudde for the first time that it was a shame Tepres was not an instrumentalist. Unspoken truths were just the ones that might best be poured into music.

Karah said gently, "A father has a duty to try, at least. But in the end, surely every man is master of his own heart."

"There we can agree," Tepres said smoothly, recovering himself.

"Well, and Prince Telis?" asked Irelle, also quick to move away from too great an exposure of the heart. "Everyone speaks of Prince Sehonnes, but what is the chance that Prince Telis will put forward a claim?"

"Oh, no!" said Karah at once.

"No," Tepres agreed. "Telis is more intelligent than Sehonnes, but he is neither trusted nor popular—neither within the high court or the low, not among the merchants, nor among the common people, who find him cold-hearted. No claim of his will be accepted. He must know this. He cannot help but know it."

"And is therefore the more bitter?" suggested Taudde.

"Perhaps." Tepres hesitated, then added, "Telis will not attempt to claim the throne, but he will have his own plans. He is always subtle. Serpents have many turns and sharp fangs."

Irelle said thoughtfully, "A dangerous enemy, then, if he is allowed to go on with his plans. I see why you would prefer to move quickly."

"Indeed. Geradde—our youngest brother, my younger half-brother Geradde, is far more popular. *His* claim might garner considerable support, were he to make it. Sehonnes will know this also, and Telis . . . he and Geradde never liked each other. I think . . . I think Geradde has not likely survived."

Irelle gave a sympathetic little nod. "I think Berente told you we have no news of Geradde. That was still true last I heard."

Tepres bowed his head in polite acceptance of this statement.

"I think," Irelle said thoughtfully, "From all you have said and all we have heard, that it would simplify my grandfather's life considerably to deal with the particular Seriantes prince who happens to be most conveniently at hand for argument, and most inclined to offer concessions to Kalches in return for . . . whatever considerations seem most important. Suppose we—that is, Kalches—agreed to return your living person, with all your parts attached, exactly as you stand today, to Lonne, with such a force under your command as to ensure you and not your half-brothers secured the throne of Lirionne. In return for this, Lirionne might agree to return the borders between our two countries as they lay in the time of your great-grandfather. Would you find that agreement acceptable? Would your people accept it?"

Tepres, his face still, did not move for a long moment. Then he said, "If I offered so much, many of my people would find they had lost titles granted by my great-grandfather and grandfather and father. They would be reduced; some would be impoverished. Such a proposal would cast the throne to Sehonnes and guarantee war. The borders might be redrawn as they lay before Brenedde, though even that . . . or, better, if the claims and titles of my own people were upheld, no matter where the borders were drawn—"

"Insufficient," snapped Irelle. "Impossible."

"Kalches must have at least the lands east and south of Anharadde, and north of Teleddes," Taudde put in more quietly. "And Brenedde. We must have Brenedde. Nothing less will be acceptable to my people."

"Giving up so much will not be acceptable to my people," Tepres said, reluctantly but without any shadow of doubt or deceit in his voice. "It would be seen as shameful. *I* would see it so. I could not agree to concede so much." His lip curled. "Certainly not for any mere threat your grandfather or father or uncle might offer—"

Irelle held up her hand. Smiling a bland smile worthy of a keiso, she tipped her chin up, and said with perfect composure, "There's more than one way to fall down a mountain, as we say. Let's not speak of *threats*. Surely we all agree that the *right* sort of agreement must give the King of Lirionne a way to return Kalchesene land to Kalches without shame, and the King of Kalches a way to accept our own lands as a gift, also without shame."

It took Taudde a long moment to understand exactly how Irelle was suggesting they might—fall down this mountain. He said sharply, "And how do you suppose your father would feel about this idea? Or your mother? Or *Grandfather?*"

Irelle said mildly, "Mother and I discussed the possibility yesterday." She looked briefly bemused. "*Was* that only yesterday? I admit, events seem to have gotten away from me a little. I mean, practically as soon as Prince Tepres claimed that ring of his." She gave Tepres a small nod. "I assure you, O Dragon of Lirionne, I am quite serious."

Tepres was sitting very still, regarding Irelle with a new intensity. He said after a moment, carefully not looking at Karah, "I believe the suggestion merits consideration."

"Oh!" said Karah, suddenly understanding. And then, "If it would work, then certainly you should consider it! But isn't Irelle her father's *heir?*"

Tepres did glance at her when she spoke, and looked away again quickly, his lips thinning. Karah blushed and looked down, but not as though she were hurt—more as though she were shy. She said quickly, "*I* wouldn't mind. *I* think it's clever—if Irelle and you think it would work." Taudde couldn't quite decide whether he thought she sounded as though she meant it.

"My brother could become my father's heir, just as he'd have to if I died. In a war, perhaps. And my sons would be the heirs of the Dragon," Irelle said steadily. The color had mounted into her cheeks, and she glanced at Karah and then away, but she didn't lower her eyes. "It would provide an answer for the anger of my people, to see the throne of Lirionne go to a Kalchesene child. It would have some hope of giving us all an assurance of amity for a generation or more. And it would establish a tie between Lariodde blood and the . . . other dragon of Lonne. All this," she finished, "provided we were confident we might rely upon one another, Tepres Nemedde ken Seriantes."

Taudde had been staring at his cousin. Now he turned his head, fascinated, to gaze at Tepres.

"Do you think then that we may be confident?" asked Tepres, his tone rather dry.

Irelle lifted her shoulders in a considering sort of shrug. "My cousin approves of you. He's made that plain. Karah has been living in my mother's household for three days. I like her, and she loves you, so that surely speaks well of you. The customs of Lirionne seem strange to me, but I suppose I could become accustomed." Her blush heightened, but she ignored it, adding instead, "And there is the dragon, or my cousin insists so. There's *something*, without doubt, for I hear it behind your heartbeat, Prince Tepres, Dragon of Lirionne. I hear it within the undertones of your voice."

Tepres inclined his head a minute degree. "There *is* a dragon. It is not mine to command. No one commands it. It is the heart of Lonne. Its heartbeat lies behind mine, perhaps. But we none of us desire it to stir itself. Believe that this is true."

"I think I might believe you," Irelle said, about more than that, Taudde thought. She rose to her feet, a little stiffly after so long sitting on the floor. She had put her hand on her flute; not meaning to use it, Taudde could see, but simply for comfort.

Tepres rose as well, at once, gracefully. He held out one hand to Irelle, not looking at Karah. The ruby eyes of the dragon ring glinted on his hand. Irelle offered her hand in return, a little uncertainly, and the Seriantes prince touched the barest tips of her fingers with his and bowed. He said, "Though nothing has been decided, yet I honor your courage." He dropped his hand, but he did not step back.

Irelle slowly lowered her hand to her side. Her expression was unreadable. She said in her blandest tone, "Karah and I will retire to the other room. I'm sure we all need rest if we are to confront Uncle Manaskes in the morning. Or even if we must merely confront my father."

Taudde wanted to laugh, though nothing about this was funny. "Cousin! You haven't discussed this with your *father?*"

"I discussed it with my *mother,*" Irelle said, sounding faintly harassed. "And then, perhaps you noticed, but we ran out of time! You can discuss it with me, too, Cousin, tomorrow, after you've had time to consider it, and I'm sure you'll give me your most honest and considered opinion!"

Taudde held up his hands in alarm that was only half feigned. "If you and Aunt Ines think it's the best way to—fall down the mountain, I would hardly argue!"

-15-

Three full days and another whole night passed while Sa-Telis and his horrible thugs and his even more horrible mages held Nemienne and Prince Geradde prisoner in the tomb of Kerre Taum, high above Lonne.

Nemienne lost track of the days, because the light of the sun never reached into the deepest part of the tomb, which was where they were held. The mages were using magic to bind something to the bones, or to bind the bones to something—Nemienne tried to understand exactly what they were doing, but it was a kind of magecrafting that was well beyond anything she understood. Except they were using Geradde's blood in the binding, too, so obviously it had to be something about the Seriantes line, or the dragon, or most likely both.

Geradde tried to fight the mages at first. But he couldn't fight his brother's thugs. Nemienne despised the mages, Isonne and the man whose name she learned was Perodde and the others that came and went, but she was afraid of the thugs. They really were criminals, she was sure of it. Usually there were three of them, sometimes four, always at least two. Even after so many days she didn't know their names, because they called each other by coarse terms that made her blush, or else by casual names like Dog or Rip. All of them were big, and all of them liked hurting people, and all of them made it clear that they especially liked it when Geradde gave them reason to hurt him. After the first time, she begged Geradde just to let the mages take his blood, and after the second time, he did.

Geradde's shame was painful to see. He was brave, but there was nothing he could do. Nothing was his fault, but Nemienne could see he didn't believe that.

It was her fault, of course, for letting herself be caught by his brother's trap. Her fault, too, for bringing Geradde with her.

He never said so, but he didn't have to. She knew it perfectly well. If she had realized faster what was happening—if she had tilted her steps in a different direction—if she had pushed Geradde away from her when she'd realized her attempt to get out of the caverns had gone wrong, then she could have stopped the trap from closing around them both. Or if she could only be cleverer now, she would be able to get them out of this prison, instead of being helpless to cross the magecrafted boundary Isonne had made.

But she could do nothing.

If she hadn't known this already, the mages would have made it clear. Especially Isonne. All the mages hated Nemienne, but especially Isonne, who took pains to point out Nemienne's ignorance and helplessness. Isonne said there was nothing worse than an apprentice who turned on her master and betrayed him; she said Mage Ankennes' death was all Nemienne's fault. Nemienne couldn't answer anything Isonne said; she couldn't have made any answer even if she hadn't been the woman mage's prisoner. It was all true. She *had* betrayed Ankennes, and it had been horrible.

But Mage Ankennes had betrayed Nemienne, betrayed them all, first. What he'd tried to do—he'd been wrong about the dragon and entirely, terribly wrong when he'd tried to kill Prince Tepres. Nemienne had had to make up her own mind about Mage Ankennes right then, right that moment, because if she hadn't done something to stop him, then no one would have been able to stop him. But Isonne didn't think anybody should have stopped him, so it wouldn't have helped to say so. And she'd been one of Ankennes' other students, or so Nemienne guessed. So there was no arguing with her.

If only she could think of something to do now to stop Prince Telis. But Nemienne had no idea what she could do. She couldn't even find a way around the binding Isonne had set up to keep her and Geradde pinned up in the deepest chamber of the tomb. It was even a simple binding; Nemienne could *see* how simple it was. But sometimes the simplest kinds of magic were the hardest to work against, and she could find no way around or through or across Isonne's magecrafted boundary.

The tomb was a terrible place to be held, and this part of the tomb was the worst. It was dark. It was an ordinary darkness, and even Nemienne could summon light into it though she had no particular skill with light. So the darkness wasn't so bad. But summoning light only let her see the bones that surrounded them.

The bones were old, they were the bones of the long-dead Seriantes kings, but despite their age some of them were still bound together with . . . dried tendons or something, and the dusty remnants of clothing, and surprisingly bright links of mail. The skulls were particularly awful. Magelight was steadier than candlelight, but it wasn't so steady that shadows didn't shift within the empty eye sockets of the dead kings. They seemed to *look* at you. It was *horrible*. Nemienne tried not to look at the bodies, but it was impossible to avoid looking at them—except by letting the light go out, and that was far worse. It was probably even worse for Geradde. After all, they were his ancestors. He knew all their names. It was worst of all when you knew their names, somehow.

The bodies were all laid out on roughly carved stone plinths, each about four hands high. The highest plinth held the body of Taliente Neredde ken Seriantes himself. Or most of it. His were the bones that Prince Telis had taken away to use in his horrible magic. King Taliente's arm bones were missing, and one of the bones from his lower leg, and his skull. His mail had been lying tumbled beside his plinth when Geradde and Nemienne had been forced into this deep chamber. His clothing must have fallen to dust long ago, all but fragments. Geradde had laid out the rest of his bones in better order, and arranged the mail properly. He had set the long-dead king's sword back at his right hand and placed his helm where his skull should have been, and . . . that was a little bit better somehow than letting the body lie in disorder, but it was still terrible. Nemienne knew she wouldn't have had the courage to neaten the bones, if she'd been alone. She was very glad Geradde was with her. It was wrong to be so glad when she should have wished him anywhere else, but she couldn't help it. His courage made her a little braver herself.

Prince Telis came and went in the outer part of the tomb; they knew that from things the others said and did; but he never came into the deep chamber where Geradde and Nemienne were prisoned. Nemienne was glad of that, too. She was afraid of Prince Telis. Sa-Telis, the serpent. She was more afraid of him than even of Isonne. But that wasn't why she was glad he never came into this part of the tomb. She was sure that when he came for them himself, it would be because he was ready to do . . . whatever he meant to do.

And then, three or four or five days after he had captured them, Sa-Telis finally came.

The days had blurred together for Nemienne. Neither she nor Geradde had thought at first to mark off the days, and it was impossible to tell whether the serpent-prince's men brought bread according to any kind of schedule or just when they had nothing better to do. The intervals didn't seem predictable to Nemienne, but she thought that might have been just because it was so hard to tell what time of day or night it was, in the dark tombs of Kerre Taum. She had asked Geradde what he thought, but he had no better idea than she did. So it might even have been more than five days when Prince Telis came for them.

He looked exactly as before: cold-eyed and elegant. He looked like nothing had ever bothered him and like nothing ever would. She could see just why people called him Sa-Telis. It astonished her that he was Geradde's full brother, even more now than it had at first. But he did at least look attentively at Geradde, instead of ignoring him as he did Nemienne.

"You look well enough," he said to Geradde. "Good. It's a long way down the mountain to the city."

Geradde stood up slowly. He was thinner, Nemienne thought. His face looked narrower and sharper-boned. But it was true that Telis' people had brought enough food, at least mostly. Geradde moved slowly, but he moved like a cat wondering if this would be a good time to spring and not like a cowed prisoner wondering how to avoid punishment.

"Don't," said Sa-Telis, sounding bored. He glanced meaningfully at Nemienne. "I need her. But I don't need her on her feet. A little girl like her wouldn't be too difficult to carry down the mountain."

Nemienne privately resolved that if anybody tried to carry her anywhere, she would make sure it was very difficult. But she didn't want Sa-Telis to do anything awful to Geradde, or to her.

She said nothing, and Geradde straightened his back and looked coolly at his brother, but he didn't move to defy him. They had to descend from the tomb by taking the long, long flight of stairs that cut back and forth across the face of Kerre Taum. The stairs were terrifying. Nemienne was very glad after all that no one was trying to carry her, because she was sure even the strongest of the serpent-prince's thugs—that was the one they called Dog—would have fallen in the attempt. She couldn't find a way to escape—she was too distracted by a sudden unexpected terror of heights to even try.

From here, one could see down and down, to where the white bulk of the Laodd was tucked against the side of the mountain, appearing from this height no bigger than a shepherd's cottage. Below the Laodd, mist from Nijiadde Falls half-hid the townhouses of the King's District, but then the mist would blow aside to reveal houses like toys. The rivers cut through the city like silver ribbons, and the bridges might as well have been made of wire and paper.

From such a height, it was easy to believe that all the works of men were ephemeral and vulnerable. Nemienne did believe it. She wished she could think of something to do to stop Prince Telis. But the thundering voice of Nijiadde Falls drowned thought even when it was desperately important to think.

The face of the mountain was rugged, the stairway narrow, the carved steps steep and often cracked or broken. There was no railing, not even a bit of rope strung between the stairway and the sheer plunge. It was worse for Nemienne because she was small and often the steps were too far apart for her. Isonne had the same trouble, especially since she was carrying Taliente's skull in a leather bag slung over her shoulder. Nemienne wished the woman mage would stumble and drop it; she could imagine how furious Prince Telis would be. But Isonne went carefully and one of the men helped her over the worst bits.

Prince Geradde helped Nemienne. His brother did not stop him, nor even seem very interested. There ought to have been something Nemienne could have done, when Prince Geradde held her hand over a broken step and no one else was within arm's reach. She knew she should be able to step away from these cold heights back into the darkness beneath the mountain, drawing him with her and leaving their enemies behind. She ought to be able to take both the prince and herself down a not-quite-seen path, from the chill brilliance and the rainbow-edged mist veiling Nijiadde Falls toward the memory of warmer, more comfortable lamplight.

She had been afraid to take Geradde to her home and let him see where her sisters lived. But after the past week or however long it had been, she thought, stealing a glance at Geradde's closed, ironic expression, that she would be glad to risk taking him there, as long as she could be certain of leaving Prince Telis and his entourage of mages and thugs behind. But she didn't know even how to find that half-felt pathway in the first place, far less how to stop an experienced mage following her. She could imagine, far too vividly, stepping off the steep pathway and into the light, and into her sisters' house—but with Isonne and King Taliente's skull right behind her.

Or, if not that, then she could imagine simply making a mistake and falling instead. Falling and falling, through light and mist, into the lake where she would drown or else, worse, onto the shore of the lake. It was a long way down, either way. And not only herself to risk, but Geradde as well.

She couldn't find the courage to act. She only let Geradde help her over each particularly broken section of the stairway, while her legs and back began to ache with the strain of all this unaccustomed exercise of going down and down and down. She began to feel as she had in the caverns: as though she had been making her way down endless steps forever without any hope of ever reaching any kind of destination.

Her head ached, too, right behind her eyes, with the dazzle of light from stone and mist and the ice that glittered along shadowed faces of the cliffs. She paused, one hand on cold stone, and rubbed her forehead. It didn't help, and she couldn't stop for long because of Prince Telis' people behind her. Geradde gave her a concerned look and half-extended a hand to her, but the steps right here weren't too frightening. Nemienne shook her head, tried to smile and began to make her way down once more.

The stairway ended at last very near the Laodd, by the shores of the lake where Nijiadde Falls came down in all its deafening clamor. Nemienne thought it should be possible to get away from Telis, now that they were no longer trapped by the narrow confines of the stair. Of course, there were still the thugs and the mages, and Telis himself. But she thought it might be possible to call out for help, because after all Geradde was just as much a prince as his brother, and everyone in the city liked him better anyway.

But the wide sweep of flagstones between the lake and the roadway that led up to the Laodd was empty. Or nearly so. In the distance, she could see a small group of red-uniformed soldiers, but they were too far away to hear even a loud scream, even if the thunder of the falls hadn't masked all other sound. And someone in keiso blue hurried along the wrought iron fence that guarded the nearest great houses of the King's District, but she was even farther away. That was too bad; a keiso might not be able to get Nemienne and Geradde away from Telis by herself, but a keiso certainly could tell everyone that Sa-Telis had taken them prisoner. *Then* let Telis try to keep them in his hand!

But the keiso, whoever she was, turned away from the Falls and vanished into some narrow servant's alley, almost certainly without ever noticing anything that might be happening here at the foot of the stairway, and there was nothing Nemienne could do about that, either.

She was completely helpless. She knew a little magic, but she still was completely helpless, because what could she do against two experienced adult mages? And Geradde was even more helpless than she was, because he didn't even know any magic at all. She wanted to be angry at Telis; she wanted to be furious with the mages who were helping him. But mostly she was just afraid.

Prince Geradde didn't seem to be afraid, though he had even more reason for fear than Nemienne. She knew he had to be afraid, but he hid his fear behind a mask of scornful annoyance. No one held him now; when one of the thugs has reached for his wrist, Geradde hadn't moved, but had flicked a glance sharp-edged as a knife at him. The man had actually stopped, looking to Prince Telis for direction. Sa-Telis, lifting an amused eyebrow, had gestured him back. Now the thug stood watchfully close to Geradde, but did not touch him.

Nemienne wished she knew how to deliver a look so filled

with contempt and authority that it would stop a brute like that in his tracks, but unfortunately she didn't have the trick of it. Probably Leilis could have done it, but one of the men grabbed Nemienne's right wrist in a grip that bruised and she had been too afraid even to *try* to stop him. Now, as Telis gestured, they all moved south away from the Falls, skirting the lake. The man dragged Nemienne along without regard for her shorter legs, and the rocks here were rough and slippery, but at least his grip on her wrist kept her from falling.

To her surprise, Prince Telis didn't lead them toward the Laodd, nor toward the King's District, which might have made sense—Prince Telis most likely owned a private house in the District—but instead toward the bridge that would take them across the river and into the part of the city that lay hard against the mountains. Nemienne tilted her head back and gazed up at Kerre Taum and Kerre Maraddras and the lesser mountains that stood against the sky. It was still early in the day, so that the shadows of the great mountains lay across half the city.

Once across the bridge, they might go anywhere. But she thought . . . she thought she knew where they might be going.

Because once they crossed the bridge, they could very easily turn straight east and walk back into the shadow of the mountains. Straight into the shadow of Kerre Maraddras, right toward the Lane of Shadows that ran along the base of the mountains. The Lane of Shadows, where stood the house of shadows, where Nemienne had so briefly been Mage Ankennes' apprentice before she had become Taudde's.

It was exactly where Prince Geradde had wanted her to take him: the house whose windows looked out onto many different hours and whose doors came and went according to no rules she understood. Where the newest of the doors was made of pine set into a granite lintel, and no doubt was marked even now with a smear of dried blood. That was probably not the door Telis wanted, though. Always assuming she was right about their destination at all, she doubted very much that Sa-Telis had any intention of opening, or trying to open, the door into Kalches. No. She was nearly certain he had another door in mind. The black one, the one that opened into the dark. She was almost sure that was the one to which he meant to lay his hand. He and his ghastly mages with the bones of dead kings in their hands.

Nemienne wondered what Geradde would think when his horrible brother took them into that house. So close to the door into Kalches . . . he would surely try then to get away from his horrible brother.

She hoped she might find a way to help with that. But she was certain Sa-Telis would expect her to try. He would expect them both to try. She doubted very much that any attempt either of them made could work.

But she thought about it anyway. Because it was a strange and capricious house, and one never quite knew where any of its hallways or stairs might lead, or when its doors might come or go.

And Enkea might be there, too. It was *her* house more than it had ever been Ankennes' or Taudde's, or Nemienne's. Nemienne couldn't quite see anything that the cat could do to help, and Enkea was, after all, just as capricious as the house. But then, the other time . . . Mage Ankennes hadn't expected Enkea to get in his way then, either. She wasn't *just* a cat. And one never knew. It was important to remember that one really never knew what might happen, or what chance might come.

Prince Telis turned out to be interested in the dragon harp that occupied pride of place in the music room, which Nemienne ought to have expected.

Though she knew it was stupid, as they had approached the house, Nemienne had almost expected the delicate ripple of music from a harp or kinsana or pipes to come spilling out of the door to greet them. There had always been music in the house, once Taudde rather than Mage Ankennes lived there. For Mage Ankennes, music had been a half-understood weapon and tool, but Nemienne thought that for Taudde it had been as natural and essential as breath. Somehow the silence of the house seemed now to make her feel even more lonely and abandoned—proof Taudde had not come back and did not know Sa-Telis was here, or that she was. Proof that no one was going to come save her. Nemienne knew she had to find a way to save herself—and Prince Geradde, too—but she only felt small and hopeless. She knew she wasn't going to find a way to save either of them.

Sa-Telis strode through the front door of the house without even glancing to either side, just a jerk of his head to bring the two men guarding the door inside with them. Then he went straight to the music room, Nemienne and the rest perforce following him. And then he went straight across the music room to the harp.

It was a floor harp, a great harp, taller than Nemienne was herself. The dragon carved into its face was inlaid with opal and mother-of-pearl, lapis and jet. Anybody who had ever glimpsed the true dragon below Kerre Maraddras would have recognized it instantly: long and serpentine, delicate antennae nodding above its eyes; not an ordinary sea-dragon—if sea-dragons could be said to be ordinary—but a far less familiar sort of creature.

Above the carved dragon were set three beads, one above the next: a bead of smoky glass, a bead of hematite, and a silvery pearl. Nemienne knew what each stood for: the ephemeral and the eternal and the immanent. She wished now she had read more deeply about the way magery defined the interrelationships among the three concepts . . . she had thought she would have more time to learn about such things! She had always expected to have more time! And now they were here, and Prince Telis would go on with whatever his plan comprised, and she didn't know what she could even begin to do about it.

There were other instruments in the music room, of course. The bone flute was gone now . . . fortunately. Considering the harp and the bone flute, Nemienne supposed all the other instruments might be magical, too, but if they were, Taudde had never explained them to her. But she didn't know how to play any of them anyway; she'd never been interested in music.

If Karah had been here, she would know about harps and things. Keiso all learned something of music. But Karah wasn't here either. And even if she had been, Prince Telis already had his hands on the great harp, and Nemienne doubted any of the other instruments in this room could possibly equal that ornate and massive instrument.

Besides the harp, there were three sets of pipes, a flute made of rosewood with fittings of brass, an unstrung kinsana, and, on a stand near Nemienne, an ekonne horn carved of shining black wood. That definitely looked like it must be magic. There was a set of feather drums, too, each hanging on its own hook on the far wall—those were new; Nemienne didn't remember ever seeing them before. She thought perhaps Taudde had made the drums, though she didn't know. Taudde was always picking up odd instruments in the Paliante and from stalls in the open-air markets down by the docks.

She wished fervently that Taudde were here now. Not a prisoner, obviously. Free, and with his flute in his hand. Or any instrument. Or just his voice. She was certain *he* could have dealt with Prince Telis and all his people. Even though Telis had those two extra men now. He must have brought them in along with the rest of his people to help carry things, Nemienne guessed. That harp was enormous; it must be very heavy, and a prince wasn't likely to want to heave it around himself.

She was certain Taudde could have dealt with any number of common thugs, though, and surely he could have managed three mages, even if one of them was also a prince. She *wished* Taudde were here. But he wasn't, and she still had no idea what she could do by herself. Or even with Geradde to help her. She was sure he would try to help, if she could only do something. Sound that black ekonne horn, kick Telis in the shins and duck out the door and get clear away, anything. Break the harpstrings, maybe, or smash the carving, or tear the beads out of their settings.

Mage Ankennes had made the dragon harp. Or, no, that wasn't right. He hadn't made it himself; he'd told her he'd had it made. Not in Lonne; he'd commissioned it from an Erhlianne craftsmaster, he'd said. It was magic, but not a thing of magecraft. That's what he'd told her. *That harp isn't really a thing of magecraft at all. It's meant for a different kind of magic altogether, more akin to the sorcery of Kalches.* Something like that. He'd explained about the harp before everything else had happened, last winter. But Mage Ankennes hadn't ever used the harp for anything, not even when he moved to destroy the Seriantes' dragon. And she hadn't even wondered why.

Nemienne knew she wouldn't like to find out what Prince Telis meant to do with that harp. He might even know exactly what Mage Ankennes had intended for it; he might know exactly why the mage had had it made. For the first time, she wondered whether Prince Telis had been part of that other conspiracy, only no one had ever realized because both Mage Ankennes and Lord Miennes had died without saying so.

For the first time, she wondered whether Mage Ankennes had actually been the man driving that conspiracy. She knew he had used it for his own ends. But now she wondered if Prince Telis had been part of it, too, and using it for *his* ends. Now that it was too late, she wondered exactly who had led or persuaded the other three right-hand princes into the treachery and attempted usurpation that had led to their deaths. Indeed, *now* she wondered exactly when and how and why it had occurred to Prince Sehonnes to lead his own more successful coup. She looked measuringly at Prince Telis. Just how far and how wide and subtly did the net of his ambition stretch?

She glanced at Geradde, standing to one side between two of the thugs. Geradde, too, was watching Telis steadily. Maybe he guessed or knew what his brother was about, but Nemienne couldn't read anything from his face. He stood patiently, his arms folded over his chest, for all the world as though he were prepared to stand just there for the rest of the day and into the night. Nemienne suspected that if he saw a chance to do anything, he would move fast enough. If he did, she would try to help, but she couldn't see anything he could do either.

Prince Telis either did not notice or did not regard his brother's intent gaze. He was running his hands over the harp, tracing the dragon carved down its face, testing the strings. Without sounding the notes, Nemienne noticed, and wondered whether that was chance or caution, and what the latter might imply about that harp. She had never heard Taudde play it, either.

The two mages, Isonne and the other one, the man, Perodde, stood to one side, murmuring to each other, not touching anything. Perodde reached out once with the bone he held as though to prod the ekonne horn, but Isonne hissed at him and he stopped. It all made Nemienne more certain than ever that all the instruments in this room were magical in some way: magecrafted, or made by and for bardic sorcery, or maybe infused somehow with the even stranger enchantment of Enescedd. Nemienne had no idea how to even look for

Enesceddi enchantment. That black ekonne horn looked a bit like something that might have been made with some kind of unfamiliar wild magic. She wished Perodde *would* touch it. Maybe something would happen.

But he didn't. And Prince Telis straightened and beckoned to him, ordering, "Give Isonne that bone and help me with this." The mage moved to obey. And Nemienne, impulsively, more than half surprised by her own actions, suddenly stomped her heel down on the foot of the man who held her, twisted her wrist free of his grip as he yelped in surprise, leaped forward, and snatched the bone away from Perodde just as he handed it to Isonne. It felt dry and brittle; it felt, in some indescribable way, *dead*. But it felt powerful, too, though she couldn't have explained what she mean by that. She made a little noise of dismay at the feel of the bone in her hands, but she also jumped sideways as Perodde and the thug both grabbed at her. She jabbed the bone at the thug—he flinched back—and then whipped it around and across the strings of the dragon harp. Discordant notes tangled, all at odds: metallic, strangely muffled and flat, but somehow lingering in the air, too, as though they would never fade.

-16-

The house that had recently belonged to Mage Ankennes—
or that Mage Ankennes had lived in, at least—was the third
along the Lane of Shadows, at the steep foot of Kerre Maraddras,
where sun rarely fell.

After Ankennes had died, Geriodde Nerenne ken Seriantes
had given Taudde leave to dwell in that house, perhaps because
he felt it unwise to leave it empty but, Leilis now suspected,
more likely because he did not quite trust any mage of Lonne
who might want to dwell there. It was not the sort of house
where one would wish to leave an enemy. It had too many doors,
and too many of them led in unexpected directions. She doubted
very much that Prince Telis would have left it unguarded, but no
guards were in evidence outside the house. That absence of
guards did not make the house seem inviting. It made it seem
like a trap.

"How very quiet it is today," Gerenes Brenededd murmured
in her ear, his tone dry.

Leilis smiled despite her nervousness. "I suspect that will
not last."

"You are undoubtedly correct." Gerenes paused. "You are
prepared?"

Leilis nodded, hoping it was true. "You?"

"Indeed." He, at least, sounded as though he thought this
was true.

From the outside, the house seemed small. It had been built
of weathered gray stone, the same stone as the mountain's face,
so that it looked rather as though it had been carved straight out
of the mountain rather than built in the normal way. Its angles
seemed odd and possibly crooked, though when one looked more
closely, one could not quite find any specific fault. Leilis had
never noticed before how the light that did make its way past the
mountain slanted obliquely across those windows, so that it was
impossible to see through the glass. Anyone could stand inside

and look out, and no one in the lane would ever know. She didn't like those blind windows. She didn't like the house itself, in fact, though she had come here now and again in the past few weeks and never minded the house then.

But Taudde had been in this house, then. Now no one was here. Or if anyone was, it would be an enemy. Leilis looked at Gerenes Brenededd, raising her eyebrows in silent query.

"No one on the porch," he murmured. "Neither soldier nor guardsman nor mage. That house is altogether deserted, it seems."

Leilis inclined her head. "The better to coax the unwary to enter?"

"Just so. There is no other door for tradesmen or servants, you understand, young woman." He did not use any name for her, neither her keiso name nor her birth name. Either might be dangerous, if anyone happened to overhear. He merely went on, "Such an entrance would be at the rear, and all the houses here are built directly against the mountain. And those blind windows do not invite experimentation. Still, as our enemies invite us to enter this house, so we shall." He offered her his arm and added, "Slowly, slowly, young woman. Remember you are keiso. Think of this as you would think of a public performance."

Leilis forbore to remind Gerenes that her curse had not permitted her to offer public performances; that, though born into the flower world, she had not become a true keiso until very recently. Besides, in a very real sense, she had been offering a public performance to the world all her life. A woman did, in the flower world, whether she was keiso or aika or an actress in one of the theaters. She thought of that and smiled, and took her companion's arm, and allowed him to lead her toward the house.

The steps of the house were stone, rough-fitted and not quite even underfoot. The door itself was . . . ajar, it proved, when they crossed the porch. That seemed . . . fraught. Just as no one appeared to guard the house from without, there was no sign of anyone waiting within. Leilis slanted an ironic look at her companion.

"Indeed," Gerenes murmured. He pushed the door wide with his foot and tossed three delicate little glass vials into the house, one, two, three, as smoothly and fast as a boy shying pebbles at sparrows. From within came the sound of shattering glass, a less identifiable hissing sound, and a startled oath. Ignoring this, Gerenes tossed similar vials behind them and to either side, then guided Leilis rapidly through the door and the dimly-lit entryway and into a hallway that seemed to run back an implausibly long way for so small a house.

At the moment, the end of that hallway had vanished in billowing mist. The hallway was always long, but the mist was new. It was greenish and whitish and smelled rather pleasantly musky, in small amounts and at a distance. Close to, the smell was much less pleasant. If one was that close, it also blinded ordinary vision—only for a few moments, but quite reliably. Gerenes Brenededd had not been quite so confident what this mist might do to a mage's sight, which was not entirely like the sight of an ordinary person. But Leilis had agreed his mist was a clever trick despite this uncertainty.

To Leilis' eyes, there were only two windows and one door along the whole improbable length of this hallway, though she knew it had not been the same for Taudde or even for Nemienne. Leilis knew, because Nemienne had described it to her, that various windows here might reveal brilliant sunlight and silvery moonlight and the pearly lavender light of dawn, each looking out into a different day. To her, both the narrow windows showed the plain light of the ordinary world—indirect and rather dim because the mountain's shadow lay over the house.

The only door that had ever been apparent to her eyes was the one of mountain cedar, with stylized animals and intricately branching trees carved on its ornate panels. That one led to the music room. Taudde had loved that room. Leilis thought perhaps that was why she had been able to see that one, to go freely into and out of it. Now she found herself unexpectedly furious to see that door standing open, with a man in a mage's robes gripping the doorframe. At the moment, he was bent a little, clutching the doorframe with one hand, his other hand pressed over his eyes. She hoped the smoke hurt his eyes—she was *furious* to see he had been snooping around in Taudde's favorite room in the whole house, and knew it was silly to feel that way when no doubt enemies had been everywhere in this house and made themselves quite at home. But she was still bitterly angry.

She knew, because Nemienne had described it to her, that somewhere along the length of this hall stood a door of beech wood, carved all over with beech leaves, that opened to the enchanted forests of Enescedd. Nemienne had also told her that there was a third door, this one of perfectly plain midnight-black wood, that opened to the lightless caverns below Kerre Maraddras. Leilis had never seen that one, either. And now, of course, there must be the door that led into Kalches. Somewhere. She did not see it, though she looked as hard as she could; and told herself that her heartbeat echoed with the heartbeat of the dragon and so she had to be able to see it; and reminded herself that she, of all people, ought to be able to find any door so special to Taudde. None of that helped her find it.

Gerenes had set one hand on the flat of Leilis' back, but in the other he held another handful of glass vials. He threw one of these, coolly and with startling accuracy, as they strode forward. It shattered at the feet of the mage, who coughed and swore and stepped back sharply, shutting the music room door sharply behind him to get away from the smoke.

"Ah, we are no doubt prepared for both magecraft and swordplay, but not, I see, for boy's pranks. And your door, young woman?" said Gerenes, his tone blandly calm. Under the calm was intense satisfaction. "I trust you will be able to locate it. Quickly, if you please. I doubt our friend there is alone."

Leilis doubted it, too, though she thought that, considering the other boy's tricks Gerenes had up his capacious sleeves, it might not matter so much, at least not at first. They were close, now, and no one but the one mage had yet appeared—and he had retreated back into the music room. Rage still stirred at that intrusion, but there was no time for that now. She put the rage aside, as she had learned by long practice to do, and looked for the door they needed. But though she knew it must be here somewhere, she could not *see* the door into Kalches. It *must* be here—

Then she saw it. A bloody handprint marked the place, smeared across the wooden paneling, but clearly visible. She remembered Benne saying, *The blood marked it . . . the blood drew my eye.* And it did. Leilis could see the door after all, once she saw the blood. It was perfectly obvious. It was a door of plain pine, neither carved nor painted, not even quite smooth. It should have looked out of place in this dark-paneled hall, but somehow it seemed to fit: a plain pine door with a granite lintel and a granite knob. Though the blood smeared across the wood and dried on the knob did not fit so well.

"There," Leilis breathed, and strode forward.

"There *is* a door?" said Gerenes, plainly not yet able to find it himself, despite the blood. He followed, but guardedly, most of his attention on the unseen reaches of the long hallway and on the carved door behind which the mage had retreated. Rather casually, he tossed another vial down the hallway. The smoke this time was thicker and distinctly greener, and surprisingly abundant to have come out of that little vial. "That should surprise anyone who tries to come that way," he observed, sounding rather satisfied, and turned to Leilis.

Leilis was just discovering that the knob would not turn for her hand, and that the door had no give to it at all.

"That could present a difficulty," murmured Gerenes.

Leilis hardly needed him to point that out. She pressed her palms flat against the door. The pine wood was rough under her fingers. It smelled of pine forests and woodsmoke and snow. She knew the kind of country this door must open into: high jagged mountains and snow and wide frozen lakes, and below the mountains, the close-gathered homes of men. She could almost see that country when she closed her eyes.

Taudde had been born there, in that land of stone and snow, of cold pine forests and roaring winter fires in every hearth. But he had heard the sea calling from across the mountains, and so he had left Kalches and entered Lirionne, and come at last to Lonne. And then everything that had happened . . . had happened.

It was the heartbeat of the dragon he had truly heard. He had not precisely said so, but Leilis thought so. Her own heartbeat was supposed to echo the heartbeat of the dragon. He had said that. Sometimes she thought it was true. Sometimes she thought she could hear that rhythm in the rush of blood through her veins. Sometimes she thought she could close her eyes and step forward, wherever she stood, and find herself once more in the dragon's cavern, in the heart of darkness, with the black waters of the dragon's pool washing against the toes of her slippers.

"Ah, here we are," said Gerenes, his voice taking on a light, calm tension. "Young woman, now would be an excellent time to open that door—or some door—" She felt him move behind her, a sharp, urgent gesture, and dimly heard the sound of shattering glass. Even more dimly, she heard someone shout: a coarse, loud voice that had no place in the lightless caverns. Her heart's living rhythm matched the rhythm of the dragon's heartbeat, and behind that, the rhythm of the sea. Leilis drew a long, slow breath and let it out, and felt the dragon sigh and the tide run out. And she opened the door, reached back to catch hold of Gerenes' hand, and stepped forward.

She did not know, afterward, how it was Gerenes Brenededd did not come with her: whether one of their enemies had dragged him back at the last moment, or whether the door had opened only for her. She only felt him jerk back and away from her. She turned immediately, reaching, dismayed, but it was already too late. Her foot came down on hard-packed snow, and snow came into her face on a driving wind, and a hard, cold light like polished pewter lay over a world of stone and snow. Gerenes was not there. The door was not there, either. There was nothing where it should have been save for a long, long sweep of empty air and, far below, dimly visible through the blowing snow, the curve of a road along the side of the mountain.

Leilis put a hand out blindly to the freezing stone beside her, steadying herself against the dizzying height. Tears prickled at the backs of her eyes, hot against the cold. Her heart beat fast now, nothing like the slow rhythm of the dragon's heartbeat. She was afraid for herself, alone in this unfamiliar country. But she was more afraid for Gerenes Brenededd, the king's cousin, who for his cousin's sake had risked everything to help her, and had perhaps lost everything. And she was angry, she was *furious*, at whatever ridiculous slant of magic had stopped him from coming with her—or if it had been an enemy, catching hold of him at the last moment, that was *worse*.

He knew her name, and what she had come here to do. And he knew his cousin lived—though fortunately not where he lay, or in whose care, so that was a little better at least than if Leilis herself had been caught. But she had never meant to put the king's ironic, subtle, generous cousin into such peril—well, but whatever her intention, she *had* drawn him into danger, and he had accepted it on his own account, but neither of them had expected him to be *caught*.

Though, come to that . . . even at the end, Leilis did not think Gerenes Brenededd had quite used all his tricks. That was a thin hope. But it was one she clung to, thin as it was. Certainly there was nothing at all she could do now to help him.

She could see, in fact, that she had better think at once of what she might do to help herself. It was bitterly cold in this place to which the door had brought her, and that town was far below, and, Leilis now realized, though she had been warmly clad for Lonne, she was not nearly adequately prepared for Kalches.

How abysmally foolish.

And how ironic, to freeze to death here on this foreign mountain, no doubt nearly within sight of warmth and help. Perhaps within a day's walk or less of Taudde, and of Prince Tepres. Though she thought possibly her sheer anger would keep her warm.

There was no door set here, into the air or the stone, to take her with one step where she would go. Leilis wrapped her robes more tightly about herself. She was reluctant to bring out her keiso robes unless the cold proved too fierce. Those robes were her weapons, and she had no intention of trailing even the hem in the snow unless she truly had no choice. For the moment, she only slung her satchel more comfortably over her shoulder, and began to pick her way down the face of the mountain, toward the road far below.

-17-

Nemienne had had no idea what that harp would sound like when it was finally played, but she knew she hadn't expected the strange, discordant noise she produced. She was sure the bone she had raked across the strings had belonged to Taliente Seriantes himself, and the instant she touched it, she could feel the power that clung to it. Even if she were wrong and it was someone else's bone, all the Seriantes were similar things to the dragon, and the dragon was carved all down the harp's face, and she couldn't think of anything else to do, and she was desperate to do *something*. But she had no idea what the discordant clamor of notes might have done. She tried to rake the bone across the strings again anyway, but one of Sa-Telis' men grabbed her.

Geradde was moving, too, she was dimly aware of that, but she was completely unable to keep track of anything. The harp notes were swelling, and she thought the feather drums were thrumming in answer, but every sound in the room, every sound in the world, seemed somehow to become somehow muffled and flat, too. She couldn't tell what that might mean. The man—it was the one called Dog—had her by the arm. He dragged her back, and she hit him with the bone and only then realized that of course she ought to try to *break* the bone, maybe *that* would interfere with whatever Prince Telis had planned, only Dog had hold of it now, too. She struggled to get it back, she hoped between them they might still break it in their struggle, and she even got away for a minute, but someone else gabbed her hair and pulled her head back so hard she thought her neck might break—she couldn't get her breath—all kinds of things were happening all over, she couldn't tell what, but she hoped at least Geradde might have gotten away. But people were still struggling. Someone cursed, and someone else grunted, a pained sound, and then the thug she was fighting grabbed the back of her neck and squeezed and Nemienne cried out and stopped fighting.

It took her a moment to blink her eyes clear of tears and focus on the room, and then she wanted to cry in earnest. Because she hadn't achieved anything. Not anything.

Or, well, maybe *something*. Dog, who had struggled with her for possession of the bone now leaned against a wall, his eyes closed and his face gray, his hands cradled against his chest as though the bone had burned him. That seemed strange. Nemienne hadn't liked the dead bone—she had hated touching it—but it hadn't *hurt* her. But she was angry and frightened enough to be glad it seemed to have hurt *him*. Though it hadn't been enough, because plainly the remaining thugs were enough to control her and Geradde.

Geradde had failed to get away. Nemienne hadn't really expected he would, but she was terribly disappointed anyway. Poor Geradde was on his knees, pinned by the oldest and meanest-looking of the thugs, a grim-looking man called Lob. Geradde wasn't struggling, and she didn't blame him, because Lob had his arm wrenched up behind his back. Geradde's face was white with pain, though he wasn't making a sound.

Mage Isonne had the bone, now. She cradled it in both her hands. She ran her finger anxiously along its length, but it did not seem to have been harmed, unfortunately. The leather bag with the skull in it was still securely over her shoulder.

And Perodde and Telis stood, one on either side of the dragon harp, their hands spread, their fingers laid flat against the strings. No wonder the notes had sounded stifled. Whatever might have happened, or might have been about to happen, they had plainly stopped it.

Or mostly stopped it. Despite everything, Nemienne couldn't help but be a little bit pleased to see how pale Prince Telis looked now. Pale and strained. Maybe she had managed to do something useful after all. Maybe she had at least come close to doing something useful. He looked angry, too. That wasn't so good. She tried not to cower when he sent a thin-lipped glare her way. At least he hadn't moved, yet. His hands still rested flat on the harpstrings, as though he feared that if he lifted them, the strings would sound again and this time the notes become impossible to stop. Nemienne wondered if that could be true. If she'd been able to think of a way to get Prince Telis away from the harp, she would have been glad to test the idea, willing to see what would happen if she let the harp sound. Unfortunately, no ideas sprang to mind. Probably it was too late anyway—and anyway, there was Mage Perodde right there, too.

Prince Telis drew a breath and cautiously lifted one hand from the harp. Nothing happened. Another breath, but the prince was clearly beginning to relax. He began to speak, but suddenly there was a brittle smashing noise from the outside hallway, and immediately another, and then another—it sounded exactly like someone had flung down three pottery cups or glass bowls, one after another. Everyone jerked and stared. The man holding Nemienne swore, startled, and she twisted and struggled, but his grip tightened and she couldn't get away.

Another smashing sound, and now she could see a thick mist, milky green, just beginning to billow through the open door of the music room.

"Perodde!" Telis commanded, sounding tense, and the mage nodded quickly, took his hands away from the harpstrings and went quickly to the door, followed by the thug called Rip and another man. Prince Telis had spread both his hands across the strings again, as though wary about losing the other mage's support with whatever he was doing to keep them quiet.

Perodde, though coughing and with a hand up to his eyes, started to leave the music room, but there was another smashing sound, and suddenly more mist billowed up, much more thickly than before. Perodde stepped back hastily, coughing, and slammed the door against the mist.

"That's not helpful," Prince Telis said sharply.

Perodde tried to answer him, but he was still coughing and unable to speak. But he clapped his hands and blew between them. A swift breeze came across the room, rushed around the walls—the feather drums thrummed again, and Telis swore and pressed all his wide-spread fingers against the harpstrings. But Perodde flung the door open again, and this time the breeze whipped out the door, carrying the mist away, and Perodde ran out, followed by the two thugs.

Isonne glanced at Prince Telis, hefted the long bone in her hand like a club, and moved cautiously toward the door. Geradde made a low sound of pain and Nemienne knew he had tried to break away from his captor, but he hadn't succeeded and she didn't think he could. Lob was too big and too alert. She couldn't do anything, either; the one now holding her by the neck had tightened his grip until it really hurt. She could hear things—a banging, and a scraping noise, and someone cursing, she couldn't tell whether it was Perodde or one of the other men or someone else. Then there were several dull thuds, not very loud. Then, at last, quiet.

Isonne peered out, then stepped back hastily. Everyone was coming back, and Nemienne as much as anyone tried to see.

The thugs came back first. One of them dragged along someone new, no one Nemienne knew, an elderly man in plain brown and beige robes, but with fine-boned elegant features and, from his rigid fury, undoubtedly someone with high-born connections—he certainly had all a well-born man's anger at being manhandled. Nor was he troubling to disguise his anger. He staggered when the thug shoved him into the music room, but once he caught his balance, he straightened his shoulders, sent a sharp glance around the room, saw Prince Telis, and tilted his head in contempt. He must have seen Geradde as well, and Nemienne, both of them pinned and helpless, but if so, this sight did not elicit so much as a flicker of overt attention.

Perodde came back in, then, looking rather disarranged, and said without preamble, "Eminence, the other one got away. A woman. I don't know how she got it open, but she went through the door into Kalches. "

"Of course she did," Prince Telis answered. His tone was dry, but Nemienne could tell that underneath the pose of patience, he was coldly furious. But he said, "It doesn't matter now." Even so, he added, to the other thug, the only one now not occupied with a prisoner, "However, let us try to avoid further interruptions, yes?" The man shrugged and nodded and went away, to resume guarding the door of the house, Nemienne guessed.

Prince Telis rather warily lifted his hands from the strings of the dragon harp. Nemienne listened hard, but she could not hear even a whisper of sound. Neither could the prince, evidently, since she saw his shoulders relax. He didn't look at her, so she thought the interruption had distracted him at least from her attempt to interfere with things. So that was good.

At least, it was good for her. The look Prince Telis turned on the old man was not kind. "Gerenes Brenededd," he said after a moment. "Well. Who would have expected this? Who was the woman? What was your intention? What does she mean to do now? Do you know anything of what has been happening in Kalches?"

To all these questions, the man only lifted a silently disdainful eyebrow. His name sounded faintly familiar to Nemienne, but she could not remember where she might have heard it. She, too, wanted very much to know about the woman and her intentions and what was happening in Kalches, but she was impressed at his elegantly silent defiance. And afraid for him, because she couldn't guess what Prince Telis might do.

"I can make him answer," offered the thug

"It doesn't matter. And we can't take the time. No. Let's simply be rid of him—"

"No!" Geradde said sharply, and everyone turned to stare. "No," he repeated, more quietly this time. "Leave him be, brother, and I'll do as you wish."

Telis regarded him for a moment. "The moment you annoy me, *brother*, I'll put a knife in his belly and leave him to die."

"I know you will. I don't doubt it. Leave him alone, and I'll do as you wish."

"Well," Telis said after a moment, "I hardly think that's likely. But if it will keep you quiet for ten minutes together, then he's not without use. You understand, his life is now measured by that use."

Geradde, his expression grim, nodded understanding. The man—Gerenes Brenededd—was regarding the younger prince with dispassionate calm. Nemienne wondered what the man thought, and why Geradde had made such a promise for him. In a play, a prince would keep exactly that kind of promise even unto death. There was a scene just like that in Geselle Maniente's "Four Seasons of the Heart." But that was a play, of course. If Nemienne had made such a promise, under the circumstances, *she* definitely wouldn't hesitate to break it. But she wasn't a man, or a prince.

But it was something else to worry about, because she wasn't *entirely* certain if Prince Geradde would seize a chance now, even if he got one.

Prince Telis nodded to Mage Perodde, then gestured to Dog, who seemed to be recuperating at last from whatever touching the bone had done to him. The prince said, "If you have quite recovered? Can you manage the weight? We must take care. We don't wish to sound the strings before time. Perodde?"

"Yes, eminence," Perodde said earnestly, and Dog grunted and nodded and straightened, though he still moved rather creakily.

Nemienne only wished she had managed to do to all of the thugs whatever she had done to Dog. She glanced at Isonne, trying to be subtle, but the woman was too far away and Nemienne couldn't see any way she could get the bone back again for a second try.

"Very well," said Prince Telis. "We have been delayed enough and more than enough. It's time to finish this. Perodde, if you are ready?" As the other men moved to help him, Telis laid his hand on the face of the harp with a proprietary air and then carefully shifting his grip to help lift it.

Nemienne had not been in the dragon's chamber since that dreadful night when Mage Ankennes had tried to kill Prince Tepres and died instead. She had felt so helpless and alone that night, especially after Karah had vanished and everything had gone so wrong. But this was worse. Because last time, even if she had felt alone, other people had been there, trying to help. Leilis and Taudde—she hadn't even known them then, not as she did now; but she had known that Taudde was a real bardic sorcerer and that Leilis was the sort of person who always knew what to do.

And Taudde had saved them all, in the end. Or Karah had saved them all, in a way. Or King Geriodde himself had.

Well, and Nemienne had done things, too, that might have made a difference. But she had hardly known, at any time during that grim night, what it was she did. She had not known anything. But the dragon had woken. And then everything else had followed from that.

Now Telis had brought them again through the black door that led from the house of shadows into this heavy, powerful darkness, and once more into the dragon's chamber.

And the dragon was here—neither truly asleep nor precisely awake. Drowsing, it had gone halfway back into the stone, so that most of its long tail and part of its back and haunches seemed to have been carved into and from the pale stone of the mountain. But its head and neck and most of its forequarters could never have been mistaken for anything made by the hands of men. Its long head, more than twice Nemienne's height, lay between its black pool and the cavern wall. Its jaw rested on one curled forefoot, its elegant neck curved into and out of the stone. Where it was clear of the stone, the dragon glittered in jewel-tones: lapis and amethyst shading from jaw to throat, sapphire and darker amethyst and emerald shimmering down its long neck and shoulder. Its nearer wing, half visible, was sapphire netted with a tracery of gold. The antennae that arched over its long, narrow eyes shifted gently as though in an unfelt breeze, sapphire and aquamarine and emerald. Its eyes were closed. Nemienne knew that if they opened, they would be black as the darkness that lived here below Kerre Maraddras.

She did not quite know whether she wanted those eyes to open and see her, as they had seen her once before. She would not exactly mind if the dragon woke and noticed Prince Telis and his people. It could destroy them all and she would not mind. It was the other things the dragon might do that frightened her. She remembered, vividly, what it had almost done the other time. Except they had persuaded it otherwise. Nemienne had never, ever guessed that anyone would be so bold or so foolish as to risk disturbing the dragon yet again..

But she should have. It should have occurred to her that if Mage Ankennes knew about the dragon, other mages must, too. That if King Geriodde knew about the dragon, his sons might as well.

Mage Ankennes had hated the dragon. Nemienne couldn't begin to guess at the exact relationship between King Geriodde and the dragon, though she knew the man who was called the

Dragon of Lirionne was, in a way, a similar thing to this true dragon—that had been key to her first master's plan to destroy it. What Sa-Telis, both prince and mage, thought about this dragon . . . she hardly knew. Though, no matter what he said, she could hardly believe he could look at it and think he might *control* it. And it was almost harder to believe his mage allies thought he could do anything of the kind. Yet they were all here. And the dragon did not seem truly awake.

Nemienne thought Prince Telis might have done something to keep the dragon from noticing him, or any of them: there were spiky, strange lines on the cavern floor that she did not remember, painted in black ink, or perhaps carved right into the stone so that the blackness was not ink but shadow. They cut across the cavern, those lines, curving along the outer edge of the black pool, dividing the dragon's half of the cavern from the half where the men stood.

Mage light broke the darkness on this half of the cavern, though the light did not seem to cross those spiky lines. It wasn't the kind of light Nemienne could summon into the dark. The kind of light she could bring into the reaches below the mountain was . . . not exactly light. But it was better, here. Her light might not be *exactly* light, but it was not a disturbance to the darkness.

The brilliant light which the prince's mages had summoned was different. That light was all wrong, here. It fractured the dark and drove it away, rather than making a soft place for itself at the roots of the mountain. It gleamed harshly off the surface of the black pool. The water of that pool was not exactly water. Under the pressure of that bitter light, it looked more like iron, except that slow ripples spread out from where one drop of water and then another fell from the cavern heights. The sound was not quite the sound of droplets of water falling into a pool: each falling drop struck an echo from the darkness that was more like the ring of iron against iron. The ripples ran against the edge of the pool with a faint, high chiming sound that was nothing to do with water.

If *her* light touched the black water of the dragon's pool, it would slide right through the water's opaque surface and . . . become something else again, Nemienne thought. Some kind of sound, or magic. She might have tried to summon light and cast it across the pool, except she was too far away from the pool and too close-guarded. Nemienne shivered, listening to the sound of those drops of falling black water.

She could see no sign that Prince Telis or his people heard anything strange behind the sound, or saw anything wrong with the way their harsh light struck through the darkness. Or that any of them feared the dragon. Though, when she looked carefully, she saw that none of them stood too near the black pool, and none of them ever seemed to glance across the pool to look directly at the dragon, either.

Prince Telis stood, speaking to his mages, near the passageway that led up, by a long but simple path, to the light and air. Up to the ordinary places where men ought to be. Nemienne wished they were back up there now, except then she and Prince Geradde would still be in the hands of Prince Telis' men, and what good would that do?

A torch burned on either side of the entry to that passageway, and below the nearer torch Telis had set the great harp. Comparing the carved dragon now to the one half free of the stone, she could see that they were not *exactly* the same. The long, elegant head was the same, the serpentine curves of its body, the angle of the claws, all that was very nearly echoed by the carved dragon. But the real dragon was more complicated, its colors more subtle, than anything that could be made out of wood and inlay.

Prince Telis stood with his hand resting familiarly on the smooth curve of the harp's frame, his thumb stroking the black pearl and the beads of smoky glass and hematite set into the face of the harp, above the dragon. It was a possessive, satisfied gesture.

Nemienne glanced up at Prince Geradde, who returned her look. Geradde's expression, blank and neutral, did not change. But he shifted half a step closer to her. She felt better somehow, even though the men guarding them stood too close for either her or Prince Geradde to do anything useful. Gerenes Brenededd stood not far away. One of Telis' thugs stood at his back, holding a knife at the old man's throat in naked threat. Gerenes stood with his back straight and his arms crossed over his chest. His mouth was pressed thin with anger. He did not speak to Geradde, however. None of them could speak to the others. Geradde had tried, and one of the other thugs had hit him across the face and ordered him silent. How the man dared strike a prince or speak to him so, Nemienne still could hardly imagine, but Geradde's brother had not reprimanded him.

No one had hit Nemienne, but the third guard leaned against the cavern wall not far away, watching her with casual attention. She could think of nothing she could do, even if he happened to look away. This time, she didn't even have beads. She wanted the ones set into the face of the harp, but even if she could have reached it, she might not have had the nerve to pry loose those beads. She was almost sure that tearing them out of the harp would release some kind of sorcery, and almost sure that would be disastrous.

But she might have tried, if she had been able to reach the harp.

Isonne had taken the skull out of the leather bag and now held it in both her hands. Perodde had taken back the other bone. Both mages stayed close by Prince Telis. They were talking about something. Nemienne wished she could overhear them. Telis was clearly worried about something, or angry about something. He scowled all the time, and sometimes he rubbed his forehead as though he had a headache. Nemienne hoped he did. She wished she thought he had run into a real problem that would stop him doing what he intended, but he didn't look *that* upset.

"What are those bones for, I wonder?" Geradde murmured. "Seriantes bones in this cavern, that seems rather fraught—"

"Shut up," Lob said, and shoved him, not hard, but enough to emphasize the order.

Geradde gave the man a scornful look and Nemienne a small, reassuring smile, but he didn't try to speak again, and Nemienne didn't dare try to answer. Gerenes Brenededd said, "Boar-pig," in a reflective tone, but the man holding him pretended not to hear.

Nemienne did not, of course, know exactly what Telis intended to do, or try to do. But she was afraid she might be able to guess. Even if their guards hadn't been listening, though, she wouldn't have wanted to put her guess into words because it was all too horrible. Dead Seriantes bone, living Seriantes blood, and a harp tuned to the darkness beneath the mountain—to the heartbeat of the dragon—to the surge of the tides that ran through both the darkness and the dragon's blood. She was afraid she had a fairly clear idea what kind of magic Sa-Telis meant to work.

Mage Ankennes had used a bone like that—well, not quite like that, he had made his into a flute—but he had used an old bone in a strange blend of magecraft and sorcery. Taudde had been horrified. He had explained that to Nemienne later, when he had started to teach her sorcery. Sorcery, really powerful sorcery that you anchored in a living person, you had to ground that kind of sorcery very carefully in the earth as well as in the person, and you had to know just what you intended your sorcery to do.

Sorcery was very different from magecraft, different in ways that Nemienne knew Mage Ankennes hadn't really understood. Or hadn't really believed. Nemienne doubted very much that Prince Telis or his mages knew anything about grounding sorcery. She knew Telis had an idea what he was doing, but if he tried to blend sorcery and magecraft as Mage Ankennes had, she was afraid he would do something terrible. She was sure that was exactly what they were going to try, and if they didn't understand what they were doing, that was fine—except that she and Prince Geradde were right here, too, and would be caught up in whatever Telis did. And the dragon, too, which was the whole point. What might happen when the dragon's magic was trapped in whatever Telis planned . . . Nemienne didn't want to think about it.

Kelle Iasodde had written a whole chapter on sympathy and similarity. Nemienne had read it twice, and thought she understood some of it. She guessed that Telis meant to establish sympathy between those old bones and Prince Geradde, with the bones standing for the eternal and the living prince standing for the ephemeral. And she was afraid she could guess how Telis meant to define the immanent: she thought he was going to define that as breath and life and spirit and will.

That was how *she* would define the immanent, if she had a harp tuned to the dragon, and old bones, and a living prince. And a wish to cast down everything and everyone else, and rule.

But she had nothing. Prince Telis had everything, including, plainly, ruthless determination. He seemed mad, perhaps he *was* mad, but Nemienne couldn't think of anything to do to stop him. Geradde was brave, but what could he do, guarded by two men?

"Ah. Here we go," murmured Geradde, and Nemienne saw that Telis had evidently finished arranging other things and was coming toward them, trailed by those two mages, Isonne and Perodde. Perodde held the long bone in one hand and a small silver knife in the other. Nemienne didn't want to think about what possible use he might have for that knife and tried not to look at it. Breath and life, blood and spirit and will—all the things Telis meant to steal from his brother. It was horrible. Even yet, she doubted that Geradde quite guessed how horrible it was. Nemienne almost wished she didn't, either. She thought perhaps Gerenes Brenededd did, because he was looking at her, his lips pressed thin and his expression intent.

Perodde, in contrast, seemed pleased with himself, as though he'd worked out some difficult theoretical question that had nothing to do with murder, or worse than murder. Isonne held Taliente's skull in both hands, carefully, not so much as though she feared to drop it as though she just feared it. Maybe she had more of an understanding of what might go wrong with this kind of magic than Perodde, who was younger than she. Nemienne wished she found that thought more comforting.

Prince Telis mostly looked impatient and satisfied. He nodded to Geradde—no, Nemienne saw, he nodded to the men guarding his brother. Geradde himself, he ignored completely.

Then Telis reached out without looking and took the little silver knife from Mage Perodde.

Geradde didn't draw back. He didn't glance at Gerenes Brenededd, hostage for his cooperation; nor did he look at Nemienne; but Nemienne sensed the effort it took him to stand still, not to fight. The old man wasn't watching the two princes, but still gazing straight at her. Even at this moment, Nemienne thought that was strange. She stared back, questioningly.

As his brother took his arm, Geradde asked, as though he couldn't help himself, "What are you going to do?" His voice shook just a little, right at the end, and he cut the last word off short.

Telis ignored him. He said to the men, "Hold him still," and twisted his brother's right wrist, forcing him to turn his palm upward. Geradde immediately clenched his fist, but Telis only gave him an impatient look and said, "I shall cut across your fingers, then, and if you are crippled, you will have only your own cowardice to blame."

This was patently unfair, but Geradde plainly believed his brother would do it. He set his jaw and opened his hand, and did not flinch when Telis sliced across his palm. It was not a deep cut, but it bled freely. Here beneath the mountain, where the harsh magelight drove back the dark, the blood was a crimson so deep it was almost black.

Taking the bone from Mage Perodde, Telis stroked his fingers through the welling blood from his brother's hand, and then ran his bloody fingers along the length of the bone. The blood clung to the white bone, and light ran suddenly along the bone, along the streaks of blood—not the brilliant magelight, but the pale greenish light that wasn't truly light at all.

Then Isonne stepped forward, holding up the skull.

In that moment, that one moment when everyone's attention was focused on the skull, on the knife and the blood and the glimmering bone, Gerenes Brenededd lunged forward and drove his own throat against the knife his captor held.

The man jerked back as the blood poured over his hands, cursing, and everyone but Nemienne pivoted to stare, their attention completely captured by the old man's act.

Nemienne was the only one who had almost seen that coming—who *had* seen it coming, an instant before it happened. Catching that moment where everyone's horrified attention had been jerked away from Prince Geradde and from her, she reached out, dabbed her own fingertip in the blood that filled Geradde's palm, dropped to her knees, and drew on the stone, quickly and without thinking very much about it, the rune for summoning. And what she summoned, as she had once before in this very cavern, was the powerful, heavy darkness that lay, still and forever beyond the reach of any light.

All through the wide reaches of the dragon's cavern, all the magelight died. The torches by the entryway guttered, sank, and went out. The darkness swallowed it all, and grew vast. The greenish light that clung to the bone dripped like water or like blood, and ran in a thin rivulet across the pale stone.

Prince Telis shouted wordlessly, sounding furious and shocked. Someone else shouted, too, but Nemienne could not tell who it was. She wasn't listening. She grabbed Geradde's hand, not minding the blood, and pulled him away with her into the dark. She knew where she wanted to go—*home*—but under the tremendous weight of this darkness, she couldn't remember light—not right now, not yet—and anyway, she was terrified that if she tried to lead Geradde there, Prince Telis would follow them. So *away* would do, just away, anywhere, out of this fraught cavern and right into the secret dark.

Only almost at once she found something in the way, something spiky and difficult, like a dense hedge of thorns. It stabbed and pricked like thorns, only it was made of a different kind of darkness, something bodiless but inimical. Nemienne tried to find a way around this barrier, then a way through it. Behind them, not nearly far enough away, people were shouting. The greenish light made from Geradde's blood glimmered. In a minute, Telis or his mages would surely come after them, find them, and the poor old man's bravery would be for nothing. Nemienne didn't know what to do. There was a rune that would let someone step from one place to another, but she couldn't *remember* it—and it took real magic, real power, to step across any great distance—but she would have been glad to step even a little way, if they could only get out of the dragon's chamber and away into the farther reaches of the caverns—

Geradde closed his hand hard on hers and dragged her sideways, away from the shouting. That seemed like a good idea. Nemienne clung to him, put her other hand out to fend off unseen walls, and ran with a will.

Light bloomed before and behind them and around them, greenish, gleaming through the dark. Nemienne pulled Geradde away from it, keeping to the dark, but almost at once they ran again into the thorny barrier. This time, Nemienne recognized the spiky lines drawn out on the cavern floor, dividing the dragon's half of the cavern from the mages' half. Runes, she guessed, to divide one kind of magic from another. She could *feel* the antipathy between those runes and the heavy darkness.

Furious and terrified, she dropped to the floor, dragging Geradde with her, pulled his hand down, and smeared his blood right across those lines.

The runes . . . shattered. It was like that, like throwing a rock against something delicate and brittle. Nemienne thought she might have cried out, but she wasn't sure. She ducked down low, covering her face with her arm, and only then realized that the thing that had shattered had never actually had physical form or substance. She thought at first she had been stabbed somehow; then she thought the darkness, slamming down, might crush her. Then someone—Sa-Telis—grabbed her arm, and she screamed, and Geradde pulled her the other way—for a moment, she thought he and his horrible brother might pull her apart, just like disjointing a hen for the pot—she kicked Sa-Telis, twisting to get free, and then she was stumbling through a shock of cold that wasn't water, but *like* water. One could drown in it, but it would be like drowning in darkness. Or in light. It was like both. It wasn't like anything. It splashed around her knees and soaked her robes, and then she and Geradde were staggering up out of the dragon's black pool, and Geradde let her go at last because there was nowhere else to run. He turned, then, to face his brother, his back to the dragon.

Nemienne was terrified of what Sa-Telis might do, of what his mages might do. But she found it impossible to turn away from the dragon. This close, she might have reached out and touched it. She wondered if her touch would rouse it, and whether she dared. She might, to stop Telis. The dragon frightened her much more than Prince Telis, but not the same way; she feared it, but she trusted it, too. Not to help, exactly, but to be powerful and . . . uncorrupted. Pure. As the darkness was pure, here beneath the mountain.

Telis was saying something, and Geradde answered, but Nemienne didn't listen. All her attention was bent on the dragon. Its nearer eye hadn't opened . . . yet, but she had the sense it might at any moment. Its antennae swayed gently overhead, as though to an unfelt current that stirred through the darkness as through the sea; greenish light glinted along their length, aquamarine and emerald. One slow drop of water ran down the length of its nearest antenna and fell, with a reverberating *plink*, into the dragon's pool. As though in deliberate echo, a single drop of blood ran down Geradde's cut hand, spiraled around his thumb, and fell into the pool as well. *Plink.* Ripples ran sluggishly through the black water and against the pale stone.

The dragon's eye slitted open.

It was black, black, black. No light had ever gleamed in those ageless eyes. Nemienne clutched Geradde's arm convulsively.

"The harp!" Prince Telis said, urgently, too near. "The knife and the harp!"

Nemienne turned at last, to see Prince Telis snatch the long bone from Mage Perodde's hand and stride across the length of the dragon's cavern, to the dead torches and the great harp. He didn't run, but he moved fast. Mage Isonne called out, sounding urgent, even frightened, but Nemienne didn't understand what the woman said. She was caught by Telis, by what he would do and what he intended to do. She watched, with a frozen sense of inevitability, as the prince raised the bone, glimmering with blood and light and swept it deliberately across the full span of the harp's strings.

Each note fell separately into the deep silence of the caverns, reverberating like a drop of water falling into a depthless pool, sending ripples through the darkness as through water. Each note seemed to Nemienne to be pitched to the echoes of light that run through the long span of a day or a year: the soft pearlescent light of dawn and the sharp, clean light of morning; the golden light of noon and the lavender of dusk. Light and the memory of light ran into the caverns like a rising tide, and then ebbed as the tide might ebb at the dark of the moon. Over all those notes that rose and subsided, the deepest string sounded, made of darkness, pitched to the memory of darkness. *That* note did not ebb, but lingered, reverberating and gathering strength.

Behind Nemienne and Geradde, the dragon opened its eye and lifted its head: Nemienne felt it stir and flinched, both glad it was roused and desperately frightened.

Geradde cried out, a sharp wordless cry, clutching his cut hand to his chest.

Prince Telis cried out, too, something with words in it, as

the dragon shifted the long coil of its neck and began to turn its immense, elegant head.

Nemienne caught Geradde's hand and pulled him with her along the endless undulating length of the dragon and into the dark, and out of the dark, one step and then another, following the lingering reverberations of the deepest string of the harp, stumbling from the dark into a memory of light, following the echo of the dragon's heartbeat and the rush of the tide. Behind them, Prince Telis shouted. Nemienne didn't listen, but shoved Geradde so that he staggered and fell away into light. The dragon rose, she *felt* it rise, she knew it was pouring itself out of stone all around them, but she leaped after Geradde, out of darkness and into piercing brightness, away from the rising tides and into brilliant cutting winds, with all around them the echo of the dragon's heartbeat and the sound of the harp.

-18-

As soon as Irelle and Karah had retired to the other room of Toma's tiny apartment, closing the door gently behind them, Tepres looked at Taudde and raised one expressive eyebrow.

Taudde raised his hands. "No," he said firmly. "My cousin did not discuss her ideas with me. I had no idea she was thinking along such . . . poetic lines. Quite like something from a song, really. Now, don't give me that look. Any bard would say the same, I'm sure."

And, whatever Irelle might think of the keiso of Lonne, he suspected she would dismiss any such concern if she thought this political match important enough. Women could be ruthless. He believed now that his cousin certainly could be. He asked cautiously, "Do you . . . think you might like Irelle?"

"Does it signify?" Tepres asked coolly. "I don't imagine fondness is foremost in your cousin's mind."

Taudde did not entirely believe in the Seriantes prince's cool tone. He said, "I never knew her well; she must have been about fourteen when I left Kalches—too young for me to notice. I was as self-centered as any young man, I suppose," he added reflectively.

"I have no doubt of it," murmured Tepres, who was some years younger than Taudde.

Taudde grinned, but declined to rise to the bait. He said only, "She was an intelligent girl, much focused on her music, as I recall. But of course, as Heronn's eldest, she would have been raised to set her duty as a Lariodde before any passion for music or sorcery."

"Indeed? She might have made a good keiso."

"Irelle?" Taudde could not quite keep the surprise out of his tone.

This earned him a sharp look. "A keiso need not be beautiful," Tepres said, faintly chiding. Taudde could clearly hear the undertone behind his spoken words: *uncivilized foreigners*. But after a pause, Tepres added, more kindly, "Your cousin has the confidence and the poise. And, I think, the passion for her art."

"You see that? Yes, Larioddes are often powerfully torn between sorcery and duty, and Irelle's learned metalworking in service to her art, did you mark that? That's rare for a girl."

"Is it? Then it's a pity she must put blood and rank before her own desires. Well, that is the lot of a daughter of high birth, as it is for a son. But she might do well in Lonne. Do you think she understands that, in Lonne, she would be able to put her passion for music or sorcery foremost?"

"I'm almost certain she's thought the whole thing through from every direction," Taudde said honestly. "Or her mother has. Aunt Ines doesn't miss much, and I think Irelle must take after her."

"Indeed." Tepres paced across the room, swung around, and came back. "Well, I will tell you, it pleases me that your cousin has a passion for music. Or sorcery, or both. She might perhaps learn to be sympathetic toward the keiso. And toward Karah."

"Ah!" said Taudde, and paused.

"A king need not be greatly fond of his wife," Tepres said, an edge coming into his tone. "Especially a queen who has her own resources and interests. Goodwill and cordiality are sufficient. But it is better if queen and keimiso are friends, one with the other. Then all of Lonne is happier and more pleasant."

"Shall I point that out to Irelle?"

Tepres gave him a look. "Do you think she requires you to make it clear to her?"

Taudde wanted to laugh. But he restrained himself.

"Tell me of your cousin," Tepres said abruptly. "Of your family. This troublesome uncle, Manaskes. Your Uncle Heronn. Tell me of this house and this town." He gave Taudde a shrewd glance. "Nothing you would not care to lay out for a Seriantes. An ordinary tale of ordinary life. What is it like to grow up a Lariodde of Kalches?"

Taudde resisted the urge to say, *Well, after the field of Brenedde . . .* Nothing that had happened at Brenedde was any fault of Tepres.' He said after a moment, "Next to my grandfather, my uncle Heronn probably seems very quiet, perhaps even insignificant. But I imagine Uncle Manaskes is finding out right now that Heronn never forgets a detail and can always lay his hand right on any dangling thread, and always knows just how to resolve any dissonance that might have gotten started. I'll tell you about the time Penad and I had reason to be grateful for Heronn's imperturbability. It had to do with a bell, a mirror, and a goat—"

Tepres interrupted him. "Does your cousin Irelle come into this tale?"

Taudde gave Prince Tepres a severe look. "Not this one. She was a child of ten or so at the time. If you want Irelle stories, you can ask Aunt Ines, if you should get the chance and have the nerve. Do you want to hear my story or not?"

"A . . . goat," Tepres said musingly. "Already it sounds like a story of Kalches." He tipped his head toward the closed door that led to the bedchamber. "Do you suppose they are telling stories in there?"

Taudde laughed. "Undoubtedly. Probably about us."

Tepres answering smile seemed a little forced. Of course, it was quite true that any tales Karah might tell Irelle would almost certainly be about him. Taudde was just as glad Leilis was not at the moment trading tales with the others, and while this was mostly because he preferred to hope she was safe in Cloisonné House, he had to admit that it was also a little bit because he would just as soon not feature in too many of those stories.

***

Karah perched on the end of the flat bed, watching Irelle, who was pacing from one side to the other of the plain little room. She wished she had something to do with her hands. Irelle had her flute; as she paced, she was running absently through different fingering exercises. The flute was not like any instrument Karah had ever seen. One held it sideways to play it, she surmised from the way Irelle handled it, which seemed peculiar; and it was made of silver, with all kinds of complicated fittings. She wondered what a silver flute would sound like. She couldn't imagine it would be very similar to the warm voice of an ordinary wooden flute. The voice of a silver flute would no doubt be pure and clean and cold, like the voices of stars, if stars could sing.

She would have liked to ask Irelle to play a little, but perhaps bardic sorcerers—or sorceresses—did not like to play just for the joy of the music. Irelle had not played that flute at all during the nearly three days Karah had spent in the household of Lady Ines. But then, Karah had not wished to put herself forward and had kept to her room a good deal, and Irelle had spent little time in her mother's household in those days, and so there had been little opportunity for Karah to hear her if she had.

Irelle stopped pacing abruptly, thrusting the flute back through its loop on her belt and turning to face Karah. She held her shoulders back and straight, like a man—like a man facing an enemy, or something he feared. Karah clasped her hands in her lap, lowered her eyes, and tried to look harmless. She wished she were wearing her keiso robes and not this immodest foreign garment that curved around her breasts and hips, but she had to acknowledge that this style of dress suited the Kalchesene princess, accenting her slighter curves and preventing her from looking like a boy even when she stood in so aggressive a stance. Perhaps any garment or style would seem appropriate, to a woman who had grown up wearing—

"So the flower girls of Lonne marry noblemen and bear them bastard sons, do they? Sons that turn against them and against their legitimate sons, one gathers! And where are the *wives* in all this?" Irelle demanded.

It was much more open anger and suspicion than a woman of Lonne would show—certainly much more than a keiso would consider fitting. Karah admired her more than ever. Keeping her eyes lowered, she answered softly, as she would have answered a man. "I am amazed to learn that brothers never quarrel in Kalches."

After a moment when it might have gone either way, Irelle laughed in reluctant appreciation, lifting a hand to concede the point.

Karah smiled at her. "The sons that keimiso bear on the left should be friends to the right-hand sons of her keisonne. It is not always so, but that is how it should be. It is better if the proper wife and the flower wife are friends. That is not always so either, but that is how it should be."

"Do they all take . . . flower wives? All the noblemen of Lonne?" Irelle's tone was not so hostile now. Now she mostly sounded curious.

"No, not all. But important men take wives as they are directed by their families. Keimiso they may take as their hearts desire, if the keiso and her Mother agree."

"But they don't, always. They can choose otherwise, you say. This Rue you mentioned, who prefers dancing to marriage—"

"It is easier for keiso to make their own choices," Karah said sympathetically. "Women born to the high or low court marry, like men, as their families direct. Occasionally a girl will not accept her family's choice, but runs away to become keiso. There is a famous play where that happens; I have been learning the little gaodd poems from it. It is rare that a family will press a girl so hard as to persuade her to renounce the family of her birth and take a flower name. But I know a keiso who made that choice."

"Do you? Is she . . . happy?"

Karah lifted her hands in a gesture of uncertainty. "Happy? I do not know, but she seems content. She is older, now, and retired from the public eye. She teaches the deisa. She teaches them deportment, and the gaodd poems, and to converse intelligently about poetry and the classic plays. She was teaching me, too, because I became a keiso without really being a deisa first and so I am still learning."

Irelle came closer, hesitated, and at last sat down at the other end of the bed. "Can a man take many flower wives at the same time?"

Karah stared at her. Finally, finding her voice, she said in a tone that came out hushed, "But that would completely—no one would *ever*—" She imagined what Narienneh, Mother of Cloisonné House would say if a man proposed to her that he should take one of her daughters as a *second* keimiso, and couldn't help but laugh. "Oh! It would *never* happen. Even if a keiso would accept such an offer, even if a man were *so* wealthy as to buy *every* woman her own house and set up *all* their sons in professions and buy *every* daughter into a proper House . . . even if he could do that, the entire flower world would be *terribly* offended." Irelle's open astonishment made Karah laugh again. She added quickly, "I am not laughing at you! I'm just, I'm thinking of what a man's life would be like if he suggested such a thing. If he were married, his wife's family would be *so* angry, but even if he had no true wife, the Mother of his first keimiso would be just as offended. Someone would write a play, I'm sure. No one wants to be famous because of a *comic* play! I know a playwright who would probably be very amused at the idea; I will have to mention it to him . . ." then she thought of how far away Lonne was, how far away Cloisonné House was, and the bubbles of laughter died away.

But now Irelle was looking faintly amused herself. Much of her stiffness had eased. She leaned back against the headboard of the bed and observed thoughtfully, "So a man only ever has one . . . flower wife. And he buys his flower wife her own house. She doesn't live in *his* house. And he supports her sons and dowers her daughters . . . the arrangement sounds more civilized that I'd imagined."

Karah tried not to laugh again. "Of course it is civilized. Lonne is the Pearl of the West! Though I am sure your town here is very nice as well," she added with painstaking courtesy.

"Well, we think so," Irelle said drily. She gave Karah a searching look. "You are in love with Tepres Seriantes, of course. Perhaps . . . perhaps that may speak well of him."

Karah blushed, unable to answer this at all.

"He seems very polite, at least," Irelle mused. "And thoughtful, once you get a glimpse beneath that icy manner. He is very arrogant, of course. And so formal. I suppose it's only natural a Seriantes prince would be stiff. Or perhaps he only seems so because his position is a little uncertain just now . . ."

"No," Karah admitted. "He *is* arrogant. He is proud, and vain, and strict, and always . . . correct in everything. He always knows people are looking at him—they always *are*, you know, as though he were an actor who could never leave the stage . . ."

"You're smiling. You *are* in love with him."

"Well, he is also kind, and brave, and intelligent . . ."

"Stop!" ordered Irelle. "Before I decide this is the hero of an epic." She went on thoughtfully, "Whatever his quality, there *is* an echo underlying his voice and his heartbeat, though. I do hear it."

"Like the tides of the sea, Nemienne says. Nemienne is my sister," Karah explained. "She was—she was with us, when Prince Sehonnes came, but we all—we all came through the door into Kalches, but I don't know if Nemienne ran through some other door or . . ."

"I'm sorry."

Karah tried to smile. "I'm sure she is all right. She must be. She'd lived in that house for months, she knew all its strange doors, some only steps away . . . and Prince Sehonnes had no reason to care one way or another about my sister . . ." except Nemienne knew a little bit about magecraft and a little bit about sorcery and a little bit about the dragon of Lonne. Karah could think of more than one reason a prince might have cared very much about Nemienne. She picked up the flat pillow and hugged it to herself in a vain attempt at comfort, all her fears crowding back into her mind now that she had a moment to think of them.

"These days are filled with dangers for us all, and the perils our friends and family face are worse for us than our own," Irelle said, more kindly than she had yet spoken to Karah. Her own family and friends were in peril, too, of course.

After a moment of silence that was uncomfortable yet somehow companionable, Irelle tilted her head thoughtfully. "You've met his father, too, I gather. A ruthless man, Geriodde Seriantes; so everyone agrees. Pitiless toward his enemies, equally so toward his own sons. A hard man. But honorable, my grandfather says. He kept every promise he ever made to us. My cousin seems to have trusted him to keep his word to him, though I know Taudde hated him when he was younger."

"The king . . . it was . . . it is complicated, between Prince Tepres and his father." Karah did not feel it would be right to tell this Kalchesene princess much about that tense relationship, so she let this diplomatically vague comment stand on its own.

"Yes? One suspects this young Dragon is much the same as his father: honorable and ruthless and powerful. Or that he will be, when he grows into himself. Provided he has a chance to grow into himself, but surely among us we can all . . . make everything come out the way it should. But . . . this connection between the Seriantes line and this dragon . . . I suppose it exists between the, what is your term? The left-hand sons and the dragon as well."

Karah spread her hands to show she had no idea. "My sister would know about such matters, perhaps. Or your cousin. I think he understands the dragon as well as anyone."

"He thinks so, too, I'm sure. Still, Taudde is almost as gifted as he thinks he is, my mother says."

"I hope he is even more gifted," murmured Karah. "I think we will need him, your people and mine. I think he understands both Kalches and Lirionne as well as anyone, and I think we will need that." She hesitated, and then added, "I wish we knew how . . . how matters stood now, between your uncle and your father and . . . everyone. Do you suppose your grandfather's man will come back soon?"

"I hope so. I want to know how Grandfather is." Irelle, now less angry and nervous, eased down to lie on the bed, propping herself up on an elbow. "Tell me more about the dragon, about what happened. Taudde barely said anything, and you know we weren't supposed to go up to the tower to ask him about it—though I thought about it! I know you said you don't know everything, but you must know something. Will you tell me?"

Karah thought about this. Then she smiled. Storytelling was an art much practiced by the keiso, and she thought she could tell this one in a way that would make Irelle see Tepres and his father and even her cousin Taudde a little more as they really were. She began, "In a city of gray stone and mist, between the steep rainswept mountains and the sea, there lived a merchant with his eight daughters . . ."

***

It was a long, uncomfortable evening, and, as the girls had taken over Toma's bedchamber, an extremely long and strikingly uncomfortable night. Taudde would not have dared venture out of the guard captain's apartment even if he'd had the key to the door, but since Irelle had the key, the temptation was negated anyway. But, though one could nap a little sitting against the wall, Taudde found it impossible to sleep. Especially when worries and fears pressed all about him. He expected every moment for Toma Piriodde to reappear, but this didn't happen. Taudde could hardly believe that Uncle Heronn and Aunt Ines hadn't yet forced Uncle Manaskes to back down . . . unless Grandfather was worse, and they were too distracted by that. Or unless Uncle Manaskes had far more support than Taudde had hoped.

Tepres had declined to take the chair, though Taudde had offered it to him. The chair was as uncomfortable as the floor, after a little while. The night stretched out. Taudde had an endless supply of tales, but not endless patience for telling them. Fortunately there was water in the accommodation, but the hours seemed even longer once he had realized he was hungry. How provoking that no one had thought of such elementary matters when they might have done something about it. He forbore to mention it now, and of course Tepres would not complain.

There was an hour-glass on the shelf near the ledgers. Taudde turned it when he heard the house bell strike once to indicate the hinge of the night, but later he dozed and the next time he glanced at it, the sand had all run down into the base and he had no idea what hour it might be. The lamp was still lit, but an oil lamp like that one might have any size reservoir. There was no window by which one might glimpse the dawn . . . he turned the hour-glass anyway, for something to do, shrugging at Tepres' ironic glance.

The sand had nearly run down again when a faint scratching at the door brought both Taudde and Tepres to their feet. Of course Taudde expected Toma Piriodde, or if all had gone very badly, it might be anyone . . .

The door opened just enough, and Aunt Ines whisked through. After the first startled instant, Taudde found he was not at all surprised. He was also pleased, especially when he realized that she was burdened with a highly promising basket over her arm and an equally promising pottery jug in her other hand.

"Taudde, my dear, how very uncomfortable," she said warmly, in a low voice, after shutting the door behind her and sending a keen glance around. "How like Toma not to think of extra pillows! Where are the girls? Oh, of course. No, don't wake them, they may as well sleep, I fear it will be a long day as well as an interminable night. Eminence, I do apologize for leaving you to wait without word. I hoped to come—or send someone—long since."

"Not at all," Tepres said politely. "We have been quite at ease, I'm sure. I hope your night was equally uneventful, Lady Ines. Or rather, may I offer my hope that the night was happily eventful?"

"Happily eventful! What a nice phrase." Aunt Ines smiled at Tepres, though with, Taudde thought, a shrewd glint in her eyes. But there was no obvious calculation in the undertones of her voice as she went on, "Yes, I'm pleased to say that Berente is, if not actually back on his feet, at least rational. Or, well, one would not like to overstate the case—articulate, I should say, and he would be far more rational if he were far less impatient."

"He's better, then?" Taudde was immensely relieved to hear it. "Aunt, this is probably not the time to convey my sincere apologies to him, but I do beg his pardon, and yours, and Heronn's as well."

"So you should," Aunt Ines told him severely. "Really, Taudde, one would think you'd have learned to contain your temper by this time. Did you think Berente wouldn't have answered that young idiot Penad as he deserved?"

Taudde bowed his head, accepting this rebuke.

His aunt said more gently, "Well, it was not entirely your fault, Taudde. Penad's idiocy might have done it right then, even if you hadn't added your own. Something of the kind was bound to happen soon enough. Berente isn't the sort to avoid excitement, which unfortunately this year does seem guaranteed to provide in abundance. It might even be better that he's had this warning before the solstice."

"I am most relieved to hear King Berente is recovering," Tepres said politely. "It was his heart, of course?"

"Of course, and if Berente would avoid agitation, it would no doubt be easier for the bardic surgeons to keep him in order.

Alas, that doesn't seem at all likely. However, the surgeons thinks they have managed to calm the spasms of the heart for, well, for the next little while, we shall hope." Aunt Ines handed Taudde the jug. "This should soothe your nerves, which no doubt, like all of ours, have been tested by this night. It's ale; not quite suitable for breakfast, I suppose, but perhaps we can consider this a very late supper rather than a very early breakfast. I hope I remembered to include some mugs . . ." Setting her basket on Toma's desk, Aunt Ines began poking about in its depths.

"What *is* the hour?" Taudde helped her lay out an eclectic assortment of foods, some indeed more suitable for supper than breakfast: mutton and turnip pastries, onion turnovers, and little pies of eggs and dandelion greens. But there were also boiled eggs still in the shell and dark rye loaves still hot from the ovens, along with a crock of sweet butter and one of honey.

"Well after dawn, but the morning is all at odd angles, as you might imagine," Aunt Ines said briskly. "It's a wonder anybody managed to set the bread to rise, or remembered to bake it. That fool Manaskes is still ranting up and down—I thought he would wear himself out last night, but unfortunately he seems to have gained a second wind this morning, probably because he finally persuaded Peranne to come in on his side."

"Did he? I'd thought better of Aunt Peranne."

"So had I, but to be fair, it *has* been very unsettling having Berente out of the way, and my husband is quite determined— rightly so, I would say—to keep the whole business completely out of his sight for a little while longer, but that does mean Heronn hasn't been quite able to exert himself just yet. It's doubly unfortunate about Peranne, because of course she's so much better than Manaskes at thinking things through and sorting out complications into neat little lists. Quite a lot of people find a competent, organized woman reassuring, you know, and are inclined to listen to Manaskes now that they can see he's got Peranne to stop him going off with only half his harp strung and no way to get the rest of the strings."

Taudde, who was quite willing to have the supper he'd missed and then the breakfast suggested by the hour, held up a mutton pastry and looked inquiringly at Tepres, handed it over and bit into one of his own. The ale was the best the king's larder had to offer, pleasantly bitter and with a clean aftertaste.

"And, of course," Aunt Ines added, breaking open one of the rye loaves and opening the crock of butter, "Heronn is having a terrible time without Irelle."

"Irelle, Aunt?"

"Yes, Irelle. My daughter, your cousin, Irelle. I believe you know her."

Somehow Taudde had not remembered Aunt Ines being quite so sarcastic.

She added, "Irelle is a steady girl, you know, and such a help to her father. She would be able to counter Peranne quite effectively, I'm sure, except that all things considered it doesn't seem wise for her to show herself just yet."

"She certainly has made her opposition to Manaskes clear. I did wonder if the notion was yours, Aunt."

"Oh, Irelle is entirely capable of coming up with such designs entirely on her own, I assure you, though I'm glad to say she did discuss this one with me. I admit it was difficult to know how to advise her."

"I'm a bit surprised you didn't suggest that, after all, Grandfather has a good many other granddaughters, some of perfectly suitable age and adventurous temperament. Or did you?"

Aunt Ines lifted an amused eyebrow. "You've been away too long, Nephew. Miskelle is married now; Janne is both married and carrying; she will come to her time in another month. I doubt you would seriously suggest Tarina, but if you would, allow me to disabuse you of the notion: she would be completely unsuited as the lynchpin to such an extraordinary alliance." She smiled suddenly at Tepres. "Is it true your palace has a thousand rooms, all carved into the mountains above Lonne?"

"Not quite so many," Tepres told her. "Perhaps two hundred. Some are merely storerooms, of course."

"It's a very impressive fortress," Taudde assured his aunt. "But—"

"Taudde, my dear. No other girl would do, you know. If Berente permitted any other granddaughter to enter into such a bargain, it would be taken as a shameful act. Sacrificing a daughter of Kalches in return for a heartless peace with Lirionne! No, it wouldn't do."

"But—"

"Hush. Listen. It's different if it's Irelle. If Heronn's daughter, Berente's heir, goes to Lirionne, it will because the young Dragon has given his throne to Kalches in return for a sensible peace." She glanced at Tepres again. "Or so it will be perceived by my people."

He inclined his head, acknowledging this without commenting on how the people of Lirionne would perceive such a match.

Ines didn't ask. She only gave Taudde a thoughtful look and added, "Besides, during these past few months, Irelle tells me, she has begun dreaming of the sea."

Taudde was caught by this. "Dreaming of the sea? Only recently? Since the dragon was stirred to wakefulness, perhaps. But she didn't mention that to me."

"Well, she wouldn't, would she? To you least of all, perhaps, since you were free to defy Berente and she was not. Or had no reason grave enough to consider it, at least, until now."

Taudde nodded understanding. "Now that the sea has entered her dreams, you may find those dreams do not fade, Aunt Ines. You mustn't think less of Irelle, if—"

"I am hardly likely to think less of my daughter under any reasonable circumstances. Nor is *she* likely to give me cause."

Unlike Taudde. To be sure. He made no attempt to answer this.

Aunt Ines added, in quite a different tone, "These flower girls do present a challenge to a young woman's pride, I admit. Though, given a political marriage, one can see the benefit of codifying the, shall we say, supplementary arrangements that are so likely to occur. At least this way a woman does not have to *wonder.*"

Tepres, stung at last, said stiffly, "One would naturally be dismayed to think that any woman, whether a foreign princess or a keiso of the flower world, should feel her pride in any way damaged by connection to the throne of Lirionne. Whether arranged for political considerations or otherwise, any civilized man would be ashamed to bring embarrassment to any woman who had honored him with her trust."

"Yes, provided we all go on with Irelle's notion, I do find that sort of statement heartening. I will assure Heronn of that. Fathers, you know. He has not yet quite begun to consider the possible advantages of this . . . arrangement, and of course, it's been difficult to argue it through, what with not quite wishing to invite every possible cousin to join the argument."

"One rather imagines that many fraught discussions are taking place just now, as we say, beneath Nijiadde Falls," Tepres observed drily.

This meant, covered by the thunder of the cataract, Taudde knew. "We say here, to speak behind the avalanche."

"Of course," Tepres acknowledged. "I shall be most interested to hear Prince Heronn's response when next we meet. Or King Berente's, perhaps; I am sure we all wish him a rapid recovery from his illness, as well as a moderate temper."

"I'm sure we all do indeed," Ines agreed, smiling, and began to gather up some of the oiled papers that had wrapped the mutton pastries. "I'm sorry that I must ask you to remain in these rooms for just a few hours longer—I hope not another night, though I will see to additional pillows if so. Do make free of all this food. Toma or I will bring more, and news of Berente's recovery, I trust."

***

When she and Irelle finally ventured out to the other room, Karah was very glad to find Lady Ines had been before them, with food and word of poor King Berente—Prince Heronn must be having a terrible time. Karah had hardly met the quiet, responsible heir, but she liked him and wished he might very soon find a chance to haul the other prince, Manaskes, up sharply. "Perhaps today your father will feel he may answer your uncle," she said hopefully to Irelle. "It sounds as though your grandfather is much better."

"Better, anyway," Irelle acknowledged. "*Much* better, I

doubt. He needs to think of peaceful things and not enrage himself, but I grant, no one would recognize him if he tried. My father does better with him than anyone, but I also wish he would put a stop to Uncle Manaskes' posturing. Aunt Peranne has persuaded herself Manaskes is right, you say, Taudde? That's enraging enough right there. My father's patient, but my mother must be livid, too. But you don't see her working herself into apoplexy." She picked up the crock of honey and looked into it critically. "You might have left a little more honey, Cousin."

"It wasn't full to start. I left more than half. Have an egg."

Irelle sniffed, but she also perched on the edge of the guard captain's desk and began to peel eggs. Karah accepted the first one, untwisted the paper with the salt, and ate the egg gratefully. Despite Taudde explaining how late it was, she *felt* it was early in the day. She never slept so late, but without windows . . . and of course she and Irelle had stayed up late telling each other stories. She would have liked the warm comfort of rice porridge, and she didn't quite feel up to the onion turnovers, but the eggs were good. And the bread was still a little bit warm. No one had a knife, but one could pull the loaves apart and spread butter— and honey, despite Irelle's complaints there was plenty—on the chunks.

"Irelle thinks she would like to visit the sea," she told Taudde, carefully not looking at Tepres because she didn't want to embarrass either him or Irelle.

"Aunt Ines said something of the kind," Taudde agreed, and lifted an eyebrow at his cousin. "Dreams, I hear. You didn't mention that to me."

"I hardly had the chance." Irelle regarded Taudde, her expression thoughtful. "Tell me, Cousin, did *you* learn from the sea what you went to Lonne to learn? Was it worth what you gave up to go there?" She didn't look at Tepres either, Karah noticed. Nor did Tepres put himself forward. He leaned against the wall near the door, listening. She saw how he didn't seem to want to look at her, how his gaze lingered on Irelle instead. Poor Tepres. Everywhere he turned, another duty lay before him. She wished he weren't a prince at all. Everything would be so much simpler if he'd been born on the left. Though then he wouldn't be who he was. Everything was so complicated.

Irelle was a little like him, really. Or actually, perhaps quite a lot like him. Karah had only realized this last night. It shouldn't have taken her so long, but they'd all been so distracted . . . but Irelle also had one duty after another lined up before her feet. Except her most important duties opposed one another. Poor Irelle.

Taudde had been considering his cousin's question. Now he said at last, "I learned something, certainly. I think I had . . . begun to learn how to listen to the sea. Sometimes you half-hear in your dreams a kind of harmony that forever after you seek in your heart . . ."

"Yes, that's true," Irelle conceded, sounding faintly startled.

"Of course you would feel that, too." Taudde plainly wasn't a bit surprised. "A *silver* flute, cousin?"

Irelle ran her thumb caressingly along her flute. "I like the purity of tone. I like how you have to wring that purity out of fire and pay the cost of it with the occasional burn."

It occurred to Karah that this was the kind of thing Rue might say about dancing, and that if Irelle had been born to a good family in Lonne, she would very likely have become a keiso. The thought was reassuring. Of course if Irelle married Tepres and became his wife and queen, she could hardly become a keiso. But she might be *like* a keiso, perhaps. She might be like the keiso who gave the greater measure of their passion to their art. Karah liked that idea very much. Women of good birth did not ordinarily venture much into the flower world or mingle with the keiso, but Karah could hardly see why Irelle should care for that particular custom . . . she would introduce Irelle to Rue and Bluefountain, and they could *all* be friends, and everyone would be happy because of the friendship between the king's queen and his keimiso . . .

Then Irelle caught Karah's attention by asking, "Eminence, if it came to war and there were no dragon, who do you think would win?"

Tepres answered courteously, "We of Lonne believed that when the solstice arrived, Kalches would test our resolve. Then we would crush Kalches completely."

"We of Kalches believed we would win back our bloody

fields with bardic sorcery and edged steel, and humble Lirionne arrogance."

Tepres opened a hand. "And so men quarrel."

"But there is this dragon."

"Just so."

Irelle pulled her flute out of her belt and turned it over in her fingers. Lifting it, she breathed a note into its mouthpiece. A single note, heart-stoppingly pure.

Taudde closed his eyes, hearing all the minor keys of loneliness contained in that one silvery note.

"Anyone might have heard that," Taudde rebuked her, but gently.

"I limited it," Irelle said absently. "I would like to see this dragon, I think. Or hear music written to evoke it."

"I'd like to evoke it for everyone to see," Taudde agreed. "That should certainly slow Manaskes down quite a lot. I've given it some thought—a great harp, perhaps underlain by your flute . . . that might indeed encourage both Uncle Heronn and Grandfather to agree with you, Cousin. You haven't actually discussed this with Grandfather, yet, I'm sure."

"The chance hadn't presented itself, and then suddenly it was impossible. It's important to choose the right moment for these conversations, Taudde. If you had ever learned that, you wouldn't have had to defy him to go on your little adventure."

Taudde opened his mouth and closed it again. He didn't know whether to laugh or throw something at her. He began, perhaps a trifle intemperately, "I think I—"

But then he paused, turning his head sharply as a slow, deep vibration began to tremble through the room. Not through the air so much as through the very wood of the floor and the walls; not an audible sound at first so much as a half-felt reverberation.

"The horns," Irelle said, sounding astonished. "The horns at the door. Some stranger has come into the house." She rose, quickly, and Taudde with her.

Karah, too, found herself on his feet. She was immediately afraid that this might be some envoy sent from Lonne to bargain with King Berente for Tepres. For his death, more likely than his life.

Then she realized that made no sense, because people came

and went all the time, so this must be different. Surely no official envoy would try to enter the king's house secretly.

Irelle's flute was in her hand, but she didn't seem afraid. Only surprised. She tilted her head, listening, and then slipped her flute through her belt. "A puzzle more than an alarm, I think," she said to the rest of them. "That's not so very urgent a tone. Still . . . still, a foreigner, one can think of one or two exciting possibilities. *I* think this may be precisely the right moment to stop hiding. Grandfather will hardly keep to his bed *now*. I think this is *just* the time go down and find out who this is. All of us."

-19-

Leilis had never been more grateful for the training she had absorbed from her earliest childhood. For all she hadn't changed her robes until this very year, she knew the keiso role so well she could not be shaken out of it merely by stepping out of Lonne into an entirely different country. Even though she had been dressed in the manner of a servant when she stepped through the door into a shock of cold light that could hardly have been more different from the soft warmth of Lonne.

A woman alone in a strange country, whether servant or keiso, had no choice but to depend on the kindness of strangers. Leilis knew how fortunate she had been, to find a Kalchesene man and his two sons almost the moment she had set her foot on the road that led down from the heights of the mountain. The man was some sort of merchant; so much she had gathered, though she had never known what goods might be bundled, tightly wrapped, on the sledges that must surely—so it seemed to her first startled glance—weigh far too much for the shaggy little ponies that drew them.

She had asked him why he did not wait for kinder weather to venture the mountain road, and he had laughed and answered that the strength of the winter had already broken and a man who wished to prosper had better not wait for high summer to cross the mountains. Then she had worried that surely she must weigh too much for any of the ponies to pull a sledge with her sitting on it, but the man had laughed again and said no, the road was good and Kedres only a little way, and the ponies would hardly notice her weight. He had picked her up himself and set her atop the leading sledge, first handing a bundle to each of his bashful sons to make room, and after that she had been surprised how easily the ponies went on and how quickly the town appeared below them.

Perhaps the people of Kalches were naturally generous to strangers. But Leilis doubted whether a man with her accent and her foreign mode of dress would have met with such hospitality. Particularly not on the very eve of the solstice.

It was hard, here, to believe the solstice was all but upon them, even once they had made their way down from the cold heights. It was almost like magic how the sledges ran bumpily from winter into spring, and then from spring into earliest summer—pressing an entire change of seasons into mere hours. In less than a day, the snow turned to rain and then blew away, the wind gentled, the sun came out bright and not entirely without warmth, and Leilis shyly gave the man back the blanket he had thrown over her feet. He laughed at her, not unkindly, and said girls had no business wearing house slippers up to the heights—the only comment he had made about her manner of dress or inexplicable appearance in the heights. She had no idea who he thought she was. It seemed part of his hospitality that he did not ask.

The man took her to his own home—where else; but it seemed to Leilis another mark of his generosity. His wife, startled to discover that her husband had brought home a half-frozen young woman, was nevertheless all that was kind. She installed Leilis in her own daughter's room and brought, in a hospitable rush, warm water and heated towels, salve for feet blistered from the too-long walk down the slopes of the open mountains to the high road, hot broth and bread, and a robe that was nothing like the proper robes of Lonne, but pleasant for a chilled woman who wanted nothing but to sit close by the fire and warm herself through.

"I've hung your things by the fire. They're light enough, they should dry in an hour or so," she told Leilis. "And they should be warm enough now you're down from the mountains. Do you have people here? I can send one of the boys with a message—" she paused invitingly.

"I am so grateful," murmured Leilis. It was true, but she hesitated over what else to say. At last she said diffidently, "I should . . . is this . . . is it far from this place to the house of the King of Kalches? I think I must go there, as quickly as I may, if you would be so kind as to set me on the proper road."

"So you *are* from Lirionne," declared the woman, sounding rather pleased about it. "You've brought word of the doings in Lonne? It's one after another these past few days, rushing up to the king's house; we wonder Lirionne isn't empty, with all the men who've hurried to bring word of one kind or another. But you're the first *woman* we've seen on that road. Brave or foolish or both, I'd say, and how you got as far as you did in those slippers, I'll never know." She handed the empty mug to her daughter, a girl of fifteen or so who was desperately excited, and sent her for more broth. The girl whisked off and back so fast that Leilis was still considering exactly what to say when she returned.

"I am from Lonne, yes," she murmured at last. "And very fortunate to have encountered your husband. Brave and foolish, I grant you both, but mainly driven by need. I do have word, though I would wonder, first, if you have heard of what might . . . of who . . . that is . . ."

"You've heard Taudde Lariodde's come home, have you?" asked the woman wisely. "Both a comfort and a trouble to his grandfather, that one, and we all know he's brought one of the Dragon princes back with him, which ought to sweeten his grandfather, one would think, but for all the confusion, we hardly know from one hour to the next what all's going on. Now, careful there, those blisters need gentle treatment and bandages!"

Leilis smiled at her and began to take things out of her satchel. Scented lotion for her hands and feet, her softest and most intricately embroidered slippers, her proper robes, powdered lapis and pearl, delicate bangles for her wrists and her jeweled gull pin and strands of pearls for her hair. "Have you a mirror?" she asked. "I would be so grateful."

"None of the *men* from Lonne were at all like *you!*" exclaimed the daughter, and blushed fiercely, but her mother was speechless.

"I am a keiso of Cloisonné House," Leilis agreed, smiling gravely at the daughter. "No one else is like the keiso of Lonne, and we of Cloisonné House are the most elegant of all. For a man, it is different, but for a woman, beauty and poise are both weapon and shield. Where natural beauty is insufficient, poise and artifice will do. Let me show you."

And very soon, Leilis was clad from top to toe with the sweeping elegance of a keiso of Lonne. She showed the women how she draped the slate-blue and dark silver-blue overrobe so that the darker slate-gray of the underrobe showed at throat and wrist. "We of Cloisonné House prefer restrained elegance to a vulgar show," she murmured. "Darker colors, plainer robes . . ."

"But the birds!" cried the daughter.

"This is restrained," Leilis assured her, amused, glancing down at the lacework of ocean spray all around the hem and the narrow-winged gulls flying from knee to shoulder. "Older keiso are generally more subtle." She had put the three silver bangles on her right wrist, and the three of pewter and bronze on her left. They all chimed delicately when she moved her hands.

The daughter helped her take down and rebraid her hair, this time with the strands of pearls. Leilis herself carefully put her hair up afterward, and arranged the strand of tiny slate-colored pearls to swing behind one ear while the daughter held a mirror for her. Then she dusted the lapis and pearl powders on her eyelids and spiraling up her cheek.

"So beautiful!" the daughter declared, stepping back to view Leilis with awe. "Are you to *marry* him, then, the Dragon prince? Is that why you came—to find him?"

Leilis saw that the girl wanted it to be so: a tale of romance, true love that had set wings on a woman's feet and carried her across the mountains to find her beloved. It would have made a wonderful tale. It *would* make a wonderful tale; she could see a play like that being performed in the theaters of Lonne, eventually, with Moonflower of Cloisonné House in her place and the brave Prince Tepres waiting in durance for her to find him. She *hoped* such a play would be shown eventually in the theaters.

But she answered with the truth: "The one who would wed the prince is more beautiful than I. But no one knows with certainty where she is. So I came, in hope that your king would hear me."

"Oh, he will have to listen to *you*," the girl promised her earnestly.

"A weapon and a shield, eh?" said her mother, not exactly skeptically. "I'd say it was wise of your people to send you after all—and it's as well our king is an old man and his heir firmly married! Even so, I wonder if my man did so well as we thought, bringing you off the mountain, or if he ought to take you now to the king's house as you wish."

"Mother!" said the girl, embarrassed.

"Surely it is for your king to judge whether he will hear what word I bring?" Leilis said gently. "But the keiso of Lonne hope for peace between our peoples. And our prince hopes for the same, I know." She glanced at the daughter. "Our Dragon prince has no hold on my heart. But *your* prince does."

"Taudde Lariodde?" exclaimed the woman, putting the tale together with admirable swiftness. "So that's why he was away from home so long!"

Leilis lowered her eyes modestly and murmured, "So you see why I wish for peace. Will you help me come before your king in good order? I would be very grateful."

Her whole family agreed. The man had been kind to her on the mountain road because she was a woman. But he hitched up his ponies again, this time to a wheeled cart, and carried Leilis from his doorstep to the cart, and brought her through the town to the king's house, because she was a keiso.

Leilis wished to thank the man and his family, but feared to give offense. So she waited until they came to the king's house. Then she let the man help her from the little cart, took the jeweled gull from her hair, and folded it into his hand. "For your daughter," she murmured when he tried to demur. "No, please permit me. It is the custom in Lonne. Quite possibly your kindness saved my life—certainly you and your family saved me a great deal of time and difficulty. Cloisonné House would be ashamed of me if I offered no token of my gratitude. Would you shame my Mother's teaching?"

This seemed a telling argument, for the man let her press the gull into his hand after all, and Leilis inclined her head to him once more and then turned and stepped between the immense curled ekonne horns that stood on either side of the door.

A long burring note sounded in challenge and warning as she passed between the horns. Leilis was not surprised. But she was not afraid, and she was most sincerely grateful to the man and his family, who had helped her come to this place in such beautiful order. She would look exactly as though she had stepped directly from Cloisonné House to the Kalchesene King's doorstep. She liked that idea very much. Let it seem that she had come straight to the door of this house by some unknown, inevitable magic.

No guardsman appeared until she had come all the way into the house, though the slow, mellow notes of the ekonne horns still lingered.

Then one came, hurriedly—unmistakably a guardsman, though not in anything Leilis could recognize as a uniform. He carried a flute in his hand rather than a sword. This amused her. She did not doubt the man's competence, and she knew well what bardic sorcery could do, but the idea of guardsmen answering an alarm with a musical instrument to hand rather than edged steel . . . she had to concentrate to suppress a smile. Then she changed her mind and smiled after all, a composed smile that brought the man skidding to a surprised halt.

Casting a covert glance around, Leilis found that she wasn't standing in a reception room as there would have been in a great house in Lonne, but only a broad hallway, perhaps twenty paces across, that led off to the left and right at strange not-quite-even diagonal angles, perhaps for some reason of magic or perhaps because of some whim of design. She frowned, having no idea which way to go. So she said to the guardsmen—there were three now, and one was armed with what seemed an ordinary sword rather than an instrument—"I am Seathrift of Cloisonné House. I am come with word of Lonne. I am come to speak to your king, if he would be so gracious as to grant me the favor of an audience." She spoke in the cadences of a tale, for she knew well that Kalches was a land of music, of bards, of poetry, and so she hoped to capture the curiosity of these men in that way.

The guardsmen looked at her and at one another in bewilderment. Leilis folded her hands inside the sleeves of her overrobe and waited. She was not afraid at all.

Yet another guardsman arrived, seeming in no great hurry. That was an illusion as much as any keiso pose, she thought. This one, Leilis was certain, must be the captain. He bore no weapon that she saw, neither instrument nor steel, but he had that air of unruffled command and the others deferred to him immediately and with obvious gratitude: *Here is this strange and beautiful woman; you deal with her.* The man pursed his lips, regarding Leilis with no sign of either favor nor disfavor, nor even a flicker of surprise.

"Says she's come with word of Lonne," muttered one of the other guardsmen to the captain. "Says she wants to speak to King Berente."

"Of course she does," acknowledged the captain without inflection. He looked Leilis up and down. "A keiso, I surmise," he said in a dry one. "Taudde's keiso, would you be?"

This was a genuine surprise. Leilis answered unhurriedly, "I am a keiso of Cloisonné House and of Lonne, but it is true that I am acquainted with Prince Chontas Taudde ser Omientes ken Lariodde. It is he I seek, but also I seek your own king, Berente ser Omientes ken Lariodde. For my House and my city and all my people, I seek converse with the King of Kalches."

The captain tilted his head. "I expect he will wish to speak to you as well. I expect it will not be possible to dissuade him from doing so, in fact. But he was bound to insist soon on rising from his bed in any case, I imagine." Dismissing the other guardsmen with a lift of his hand, he added, "Go find—"

But at this moment, another group of Kalchesene folk arrived all in a clump. These were young men and older men and two women of middle years, but the one foremost was perhaps in his fourth decade, by no means old enough to be the king. He was heavyset; imposing in that bluff, hearty way some men developed as they grew older. Leilis imagined she might see something of Taudde in the angle of his bones; indeed, she saw a general resemblance among all these people. But this was a man who seemed energetic without seeming assured; confident without seeming poised. She could see, from the way the guard captain's eyes narrowed and the slight stiffening of his back, that he was not pleased by the advent of this man or his entourage.

Then the man's gaze crossed Leilis, and he stumbled to a halt, all his people scattering around him in no particular order. "Toma! *Who* is *this?*" he demanded.

The captain said briefly to the nearest guardsman, "Go inform Heronn." Then he said to the newcomer, with a very slight inclination of his head, "Lord Manaskes."

"There's no need to disturb Heronn," snapped the man.

"I beg your pardon, noble lord," murmured Leilis. "But surely you speak of Prince Heronn Lakadde ser Omientes ken Lariodde, heir of King Berente ser Omientes ken Lariodde. I know that name. I do not know *your* name, noble lord."

There was a brief, sharp-edged pause. Other people were arriving, wide-eyed and curious: another guardsman or two, a scattering of women, a pair of young men. The man who had brought her had edged through the great doors as well and watched in fascination. Leilis was pleased. She suspected a wide audience was best, now.

"*You* are an emissary of Lonne? From Prince Sehonnes?" The man, Lord Manaskes, looked Leilis disdainfully up and down. "You are another of those flower girls, are you, and your prince sends *you* as an emissary? You may come with me, young woman—"

Another flower girl, Leilis thought, and wondered if she should go with this man after all—he undoubtedly knew something of Karah, which seemed promising—

"We shall wait to hear the king's pleasure," the guard captain said inflexibly. "Or his heir's. As this keiso of Lonne has pointed out, you are not he."

"Toma—"

"Lord Manaskes. You are not the heir. It should not take a foreign woman to point that out."

For a long moment, no one moved. No one in the growing gathering seemed even to breathe. If the guard captain noticed this, he didn't show it.

Then Lord Manaskes laughed, sharp and uneasy. "*Heronn* will not—"

"Stand by and let you claim Father's throne?" asked a level voice, as another man came into the increasingly crowded hallway. "No, I won't. Nor should you expect it. And the rest of you should be ashamed to support it." This was a man about the same age as Lord Manaskes, but with a contained, quiet presence that Manaskes entirely lacked.

"I should hope no one supports such foolishness! I'm sure Grandfather will have something to say about it!" declared someone else, a girl, but Taudde was with her—and, Leilis realized after that first startled instant, Karah and Prince Tepres as well.

Leilis immediately longed to go to Taudde. She was amused at herself when she realized she wanted to ask him first about the girl who had come with him. How ridiculous.

The girl, perhaps Karah's age, was striking, for though she was not pretty, she had the sort of poise that the best keiso owned. But anyone could guess she was probably a cousin or niece or something of the sort, for she had the long Lariodde face, those sharp bones. She wore the style considered proper here for women, the garment that accented breast and hip and then fell straight to the floor. It was not unattractive the way she wore it. Karah was dressed similarly, but with an air of being in costume, like an actress. Naturally, being Karah, she made the style look charming.

Prince Tepres also wore the Kalchesene style, though for men. He looked well, she thought. A little thinner, a little older, a little harder-tempered. But he looked well enough. Half the driving fear that had followed Leilis through the doorway of Ankennes' house fell away at last.

She could not run to join them, of course. That would not suit the graceful image she was building, and of course for a keiso, image was everything.

"You!" snapped Lord Manaskes, addressing the girl, moving aggressively forward. Prince Heronn matched him immediately, and the entire gathering shivered with uncertainty.

Leilis did not wait to see what would happen. Plainly there was conflict in this house; no doubt because of Prince Tepres. Plainly the rivals were this Lord Manaskes and Prince Heronn, and everything she had seen and heard so far made her wish to set Lord Manaskes back and enhance Prince Heronn's position. So she glided forward with keiso grace, her back straight and her head high and every step precise. She meant to draw all eyes and halt all other movement, and she did.

Walking gracefully in elaborate keiso robes was in some ways almost as exacting as a dance, but Leilis had learned how to move so softly that her robes barely rippled with her steps. Her delicate slippers, embroidered with silver and beaded with pearls, made almost no sound on the flagstones of the hall.

Someone unseen brought out a finger harp and scattered delicate silvery notes like flower petals beneath Leilis' feet, and she wanted to laugh.

Approaching Prince Heronn, Leilis bowed her head in a show of grave respect. Then she lifted her head again, met his eyes, and said composedly, "Prince Heronn Lakadde ser Omientes ken Lariodde. I bear greetings to you and to your king from the folk of Lonne. From the flowers of Lonne, I bring you greetings. From the sea that runs against the shore, I carry greetings to the frozen heights of the mountains."

"And from your king?" Prince Heronn inquired, his tone blandly neutral.

"No king holds the throne of Lirionne," answered Leilis. "No king has stepped forward to claim the throne in Lonne. No king sends across the wide distance between the sea and the mountains. Yet we have heard, far in the west and the south, that here in the east and the north waits our king's heir." She did not look at Prince Tepres, but went on in the same measured cadences, "We have heard that he tarries here where the long winter tarries. Behind mountains and beneath the high reaches of the stars he awaits our call: this we have heard, Prince Heronn."

Those lines echoed Geselle Maniente's "Four Seasons of the Heart," the most famous play in Lonne. In 'Four Seasons,' it was *We have heard that he tarries here where the long waves run.* But Leilis was rather pleased with her improvisation.

These lines were not a spell. But Leilis might as well have been weaving a kind of ensorcelment, because no one could possibly break into her smooth, resonant lines with any coarse insult or rough command. Certainly Lord Manaskes did not seem able to. He was as caught by the rhythm of her words as any of the others. Small-witted, Leilis decided, for all his aggressive manner. She could see Taudde bite his lip against a desire to laugh, and looked quickly away lest his inconvenient sense of humor affect her as well.

There was, she thought, a hidden amusement in Prince Heronn's eyes, too, though his expression was unchanged. He said mildly, "So he does. Here he is, indeed, flourishing in our hospitality." He nodded toward Prince Tepres and went on, raising his voice slightly, "Naturally the people of Kalches would take no hasty or unconsidered action even when the heir of the Dragon of Lirionne came asking succor against treachery within his family. Indeed, we of Kalches have been shocked to hear of events in the Pearl of the West, for here in the north, brother never turns against brother."

Someone in the gathering laughed, and quite a lot of the people near Lord Manaskes shuffled uneasily. Leilis smiled as gravely and calmly as though she noticed nothing, turned smoothly, and walked with small, gliding steps toward Prince Tepres. Ignoring Taudde—though she gave Karah a brief smile—she sank down to kneel with exquisite grace at her prince's feet.

Prince Tepres had not lost his customary self-possession. He took her hands at once, lifting her to her feet, and said quietly, "Seathrift of Cloisonné House. You are well come. All men know the graciousness and honor of your House. And how fares Lonne? Word has been scant of late."

Leilis hesitated very slightly. She had not noticed until he took her hands. But now she could not miss the ring he wore. The iron ring, the dragon with its ruby eyes. She was appalled, and for the first time uncertain; Prince Tepres believed his father dead, clearly, or he would never have put on that ring. She hardly knew how to tell him he was mistaken. She wanted very badly to speak to him privately. But this was all a show, and she dared not even request privacy. Nor did she know anything of the political situation here. She could not judge what ill might come from telling everyone in this gathering the truth.

So what she said, gravely, was only, "It is said that Sehonnes will claim your father's throne; that he will claim the throne on the solstice, on the very day; that he will take it and hold it. It is said that no one challenges his claim, because it is Telis who struck down the king—so it is said. And because you are not there, eminence, Sehonnes may act according to his desires. But few men are pleased by this, or trust his word that the blood is not on his hands."

Prince Tepres, inclined his head. His mouth was tight, but his voice was flat and distant. "Geradde?"

"Missing, eminence—so it is said. And Meiredde, of course, has not appeared."

"I do not expect that he will."

"Indeed, no one expects that, eminence. So Lonne is quiet—men step into and out of the shadows, but I think there is no one anywhere who knows all the measures of the dance. Thus your people wait to see what will come." She glanced at Prince Heronn, who gave her a little *don't-mind-me* flick of one hand. Leilis did not permit herself to smile, though she was amused. She said clearly, speaking ostensibly to Prince Tepres but actually to the Kalchesene gathering, "I am glad to find you well, eminence. There are many in Lirionne and in Lonne who will be astonished by the measure of Kalchesene courtesy, and eager to repay generosity with generosity."

This, however, proved a miscalculation.

"Kalchesene *generosity!*" Manaskes strode forward suddenly. Though one of his people caught at his arm, he shook her off and continued forcefully, "If Lirionne *dupes* Kalches into obedience without ever spending a drop of blood—if Lirionne wins the war by *asking* for the victory, and Kalches simply *gives* it to them—then we deserve to be a subservient people! I say, let no one mistake our reluctance to act hastily for lack of the will to act! I say—"

Drawing herself up with injured dignity, Leilis prepared to reclaim the attention and momentum Lord Manaskes had taken from her. But before she could try, the girl with Taudde snapped, "We've all heard everything *you* have to say at tiresome length! Hasty action is *just* what you promote, Uncle, or why not wait for Grandfather to make his wishes known? Could it be because you know he won't support you?"

Lord Manaskes made a derisive gesture. "What Berente can't support any longer is the weight of the crown, as we all know! Or he'd not—"

"I'd like to see you tell Grandfather so to his face—"

"*You* have nothing to say to anyone, Irelle, making common cause with the Seriantes dragonling and that unreliable fool Taudde, sneaking around behind everyone's back—"

"Oh, no, Uncle," the girl said sweetly. "I've just been sneaking around behind yours. Someone had to see to it that you didn't drag us to war without even thinking about any other course of action!"

"You've done your best to take advantage of Grandfather's indisposition," added Taudde, his tone edged with scorn. "No decent man would do such a thing, and no decent man support it."

Lord Manaskes started toward him. Taudde shifted forward to meet him, his hand falling to the flute at his belt, but Prince Heronn stepped suddenly forward and caught Manaskes' arm, jerking the other man to a halt. "This is enough," he said, quietly, but with considerable force.

"It does not *begin* to be enough!" declared Manaskes, knocking Prince Heronn's hand loose. He pivoted to the group of people who had all come into the hallway with him. "I say there *is* no other course but war, and if there were, we would be cowards to take it! I say—"

"Rather too much, and far too loudly, and without the slightest sense of discretion!" snapped Prince Heronn, losing his temper at last. "You are neither king nor heir, Manaskes, and I've had enough of you! You *will* keep your peace or you may retire to your own apartment, but in neither case will I permit—"

"*You* won't permit!" said Manaskes contemptuously. He turned again to his supporters. "*I say* there's no peace with Lirionne and no place for a Dragon in Kalches! *I say* we send the Dragon we have here straight back to Lirionne, turn him loose naked at the border, and if there is civil war in Lirionne, all the better! *I say* we don't need a Dragon to *give* us what we should *take*, and teach all of Lirionne they'd better treat Kalches with more—"

"*You do go on, Uncle,*" Taudde drawled, somehow making each amused, scornful word stand out clearly amid this diatribe. "I've a notion: let's have every man here—and every woman, too—step up and say clearly whether they care more for what *you* say than for law, tradition, and Grandfather's clearly expressed wishes. Then we'll know where we stand, won't we?—and so will Captain Toma Piriodde and Uncle Heronn and Grandfather."

This was effective in a sense, for it produced an immediate pause. But Leilis, casting a covert glance around the hallway, was by no means certain that Taudde had been right to call for such a firm decision at just this moment. This was not her country and these were not her people, but she felt that the mood had not yet shifted enough. It was her fault—she should have never allowed Lord Manaskes to break in on her performance. But this confrontation had gotten away from her, and she did not know how to get it back.

-20-

When the dragon tore itself free of the shadows beneath Kerre Maraddras, it was as though all of Lonne poured up into the sky through curtains of fire. It was as though the city fell into the sky. It was as though the very air turned to light. That was what Enelle thought. The light was so brilliant and the shock of the dragon so enormous. The city itself did not actually shatter, for the dragon moved through darkness and light, not through stone. But it *felt* as though Nijiadde Falls had reversed its course; as though the mountains shattered and fell; as though the earth cracked through and crashed into the sea.

It was like that, when the dragon tore itself free. Nemienne and Karah had told their sisters about darkness and water and silence, but when it rose, Enelle saw they had been wrong, for the dragon was actually a thing of light, of fire. When it rose, it turned the sky to fire and the sea to light; it turned the city and the Laodd and the pale cliffs of the mountains all to jewels.

Enelle stood rapt by the wide window of the gallery, the coruscation of light playing across her face and felt that all of Lonne was rising in thunder to follow the dragon.

Then it was gone. And the city fell at once back into dimness and silence, as if the very sun had gone out of the sky, though she could see perfectly well that it had not moved even a finger's width in that moment. Not even a single cobblestone had cracked, though she would have sworn she had felt the very streets heave up into the air.

The Laodd still loomed above the city, where it was carved into the mountains. Not even its glass windows had shattered, but now even that glitter seemed a quiet, timid thing. She would have *sworn* the dragon had torn a path through the stone. But if it had, the earth had closed up again and every cobble dropped back into its place. She pressed her hands over her ears, not to keep out the great rushing roar of the dragon's departure, but because the silence it left in its wake was too great to bear.

Behind her, Geriodde Nerenne ken Seriantes said flatly, "I will get up. Now. I will take back Lonne. Today. I will not be gainsaid." The king was on his feet, as though the dragon's rising had lifted him, too, to his feet. He gripped the bedpost, but he stood straight, and before or behind or within him, Enelle, turning to stare at him, thought she could see the long, elegant lines of the dragon. Dark Of The Moon had leaped up on the bed close by the king's hand, but he no longer looked like anyone's tame pet. The cat looked twice as big as a moment before, his back arched and his fur fluffed out so that the shimmering white undercoat showed through, light through the dark. Both his eyes blazed, the green no less than the gold.

Enelle's heartbeat thudded in her ears in time with the heartbeat of the dragon—in time with the heartbeat of the king. "Yes," she said. "It's time for the Dragon of Lirionne to throw down his enemies. But are you strong enough?"

"I will be as strong as I must be," the king stated, not so much as though he were answering her, but more as though he were speaking to himself. His tone was flat and cold. "This is the time. I will make it so. If Neriodd lives, he will have been working on my behalf. When I declare myself, he will come to me—yes, and he will bring all of Lonne at his back. Let us see what allies stand with Sehonnes now, when *I* set my foot on the road that runs to the doors of the Laodd." Then he looked at her and asked, still coldly, "Is the Laodd still there?"

From this, Enelle surmised that he, too, had felt he dragon's rising as a huge and motionless shock, and was still sorting out the feeling that the city had shattered from the truth that it had, apparently, not. She said quietly, "It's still there. Lonne is still there. The Nijiadde hasn't changed its course. The mountains have not fallen."

Geriodde Seriantes nodded. "Then I will claim the Laodd and the city and Lirionne entire. I have never given it up. It is all still mine and in my hand." From his grim tone, he did not expect anyone at all to stand with his usurping son. He expected to walk out into the city and step into the Laodd and find every single guard and soldier and courtier and noble rushing to his side, leaving Sehonnes entirely alone. His tone promised dire fury if he did not see that.

Enelle thought he would see *exactly* that. If he could make it so far. That was the part that frightened her. Or the part that frightened her the most. But she wanted him to be right. She wanted to see Geriodde Nerenne ken Seriantes set his foot on the high narrow road that ran high above Lonne and through the spray of Nijiadde Falls; she wanted him to lay his hand on the great doors of the Laodd and see those doors leap open at his touch.

He *was* on his feet. So that was the first step. He was slow about moving, and careful, and he didn't argue when Enelle matter-of-factly helped him dress. Miande and Tana, who did the neatest needlework, had cleaned and mended his robes, tiny stitches that did not show even in the saffron-yellow of the cloth, so he could be clad as a king. The wound across his chest was still livid beneath its bandages, and his broken ribs could hardly have begun to knit, and his maimed hand was still bandaged. But he stood straight, and if his mouth was tight, that expression seemed only his natural severity.

His age had come upon him with those terrible injuries, though. Or perhaps with his sons' treachery. Pain had carved ruthless lines alongside his mouth. But that, too, only made him look severe. And Enelle had learned to trust his stark, hard patience. It was this that led him to accept her quiet assistance, which he no more acknowledged than he acknowledged the air he breathed. He would not acknowledge it because he would not acknowledge his own weakness. It might have been vanity, but it was not. It was ruthless patience, and Enelle knew that he would not fail. Not even though the dragon had torn itself free of Lonne and gone into the sky. The dragon's strength might have sustained the king; she did not know. But if it had gone, he still possessed his own harsh strength, and that would not let him fail.

Besides, *she* would not let him fail, either. She thought of Karah and Nemienne, lost in Kalches and probably safer there than they would have been in Lonne, and she was ready to forget practicality. She wanted to help the king set down his enemies.

Of all Enelle's sisters, Ananda was the most horrified to see Geriodde Seriantes on his feet, descending the stairs with slow, measured dignity. "Enelle! I thought you had more sense!" she said, hurrying forward in alarm, holding up her hands in case the king should fall.

"I couldn't stop him," Enelle protested. Dark Of The Moon perched on her shoulder, his tail curling around her neck. She held one hand up to help him balance and also to guard against his trying to jump from her shoulder to the king's. She had only with difficulty managed to persuade the heavy cat that the king should not carry him, and hoped to prevent any further attempts Dark made to leap back to his rightful place. But though she knew the king wasn't even fit to lift his own cat, she added firmly, "And besides, he's right! Didn't you see the dragon? We could wait a hundred years and never again get a moment as perfect as this! This is *exactly* when the king should move!"

"But he—but you—" Ananda didn't know what to do, and hovered, making small distressed sounds.

"Neriodd will have already begun," the king said grimly. "Or if he has not, then he cannot. But if he lives, he will meet me at the road to the Laodd. If he does not meet me, though his loss would be grievous to me, other men must do." He descended the last step, gripping the railing carefully, ignoring Ananda's terror that he might fall, ignoring the swift, worried arrival of her husband Petris and the sudden clutter of little girls appearing from the far reaches of the house.

"*Oh*, good," Liaska cried, the only one of them who didn't seem concerned at all for the king's safety or well-being. She clapped her hands and darted away, but returned almost instantly, offering the king a slender cloisonné dragon barely as long as her hand.

The dragon had been a gift to Liaska from Karah. Prince Tepres had given it to Karah, and she'd passed it on to her littlest sister. It was a beautiful thing: jewel-toned in sapphire and amethyst, turquoise and emerald, with delicate golden antennae curving above onyx eyes. Liaska loved it beyond anything; she slept with it on her pillow and set it carefully on the windowsill during the day "so it can see out and won't get bored." But she held it out now to the king.

"Look!" said Liaska. "It's a dragon—it's *your* dragon. Did you see it go up into the sky? It turned into light. It was always made of light on the inside, wasn't it? This one isn't made of light, but it's almost as beautiful. Dragons are stronger than anything. It will make you strong, too."

The king took the little figure, slowly. His mouth was still set in stark lines of ruthless endurance. But curiosity and even warmth had come into his ice-pale eyes. "I think it may. I think it will," he said to Liaska. He touched her cheek, a light, quick touch with the two remaining fingertips of his crippled hand. He said, "You are a remarkable child. Perhaps I might have done better to have had daughters and not sons."

"It's being king," Liaska said wisely. "That was the trouble. Your sons learned to hate each other because they couldn't all be king later."

No one else would have had the impertinence to say it, but the king did not seem angry. He only nodded slightly and tucked the little cloisonné dragon away.

Then he said, to Ananda because she was the oldest and to Petris because he was her husband, "I am grateful for your care and for the care of your sisters and your household. I will not forget my sojourn in this house." And he said to Enelle, holding out his good arm to take Dark Of The Moon, "Do not worry. I shall not falter. Nor, I promise you, shall I draw unwanted attention upon this house."

"Well, I know *that*," said Enelle, taking a quick step back to prevent Dark from leaping to the king's arms. "But, well, won't you sit down, the kitchen is just along here, it's warm and there are chairs, Tana and I can go around and get our carriage for you, it's open and our horse is old, but it's far better than trying to *walk*, you don't want to use all your strength just getting to the Laodd. Do please be *sensible*."

"I cherish your good sense," murmured the king. He sounded faintly amused.

"I'll drive you," Petris said nervously. He held up his hands when Ananda began to protest. "Our horse may be old, but he can be stubborn, and besides, it wouldn't be right for our king to drive himself!"

"I could—" Enelle began.

287

"You can't drive, the king will need you to hold Dark, and anyway, if you went by yourself, who'd take care of *you*, if there's trouble? You can go to help the king and I'll go to drive, and," he added firmly to Ananda, "I'll make sure she stays safe even if there *is* trouble, though of course there won't be!"

Enelle thought Ananda would keep protesting, but instead she only gave Petris a proud little nod and said, "Yes, that's right. Of course you must drive. Only be sure and—and be careful, and if there's fighting, stay out of it! I know you're brave enough, but you're not a soldier, and we need you! I need you," she added, more softly, and her husband smiled and went to her and touched her cheek.

Somewhat to Enelle's surprise, the king also allowed himself to be persuaded to this plan. She guessed by this that he might have barely made it down the stairs at all, but it might also have been a kind of generosity, not to shut out from the end of the play those who had helped him.

So Miande stood on her toes to kiss the king's cheek, for luck, and Jehenne whispered that he had to come back someday and let her try again to beat him at tiles, and Tana pressed his hand and looked solemn. Only Liaska bounced with excitement and was plainly delighted to see him on his way. "I want to come, too! Can't I come? Oh, *why* can't I be grown up and do all the interesting things!" But fortunately the king refused her, and even Liaska seemed at least a little impressed by his authority.

So, once the carriage was ready and a warm lap-rug had been brought, and the king had taken his leave of all the little girls, Enelle nodded to Petris, and Petris held the door open and stood back like a man-at-arms, and she put her hand under the king's elbow, and he made his way slowly out and mounted into the carriage. But, though the king did not turn his head when the carriage started forward, she could not resist a look back.

She watched her youngest sister bounce and thought of the little cloisonné dragon, and the other dragon, and of her littlest sister saying, *It's stronger than anything. It will make you strong, too.* And she knew that whatever or whoever might fail, it would not be Geriodde Nerenne ken Seriantes, the Dragon of Lirionne.

It was a long way from the tall, narrow house near the stoneyard to the Laodd. Even from street level, though, they could see the Laodd whenever the cobbled streets turned that way: high above the city, imposing in its sheer massive size even at this distance. The Laodd hardly looked like anything mere men had made. Its stark white walls and glittering glass windows seemed like something fashioned out of ice and white snow and the crystalline air of winter. The mountains themselves, looming above the city, seemed hardly greater or wilder or more distant than the white Laodd. Beyond the Laodd, the great cataract of Nijiadde Falls poured down, the water glittering like glass where it fell, and where it broke the mist rose up in clouds and eddies, veiling even the Laodd itself from time to time so that the fortress seemed to float suspended above the city.

Everything was the same. Nothing had changed. The mountains had not been torn open, Nijiadde Falls had not been shattered and left to find another way down from the heights, the Laodd had not been cast down from the face of the cliff.

But everything was different, too.

Where they drove through the streets, it seemed in one way an ordinary world, a world of ordinary men. Except that today, Enelle could almost have believed that they traveled through a city peopled mostly by spirits and memories—or that they were spirits themselves, though the hooves of the horse struck echoes from the cobbles. The air smelled of summer, of recent rain and damp earth and the trees blooming along the streets and the rivers, of horses and baking bread and simmering broth, and fish, and always, above everything else, of the sea. The smells were those of the ordinary world, but everything else seemed strange. As though the real city had been carried away by the dragon and they traveled now through merely an echo or a memory of Lonne.

Ordinarily, Lonne would be crowded and busy at this season and this time of day. The city woke early: at sunrise, women selling warm bread or pastries or fresh fruit, men selling noodles in broth or fresh-laid eggs, would all have begun to call their wares through the streets. The fish market down by the harbor would be busy almost before first light, and then, not long after dawn, the other market, where everything else was bartered and sold, would be busy and bustling as well.

But today, though the weather was fair and the sun already high, the people were quiet. Everyone, from the youngest infant at the breast to the most elderly of grandmothers sitting by the fire, had felt the shock of the dragon's rising. Everyone had come out into the streets. But the people were greatly subdued. They murmured to one another, but very quietly. And somehow they knew the king, though the carriage was a plain one and the horse old. Their low murmuring came to Enelle dimly, as though heard through glass, or distance. Or time. It was as though she heard not the people themselves, but only echoes of the voices that had filled the city in ordinary days, before everything had become so frightening. And she saw how all the people stopped whatever they were doing and turned and followed the carriage.

Enelle risked a glance across the open seat of the carriage, at the king. Even here in this ordinary carriage, with no one to serve him but her and Petris, Geriodde Nerenne ken Seriantes looked exactly like himself. By every possible measure a king. He should have men about him, men of the grimly efficient King's Own Guard, and perhaps soldiers, and certainly servants and bodyguards and courtiers.

She dared another glance at the king. He looked like he knew exactly what to do and how to do it. That was reassuring . . . although it was also a little frightening. She was not frightened of *him*, precisely, but she saw that in his ruthless focus, he might become frightening.

They took the bridge across the narrow Niarre River, gentler than the Nijiadde, and beyond the Niarre, the Paliante, and beyond that the King's District, and then at last the long narrow road to the Laodd. Enelle had never come all this way before. It seemed a long way. The Paliante was quiet. All the shutters were latched back and all the doors and gates stood open, but men stood alone or in small groups, simply watching and waiting. One man left his shop and followed the carriage, and then another, on foot. And then a handful. Enelle glanced back, and saw others moving quietly in their wake, and was not even surprised.

They saw one small group of soldiers in red and gray, but

only at a distance. The soldiers stared at the carriage, the only one moving in all these empty streets. Enelle watched them nervously, but they did not approach, but turned instead and rode away in another direction, slowly, not looking back.

Enelle glanced at the king. He returned her an abstracted nod. He seemed now fine-drawn and weary, his ferocious will not ebbing, but . . . banked, she decided. He was waiting. Though his glance after those soldiers was thoughtful. He said abruptly, "They turned away deliberately; did you mark that? They deliberately turned aside rather than meet a conveyance traveling openly through the streets."

Enelle hadn't realized this. She wasn't sure what he meant, and asked tentatively, "You mean, they have orders to pretend not to notice carriages? At least those that belong to ordinary people?"

"No," said the king tersely. "They have orders to stop any conveyance they meet. So they turn aside so as not to meet us."

"Oh . . ."

"They are *my* soldiers," said the king.

"Oh," Enelle said again, relieved. She thought she understood, and anyway . . . today, of all days, she thought he must be right. So when the king gave Petris a curt gesture to turn and follow the soldiers, though she bit her lip and worried, she did not protest.

When Petris first turned the horse to go after them, the soldiers pivoted immediately back to meet it—so they *had* been watching, though pretending not to. Their captain reined ahead of his men, lifting his hand to halt them, and shaded his eyes against the sun to peer at them. Enelle thought his glance was quick and shrewd, but not unkind. Then the officer noticed Dark Of The Moon, glowering from Enelle's arms with his odd-colored eyes set wide in his broad head and his white-behind-black fur. *Then* he looked at Geriodde Seriantes, and she saw him recognize the king. His hands must have tightened on his reins because his horse sidled and backed. The captain's expression had gone blank and still.

"Well?" said the king, without expression.

The man swung wordlessly down from his horse and went to one knee on the cobbles, the reins gripped in one fist, his other held across his chest in salute. All of his men did the same, one ragged movement that ended with them all kneeling in the street.

"Good," said the king. He raised his light, ruthless eyes and looked past the soldiers, at the ordinary people coming cautiously nearer, and they knew him, too. No one shouted, but a low murmur began, like a wind across the stone, or like the tide coming in against the rocky shore.

So Geriodde Nerenne ken Seriantes took back the first of his people. After that, word spread out and out, faster than seemed reasonable to Enelle, so that as they passed through the King's District, the streets grew more and more crowded.

Nor were all of those who came to join the king soldiers; indeed, most were not. Some of the men were mounted, but many were on foot; and some women appeared, too, one or another even holding a child up to see. So Petris drew the horse back to an easy walk, and they went on, but now Lonne did not seem like an empty city of spirits and sunlight. No one spoke loudly, but the murmuring was like the voice of the sea, and men's boots rang on the cobbles, with here and there the loud metallic clatter of a horse's hooves. The sun seemed brighter, Enelle thought; and the mist where Nijiadde Falls came down beside the road shone silver and white; and she could see that at the other end of the high road, the great doors of the Laodd stood open before them.

Thus the king returned to the Laodd at last, escorted by men in red and gray, or in black, or in the plain colors of ordinary people, or in the elaborate jewel-tones of the lesser nobility. And though at the last moment, a scattering of men ran out and tried to shut the doors of the Laodd, other men came out after them to stop them. And then the king's own people were there, and there was no question of shutting the doors after all.

Petris drove the open carriage right through the wide doorway and directly into the entry hall of the Laodd. He did not look around, but only forward. If his heart was beating fast, he didn't show it. Enelle's heart was racing and she could hear her blood rushing in her ears, but she found that somehow she wasn't at all afraid—she was fiercely satisfied. No one knew her, but s*he* was the one who had brought back the king.

Petris got down and held his hand to assist the king, and

then to assist Enelle, as though it was just a courtesy and Geriodde perfectly able to get down by himself. But he knew what he was about. He made sure Enelle had Dark secure on her shoulder and was also near enough to the king to support him if she needed to, and only then took the horse's reins and led it aside. Enelle was proud of him. She had always liked her sister's husband, but she had never realized he had so much sense, or understood how to be subtle.

One of the black-clad King's Own moved forward to take her place beside the king, and a heartbeat after him a man in the sapphire and primrose of the high court, and she thought the king might let one of them help him instead and send her away with Petris. But the king gestured both men back with a tiny, sharp motion of one hand, and took her arm instead, so she understood he still did not want anyone to guess his weakness. He let her take a good deal of his weight, but carefully, so no one could tell. Enelle stiffened her back and supported him as subtly as she could. She worried that he might hardly be keeping his feet, but he leaned his weight covertly on her, and neither of them let his weakness show. The king looked grim, but he stood straight and looked directly at this man and that one, until they all knelt attentively, waiting to hear his will.

Then he asked at last, "Where is Sehonnes?"

And all the crowd parted, to open a path between the king and the inner reaches of the Laodd; between the King of Lirionne and the throne his son had taken but would never, now, hold.

-21-

When Taudde called for everyone to declare their support for either this Uncle Manaskes of his or for his other uncle, Prince Heronn, Leilis feared the mood of the gathering had not yet shifted far enough against Manaskes. She was right.

"We *know* where we stand!" Manaskes shouted, with far too much confidence for Leilis' taste. "Against Lirionne, that's where we stand! Against Lirionne and against the Dragon and all his get!"

The mutter of support for this position was strong. A more experienced keiso might have seized the attention of everyone in this growing crowd, shaken them up, surprised them, charmed them, and won their favor—but Leilis knew, with a sinking feeling, that she did not have such skill. She looked quickly at Karah, but she had little hope the younger woman could manage this audience, either, and she saw at once that Karah was as horrified as she was. Perhaps no keiso could have won the hearts of a Kalchesene gathering, but she feared her failure of skill and imagination would cost them all—cost them all everything, and after she had won through so much even to come to this house—after they had all won through so much—

Prince Heronn said calmly, his tone penetrating, "*Against* the Dragon? Not *for* Kalches, nor *for* our own people?"

The mood shifted. That fast. Leilis took a breath, feeling the change. She had not foreseen that at all.

They were *his* people, of course. She should have remembered that.

Manaskes began to shout something else, but Heronn merely went on in that same level voice, picking out one man and then another in the gathering, "Girannes, I'm surprised at you. You lost a son at the field of Brenedde, I know. We all lost so many. But you have two more sons old enough now to take up arms. Do you truly want to rush into another war when we have every Seriantes prince left alive competing to win our good regard? Heradd, the Treaty cost you everything, as it cost so many. It's taken you and your good wife fifteen years to rebuild your family's fortunes, but you were too stubborn to let your girls go undowered and you worked hard. Do you want to spend all that you've built struggling to take Kalchesene lands back from the Dragon with blood and steel, when we might regain those lands with the stroke of a pen?

Prince Heronn was using his very restraint to make all this gathering listen to him; he spoke so softly that men had to lean forward and quiet their neighbors to hear him. More than one of his supporters hushed Lord Manaskes when he would have kept shouting. The men Heronn addressed by name became silent and thoughtful, and after them others, in a spreading ripple of quiet.

So everyone heard King Berente with perfect clarity when he said grimly, from a doorway well down the hall, "It doesn't surprise me a bit that you've been making a nuisance of yourself, Manaskes."

From quiet, the gathering because stiflingly hushed. Men and women edged to the sides, leaving a clear path between the king and his sons. Leilis did not have to be told that this was the king. Though she gathered the old man had been ill, she couldn't have guessed it from his straight posture and hard, clear voice. His authority was obvious; just as obvious as the Dragon's authority. A woman of middle years stood by his side and half a pace back, but she stood there not as though hovering over a man in uncertain health, but like a woman of rank attending a king.

King Berente regarded Manaskes for a moment longer. The man had flushed—with temper and impatience rather than shame, Leilis thought, for he did not seem capable of shame. But he said nothing. Glancing at Heronn, the king added drily, "What does surprise me is that you, Heronn, and you, Toma, let this farcical situation roll on like an uninterrupted drum rhythm!" He gave the woman who had accompanied him a dark look—which did not seem to impress her in the least—before turning back to his heir. "No doubt Ines persuaded you to stay quiet. For days! For fear of disturbing me! As though I were *fragile*." The king regarded his heir without favor and then swept his gaze across the crowd. Hardly any of his people met his eyes, though the guard captain did not seem troubled by this rebuke and Prince Heronn was smiling wryly.

Irelle broke the moment. "But, Grandfather, you *are* fragile," she said cheerfully. "You mustn't shout at people; look what it leads to! Would you like me to get you a chair?"

King Berente glowered at her. "Nuisance of a girl, no, I don't want a chair! What you mean is, I mustn't shout at *you!* Hah! A fond hope of yours, I'm sure!" He jerked a hand at the woman and added, "Your mother's been telling me what you've been up to. Don't think she hasn't." Transferring his glower to Prince Tepres, he added brusquely, "A cursed awkward situation for you, Tepres ken Seriantes, and I'm sorry for that, and commend my granddaughter for her wit in keeping you clear of the worst of it. Mind you, I might still send your head to your brother, but hardly—" the king darted a sharp look at Manaskes—"in a shameful muddle that's all temper and no thought."

Manaskes flushed but clearly did not dare answer this. Irelle, not in the least discommoded, protested, "You won't either, Grandfather."

"You think not?" the king said darkly.

"Whatever your decision, o King, I have no doubt it will arise from careful thought and be delivered generously and with honor," Prince Tepres said with perfect composure.

"Hah," King Berente growled, and turned to Leilis. "And who is this? Another keiso of Lonne's famous flower world, surely. One with magic in her toes, to come down from the heights with never a trace of dirt on her slippers! How is that, keiso? You came through my troublesome grandson's enchanted doorway, did you?"

Leilis was starting to think she might like this old king. Controlling an impulse to smile, she inclined her head. "High in the mountains stands that doorway, for the hand that can open it."

Taudde gave her an intense look, clearly longing to ask how she had in fact managed the long descent down the steep mountain road without losing a single pearl from her slippers or smudging the swirl of blue and pearl glitter on her cheek. Leilis did smile at that. *Keiso magic*, she wanted to say. Keiso illusion, more like. No keiso would let anyone know she had made her laborious way down to an ordinary road to beg kindness from the first stranger she encountered. No. Let it seem she had simply stepped out of the air and flown like a gull to the door of this house.

King Berente raised his eyebrows at Taudde. "*This* is the woman, eh? Well, well."

Taudde shrugged, but he looked faintly self-satisfied as well, which made the reference quite clear to Leilis. She did not permit herself to smile, or to say, *Why yes, I am the woman,* though she was certainly tempted. It *was* a shame anything of the sort would be out of character for a perfect keiso.

Turning to Leilis, the king demanded, far more sharply, "Well, beautiful you may be, the very image of beauty! But who shall we see *next* through that door, eh? All the remaining Seriantes princes and their armies?"

That was a concern that Lord Manaskes would have done well to raise. Leilis was grateful it hadn't occurred to him. She waited a few seconds to be sure everyone was impatient for her answer. Then she said, her voice soft but pitched to carry, "That door will open to no hand that would turn against Kalches, o king." This might even be true. Certainly no hand but hers and before that Taudde's had been able to open that door—so far as she knew. She went on smoothly, "That is why you have no army marching out of the air and down from your heights. But no army would wish to come. The heart of Lonne is here. You hold it in your hands."

"I much doubt that the people of Lonne would wish to trust *me* with their heart," King Berente answered, his tone dry.

"We might," Karah said softly. "Are you not trustworthy?"

King Berente stared at her. She gazed back, clad like a woman of Kalches, but her manner unmistakably that of a keiso. The king opened his mouth, shut it again, and turned sharply to Leilis instead. Fixing her with a glowering stare, he demanded abruptly, "On whose behalf do you speak, woman? Lonne's? What precisely is it that Lonne desires of me? To return your Dragon without cost or question? That hardly seems reasonable."

Lowering her gaze in grave deference, Leilis said clearly, in the cadences of the storyteller, "In this difficult spring, as the season rises toward the long days, surely all those who walk beneath the warm sun and the close stars share but one desire."

In the poem, it was *all young lovers* and their one desire was for the warm starlit night to linger forever. But Leilis went on, seizing her chance, altering the poem to fit her need and slanting a glance at Prince Tepres. "For in this season, what should the people of the sea or the people of the mountains desire but that the sun and the moon together, twin lights set against the dark, turn along the iron ring of passing days and hold back the reaching darkness? You shall be sure of it, o king, but not you alone; the people of Lirionne wait on your word. The people of Kalches wait on your word. You have but to declare yourself, and the Dragon of Lirionne will declare himself as well."

Was that clear enough? Or perhaps even too clear? Twin lights and turning around an iron ring; that was not very subtle. Leilis covertly watched Prince Tepres. She saw him grasp the meaning she had hidden beneath those fragments of poetry; that repetition of *wait on your word*. The prince would remember who in that poem had waited, and for what word—he must remember—he *did* remember; she knew by the way his eyes widened suddenly and sought hers. She gave him a very small nod, trusting that no one else would guess what she meant to convey. Well, Karah, but she fortunately did not make any betraying exclamation.

Nor did Prince Tepres cry out or step forward to seize Leilis' arm and demand, *My father lives? Are you sure?* But his head went back slightly, as though he had been struck.

Neither King Berente nor Taudde were of Lonne. Neither of them knew the rhythm of that poem; neither of them had the eyes of the king's dragon ring glittering in their mind's eye. But Prince Tepres, blinking, turned his head away and brushed a hand across his eyes. Karah laid her hand on his arm, and he put his own over it and bowed his head over hers, though neither of them murmured aloud. Leilis saw Taudde notice however, and she saw him pretend not to think anything of this moment, though to her it cried out to be noticed.

Leilis said quickly, to keep the king's attention on her, "Let my words ride on the winds and murmur in the tides, that generosity may replace malice and forbearance overset old anger."

Prince Tepres turned back at last. He still held Karah's hand, but he had concealed his reaction now behind a cool, somewhat disdainful expression. Taudde was gazing at him, his eyebrows slightly raised, concern in his eyes, but before his expression could catch anyone else's eye, he turned his attention smoothly to Leilis. He began to speak, but what he intended to say remained a mystery, because at that moment the great horns set to either side of the main door began to hum.

Those horns had sounded for Leilis, too, so she recognized the sound at once. They were much like ordinary ekonne horns, only much larger and somewhat more curved. Their mouths were as big around as banquet platters; their high, arching mouthpieces reached high above the heads of the gathering. The initial sound was not loud, but it was penetrating, and it rapidly rose into a long, mellow note, rich as gold, that made Leilis feel her very bones were humming in sympathy.

King Berente stepped forward, Taudde moving quickly in his wake—everyone was moving, it seemed to Leilis; a general shift toward the great doors. Someone flung them wide, and the great voices of the horns soared, redoubled. Sunlight poured in through those doors, and a cold wind came down from the heights and rushed in, carrying the fragrance of snow and pine.

Leilis took a deep breath. The horns still sounded their deep warning, but beyond and around and through those smooth voices she almost thought she could hear a sharper music, something more piercing. A harp. Not a pretty toy such as a finger harp, nor a simple knee harp on which any half-trained girl might perform creditably; this had the resonance of one of the great harps that stood taller than a woman, the kind of harp that required the whole reach of the instrumentalist's arm, the kind that led an entire orchestra, the kind a master instrumentalist might make just once in a lifetime.

The harp notes sounded right through the deep voices of the horns, each one clear and precise. Those notes plucked at Leilis' bones, pulled at her heart, vibrated in her blood. The deepest note, lower even than the Kalchesene horns, reverberated on and on, washing in and out and in again, until she was half blind with the sound. Somewhere quite near, she was aware of a thundering rhythm. Then she knew that rhythm was her heartbeat, but it deafened her and she could hear nothing else.

Prince Tepres took her hand in his. She knew it was Tepres. His heart beat in time with hers, and her sight cleared when he touched her. She knew him because she was herself tuned to the dragon, to the darkness beneath the mountain. Because she had been born with magic in her blood, because of her father; because of her curse, which, before Taudde had untangled it, had closed her in a web of magecraft and loneliness.

That curse was gone, and she had never even known her father. It was ridiculous to be blind *now*. Leilis took a swift breath and, clinging to Tepres' hand, blinked hard, and looked again through the tide of music that had risen around them all.

She discovered that she had stepped, without quite knowing it, out through the doors and onto the wide flagstones of the courtyard. Out of the king's house and into the open air of the Kalchesene town. Not only was Prince Tepres holding her hand, but Karah held her other hand, though Leilis had not noticed that until this moment. She returned the pressure now, gratefully. It made her feel more grounded in the human world, when she felt she had nearly dissolved into the air.

Taudde stood to her left, his flute in his hand—he was not playing it, but he held it like a weapon, or a shield. His cousin, the girl Irelle, was by his side, a flute in her hand, too, like a length of silver fire in the sharp light of the morning. Leilis saw King Berente and his heir, the woman Ines, the guard captain and all his men, the whole gathering, even Lord Manaskes— dozens of people, men and women both, most gripping flutes or pipes or knee harps or other small instruments. A few had swords or other weapons, though she could not imagine what they meant to do with them against the tide of magic she felt rising.

Prince Tepres held her right hand and Karah her left, both of them gripping hard enough to hurt her. Leilis welcomed the pain, which reminded her of herself and made her feel more real in the midst of the reverberating harp notes that pulled at her bones. She returned the pressure, feeling that they all clung to each other so that they should not be pulled apart and dragged out of the world. She could still feel the low harpstring pulling at her blood.

But Prince Tepres was not looking at her, but away, up, into the vivid sky. Leilis gripped his hand all the more fiercely and followed his gaze.

So she saw the dragon come.

It came into Kalches on the high wind, soaring out of shadow, far up in the distant heights where there was nothing at all to cast a shadow, soaring into light, into the brilliance of the mountain skies. It was long and lithe and flew with a swift writhing motion, as a serpent swims in the sea. Unlike a serpent, its wings stretched out and out, seeming to cross the entire width of the sky. The shadow of its wings passed across the town, but the shadow it cast was not of darkness, but of light.

The dragon burned. It was made of fire, or of something like fire. Sapphire flames trailed from its wings; amethyst sparks scattered from the snake-limber flick of its long body; emerald fire burned along the curve of its graceful neck. Its breath was fire, hot and golden. Where it flew, the very air turned to light. Leilis blinked, dazzled, her eyes tearing from the brilliance and the beauty of it.

Then the dragon poured itself down from the reaches of the sky, down and down toward the earth. It coiled as it came down, its vast form twisting and writhing, throwing great loops out to one side and then the other. It seemed to lengthen as it came down, stretching out impossibly long, until its fire washed against the roots of the mountains and across the streets of the town. It was not fire, after all; not true fire. But it was *like* fire. Or like lightning. Or like light. It coiled all the way around the town, which should have been impossible, but from every direction a coruscation of sapphire and emerald and amethyst and all the jewel-tones of light rose up in shimmering curtains, hanging in the sky, burning against the mountains. Even after the dragon itself disappeared, the vivid light hung in the sky, rippling in all the colors of fire.

Leilis found herself shaking. She remembered fire—she remembered all her bones turning to fire and gold, or perhaps to music—she had not been able to breathe, or the air had turned to

301

fire in her lungs—she took a deep breath of cool air and shook her head. That was all such perfect nonsense. Of course her bones had not turned to fire. Of course she had not breathed fire. Nothing of the sort had happened. How stupid.

But still she turned to stare at Prince Tepres, searching for fire beneath his skin and in his eyes, half expecting to see the dragon behind his arrogant high-boned face. Karah reached to touch his face, draw her fingertips along his cheekbone—so she, too, wanted to assure herself that he was still himself and not the dragon.

His eyes were the eyes of a man. But Leilis thought she saw fire in them, nevertheless: an echo of the dragon. She wondered what he saw in her eyes. He had not released her hand. She did not let go of his. There was a comfort in that touch, so ordinarily human. And something else: a familiarity, as though she recognized in him something of herself.

She said, rather blankly, quite forgetful of keiso dignity, "*I* am not an heir of the dragon."

"I think perhaps you are," the prince told her. "Your father was a mage. You have been entangled in the dragon's magic before. And if you had not been, the dragon took your heart, too, last winter."

Leilis could only shake her head. She did not know. The notes of those harpstrings hummed in the air and in the stones of the courtyard and in her bones, every note tuned to darkness and light and fire. No wonder . . . no wonder the jeweled light still rose up all around this town, painting the encircling mountains with all the colors of fire. The dragon might or might not wish to pull those mountains down upon this ephemeral town of men, but if the harp had called it up, then it was still calling even now. She could still hear every note.

"What *is* that?" demanded King Berente. His voice was hard, angry, but not altogether without wonder. He had a flute in his hand, made of ebony with silver fittings. He gripped it hard, so hard his knuckles were white with the pressure; he half lifted it toward his mouth, but Lady Ines touched his hand and he lowered it again without playing a note.

Turning to Leilis, the king demanded, "Did *you* bring this down upon us?"

"Of course she did not!" said Karah. "Why would you think so?"

"That cursed thing was a *dragon!*" Lord Manaskes declared, half shouting, pushing forward and glaring from Leilis to Taudde to Prince Tepres.

"I did warn you of it, Uncle. And it isn't, precisely, I think." Taudde was not really paying attention to his grandfather or Lord Manaskes or any of them. He was gazing into the air and the wavering jewel-toned curtains of light—looking, Leilis understood suddenly, for the source of the still-sounding harp. So was Prince Heronn, and Lady Ines, and Irelle, who stood at Taudde's shoulder. They were *all* bardic sorcerers, Leilis realized.

Irelle laid her hand on Taudde's arm and said, her tone commendably steady, "Well, that is not quite what I expected. And *I* believed you about the dragon."

Taudde smiled at her quickly and then glanced past her, raising his eyebrows at the older woman. "Aunt Ines?"

"Yes," the woman said, resignedly. "I would have been just as pleased to be mistaken. I don't think your description quite did it justice."

"I must admit, it didn't seem quite as . . . dramatic, in the dark."

"It's beautiful," murmured Irelle. "I'd like to set that light to music. But what could compass it? The harp doesn't, quite . . ."

"That cursed harp—" began King Berente. "It's still sounding! Did the harp draw the dragon, or the other way around?"

It occurred to Leilis belatedly that the harp *was* still sounding, and that she herself might have a way to silence it. She fumbled for the twin-pipes which Gerenes Brenededd had given her—pipes of ivory and horn, bound with silver and copper, inlaid with pearlescent shell and magecraft. Turning toward Taudde, Leilis held up the pipes and tried to frame an explanation of what they were and who had made them.

But it was too late. The harp was *there*, here, not far away at all, in the middle of the courtyard, and with it a harpist, wavering between light and shadow, touching one string and then another with a long white stick. It seemed an awkward way to play a harp, but Leilis assumed it was part of the magic—maybe a way to keep the magic of the harp at a distance, so one could hold it and control it without dissolving into the sound. She could feel the tug of the harp notes on her own bones, and *she* was not even playing it. And the harp was not even entirely present. Not yet. It was still wavering between light and shadow.

Then, as it came fully into focus, Leilis recognized the harp at last. It was the great harp from Taudde's own music room. The dragon was carved all down its face. The carving was immediately recognizable as *the* dragon, the same that had slept in the darkness beneath Kerre Maraddras, that had called itself the heart of darkness. The same that now, here in the light, seemed to be made of light.

The carving in some way managed to encompass both light and darkness as it coiled down the face of the harp, serpentine and elegant, inlaid with lapis and opal, hematite and jet. High on the face of the harp, above the dragon, was set a single black pearl and one bead each of dark, smoky glass and gleaming hematite. Leilis recognized those: they had meaning in magecraft, but she did not remember that meaning. And anyway, no one here was a mage.

Except the man who had brought the harp here, or been brought by it, she could not quite tell. He stood by the harp, his hand flat against the great sweeping curve of the harp's frame, and stroked the white stick he held across the strings, from the great low note to the purest high note. The sound was . . . strange. Wrong, somehow. Leilis shuddered.

He, too, had become gradually more visible, until at last she recognized him. Then she couldn't understand why she hadn't known him at once. It was Prince Telis, of course. Of course it was. He looked a great deal like his mother, Inann, whose flower name had been Skyblue; but his bones were more angular than graceful and there was a bitter twist to his thin mouth that his mother would not have recognized at all.

Tepres gave a sharp, wordless exclamation and started forward, brushing aside Leilis when she tried to stop him. Karah caught his hand and would not be brushed away, but he didn't seem to notice even her. Sa-Telis glanced around, as though at last becoming aware of his surroundings. He looked for one instant straight at Tepres. Then he smiled, and shook his head, and reached up to touch the beads set into the face of the harp. A note swelled, not exactly a harp note, something different and stranger and wilder and darker—something like the sound of a stone thrown into a lightless pool of water, if the water was not exactly water and had never been touched by light. Tepres, who had nearly reached his brother, halted as though struck, and turned, and pushed Karah sharply, sending her stumbling back.

And then both Sa-Telis and his harp faded, between one breath and the next, back into shadow and dream; and Prince Tepres, tangled in that rich and inhuman sound, faded with it. Karah cried out, sharp and desperate, like the cry of a gull, and Leilis seemed to hear something that might have been the echo of harpstrings, or of the roar of fire, or the surge of the sea; only it was not like any of those things. She shut her eyes, dizzied by the measureless echoes.

Then Taudde cursed bitterly, and Leilis, still holding the pipes helplessly in her hand, quickly opened her eyes and turned, caught by the fury in his voice.

King Berente closed his hands on Taudde's arms and pulled him around, glowering into his grandson's eyes. "Well, boy, who was *that*? Besides our enemy—or your enemy—or at the very least, the *Dragon's* enemy! What led him *here?* What *was* that harp? Where was that thing *made*? And by whom? Do you know what that was in that fool harpist's hand? That was no innocent bone! That was old bone with the death still clinging to it! And he used it to sound an instrument like that!"

Leilis started forward, but Taudde didn't need her help. He met his grandfather's angry stare without flinching. "Yes, sir, it's plain now I should have destroyed that harp when I had the chance—"

"You had the chance and let it pass? Wisdom is better born timely!" snapped his grandfather.

"Indeed, sir, you are quite right. The dragon came for Tepres, I assume—or was drawn here because he was here—and the harpist followed the dragon. If *you* had let Tepres go long since—sent him back to Lonne as he asked—" but he stopped without finishing that sentence, drawing a hard breath.

His grandfather regarded him, dour and angry. But he also

let Taudde go, with a curt nod that was not exactly an admission of fault, Leilis estimated, but at least an acknowledgement that Taudde was not at fault either. So King Berente was, perhaps, a fair-minded man. That was good to know.

Since Taudde plainly did not need her support, Leilis turned and gathered up Karah. The girl was not weeping, but Leilis thought it was because she was too shocked for tears. "He pushed me away!" she said to Leilis. "He said I followed him along the path to death once and he wouldn't permit me to do it again! But he—but I—"

"I know," Leilis said softly. "We will get him back. We will not permit Sa-Telis to win now, after everything we've suffered!"

Karah nodded, but Leilis didn't wait for her. She turned and took one gliding, graceful step to make King Berente look at her. Then she said softly, "There is nothing to be gained in asking what might have happened if we had stepped from one road to another, or if we had turned our faces toward the sunrise rather than the sunset, or if we had lifted up a flute rather than a sword. You ask who that was, and whether he knows what he does. That was Prince Telis, the mage-prince, the prince folk call Sa-Telis, the serpent, for he is clever and subtle and swift to bite, and because there is poison beneath his tongue."

"No bastard prince, mage or not, concerns me, save as he brings us a dragon," the guard captain, Toma, said, very dry, from his place by the king's side. He snapped his fingers for one of his men to bring the king a chair and then gazed thoughtfully at Taudde, his hands hooked into his belt, his expression reserved.

King Berente snorted at the chair, but dropped into it at the combined insistence of practically everyone. "Yes, yes, I know, bunch of old country mothers!" he snapped at them all, and waved away another man who turned up at his shoulder. "I don't need a surgeon *now!* You've done your best and I'm sure it was very well done, so get out of the way and let me breathe!" Turning, he demanded of Taudde, "Well, boy? Now what? It's *your* dragon, after all."

Everyone crowded close to listen, though they all cast wary glances toward the curtains of coruscating light that hung in the air between the town and the surrounding mountains. Taudde, too, studied the light. But his tone was matter-of-fact when he answered his grandfather. "Magecraft is all about similarity and sympathy, and defining unlike things as like so as to establish a connection between them. It's not much like bardic sorcery. You know that, sir." Then he looked around at all the gathering. "But I think we're all going to need to understand it better, now."

King Berente was plainly very angry, though he didn't shout, and he made no attempt to rise and pace. But he spared a hard glance for Leilis, as a representative of the foreignness and magic that brought dragons. She didn't blame him, under the circumstances. But she also said, seizing the chance he gave her to speak, "Whatever Sa-Telis intends, we must prevent him. Whatever the dragon harp may do, we must prevent it." Holding out the pipes, she said to Taudde, "I think you may recognize the hand that made these. He meant them for you. There is a touch of magic in them, I am told. I am told that properly played, they will silence all other sound."

Taudde drew a breath, flinching slightly. "Ah," he said after a moment. "*That* mageworking. Yes. A rather fraught gift, given . . . well."

"Gerenes Brenedde said you owed him a debt. And that he would take your use of these pipes in friendship to Prince Tepres as payment of that debt."

"Ah," Taudde said again. Reaching out slowly, he took the pipes from Leilis and examined them. "They're very well made," he said eventually. "So far as I can see without playing them— and I don't think I quite care to try them here." He paused, considering, and then added, "But you're quite right; one way or another, these pipes may be just what we need. That was well thought. I hope I will have a chance to tell their maker that I fulfilled exactly the terms he set for this . . . gift."

"I hope you will," Leilis said fervently, hoping that Gerenes Brenedde had been able to get clear of Ankennes' house, that Taudde would indeed someday soon be able to tell him in person that he had acknowledged the debt and found exactly the right use for the pipes. But that was not a concern for today, of course. She asked instead, "But does Sa-Telis *understand* bardic sorcery? Did I not understand correctly that Mage Ankennes did not employ sorcery quite as it should be employed?"

"Mages don't understand how fraught the use of old bone can be," Taudde agreed.

Lady Ines said drily, "Using a bone like that, he'll learn better. But not soon enough, I suppose."

"Yes, if he kept it to himself and destroyed Lonne with his unbounded sorcery, that would be well enough." snapped King Berente. "But we can't have him *here*."

"Far less the dragon," murmured Prince Heronn, with a slight encompassing gesture that took in the undulating curtains of light surrounding the town.

"So we've got to deal with both the mage-prince and the dragon," Irelle declared, as though the prospect was not in the least daunting. "The bone will be powerful if left unbounded. You can feel how it contains death and the memory of life. That part I think your serpent-prince probably understands quite well." She glanced at Leilis. "Sa-Telis, you say? That's not a name fond people give a prince they trust."

Leilis inclined her head.

Taudde made a little gesture of agreement and said, "It's not the first Seriantes bone to be pressed into such use, and if Ankennes knew so little of sorcery as to use dead bone in that way, well, I strongly suspect Telis knows less. Or cares less. We don't even know yet whether he merely followed the dragon here, or drove it here deliberately." He sent a speaking look toward the mountains and the light. "A dead Seriantes bone and a living Seriantes prince: one rather hesitates to guess what Telis intends to do with such tools gathered into his hand, but I think," Taudde said precisely, "that we are going to be compelled to stop him."

"And you have a plan for that, boy?" his grandfather demanded. "Can you even find this serpent prince now?"

"I can find him," Karah said earnestly, and when everyone looked at her, spread her hands and added, "I can find Tepres. I followed him before, onto a path that led out of the living world. I can follow him again, if Taudde will play me a path—"

"I think I can do that," agreed Taudde. "Well thought, Karah—it's a good idea when I hadn't any clear notion how to go on—"

"It's ridiculous!" snapped King Berente.

"Sir, it's plain we must act, and quickly," Taudde said, rather more patiently than Leilis could have managed in his place. "While we have time to act and room to maneuver, lest Sa-Telis achieves . . . whatever he means to achieve. Power in Lirionne, I assume—"

"Oh, yes, we must act swiftly while we have *room to maneuver!* So that we can save Lirionne from their very own serpent-prince! Naturally *you* have a plan to *save Lirionne!*" snapped Manaskes. Leilis raised her eyebrows, turned her head, and fixed him with a look, and was thoroughly satisfied to see the man take an involuntary step back.

"I think we must. I think someone must, or the danger will touch us all," said Taudde, but he wasn't looking at Manaskes or at Leilis. His attention was on his grandfather and Prince Heronn. "The Seriantes Dragon is in sympathy with the true dragon. They're similar things, even now, I suppose. And Tepres did claim that ring."

"It's not the ring that makes the man, surely—" began Prince Heronn.

"Intention matters in magecraft, Uncle. Magecraft is all about similarity and sympathy and calling things by name. The name you call something makes a difference."

King Berente said grimly, "So we hope to spend our strength and blood reining back this serpent of the Dragon's get, in order to protect your friend, who is another of the Dragon's get. Is that what you argue? And meanwhile, we have this other dragon. You didn't do it justice, boy."

Taudde spread his hands, his expression markedly neutral. Leilis found she could not tell whether he and his grandfather were actually on good terms or furious with one another; she thought perhaps both at the same time.

"Yes, I know," King Berente said roughly. "Well. This serpent-prince took Prince Tepres deliberately, did he not? Well, that's bad, I grant you, but mark me, Taudde, our concern is with the safety of Kalches, not Lirionne."

"Sir—"

His grandfather leaned forward aggressively, gripping the arms of his chair hard. "These Seriantes princes are not our concern," he declared. "Lirionne is not our concern. If that dragon wishes to tear every stone of all Lirionne from every other stone, that is not our concern. Our concern is *Kalches.*"

Karah said softly, "You cannot give Sa-Telis a free hand here and hope for any good to come of it, for Lirionne *or* for Kalches."

The king glared at her, but Taudde said flatly, "I won't permit Telis a free hand in this, in the hope we won't regret later that we allowed him to act freely. I won't abandon a Seriantes prince who might reasonably be our ally for one who must surely be our enemy."

King Berente threw up his hands. "Taudde, your duty is to Kalches! You've unwisely made a friend where you should have kept your distance—"

"It's true I wouldn't abandon a friend, either," Taudde conceded. "But that's not why I can't yield in this, sir. My concern *is* the safety of Kalches. You can't possibly feel sanguine about our ability to protect Kalches from that dragon— or from Sa-Telis, if he takes its power or masters it or whatever he intends to do. *Look* at it!"

Everyone followed the thrust of Taudde's hand, looking once more uneasily upward at the shimmering curtains of light rippling in the air between the mountains and the town: aquamarine and ruby, now, and a rich color that Leilis had no name for, between indigo and amethyst.

Prince Heronn cleared his throat. "Taudde is right." He absorbed the king's angry glare with equanimity. "He's right," he repeated levelly. "We cannot protect Kalches by turning our backs in the hope that the dragon will consume Lirionne and be satisfied. For one thing, the dragon is here, not in Lirionne. For another, this serpent-prince clearly has his own aims, which we do not know, but we dare not commit ourselves to the hope that he has not thought of conquest. All the Dragons think of conquest. It's what they do."

"Not Tepres!" cried Karah.

"Possibly not Tepres," Irelle agreed.

Prince Heronn allowed this point with a little tip of his head. "Well, I imagine you would know, daughter."

"I *do* know," Irelle said firmly, while Leilis blinked and

adjusted her understanding to include the notion that this girl was actually the king's heir, only once removed from the throne of Kalches.

Taudde began, "If you believe—" but at the same time, Ines declared, "Heronn is quite correct." And the guard captain stated, "It is absolutely not acceptable—" They all tangled up with one another and fell silent. The guard captain lifted an eyebrow, but before he could speak again, Leilis said softly, so softly they all had to listen to her, "Perhaps we have time to debate all these important matters."

Everyone looked at her. Taudde nodded, sharp and decisive. "You're right." He turned to his grandfather. "Leilis is right, Uncle Heronn is right, and I'm right. Whatever Sa-Telis is about, he's no doubt carrying it through right now, right this moment. And we stand here arguing?"

"Teaching your grandfather?" growled the old man, and began to say something else.

Taudde held up a hand, a sharp, angry, desperate gesture, and his grandfather paused, though he glowered impatiently. "Sir, I will gladly obey you, if you give me the right command," Taudde told him. His tone was steady, but not defiant, and he met his grandfather's angry stare without flinching. "I know I've shown poor judgment in the past. But not that poor. And not this time."

For a long moment, the king gazed at him. Manaskes began to speak, but Heronn looked at him, a hard, forceful look, and he shut his mouth again with a snap.

"Your duty *is* to Kalches," King Berente said to Taudde. "You have not forgotten that."

"No, sir," Taudde promised him. "I have not, and I will not."

"Then go," said the king. "Deal with all the Lirionne Dragons as you see fit, and as you must."

Taudde let out a breath. He held out one hand to Leilis and the other to Karah. They both moved to join him, but so did Irelle. Taudde, plainly disconcerted, said, "Irelle?" He glanced at Lady Ines and Prince Heronn.

Irelle didn't look to anyone for permission or approval. "You were right about the dragon, Cousin, and I think you're right again. I think I need to go with you." *Now* she turned and looked at Lady Ines, raising her eyebrows. "For more than one reason," she said.

"Yes, dear, you may be right," the lady said thoughtfully. "Especially if all goes well."

"Ines!" snapped Heronn.

His wife—for by now Leilis found the relationship more than obvious—tilted her head judiciously. "Well, these things are hard to judge, aren't they, and of course one does worry, but sometimes it's wise to plan for several different possible outcomes, don't you think? Irelle is really quite accomplished. And no one—no one at all—can possibly doubt her loyalty. Or her good sense." She glanced around thoughtfully, and no one in the entire gathering argued, not even Lord Manaskes.

Irelle said, not apologetically, but simply as though she were stating a fact, "I can help. I think I have the right to try." She held up her silver flute. It was very plain, with no fittings at all—but she held it up to show Taudde as a man might offer a weapon to a superior officer for inspection

Taudde nodded sharply.

Prince Heronn, said sharply, "Ines, this is impossible! Irelle, I forbid it!"

"I give her leave," King Berente said, and, when his heir turned to him in surprise and anger, "You were right the first time, Heronn." He said to Irelle, "You, also, Granddaughter: deal with all the Lirionne Dragons as you see fit, and as you must." He looked at Taudde. "If it comes to it, boy, *Irelle* is the one whose judgment I trust."

"I'm sure that's wise of you," Taudde said wryly. But he bowed as well, a slight, formal gesture of acceptance. He said, "Raise your defenses, sir. Raise them high and hard across all the town, and remember that Sa-Telis is using sorcery as well as magecraft, and that we don't know what the dragon even *is*." Then he reached out to take Leilis' hand and draw her toward him, and Leilis took Karah's hand, and Karah took Irelle's, and they all stepped forward.

Taudde closed his eyes, lifted his flute and played a single note that spread out around them as though the rest of the world was silence and that note the only sound in all the world, except that through it Leilis could hear the faint sound of the harp. Darkness closed in around them, but not quite darkness, for light trailed from Taudde's flute and from the single lingering note. The light spread out, too. It was not exactly light, yet Leilis could see with it and through it and past it, into curtains of shimmering light.

It was Karah who led the way, just as she had said. Leilis could hear the light, quick rhythm of the girl's footsteps, like light drumbeats; and she could hear how Irelle played a single sharp note that closed the way behind them as Taudde's flute opened it before them. That seemed well thought. Leilis hadn't thought of anything of the kind, but she could see it was definitely better not to leave a clear way open between the world of men and the world of light where the dragon waited.

Or at least they hoped it still waited, and that the serpent-prince had not already achieved his aims.

-22-

Nemienne hardly knew where she was going, or even where she wanted to go. Not home, though, she was determined on that. Anything was better than leading the serpent-prince to her sisters. So away, just away, out of the darkness of the caverns and into the light, but then she did not have any direction to use as an anchor. She was lost immediately. She could still hear the swelling sound of the harp notes; in a way the sound of the harp *was* the light. Or it was a similar thing to the light, somehow. She didn't understand that, but she knew it was true. The harp, and the dragon's heartbeat, and the light, and the brilliant winds that came down from all sides, and the surge of the tide that underlay everything. Everything was in sympathy with everything else, and she wished she understood it all better because then she could have found her way through the thundering magic.

She still held tight to Geradde's hand. It wasn't actually like holding his hand, but it was a similar thing, or she thought it was. She knew where he was with a knowledge that had nothing to do with sight. She was blind, but she knew Geradde was beside her. His heartbeat echoed the dragon's heartbeat and the tide. His blood scattered through the light, brilliant and vivid, not like blood at all. She pulled him with her, or he pulled her with him, or the dragon pulled them both in its wake, she couldn't quite tell. She knew they were moving very fast, though it was a lot like holding perfectly still. The harp still sounded, though, around them or behind them, one note and another, the notes swelling up through the light. That, too, was a similar thing to the light, but twisted somehow. It was trying to frame the light into . . . something else. Something limited. Something tightly bounded.

Every note was perfect, and perfectly horrible.

Nemienne closed her eyes and took a step, one step. Away from the harp; into the light. She anchored herself to the world through Geradde, and stepped blindly forward. Or she did something like taking a step. And her foot came down somewhere solid, cold light and roaring fire and freezing winds all unfolding around her like a flower, but the stone under her foot was real, or she thought it was real. Vertigo took her, and she stumbled, but Geradde caught her. Then the world settled firmly and she found her sense of up and down shaking back into order. Blinking hard, she looked around and up, trying to understand where she had brought them.

To her astonishment, she glimpsed Karah, but Karah wasn't in keiso robes, she was in a strange sort of garment that was long enough, except it traced her breasts and waist and hips in an altogether immodest way. Karah wouldn't have looked at all like herself except she *did*, somehow, even dressed like that, and then another girl dressed the same way but holding a silver flute as though it were a sword stepped protectively in front of her and Nemienne lost sight of her sister. But there was Leilis, *Leilis* was here, too, except *she* was in her elegant keiso robes, so Nemienne should remember to call her by her flower name, though at the moment Nemienne hardly remembered what that was—Seathrift, that was it. Seathrift. The name made Nemienne think of the tide, and at once light poured down around her, so that she staggered beneath its flooding weight.

Right there beside Leilis, holding her hand, stood Prince Tepres. Nemienne didn't recognize him for a moment, because the dragon came between them then and she mainly saw the dragon. But Geradde began to step forward, and she realized that Geradde had led her straight to his brother—or maybe she had found Tepres because Geradde was a similar thing to the heir, she didn't know, it was all too confusing. But then the light flooded down, and the harp notes suddenly rose up, and all around them curled the long burning length of the dragon. Nemienne stumbled and caught at Geradde's arm to steady herself, and the dragon—or something—dragged them away into light once more, and Nemienne couldn't stop it. She tried, but it was as though she tried to push back the tide with her bare hands.

The light closed around them, and opened up again. Fire poured through the air, blue and violet fire, and bright yellow flames, and white-gold fire brightest of all. It was the dragon. It *was* the dragon. Nemienne hadn't understood that at first. It coiled all around them, looping endlessly in and out of the world, but it wasn't a creature of stone and darkness any longer. Now it was made of fire, and of light solidified, barely, into amethyst and sapphire and vivid garnet-red. The dragon's head hovered over them, massive and burning, so that she couldn't help but crouch down like a mouse under the regard of an eagle. But even the stone beneath her feet seemed to have been poured out of crystalline light, so it did not help.

"Ekorraodde," Prince Geradde said.

Nemienne couldn't have said a word if her life had depended on it, and wouldn't have dared address the dragon if she had been able to speak. She looked gratefully at Geradde. *He* hadn't knelt down. He stood straight, his head tipped back, meeting the dragon's fiery gaze, as well as a man could meet the eyes of a creature so much greater. He looked very much a prince, and to her eye very much a similar thing to the dragon. She could see its fiery power in him; she could hear the roar of flames in his heartbeat. Or she thought she could.

"Blood and fire," said the dragon. Its voice seemed to come from all directions. **"Blood and fire you have brought out of the dark and into the heights. I know you. You are of the get of Taliente Neredde ken Seriantes. He bound you to me, as he bound all his get. Do you call me out of stone and into fire?"**

"Not I, O Ekorraodde," Geradde answered steadily. "My brother, called Sa-Telis."

"Sa-Telis, indeed," said the dragon, sounding amused. **"And how are *you* called, young princeling? Are you also called after the serpent-kind? Give me your name."**

"Geradde Seriantes, son of Geriodde Nerenne ken Seriantes."

"Yes. You have walked out of stone and into fire, Geradde Seriantes, son of Geriodde Nerenne ken Seriantes, great-great-grandson of Taliente Neredde ken Seriantes. You have not the heart of a serpent nor the heart of a dragon.

Will you give your heart to the fire?

Prince Geradde hesitated, which seemed wisest, perhaps, in the face of that kind of question. Nemienne seized the chance to get to her feet, not quite steadily.

"**Little mageling,**" the dragon said to her. "**But this time it is not you who has called me out of the ephemeral and the eternal and the immanent.**"

"No," said Nemienne. She meant to say it firmly and loudly, as Geradde had spoken his name, but it came out sounding rather smothered. She cleared her throat and tried again, "Prince Telis seeks to bind you, O Ekorraodde! He seeks to bind Geradde, and you through him, and I think—I think he is still coming, and I don't know how to stop him!"

"**Would you put yourself in his way? I think you might. I think you will.**" The great fiery head of the dragon tilted consideringly. White-gold flames, amethyst at the heart, rippled along its jaw and along the elegant bones of its face. Golden sparks scattered from the long antennae that swayed above its eyes. But somehow the heat of its fire seemed contained. Distant. Its eyes burned with black fire, but they also seemed endlessly deep. "**But for all your passion, you are yet a very small mageling,**" added the dragon reflectively.

Nemienne meant to protest, but words and thoughts alike scattered in the face of the dragon's immensity. She did feel very small, even standing as straight as she could. She thought of Prince Telis, of his harp, of the old bone with which he had sounded its notes—she thought she could still hear it, even now, the harp notes sounding one by one behind the rushing winds and the roaring fire. She *could* hear it; she was more and more certain as she listened.

Mage Ankennes had come close to destroying the dragon— hadn't he? She had believed he had come very close, and for all its greatness and power, the dragon had not been able to defend itself, not without Taudde's help. But Taudde wasn't here this time, and now Prince Telis was trying to bind it, and as far as she could see, it wasn't moving to defend itself from him, either. She said helplessly, "Listen! Can't you hear the harp? It was *made* to bind you, and he's coming, listen! It's closer all the time!"

Geradde put his hands on Nemienne's shoulders, steadying

317

her. "Ekorraodde!" he said. "My brother is your enemy. I know—I know we are—are ephemeral creatures, and you are—" he stopped, words failing him.

Nemienne understood exactly how he felt, but in the moment he'd given her, she'd managed to catch her breath and her wits. She said quickly, "But still we fear he may be dangerous to you, O Ekorraodde. You shouldn't linger here to meet him. You should do something to stop him!"

"So small a mageling, yet indeed so fierce," said the dragon, in a voice as low and murmuring as the sea or the wind.

"You can *hear* the harp!" Nemienne cried. "You can hear it coming. Can't you hear it?"

In that moment, Sa-Telis came. He didn't stumble through the half-seen paths of air and fire. The light seemed merely to fold back around him. Around him, and around the harp. He had his hand firmly set on the harp's wide, heavy frame, and he strummed one string and then another with the Seriantes bone. Taliente's skull rested between his feet, the empty eye sockets shadowed by a familiar kind of heavy darkness. It was missing teeth, and behind the teeth that remained, Nemienne could see that it was filled with shadows inside. The skull was horrible, having it here was horrible, and she flinched back toward the dragon—she was frightened of the dragon, but not horrified by it, she understood that suddenly but didn't have time to think about it, because Geradde started forward. She caught his hand to stop him, but then saw, as he had, that the serpent-prince had brought with him more than just that harp.

Prince Tepres seemed at first both there and elsewhere. His brother had snatched him out of the ordinary world, but it seemed at first that Sa-Telis would not be able to draw him all the way into this place beyond the curtains of fire and light. Prince Tepres wavered around the edges as though surrounded by heat haze in the summer. Even so, he was striding toward his brother, as though he had every intention of tearing the bone right out of his hands and throwing it into the fire. Sparks trailed behind him and rose up at every foot-fall.

Sa-Telis turned his head, unhurriedly taking in the curtains of light above and the fiery translucent stone below; taking in, too, the presence of Nemienne and Geradde, and the undulating form of the dragon. Ekorraodde seemed both vast and somehow insubstantial in the fiery wind, rippling in the heat haze, hard to see around the edges. It did not speak, nor did it act, but only turned its great head to consider the newcomers. Nemienne had no idea what it was waiting for. She was terrified of what it might do, and yet wished she could think of something to say that would make it act now, right *now*. She couldn't bear to wait, and yet everything seemed to be happening so slowly. Sa-Telis struck one harpstring and then another, and Prince Tepres strode forward, and Geradde moved toward Tepres, but Nemienne just stood frozen, unable to think of a single thing to do.

Then Sa-Telis bent and struck Taliente Seriantes' skull sharply with the heel of his hand. The skull shattered, and all around them, the crystalline light seemed to shatter, too. Prince Tepres cried out, staggering, and Geradde leaped forward to catch him. Nemienne was aware of that, but most of her attention was on the fragments of the skull. Blood welled from the dry bone, streaking the translucent stone with thick crimson, dulling the light that burned out of it. The pieces of the skull scattered, but not randomly. The jagged pieces formed sharp letters, in lines that slashed out longer and thinner and more ragged than ought to have been possible for shards of bone—they were making runes, Nemienne saw: runes of containment and imprisonment. Runes that turned back on themselves, that wove into knots, that closed in on every side. The runes were drawn in blood, she saw that suddenly; a dark crimson welled up all along each jagged line.

It was Tepres' blood. She looked at him in horror as she understood that. His hands were welling with blood as though his brother had slashed across his palms with a knife. It seemed a great deal of blood. He leaned on Geradde, who had an arm around him—they did not look very much alike, but there was a similarity, Nemienne saw it more clearly now that they stood together beneath the burning light of the dragon. But Prince Tepres swayed, his face waxen. Geradde could not keep his brother on his feet, but had to ease him down until Tepres half lay on the glimmering stone, his head on Geradde's knee. Blood ran out across the stone, making more runes that Nemienne almost recognized.

Sa-Telis was a bit like his brothers, yet different. If she had been glimpsing all three men for the first time, Nemienne thought she would have guessed right away that they were brothers. But she thought that she would also have realized right away that there was something wrong with Prince Telis.

Sa-Telis was older, but that was not the difference. His eyes were his mother's startling blue rather than the more ordinary Seriantes black or gray, but that was not the difference, either. Where Tepres, even now in this extremity, wore a look of haughty disdain; where Geradde's expression was closed, neutral, and hard to read—there was a coldness to Sa-Telis that was not so much like a courtier's mask, and in fact very much, Nemienne thought, like the coldness of a serpent. He did not seem to be afraid of the dragon, and certainly not of his brothers. He did not look like he had ever been afraid of anything.

He took his hand away from the frame of the harp and stepped forward, turning the long bone absently in his hand. His eyes went from the blood slowly spreading in its runes across the burning crystal of this place, to his brothers, and Nemienne saw how he dismissed Geradde, and how his lips tightened in satisfaction at what he had done to Tepres. He glanced at her, but dismissively, unconcerned with anything she might do. Nemienne felt the flick of that contemptuous dismissal like the slap of his hand, and suddenly wondered, with a shiver of dismay, if he had made even her defiance into part of his sorcery.

She knew the beginnings of magecraft and a tiny bit of sorcery, but anything she knew was as nothing to Prince Telis. She could hardly even understand what he had done; she barely knew enough to recognize runes of containment and limitation and had no idea at all how anybody might counter runes like those he had drawn in blood and set directly into the stone. If it was still stone. It looked a little like granite, now, and a little like glass, and a lot like something that barely held back internal fire.

She wished she could reach the harp, but it was on the other side of those runes and she knew she couldn't pass those bloody lines. And she didn't know what she could do, even if she could get to it. She didn't even know if laying her hands across the strings would silence it.

For the harp was still sounding even now. The last string

Prince Telis had touched was still humming.

Sa-Telis tilted his head back and gazed up at the dragon. And what came into his face then was not awe or wonderment or a decent reverence, but satisfaction. A possessive satisfaction. Nemienne, greatly daring, touched the smooth curve of the dragon's nearest talon. It looked to her as though it had been polished out of translucent crystal, obsidian maybe, and then filled with fire. Light glimmered from it, and from the stone where the dragon's foot rested, but it did not feel hot to the touch. Warm, merely. Warm as blood. Nemienne swallowed hard and whispered, "Ekorraodde! Surely you won't allow yourself to be bound by—by the ephemeral ambitions of men?"

The dragon's head swayed above hers, but it did not answer. Nemienne didn't understand how it could be at once so immense and powerful and yet seem so helpless. But she could see that Prince Telis had expected to be able to master it. He had known he could bind his brother—both his brothers, apparently—and through them, the dragon.

Sa-Telis would have had to try to bind the dragon in the darkness below Kerre Maraddras, using Geradde and not Tepres, except for her. *She* had roused the dragon, and laid a path for it out of the dark and into the light. She had laid down that path straight to Prince Tepres because she had not known how to find any path that did not lead straight to a prince who was a similar thing to the dragon.

She had led the dragon away from her sisters and away from Lonne, into Kalches, following Prince Tepres' heartbeat. And Sa-Telis had followed her.

No wonder he looked at her with such contempt. She had tried to fight him, to get away from him, to get herself and Geradde away from his ambition. But she had only led him here, and now everything was so much worse. She said again, more urgently, "Ekoraodde!"

Prince Telis said, too, but sounding satisfied and amused rather than urgent, "You are greater than any tale could tell, O Ekoraodde, and yet here you are."

"You have my name," the dragon said to Prince Telis. **"I know yours, for all you believe you have hidden it from me. Sa-Telis, serpent-prince. So men call you. I know your name.**

I know your heart. It is a brittle thing, Sa-Telis. You should take care."

Some of the easy amusement left the mage-prince's face. He answered sharply, "Do you tell me *I* should take care, O Ekoraodde? But *you* are the one bound by blood and sorcery. By old death and living blood, I have bound you and I will hold you. My great-great-grandfather recognized your power when he first bound himself to you. Himself and his heirs. But he never realized what he had done, nor what use he might make of that binding."

"Taliente Neredde ken Seriantes was wiser than you, little serpent," the dragon said. **"Though he was not wise."**

Prince Telis propped his hands on his hips and laughed.

At that moment, a quick little melody slipped through the light and folded itself out upon the flank of the burning mountain, below the curtains of light and amid the shimmering fire, between the blood-runes and the harp, quite near the place where Geradde knelt beside Prince Tepres. The music was not harp music, and certainly not the deadly harp music struck from the dragon harp by dead bone. It was the light, quick voice of a wooden flute. Around the simple melody, a different flute spun a purer, more complicated harmony like a silvery net of notes. It was a duet born from human breath and not from some horrible ensorcelled harp, and every note opened a little more widely a path between the ephemeral world of men and this world of fire.

It was Taudde, of course it was. Nemienne knew that at once, and leaped to her feet to look for him. She had never been more glad to hear his flute in her life.

-23-

Prince Sehonnes was not much like his father. That was Enelle's first thought, when she saw him. His bones were almost coarse; his eyes set wide above a broad mouth and a heavy, rounded jaw. She had seen miniatures of his mother—everyone had known of and admired Skyblue; the prominence of Maple Leaf House within the flower world dated from the hour Geriodde Seriantes had chosen her as his keimiso from among all the flowers of Lonne. But Enelle could see very little of his mother in Prince Sehonnes, either. In Sehonnes, she thought she could see the echoes of a more distant and brutal inheritance.

Though perhaps that impression was simply the result of knowing what he had done, and what he had tried to do.

Sehonnes waited for his father in the formal throne room, perhaps meaning thereby to make himself look like a king and his father like a petitioner. Enelle thought Prince Sehonnes had made a mistake when he did that. She didn't think anything could possibly make Geriodde Nerenne ken Seriantes look like anything else but a king, and no one could possibly set foot in this hall without picturing Geriodde holding court from the massive throne at the far end.

The room was vast. Its floor was imported black marble, which was extremely dramatic and must have been terribly expensive. All that expanse of marble was broken up only by rows of red and gray porphyry pillars, magnificent accents striding across that shining black. At the far end of the hall, where it captured every eye, stood the massive throne, rough-carved of plain grey granite. All around the hall, the walls were hidden not by tapestries or by panels of wooden filigree, but by huge paintings depicting all the greatest triumphs of the Dragons of Lirionne. One caught Enelle's eye; she couldn't help but compare Prince Sehonnes to the greater-than-lifesized figure that strode across the wall behind him. There was Taliente Neredde ken Seriantes—yes, Sehonnes had much the same broad bones and coarseness of feature. The painting showed Taliente Seriantes casting down lesser kings and raising up his banner above their lands, which now were his. Enelle could see, now that she viewed the famous paintings, that the artist had managed to capture something of the fierce spirit of the first Seriantes Dragon. She could almost *see* the dragon in Taliente Seriantes. Perhaps the artist had been a mage, so that he could look past the man to the dragon.

She thought she could see the dragon in Sehonnes, as well.

Prince Sehonnes was not seated on the throne. He stood before it, between the two nearest of the porphyry pillars. He stood straight, his posture aggressive, his left hand resting on the hilt of an undrawn sword. His right hand was missing, but if Enelle hadn't already known about that, she might not have noticed, for the wide sleeves of his overrobe disguised the maimed limb and he stood and moved with the confidence of a whole man. She suspected that this assumption of confidence was part of a planned performance, but she could not see any give in the prince's posture. He stood square and aggressive, facing his father, with armed men at his back.

But he did not sit on the throne.

Enelle understood that, or she thought she understood it—as much as she understood anything that Prince Sehonnes had done or meant to do. The throne was not his, and now Sehonnes knew his father lived and knew he had no right at all to the throne himself. How hard and forbidding must that granite seem, for a man who had tried to murder his own father to take it!

She found herself more than a little surprised to find that Prince Sehonnes had any supporters left at all, for what man could bring himself to support a parricide and an usurper in the very face of the king he had tried to murder? But Sehonnes was not entirely deserted even yet. A quite surprising number of men supported him: soldiers in red and gray, a scattering of men in King's Own black, courtiers of the high court and the low. Enelle tried to estimate their number, and came up with a discouragingly high guess. And she could hardly crane her neck around and stare back over the men behind the king, but even without taking time to count the men on both sides, she could guess that the numbers were more even than she would have liked.

"What did he *offer* them?" she murmured.

She was speaking to herself, not meaning to be overhead, but the king slanted an ironic glance down at her and answered, "Power, of course. Or the bitter satisfaction that comes of casting down their rivals. There are always men who believe they deserve rank or wealth or influence that they have not earned, and so hate those placed above them."

This seemed harsh to Enelle, but she had no answer. All those men *were* with Prince Sehonnes, after all, and every one of them must know now what the prince had done. Or tried to do.

Although . . . maybe some of them were not so very solidly behind the prince, after all. Because then the gathering shifted, and to her surprise she caught sight of Namir Karonnis, not far from Sehonnes. She was certain it was him, especially when he looked straight at her across the hall. Namir stood at the elbow of an older man she did not know, but the old man's overrobe was sapphire blue touched with ruby at the throat and the hem, so he must be of the high court. She was sure he must be Lord Minarras Saradd. Some of those men must be his, then, and if that was so, then she wasn't certain whom they might support if it came to fighting.

The king had been certain of Lord Minarras, certain enough to send her to him out of all the men in the city. Surely the king could not have been so wrong about Lord Minarras, and she had liked Namir when she'd met him, so maybe both of them were over there with Sehonnes because of some ruse? She wasn't certain; she couldn't be certain of anything; but she hoped that if it came to violence, Lord Minarras would turn out to be on the king's side after all.

Surely if that wasn't so, Namir wouldn't have met her eyes.

It was not supposed to come to violence, of course. If they could stop it. Or . . . most of it. She let her gaze linger on Namir's face, remembering what she had suggested. Just a little fighting, she had suggested to him. Just enough to be certain Prince Sehonnes did not live to face his father's justice. She hoped he remembered, and agreed, and would find a chance to do something. This confrontation between father and son must be hard enough for the king—let it end here, then, and not become more dire yet. That was what she tried to tell Namir through only a look.

Namir Karonnis was in black today, the black of the King's Own; he was making no pretense now. His expression was forbidding, but he gave Enelle a tiny nod. That was vastly reassuring, on more than one count. Though she thought Lord Minarras himself looked anxious rather than resolute, she hoped Namir would not hesitate if—when—it came time to move.

She wondered where else her message had spread, and what Neriodd had been doing—she hoped he was all right, and had been doing sensible and effective things somewhere—and how quickly everyone else might have realized the king had stepped back onto the board. They were so early; that was the part that worried her. The king had said *the day before the solstice,* and that was not yet. Lord Minarras was here anyway . . . assuming he was really on the king's side . . . but how many other men in this hall with Prince Sehonnes might be like Lord Minarras: loyal to the king and ready, she hoped and assumed, to turn against the usurper? She couldn't guess. Alas, loyal men looked exactly the same as treacherous men. Of course they did, but somehow she had never actually realized that before.

The king still rested a good deal of his weight on Enelle, under the pretext that he was merely escorting her, showing her the courtesy that a man of wealth and position would naturally show any woman of Lonne. Enelle kept her back straight and her arm steady and tried to make it seem he was only gracious, but his weakness worried her. She was fairly certain he would not be able to keep up the pretense of vigor and strength for very long, even with her help. If he must step away from her, she was not sure he could do it at all.

She could not even give the king a worried glance, lest someone see and guess his infirmity. But she realized that she had now yet another reason to hope for a brief confrontation, and for Sehonnes to yield quickly. She wanted to see the king sitting in his throne not only because it was the throne, but because it was a chair.

Then Prince Sehonnes took one belligerent step forward and held up his hand in curt command, and Enelle stopped, and perforce the king as well.

She knew immediately that she had made a mistake, and that the king, who no doubt knew better, had been forced to follow her into it. She knew everyone had seen Sehonnes gesture in command, and everyone had seen Geriodde halt. The king knew it, too. Nothing showed on his face—she glanced at him, discreetly, from beneath her eyelashes, and so she knew he still showed nothing but stark, ruthless patience. But his hand tightened on her arm until it was all she could do not to flinch or gasp in pain.

Then Dark Of The Moon leaped from her shoulder, landing on the floor with a soft, heavy *thud*. He was a big cat, and looked bigger still in this moment, though he was not now fluffed up in anger. Instead, he blinked his odd-colored eyes in what seemed disdain, trotted straight past the prince, and leaped up onto the seat of the throne, where he sat very straight and stared out at the gathering, looking dignified and thoroughly superior.

Prince Sehonnes, nonplused and off-balance, immediately seemed faintly ridiculous. He half raised his good hand, as though to knock the cat from the throne, but Dark merely looked through him and past him, and Sehonnes hesitated. He must know, as Enelle knew, how much worse he would look if he actually hit the cat—bad enough he had even lifted his hand. He turned sharply back to face his father instead.

The king smiled: a thin smile without much humor to it. But he let go of Enelle's arm and walked forward alone to face his son, exactly as though he had halted for that instant only to dismiss her from the confrontation.

It was perfectly done. If Enelle hadn't known how much of his weight she had been supporting, she would have believed it herself. She made herself step aside instead, as though she weren't in the least concerned for the king. She folded her hands, straightened her back, and tried to keep her expression placid, as though she had no doubts in the world. She knew *Karah* could have done it—Karah had been learning exactly this among the keiso, and Enelle had always thought how silly and pointless all such arts were, but now she wished very much she were more like her sister, more like an elegant keiso. An ordinary girl had no place here, she knew that. She had no idea what she looked like, but she couldn't possibly manage to look *serene*.

But no one was looking at her, anyway, she realized. Even Namir Karonnis wasn't looking at her. Everyone's attention was fixed on Geriodde Nerenne ken Seriantes, and on his son, and maybe on Dark Of The Moon. So it didn't matter what she did; she couldn't give the king away after all. She told herself that as firmly as possible and almost managed to make herself believe it.

Prince Sehonnes drew a breath and took a step forward, but it was the king who spoke first. That, Enelle knew, was a mistake *Sehonnes* made—to allow his father to speak first and so reclaim the moment.

"My son," the king said in a level voice, "Let us not have bloodshed here before the throne of our father and our grandfather and our great-grandfather. This is not seemly. Lay down the knife and yield yourself to me, and even yet this day may not pass into blood and iron."

He spoke with no evidence of haste or even urgency, and Enelle saw, in the prince's darkening face, that Sehonnes realize he had made a mistake in allowing his father to speak before him. The prince strode forward a step and answered loudly. "All men know that you have lost your taste for blood and iron, *Geriodde*. All men know that you have lost your courage and your strength! Why else spare a Kalchesene spy who came into your own city and lifted his hand against your son and heir? But then, we all know how little you regard your own sons! Shall a man who does murder against his own sons call for peace in his house? Shall a king who strikes down his own sons call for an end to blood and iron?"

Enelle watched the king anxiously, afraid for him—for them all—if he could not find an answer. She could see that there was enough truth in the prince's accusations to make them hard to answer. Everyone knew there was some truth to what Sehonnes said—he only put into words the doubts that must have crept into everyone's mind after the earlier rebellion of the king's elder sons. All about the hall, there was a low susurrus as men whispered to their neighbors. She looked for Lord Minarras, and saw that he was speaking quietly to another man about his own age, but she couldn't guess what they said.

But the king only asked grimly, "What is this concern for your brothers, Sehonnes? Do you balk at murder? You come late to this sensibility." He took a step forward, with now no sign of infirmity, and asked, his tone taking on a cutting edge, "Where is your brother Tepres? Where is your brother Geradde? Whose blood drips from the knife you laid upon my throne?"

This counteraccusation went home; Sehonnes did not exactly flinch, but he braced himself in a way that was as telling as a flinch. "Telis—" he began.

"Oh, indeed, will you lay the blame for all dire acts against your brother, who is not here to answer you?" the king asked, his tone withering. "It was *your* hand that drove the blade that struck *me* down, Sehonnes. Not your brother's, for all the false tale you have been at pains to put about. You thought no one lived to contradict you, but *I* am here and I hold you to account. Shall the people of Lonne have for their king a man who is liar as well as a parricide and an usurper?"

"*I* have done no murder! Can you say the same?" snapped Sehonnes at once. "You cannot! All men know you cannot say so. You turn against your own blood, you allow Kalchesene sorcerers to snatch away your heir and deliver him to Kalches, and now you stand there—you *stand* there, and you accuse me of *parricide* when plainly you are perfectly well! Usurpation I will grant you, but of the two of us, it is not *I* who lays a bloody knife on the throne!"

Plainly he had been prepared for this accusation, but Enelle thought she heard an honest fury in his voice, too. His words were even true, if one considered that he had failed to kill his father, and also failed, perhaps not through any lack of effort, to kill Prince Tepres—though Enelle didn't know what might have happened to Geradde, or for that matter, Telis.

She could see that the king was having difficulty framing an answer to these accusations. It must be so hard for him. It must be hard for Sehonnes, too, but he had driven them all to this moment and she had little pity to spare for him. But she flinched to see how the prince's words struck his father.

So she said, quietly but clearly, dropping each word into the tension like tiles onto a game board, "I am only a girl, and I do not understand great things, but I am confused by your accusations, Prince Sehonnes. If you never raised your blade against your brother, then how did you lose your hand?"

Sehonnes had no easy answer. He glared at her with focused anger, but he could not cause her words to be unsaid. But he drew breath, and she guessed that he had anticipated this attack, too, and had some smooth answer prepared. She waited, tense, to see what he might say—or do, for he might simply call for an attack, and then who knew what might happen? For a sharp-edged instant, anything might have happened.

Then another voice said suddenly, "The girl is quite correct." It was a thin voice, an old man's voice, but firm enough for all that. It was Lord Minarras, who stepped forward and said sharply, "To do justice upon an usurper is not murder." He gave the king a firm nod and went on, forcefully, speaking now to Sehonnes, "But to strike against your king and father is to *attempt* parricide, and that is worse than usurpation. If your father had died, Prince Sehonnes, it would have been by your hand. And if Prince Tepres is in Kalchesene hands, whose fault is that but yours? What bargain *have* you offered to King Berente ken Lariodde? You have been quite scant of details on that matter, Prince Sehonnes. Let us hear now what has passed between you and the King of Kalches."

There was a biting assurance to this speech, and at the end, he lifted his hand in a curt gesture and all his men moved sharply away from Sehonnes, swinging around so that they plainly supported the king instead. Enelle was first startled, but then understood that Lord Minarras had arranged exactly this—to appear to support Sehonnes purely so that he could choose a dramatic moment to snatch his support away from the prince and give it instead to the king. She could see, too, how the prince's other supporters wavered, suddenly irresolute. This was most reassuring and in fact very satisfying, but she saw how the king only grew more grim as opinion began to fall against Sehonnes. Then she could not help but remember that there was no way for the king to bring this confrontation to a good conclusion.

Then she realized that Prince Sehonnes knew this, too.

Seeing his father's bleak expression, and seeing his own support fall away, the prince flung a disgusted, furious look around at all his people. "Let us ask rather what bargain

Geriodde Nerenne ken Seriantes would strike with King Berente of Kalches!" he declared in loud voice. Then, striding forward, he challenged his father directly: "What Lirionne has won by blood and iron, *you* would cast aside! You are no fit king, and no fit heir of Taliente Seriantes! If you would avow otherwise, then take up a sword and prove your right in this hall before us all!" And he drew his own sword with a long ringing scrape of steel and faced his father squarely.

Enelle heard the desperation in the prince's voice before she understood it. Then she realized how awkwardly he had drawn his sword, and saw that for all his strong stance, he held it awkwardly as well. *Then*—she was embarrassed it had taken her so long—she understood that Sehonnes was not, of course, left handed; and that he was not aware of his father's lingering weakness. He knew the king had been injured, but he knew also that it was his father's left hand and not his right that had been maimed, and so, though he owned youth and weight and strength, he thought the disadvantage in such a contest would be his. But he could feel all the impetus in the hall shifting toward his father, so he thought he had no choice but to make such a challenge. He thought the king had no choice but to answer him by taking up a sword, and he had no idea that Geriodde might not even be able to pick one up, far less fight. Far less fight his *son*.

Yet even so, Geriodde was already turning stiffly to the nearest soldier, the captain who had first joined them, who had now stepped forward to offer the king his sword.

Enelle wanted to run forward. She did not run. She walked, sedately, imagining how Karah would walk. She wanted to look graceful, not *desperate*. She didn't even know what she was going to do—she didn't know what she *could* do. But she knew she had to do something. She had to, because no one else knew that Geriodde could not possibly fight. She couldn't stop herself from giving Namir Karonnis an urgent look, and Lord Minarras as well, but she knew they wouldn't understand—although she saw Namir's eyes narrow, so maybe he guessed what she meant, but it didn't even matter, because what could either Namir or his lord do to help?

She reached the king's side and laid her hand on his arm,

stopping him from taking the captain's weapon. She tried to make it a graceful, urgent gesture, as though she approached him as a suppliant and not as though she was afraid he might be reaching the end of his strength. She still didn't know what she ought to do or what might be the best thing to do, so she did the only thing she could think of. She said, speaking quickly lest anyone should interrupt her and loudly enough for those closest to hear her plainly, "Eminence, will you not be merciful? If your son yields even now, will you not spare him? Surely—surely Lonne has suffered enough grief in the past year. And—" inspiration struck—"And you do not know for certain what other of your sons may live. What if Prince Sehonnes is the last, the very last of them all?"

Her words rang out with unexpected clarity because the whole hall had quieted to hear the king's answer to his son's challenge, and then, once they saw Enelle move, to hear what she would say. There was a horrifying ring to them, as though she might have spoken nothing but the truth. She shook her head, trying to believe that she had only made up that warning to spare the king and that she wasn't actually afraid it might be true.

Geriodde stared down at her, his eyebrows rising in astonishment. "I hardly imagine that is possible."

Plainly it was all too possible, but the chill in his words made it clear that he would not entertain any such idea. Enelle couldn't tell whether he understood what she had tried to do, or whether he actually thought he should be able—or *would* be able—to answer his son's challenge.

"But—" she tried to think of something else to say, something that might offer the king a better way to stop this, since her first try had gone wrong. "Eminence—"

Then the king turned again to face his son, raising his eyebrows. "Did you murder your brothers?" he asked coldly. "I believe we all know what has become of Tepres. But Geradde? I had believed you a friend to your younger brother. Where is Geradde?"

"I was! I am!" snapped Sehonnes. And, furiously, "I have no notion where Geradde may have got to, none! But his blood is not on *my* hands!"

"Sehonnes. All of this . . . disorder . . . is your doing. If

Geradde has come to harm of it, that *is* on your hands." The king paused and then added, even more coldly, "But if you speak the truth, then I may yet show mercy. Yield to me, and I will make the king of Kalches this offer: he may return Tepres to me, and I will send *you* to him in return. You may choose exile in Kalches rather than death here. And so long as you dwell in Kalches, I will not raise my banners in the north. In exchange for his agreement to keep you close-guarded and out of Lirionne, I will make *that* offer to Berente of Kalches."

Sehonnes stared at his father in disbelief. "You cannot possible expect me—"

"I do not expect it at all. But it would be best. Look about you, my son! Your supporters desert you. Thus your challenge to me. But you cannot challenge me, Sehonnes. You have not had time to learn to wield a sword left-handed."

And the king reached past Enelle and took the sword the captain had offered him. He did not lift it in challenge, but rested its tip gently on the marble floor, though lightly, not permitting himself to lean his weight on it—Enelle could imagine the effort handling the weapon so lightly cost him, but he did not allow the effort to show. Except in his growing pallor, which perhaps no one saw but her. He said, his words intense and forceful, "Take this chance I offer, Sehonnes! I do not know how many of my sons yet live, but I do not require you to join those that lie cold in the tomb. Mercy is not just. But I am weary to death of justice."

"Mercy! From *you*? Murderer that you are?" cried Sehonnes. He whipped up the sword he held and started forward, moving fast, looking, despite his awkward left-handed grip on his sword, as strong and unstoppable as a charging bull.

Enelle uttered a small sound, something between a gasp and a squeak, and tried to pull the king back, out of the way, thought the attempt was plainly hopeless. But he pushed her away with more strength than she would have expected, and brought his own sword up in a defense that must surely fail at the first stroke—

And somewhere behind them, not far away, came a short, sharp *crack*, as of wood meeting wood, and a reverberating hum as though a massive harpstring had been plucked just once, and Prince Sehonnes slammed to a halt. A massive arrow had smashed into his chest, an arrow almost more like a spear, and for a long moment Sehennes seemed to hold perfectly still, a look of astonishment on his face, his sword still in his hand, all his forward impetus halted. Then, almost as though acting a scene in a play, he dropped the sword. The blade rang against marble, and rang again, the sound almost musical. And then Sehonnes tottered, and his knees folded, and he crumpled down across the fallen sword.

Enelle stared at the fallen prince for a moment that was probably not as long as it seemed. Then she turned, slowly. It seemed to her she still heard the ringing of the sword, though now it lay still; it seemed to her she heard . . . something. Something like the reverberation of a snapped harp string, far away and yet near at hand, so that she looked around in confusion.

Beside her, the king was standing very still, his eyes on his fallen son. He was perfectly white and perfectly composed. Enelle blinked, and blinked again, trying to understand. Then she finally did, and hesitantly touched the king's arm. Expression slowly came back into his face, then, and he turned at last, forgetful now of his infirmity, so that he swayed a little and she had to support him as he faced the doorway.

It was the other prince. It was Prince Meiredde, the oldest of the king's left-hand sons, the prince whom everyone had discounted, the prince who, everyone knew, had no interest in court or kingship or war. It was Prince Meiredde, who desired nothing but ships and sailing, and who did not remotely care who ruled. It was Prince Meiredde, who had, it seemed, cared enough about the throne of Lirionne to come home after all.

Meiredde held over his shoulder one of the powerful harpoon-throwing crossbows that were mounted on ocean-going ships. They were meant for the great fishes, those crossbows; they were not meant to be carried about like normal weapons. But Meiredde was a big man and he held it as though it weighed nothing.

The man beside him, holding a sheaf of harpoons, was Benne. On Benne's shoulder perched Karah's kitten, Moonglow. And on Meiredde's other side stood a man who must, Enelle guessed from his ashen pallor at the near calamity, be the king's man Neriodd, appearing at last to meet his king. He gripped a naked sword in both hands, as though even now he was not certain they had come in time and was prepared to do battle. Behind them and trailing out the door was a crowd of sailors, most armed with short swords or knives or ordinary crossbows.

In all the vast throne room, no one moved or made a sound.

Then Moonglow leaped from Benne's shoulder and darted forward, and Dark Of The Moon, who had never moved in all the confrontation, leaped from the throne, and the two cats met in the middle of the floor, nose to nose. Dark had a irritable air about him, though it didn't affect his dignity; and Moonglow looked nothing but smug. Enelle, though seldom fanciful, could almost have sworn Dark was saying *Left it a bit late, didn't you?* And Moonglow answering, *Don't fuss so; we were exactly on time.* Then both cats swung around, trotted straight down the hall and disappeared into the shadows behind the throne.

Disregarding this miniature drama, Prince Meiredde swung the crossbow down from his shoulder with a grunt and handed it to Benne, who, also a big man, took it easily but as though he was not certain what to do with it. Meiredde ignored him, ignored them all. His stare, hard and angry, was on his father. He strode forward, his gait rolling like any sailor's, and stopped a pace or two away. From this close distance, his anger was even more palpable.

Geriodde met his son's eyes, but said nothing. His face and manner were unreadable, but some of the color had come back into his face.

Meiredde shook his head, a sharp, exasperated movement. Then he went to one knee. "*That* was murder, if you say it was," he said flatly.

The king stared down at his son. He asked at last, "Do you expect me to condemn you for it?"

"I meant to kill him, and I did. He never had a chance. A man's not going to walk away from a harpoon. Nor did I call out a warning. But," said Meiredde grimly, "it's not like I did it for you. I didn't want him on the throne. He was a bully and a braggart as a boy, and a bully and a braggart as a man. It wouldn't have done." He glanced past his father, at his brother's body, crimson blood shocking against the black marble, and then around at the hall. "I did think it would be harder to get to him. And it—he—I didn't expect—" he stopped.

"You did not expect to feel the shock of your brother's death?"

"Not like that," Prince Meiredde said grimly. "Or I might have let you finish it. Or not; a harpoon in the chest is a good deal more certain than a duel." But Meiredde hesitated, and then added more quietly, in a much different tone, "Besides, maybe I did do it for you, a little. I think you've put enough of your sons to death."

There was a pause. Then the king said grimly, "More than enough. Yes." He handed the sword he held to Enelle, probably because he didn't have the strength to toss it back across the small distance to the captain who had loaned it to him. She hefted its unfamiliar weight, wondering what to do with it, and was grateful when the captain came wordlessly to take it back.

The king paid attention to neither of them. He turned one hand palm up, signaling his son to rise. "If it was murder, then I pardon it. And . . . I thank you."

Meiredde let out a breath, the first hint of uncertainty he had shown. But there was nothing uncertain about his curt nod as he got back to his feet. "Good. Then I'm going to go find Geradde. He's missing, I hear. If that serpent-hearted Telis has done for him, you'll have to pardon me again, for I won't stop till I put him down as well. No, don't say it. I'm not arguing. I'm finding Geradde and then I'm going back to my ship." He threw a grim look around the hall, looking suddenly much like his father, though nothing about him was very like the king except his expression.

"Stay," commanded the king. "I do not . . . I do not even know yet whether any of my other sons still live. I shall send men to search all of Lonne for Geradde. I shall send to Kalches to discover what has become of Tepres. I shall find Telis, and deal with him as he deserves. Stay by me until we know the full accounting of all your brothers."

Meiredde snorted. "Stay? Here? No. I'm going to find Geradde myself, and then I'm going back to my ship. Send me word there, if you will, if you discover my other brothers' fate. I will wait to hear. And I will send word if I find Geradde. But however events prove out, *I* am not your heir, nor will I be. Unless you order me held in the Laodd by force." He met his father's eyes and waited to see what Geriodde would do. Enelle waited too, though she could hardly believe—

"Go, then," conceded the king, granting his son leave with a small lift of one hand, and Enelle relaxed. But the king did not. He stood quite still, waiting, while Prince Meiredde gathered his sailors with a glance, turned his back on his father and the court, and vanished again through the door that led out of the throne room and out of the Laodd and back into the wide freedom of the city and the wider freedom of the sea. The whole thing had been so unexpected, and taken so few moments, that she was hardly certain it had happened it all.

Except when Enelle dared to look back at Geriodde. Then she believed it. He looked . . . as though watching his eldest left-hand son walk away from him cost him more than he had quite realized it would.

Then the king turned and strode to his throne, and turned again to sweep his gaze across the crowd, and then slowly sank down to sit. Even Enelle couldn't tell whether he took that seat to reclaim his authority, or because he was no longer capable of keeping his feet. Even in the midst of all these soldiers and courtiers and everyone; even with Neriodd coming back to his side, concern in his eyes; even with her right here, the king looked . . . perfectly self-contained, and perfectly alone.

-24-

Taudde feared at first that even with Karah to guide them, they might not be able to find any path that would lead to Tepres, and presumably to Sa-Telis and the dragon and that deadly harp. Without her, he would have no idea which way to go. The harp notes each seemed to spin out in a different direction, and he could hardly see through the dazzling, shifting expanses of sapphire and emerald, amethyst and topaz. The very air seemed to have turned to all the jewel-tones of fire, and he had no idea what part of this was the working of the dragon and what the working of the harp.

He could hardly believe that he had spent a full season in the same house as that harp; that he had even dared, once or twice, to sound the least of it's strings. He knew now that he had not known how to listen to it, and he saw—now, too late—that he had never come close to understanding it at all.

Nor the dragon. He had not come close to understanding the dragon, either.

That dragon had slept below Lonne for what? Hundreds of years, surely. Since long before Taliente Seriantes had discovered it there, perhaps. But now it had swept its fiery path through the brilliant sky and into the mountains of Kalches, and Taudde couldn't help but think it had come here as though it knew where it meant to go. That it had come here to Kedres and these sharp-edged mountains as though it was coming home. There were no Kalchesene tales about dragons of light and darkness, but . . . that was a very old dragon. Or so Taudde suspected. He could believe that it had dwelled among these mountains long before men had ever set foot in this high country.

Taudde could hardly imagine what it might mean for his people, that the dragon had coiled itself into these mountains. He couldn't imagine what might become of Kedres if the dragon stayed where it was for any length of time. Its very *presence* was a catastrophe, even if it did nothing. He could hardly imagine what his grandfather might try to do to free Kalches from it—his grandfather would *kill* himself with the effort, and then the whole country would surely split asunder between all the Lariodde uncles and aunts and cousins who would declare *they* knew what to do. Uncle Heronn would not be able to hold Kalches together in the face of that dragon.

Stubborn old man. He should have listened to Taudde right from the first. That would have . . . changed absolutely nothing, probably.

Taudde wished he knew what had happened to Lonne, when the dragon rose. It had spoken once of tearing down the mountains and letting in the sea. Taudde wished he knew whether it had done exactly that, when it came out of the darkness and became the light. He wished he knew what might happen to Kedres, if it rose again now and carried its fire back into the sky. Would these mountains, too, crash down upon the town where ephemeral men lived?

He listened for the echo of harpstrings, for the echo of the tide that rose and fell far away, for the roaring echo of remorseless burning. For the heartbeat of the dragon.

"We have to *hurry*," said Irelle, lengthening her stride to come up beside him. She gestured toward Karah, who was trying to find the way for all of them. "Can she find the path or not? Can *you* find it in her, or not? We're going to be *too late*. Don't you feel it?"

Taudde shook his head, not disagreeing, but trying to clear his mind, which was filled with the swelling notes of the harp and the roar of light that was not quite fire. Irelle's impatient courage made him feel old, though she was only a handful of years younger than he.

But he said only, "I'll find the path. I can almost hear it, in her heartbeat. We won't be too late. That would be entirely unacceptable."

Irelle rolled her eyes. She had her silver flute in her hand. Her other hand shielded her eyes from the incandescent, rippling curtains of light: gold and gold-white before them, sapphire and emerald to either side. The air tasted of fire.

Leilis came up beside Taudde and his cousin as they paused. Leilis seemed, as always, untouched by anything that had happened. Several strands of her hair had come out of its intricate braid, but even that only gave her a look of unstudied grace. It wasn't all keiso illusion, Taudde knew; that imperturbability was just part of Leilis. He wanted to wrap her up in his arms and cling to her, except he had to have his hands free for his flute.

They had come entirely out of the world of men, now, into a place of light wound about with thundering harpsong. But naturally Leilis looked perfectly calm. She murmured, her voice pitched to carry through the roar of light, "We shall do what we must do, but we must go carefully enough that we do not fall into the hands of our enemy. Sa-Telis will know that we are coming, no doubt. Yet we will do better not to go carelessly, even so."

Irelle gestured forward, sharply impatient. "He'll know we're coming if we actually manage to go to him! If we're going to find the way, we had better do it soon! Who else is there to stop that mage-prince? I assure you, I don't intend to lose the proper Seriantes heir after all *this*. We *need* him—unless Lonne *was* destroyed—"

"We cannot know what the dragon has done or might yet do," Karah said absently, coming back to them. "But my sister Nemienne was there, did you see? Just at the end." She looked earnestly at Irelle. "Nemienne would not have let the dragon tear down the ephemeral cities of men."

"How could *your sister* stop *that creature* from doing anything it wished?" Irelle demanded. Sometime in the past days, she had plainly gotten the whole story of the dragon and Mage Ankennes from Karah, but she sounded perfectly disbelieving now.

Karah only looked at her in surprise. "Nemienne would know what to say to it," she explained simply. "She understands its heart better than we do." She added to Taudde, "I'm sure I can find Nemienne, even if I can't find Tepres—but I can! I can find them both. But you have to play open the path. You did it before. Can't you do it now?"

Taudde raked a hand through his hair, harassed and impatient and completely unwilling to admit that he had brought them all into this place of shifting light and then gotten them lost within it.

Then he found he had taken Leilis' hand after all without ever quite noticing, and squeezed it now, a private little gesture, glad despite everything that she was there—that she was here—that she was *with him*. Leilis smiled at him, her familiar cool smile, but she also returned the pressure, and Taudde suddenly knew just how to open the one right path among the multitude of wrong paths.

He handed Leilis his flute. He had carved it of driftwood cast up on the shale beaches below the Laodd. It was very plain, very simple. It felt pleasant in his hand, the wood like silk. He had tuned the flute to the voice of the sea, but Leilis' heartbeat echoed the tides and the tides that washed against the broken shoreline of Lonne echoed the heartbeat of the dragon. He could hear the dragon in the undertones of her voice and the rhythm of her breathing.

Leilis looked at him, then took the flute and turned it over, her gaze growing distant.

"Play it," Taudde urged her. "Play it. Your heartbeat echoes the dragon's heartbeat. So let the melody you find in it be our path through the light. Open the way, and let Karah hear what you hear. This time, you're the one who has to play. Irelle and I will follow where you and Karah lead."

Irelle's eyebrows arched at this. She had hardly looked at Leilis before this, but now she tilted her head, studying her with intense interest. But she did not ask any questions.

Leilis lifted Taudde's flute to her lips and played a very simple melody. Taudde knew it. Everyone knew it. It was a teaching song that little children learned almost as soon as their hands were steady enough to span two notes on their first flute. He had heard it in Lonne, but there the words that went with the melody were different. In Kalches, the song was about swallows coming back in the spring. In Lonne, it was about gulls crying over the sea and the broken beaches.

The notes drifted out into the air. It was a sad song in both Kalches and Lonne, but the melody was comforting, too: a breath of childhood called into a sorcerer's instrument.

Leilis was not a sorcerer. But she had been wrapped in

magic her whole life, or nearly; she had been caught for years in that strange curse of tangled magecraft and dragon magic. Taudde kept his eyes on her while she played. But he didn't know whether he heard it when the song changed, or whether he saw that change in her face.

It was not really a change in the song, but in the voice of the flute. Taudde had tuned every note to the sea. But as she played it, Leilis re-tuned every note to darkness and then to brilliant fire, to the heartbeat of the dragon. She might have known what she did, or not; he could not tell. But Taudde felt every shift of the melody in his bones. Hearing that change, Irelle smiled, a swift angry smile, and gave him a fierce little nod, acknowledging that he'd been right after all.

Karah didn't make any such gesture, but she turned her head sharply, as though she'd heard someone call her name. Then she smiled at Leilis, a warm, sweet smile, and ran forward. Leilis followed, not so hastily, playing as she went.

Irelle grabbed Taudde's wrist and they followed, quickly, while the flute lay down a path for them that they could perceive.

His cousin wasn't afraid, or not afraid enough. Nor was Karah, nor even Leilis. Taudde was afraid for them all. He wished none of them had put herself in this peril, but it was too late, and he supposed they had the right, each in her own way— and he couldn't have found the way without them. Leilis had her heart tuned to the dragon and Karah could follow Tepres through any confusion of paths, through music and light, and together they made a path wide enough for any blind Kalchesene to follow.

And he couldn't help but remember that the last time he had faced the dragon, he would have been helpless except for Leilis and Karah and Nemienne. Though he had no idea what any of the women could do against Sa-Telis, he could not deny that they might each do *something*.

He strode forward. Irelle followed him—or she moved first and he followed her; he was not entirely certain which of them led, but the path spun out before them. He could see it plainly now. They all could, he knew. They all followed it, as it spun out along the curtains of jewel-toned light, and they followed it out of the light and into the light, into the shadow of Kerre Irelle.

The dragon had made a place for itself here, at the foot of the greatest mountain in all of Kalches. Taudde understood that, after the first confused moments when he had no idea where they had come. It was a place open to the sky, floored with crystallized light; bounded on one side by the granite slope of the mountain and on the other by pillars of fierce golden fire that seemed to pour up and down without movement or measure. The air, hot and still, smelled of ozone and fire; the air glittered, filled with light and the memory of fire. Here the dragon reclined, some long span of it, looping in and out of the mountain's flank and the brilliant air. It seemed a creature half of gemstones and half of flame. Little flickers of fire ran down the long edges of its wings and dripped, burning white-gold, to gutter against the flank of the mountain.

But for all the dragon's great size and power, it was caged by sharp runes of containment and restraint. Taudde had only begun to learn magecraft, but he knew at least what they were, and he could see more or less what they were meant to do.

The runes cut right through the light: sharp, deadly lines of black shadow—or of blood, Taudde realized, seeing the dark garnet gleam of those marks; they were not true black after all. Prince Tepres half sat and half lay by the dragon's great taloned foot, supported by another man—in fact, he was supported by his half-brother Geradde, whom Taudde recognized after the first beat of astonishment. But after his first surprise, he was then less astonished: no doubt Sa-Telis had found it useful to collect more than one of his brothers. Or had considered that he might need more blood than one brother could supply, for a good deal of blood seemed to have been poured out to make those runes. Clearly Geradde was as much a prisoner as Tepres.

The small, familiar figure of Nemienne hovered near the princes. How the girl had been caught up in this Taudde could not imagine—well, he could, of course; it was his fault; every mage in Lonne must have known that she had become his apprentice after Ankennes' death, and Sa-Telis must have guessed or deduced that she was connected in some way to the dragon. He hoped she hadn't come to any harm—yet; he could see no way to get her out of this peril now.

At the moment, Nemienne knelt by the dragon's massive

foot, her hand pressed to one curved talon. The dragon's head swayed above Nemienne, but Taudde was nearly certain that it did not threaten her. He was certain that the real threat to them all, the imminent threat, came from Sa-Telis and not from the dragon. Even if it had not been caged by magecrafted runes.

Prince Telis stood beside the great harp, one hand resting possessively on its massive carved frame, though he was not playing it now. But though he was not touching its strings, it was not silent: its voice thrummed in the air and the stone as though it was the voice of the mountains. As though it had always sounded and always would.

Sa-Telis was frowning, but it was a strangely passionless frown, as though he were neither truly angry nor especially concerned at their coming. A true serpent, threatened or balked, might look like that: aware of an enemy and yet unmoved. Or perhaps a dragon, with its impervious heart, might look like that. Well had this mage-gifted prince been named Sa-Telis by his people. Taudde guessed now that the serpent-prince had been their truest enemy all along, and Prince Sehonnes perhaps merely a tile on his brother's board. He should have guessed it at once. Had not Mage Ankennes worked against the Seriantes and the dragon? He should have guessed that the same might be true of other mages—and that a mage who was also a prince might be more dangerous still.

The harp had been made, Taudde guessed now, for whatever magic Telis intended. Ankennes had not found it apt for his purpose, and had left it aside. And then after Ankennes' death, no one had guessed that the wider conspiracy had not been broken. If indeed there had been a wider conspiracy. Maybe it had all been Sa-Telis and no one else, from the very beginning.

Ankennes had longed to destroy the dragon. But perhaps Prince Telis had aimed for a moment more of this kind: the dragon fully woken and yet somehow confined or restrained by magecraft and by that harp. That seemed likely; even obvious. *Now* Taudde could guess the sweep of Prince Telis' ambition. Now he could guess that Sa-Telis might have arranged the downfall of his elder right-hand brothers, that he might have struck down his father—or arranged for Prince Sehonnes to do it; that seemed more a serpent's manner. But that one way or another, he had meant all along to step through the measures of this dance into this exact moment.

And now that Taudde had realized this . . . it was too late. It was very little comfort to know that no one else had seen it coming, either.

Prince Telis stood right here before the dragon, with his ensorcelled harp and his bloodstained runes, and meant to do . . . precisely what? If not destroy it as Mage Ankennes had intended, then what? Those runes implied he did not mean to be rid of it, nor allow it to freely pursue its own desires.

Nor was Taudde at all certain that he wished the dragon freed. Save that whatever Sa-Telis was about, plainly it boded ill for the legitimate prince, and no doubt for the rest of them as well.

Tepres plainly would not be able to move effectively against his half-brother. He held his hands cradled against his chest. Blood streaked his fingers and the solidified light where he lay. He had turned his head to meet Taudde's eyes. His expression was stark. He looked, in that moment, a good deal like his father—and a good deal like the dragon. But there was a wry tilt to his mouth, too, that said quite plainly, *Here we are again, and this time what will you do?*

Taudde wished he had an answer.

The dragon looked far less like a dragon now than it had in the caverns below Kerre Maraddras. It looked . . . like something much greater, a force of the world, given form and shape. Ekorraodde. He had never asked himself where that name had come from, whether it was a name Taliente Seriantes had called the dragon, or a name the dragon had called itself, or what the word might have meant to either of them. *Mages* delved into history and gave names to the powers of the world, and declared that the name was a similar thing to what answered to it, and called things by their names in order to rule them. None of that was part of bardic sorcery, which was about balance and persuasion and limitation, about establishing a rhythm and a pattern to events so that the foot came down on the right path, or so that the dice simply fell as the sorcerer knew they ought to fall.

But whether the dragon was more akin or more susceptible

to magery or sorcery, Taudde had no idea. He could see now that he should have asked that question long ago.

Whatever the dragon's name or kind, the long elegant lines of its head were blurred now by flickers of blue and violet flames, and its eyes were filled with black fire. It did not seem immediately inclined to challenge Prince Telis, or tear down the mountains, or turn itself from fire back into stone. Taudde wondered whether he should find its apparent passivity reassuring. He found it . . . fraught.

And, now that he was here—now that *they* were here—Taudde had to admit to himself that he did not know what to do. He had expected . . . what, inspiration? Or if not that, then perhaps for the dragon itself to provide some riddle or challenge or command that they could meet. Or perhaps a crisis so immediate and urgent and obvious as to force them all into violent action on the very instant of their arrival. But now that they were here, it might be plain enough that Sa-Telis was their enemy, but he had no idea what to do about it.

All these thoughts rushed through Taudde's mind in little more than a heartbeat, though it seemed a very long heartbeat to Taudde, who was paralyzed with indecision and doubt.

Then Karah broke the moment, ignoring all greater questions to run to her sister where the girl knelt by the claw of the dragon.

Taudde, seizing that moment when all eyes followed Karah, took back his flute from Leilis and passed her, discreetly, the pipes she had brought him from the king's cousin. She raised her eyebrows, but accepted them. He said in a low voice, "These were magecrafted, not made for or by sorcery; they are well-made, but they were not made as a gift precisely; rather as a rebuke." Well-deserved, but he did not say that. He murmured instead, "I hope we may find them exactly suited to our need, but I think—I hope—a mage might find them more apt for their purpose."

"*I* am not a mage," Leilis murmured back. "They were made for you! Nor can I play the pipes! Just a very little."

"Your father was a mage, and your heartbeat is tuned to the heartbeat of the dragon," Taudde murmured. "Take them and see what you can do. I'll draw his eye."

Leilis took the pipes. She made no attempt to play them, not yet, but tucked them away in her robes, and walked gracefully toward Prince Tepres and his brother Geradde.

Taudde was quite willing to draw Sa-Telis' attention, especially away from Leilis and Nemienne and Karah, and most especially in the hope that sorcery alone might be sufficient to balk the serpent-prince. He glanced at Irelle.

His cousin had observed his exchange with Leilis with curiosity, but without comment. Now she met his eyes for an instant, then lifted an eloquent eyebrow and looked past him, at Sa-Telis and the great harp behind him. The deep harp note was still humming through light and air and stone; it sounded like . . . the kind of sustained note that opened a doorway, or perhaps like the kind that kept one sealed shut. She said quietly, her voice pitched just for his ears, "There's more than one way to silence a harp, so long as it isn't strung with the winds."

It was a reference to a Kalchesene children's tale. She meant, the harp was strung with wire, and wire could be cut. Taudde nodded. "Wires break, and men bleed," he murmured back. "Let's just see what we might do in that regard." And he played a fast series of notes on his flute; piercing notes at the top of the instrument's register, sharp-edged notes that slid up and up and flicked out toward Sa-Telis.

Taudde didn't really expect this to work. He merely wished to distract Sa-Telis, and find out what the serpent-prince might do. But he did not expect Telis to merely put out his hand and touch a harpstring, one of the high-pitched strings, and instantly shatter all of Taudde's own sorcery. It was so fast, and the sorcery broke so sharply, that Taudde ducked slightly, reflexively, as though the shards of his magic might rebound and cut him, though all the fragments were already insubstantial as mist the moment Sa-Telis touched the harp.

The serpent-prince said, his voice light and unimpassioned, "But it *is* strung with the winds." He had heard every word they'd said, plainly. It should have been impossible for him to overhear their low voices, but he went on in that same light voice, as Taudde tried to remember exactly what he had said to Leilis and what she had answered, "And it is strung as well with the tides and the heartbeat of the earth, and with light and fire.

All this it will bind, Prince Chontas Taudde ser Omientes ken Lariodde. Who is the girl? A relative of yours?" His tone was only mildly curious, as though he could not really imagine that Irelle's identity could make any difference.

Irelle raised an eyebrow at Telis in an unimpressed expression she had surely learned from her mother. She said blandly, "I'm no one important. So you've strung that harp with the winds and the tides, have you? You know, it's wisest to set bounds to such working."

Sa-Telis raised his eyebrows, faintly amused. "I know you Kalchesene sorcerers hedge your workings all about with limitations and boundaries, but that this is not essential we see from our observations of the elemental world, where power is neither limited nor bounded. Unless men circumscribe it, of course." Sa-Telis nodded toward the dragon, surrounded by the thicket of spiky runes. Blood welled out of the runes and ran sluggishly across the stone, but this did not disguise their shapes. "Your sorcery could do nothing like this, nor bind anything so powerful as I have bound. Look at it! Ekorraodde, my father's father's father's father called it. Do you know what that means?"

"No. What does it mean?" Irelle moved a cautious step forward. She was holding her long silver flute casually, as though she had forgotten all about it.

Taudde had never guessed his cousin was so skilled at the player's art, but even he almost believed she was really interested in the serpent-prince's answer. He hoped she had some idea about what to do, if she made it close enough to that harp to do it. To draw any attack toward himself, he turned his shoulder toward the harp and strode toward Leilis and Tepres and the others as though he had dismissed Sa-Telis as a threat. In fact his own attention was almost entirely on Sa-Telis, and so he stumbled when he reached the outermost layer of runes and found there was an almost physical sharpness to them, a sharpness that rose up like a hedge of thorns or knives and prevented him going closer.

The runes hadn't prevented Leilis from picking her way through them to where the princes were trapped. She had had her back turned to Ekorraodde's enormous lambent eyes. It was difficult for Taudde to decide whether the dragon were truly awake and aware.

Taudde reached out a wary hand, testing the barrier he had found in his way, watching covertly as his cousin edged another small step closer to Sa-Telis and to the harp.

"Ignorant as dogs, you Kalchesene sorcerers, and yet you're so vain of your learning, the whole lot of you," said the serpent-prince, in a musing tone. "Mages often have that fault as well, I've found." He flicked a hand in a little circle and a line of repeated runes cracked through the stone at Irelle's feet, sweeping around her, barring her way, trapping her behind a circle of spikes and blood. Blood, seeping from the new rune, trickled across the stone, bright in the shadowless air.

Prince Tepres uttered a low sound, not quite a gasp and not a groan, but owing something to both. His face was white and set, but there was nothing Taudde could do for him.

Sa-Telis, who had already turned back to his harp, seemed to dismiss all of them from his attention. He touched one string and then another, using as a plectrum a small uneven shard of something that seemed to be an unshaped fragment of bone. Taudde was grimly confident it *was* bone, and no innocent bone, either, but a stolen bit of Seriantes bone.

Irelle had halted, stymied for the moment. Perhaps not entirely, or for long. She turned her long silver flute over in her hands, studying the bloody runes and listening, Taudde had no doubt, to the notes that the serpent-mage drew out of the harp. Listening for those notes to resolve into recognizable melody, so that she could get a clear idea of the sorcery he was shaping and find a way to play a sharp dissonance across his sorcery and break it into meaningless, harmless phrases. It was all familiar from a hundred tales of sorcerous duels, one bard against another.

Taudde would not have wished to discount his cousin's skill, but he was fairly certain this was not like those tales. Sa-Telis was not going to let those notes resolve into a melody. He was not working true sorcery at all, but something else, something only he truly understood. It was not something that owed much to bardic sorcery, but Taudde couldn't quite see how anything of the sort could be done with magecraft, either. It was something different from either, and, Taudde feared, something that would be hard to counter. Even without that harp layering its peculiar hum across and through everything.

He turned toward Leilis, thinking that she, with her heartbeat tuned to the dragon's heart, might hear something in that music that he did not. She was frowning across at the serpent-prince and his harp, but she didn't move. Her hand shifted as though she were thinking of the pipes, but she didn't touch them. Taudde frowned at her, but she ignored him, and he had no choice but to trust her to seize the right moment. At least he did trust her to have a fine sense of timing, but he could have wished she'd taken after her father just a little more directly.

Nemienne had taken Karah's hand and gotten to her feet, and now she came a few steps toward Taudde, not seeming to regard the massive serpentine head of the dragon that swayed directly above her.

Taudde tilted his head back, staring up at the dragon. So powerful, and yet by all appearances held by the serpent-prince's bloody runes. "Ekorraodde," Taudde said to it quietly. "What should we do?"

The dragon heard him. It tilted its long, elegant head, fixing him with one great eye, like molten gold swirled with jet. But it did not answer him.

"It doesn't speak," Nemienne told him quickly. The barrier of the runes balked her, plainly more so than her sister, and she didn't try to cross them. She said, "It *did* speak, I mean it spoke to us at first, to both Geradde and me, but then Sa-Telis came, with Prince Tepres, and did those runes, and I think he must have bound the dragon to silence, because it hasn't spoken since!" She looked at him hopefully, as though he might know what to do to fix this—to fix everything.

Taudde looked from Nemienne to the two princes, then up again at the great head of the dragon. He could hardly believe that anything Sa-Telis had done had affected it. But still it did not speak. He asked Nemienne, "Did Ekorraodde bring you here?"

"Oh, no—the other way around. It was my fault, the dragon coming here. I had to find a way out of the darkness and then out of the light," Nemienne explained, not altogether clearly. "Then I saw Prince Tepres, but I was so *stupid*, I found him, but I led

Prince Telis straight to him!"

"You're saying the dragon followed *you* to Kalches and then here to this place?" Taudde hadn't expected that at all. He slanted an astonished look up at the silent dragon.

"Yes!" Nemienne said. "Ekorraodde woke, Telis was trying to bind the dragon, I mean he was trying to bind Geradde, and through him the dragon because they're similar things. He was going to establish a sympathy between them, you know, Iasodde wrote about that. I think that's what Telis was trying to do." She hesitated. "I'm sure it is. It's a bit like what Taliente Seriantes did, I think, to tie his line to the dragon in the first place. If I hadn't shown him the path to Prince Tepres, it least he couldn't have done all this so *easily*."

"Nemienne, it was *not* your fault," Karah said firmly, but her sister only shook her head.

"It was my fault," Prince Geradde put in grimly, from where he knelt supporting Tepres. "I let my brother draw my blood. I'm sure he used that to follow us. I should have made Nemienne leave me behind—"

"Nonsense," Karah said, sharply, for her. "None of this is your fault, either. This is *all* Telis' fault; let's keep that clearly in mind."

Nemienne looked at her gratefully as though her sister had said something important. She said rapidly, "It *is!* He *always* meant to do this! He was going to use Geradde as a similar thing to the dragon, but now that he has Prince Tepres, it's even worse! He has the Dragon's heir *and* that terrible harp, and we have to *do* something!"

"How?" Karah asked her, as though Nemienne might actually know, and everyone looked at the girl hopefully. But Nemienne only shook her head and looked at Taudde, plainly wanting him to declare that it was all right, that he had a plan. He wished he *did* have a plan—one that didn't depend on pipes he barely understood, and a thin hope that Irelle might be able to cut the harpstrings somehow if only Leilis could silence it. He wasn't at all confident he could deal with Prince Telis even if all the rest worked perfectly. He had not anticipated so much magic being loosed in this place, or such strange magic, or the dragon being bound to the serpent-prince's will.

When Taudde didn't answer, Nemienne said, dropping her voice, "You know, Sa-Telis wanted Prince Tepres in the first place, and now he has him! And he has the harp, too, and now he's bound Ekorraodde, or if he hasn't, quite, he *almost* has—he plainly *means* to—he *said* he meant to! He's using the blood of the Dragon's heir to bind the real dragon, and if he kills Prince Tepres, what does he care? He still has Geradde. We can't let him do *any* of this! We have to *do* something!"

"We do seem to have an excess of Seriantes princes just at the moment," Leilis murmured, her tone rather dry. "I agree we could well do with one fewer."

"I mostly just wanted to get away," Nemienne said helplessly. "To get us both away. But I didn't mean to bring us here, or Ekorraodde! But there was so much power in the caverns, once the dragon woke." She turned to Taudde. "*You* know what that's like."

He did. There was a great deal of power loose here, too, mostly to the benefit of the serpent-prince and not to theirs. So far. Taudde met Leilis' eyes for a long beat. What he meant to communicate was *Use the pipes! When I distract him, use those pipes and give Irelle a chance to act!* But he didn't dare say it out loud for fear Sa-Telis would hear. What he actually said, to Prince Geradde, was, "*You* are also a similar thing to the dragon, however. Almost as much so as Tepres. Isn't that so." He didn't ask it as a question. He already knew the answer.

After a startled moment, the young prince inclined his head. He answered steadily, "My brother seemed to think my blood might do for his purposes. If it would do for yours, I offer it freely."

"I can't pass these runes . . ."

Geradde immediately shifted to lay Tepres down flat upon the stone close by the dragon's taloned foot, rising to his feet and coming to face Taudde through the fence of the bloody runes. Tepres certainly made no protest; he seemed now to be more unconscious than not. He had taken on a pale, waxy look, very like that of a man slipping away along the path of death. He couldn't endure much longer, Taudde feared.

Taudde reached through the sharp runes, took Geradde's hand in his, turned the young prince's hand palm up, and whistled a note like a knife blade, a note that sliced across Geradde's palm: a light, shallow cut, but enough to bring the blood welling up. Telis turned his head, which Taudde pretended not to notice.

Geradde's hand twitched a little, involuntarily, but he did not draw back.

Taudde ran the tips of his fingers across Geradde's palm. "Blood to bind," he said, in a level, quiet tone. "Blood freely given, to bind or loose. Will you give your blood and your life into my hands, Geradde—" he knew the young prince's full name, he *did* know it, didn't he? Not Skyblue, obviously; a left-hand son surely took his mother's real name, not her flower name—it came to him at last, and he finished firmly, "Geradde Inann Seriantes, great-great-grandson of Taliente Seriantes."

He layered confidence and power into the undertones of his voice, and allowed his gaze to cross his cousin's, though she was standing very still in the circle of sharp-edged runes Sa-Telis had laid down around her. She would surely try to free herself the moment Leilis sounded the pipes, he knew; and perhaps she would manage it; she was her mother's daughter and her father's heir and that flute of hers was a masterwork; he wouldn't have wanted Irelle to look at *him* with the cool, predatory expression she had turned on the serpent-prince.

Geradde had gone rather pale, but he gave a short little nod at Taudde's words. "My blood and my life are yours," he said. "Do as you will, Chontas Taudde ser Omientes ken Lariodde."

And that permission, too, gave power to any sorcery Taudde chose to work. Kneeling, he drew a line in the young prince's blood, straight through the spiky runes that lay between them. The blood welling from the runes somehow did not mingle with Geradde's blood, but seemed to fold away from it; and the line Taudde made seemed to draw in light and widen and deepen, running in a suddenly broad pathway through the barrier Sa-Telis had laid down.

Taudde drew a breath, stood up, and offered his hand to Prince Geradde.

The prince took his hand and stepped through the runic barrier.

Prince Telis, frowning, lifted his hands from the harp and

turned to face them. Even now he did not seem precisely angry, nor greatly concerned. The rhythm of his breathing had not quickened. His calm struck Taudde more than ever as disturbing, and again he thought how well the mage-prince's name suited him. It was difficult to know whether anything Taudde had yet done discomposed him in the slightest, and that, too, was disconcerting. Yet he could see nothing to do but go on as he was.

So Taudde strode toward Sa-Telis, drawing Geradde with him, the young prince's blood sticky against his palm. Sa-Telis began to raise a hand, and Taudde at once halted, lest the mage-prince should create yet more runes of limitation and confinement—he was not at all certain that there was enough blood in Tepres' body to sustain another such crafting. So he halted, and Geradde stood still beside him, trusting him to know what he was doing.

Taudde only hoped he did. He raised his eyebrows at Telis. "Look," he said to Telis, layering his voice with undertones of confidence and mockery. "Here is another of the Dragon's heirs. What will happen if I spill *his* blood here in this place and weave it into *my* sorcery? Unlike Tepres, *Geradde* is willing. You are quick to accuse others of vanity and arrogance, but you know less of sorcery than you believe. You believe we limit our working for no reason; plainly you haven't realized how vast a difference the proper limitations grant, in sorcery."

And he ran his bloody palm the full length of his flute, from just below the mouthpiece to the last fret, raised the flute to his mouth, and began to play.

He did not, by so much as a glance her way, call attention to Irelle. He certainly did not glance over his shoulder to see what Nemienne might be doing, or Leilis.

And anyway, he had only spoken the truth. Sa-Telis simply did not seem to know why the bardic sorcerers of Kalches structured and limited their sorcery.

Sa-Telis slanted that unmoved glance toward Taudde, raised an eyebrow and touched just the lowest bass string of his harp. All around them the burning light boomed with reverberating thunder. That was power drawn from the harp but surely sourced from Tepres; if only to save Tepres it had to be countered.

Taudde played a light, quick melody, but he wove into that melody Geradde's lifeblood and spun it into a shield between Tepres and his brother the serpent-prince. But his shield wouldn't last, it couldn't last, Sa-Telis had bound his brother too closely and the power he took from the dragon was too great—

Behind him, the first tentative, clumsy notes of the pipes sounded.

Sa-Telis turned his head, curious. Taudde looked, too, quickly, readying himself to protect Leilis if he could—he couldn't spare a glance for Irelle and had no idea if his cousin could get herself free of the runes that confined her—

Leilis was not playing the pipes. Nemienne was.

Taudde understood that at once, because of course Nemienne was more a mage than Leilis—more than Taudde, too—Leilis had passed her the pipes while everyone else was distracted, and Nemienne, white-faced and stiff, was trying to play them.

Her sister stood behind her. Karah's hands rested on her little sister's shoulders, steadying, comforting, but her head was tilted up and her wide-eyed gaze was actually fixed on the dragon. The pipe notes stuttered and stumbled, but Taudde was almost certain he could feel some sort of magecraft trying to work itself out—if she had only known how to play—how could she have been Taudde's apprentice for months and he never teach her how to play the pipes? Leilis was not near them; she had backed away and stood now directly beneath the dragon's head, looking frightened and resolved.

Then Sa-Telis, looking faintly amused, crooked a finger, and the pipes vanished from Nemienne's hands and appeared in his own. "What *are* these?" the serpent-prince asked any of them. "They are cleverly made, aren't they?" And he brought them to his mouth and played an exploratory little run of notes.

Instantly all other sound ceased utterly.

It was the kind of magecraft that Taudde had experienced once before, in the silent prison of the Laodd, where he had thought he might go mad for lack of sound. His flute was silenced—and so was the great harp.

Leilis ducked aside from the dragon, which turned its head to watch her as she ran toward the harp, crossing the runes as though they weren't there, her steps utterly soundless.

Sa-Telis threw the pipes away violently, his expression stark and furious, looking for the first time much like his father. The silence lingered, but he spun toward Leilis, lifting the long bone like a weapon.

Nemienne stooped, drawing quick lines through the bloody runes at her feet.

Taudde couldn't see what she drew, but he *felt* it. Runes of summoning, he thought—she had always been good at summoning—but he couldn't tell what she summoned this time.

Then he could. He felt it. She was summoning darkness and light, both. She was summoning the dragon, even though it was already here. She was summoning its power or its attention or *something*. She couldn't possibly know what that would do. But neither could any of them. Telis turned sharply, plainly torn between dealing with Nemienne and stopping Leilis.

Then sound returned, rushing back upon them like the tide, and Sa-Telis forgot them both and flung himself back to the harp instead, sweeping his naked hand across all its strings, from the highest to the deepest. Behind him and around him and around them all the harp sounded, every note like thunder or like conflagration or like the keening of the high winds or like the rushing of the tide against the shore.

Desperate, Taudde swept Geradde's very life into his own music and moved as sharply as he could to take command of the storm of magic before Sa-Telis could take it all for his own. Geradde, crying out, fell to his hands and knees. Taudde ignored him, he had no time to take care; he knew he had to use these first seconds when his flute cut across the sound of the harp. In those seconds, Taudde redefined every bloody rune of confinement and control. Sa-Telis did not understand limitations and so he had not limited the intention he had set into his runes, and now Taudde seized this instant to redefine them all. Confinement could be made into shelter. It *was* shelter, and protection. Taudde wove his definition into the sorcery a heartbeat before Prince Telis could impose his own definition.

Taudde was not a mage, but he understood a little more of magecraft than he once had. So with his sorcery he defined all the magic that bound Geradde and Tepres and even Sa-Telis and the dragon itself as *similar*—similar in the way mages meant the term. He defined the binding in those runes as a similar thing to the full binding between all three princes and the dragon; he made certain that for this one instant, *all* the magic was redefined.

There was no doubt but that he had finally captured the serpent-prince's whole attention. Telis whipped around and strode toward Taudde, even now with very little expression, but his boots rang like metal against metal, sparks flying up with every step—Taudde could almost *see* the magic trailing behind him and rising up around him, like invisible flames. Telis held it, or he held *something*—he was trying to wrap it around the Seriantes bone he held; he was trying to define it all once more according to his own will, but he was not, Taudde thought, finding it so easy to wrestle unbounded, unlimited sorcery into the shape he desired.

Leilis had never yet paused, though she had slowed as the magic whirled up around her. She pressed her way on toward the harp through the storm of magic—some of it bounded and much unbounded, and all of it dangerous, and she was not a sorceress to protect herself.

Taudde tried to hold his own definition, to make his own work *true* in the face of everything Sa-Telis did to stop him. He didn't even understand what the serpent-prince was actually *doing*, except he could feel how the harp worked against him and for Telis. He couldn't hold back the storm—only for an instant, and another instant more; this storm wasn't his; *he* wasn't a similar thing to any Seriantes prince, nor to any dragon.

And there was so much blood already poured out here, and Telis had that Seriantes bone. He was taking control of his own runes already, countering everything Taudde could do.

Then the dragon lowered its head sharply.

At that moment, Irelle, no longer trapped by the runes Telis had swept around her, lifted her flute quickly to her lips and played a path for Leilis through the storm.

Though Irelle's eyes were wide with nerves or amazement, her hands did not tremble on the stops of her flute. She played a sharp descant above the melody Taudde laid down, fitting a harmony to his playing, supporting his definitions: *support, protection.* She was weaving a pathway for Leilis through the light and the darkness and the storm of power. A path that led straight to the harp.

The music of the harp built a wall of sharp edges across the path Irelle played into being, but her descant wove itself around all the glittering sharpness, turning aside the shimmering thunder of the harp. The harp was the greater instrument, but Irelle's sorcery wove around its violence, and Leilis ran down the path Irelle made for her. She had something in her hand, a flicker of fire or a shard of light—a knife, Taudde realized, its blade hardly as long as her finger, but not an ordinary knife, it seemed, for when she ran straight up to the harp and whipped the edge of that blade straight across all the strings of the harp, all the harpstrings wailed and broke, one after another.

Taudde caught the merest edges of the magic that poured out upon them all. He couldn't hold it or contain it; it wasn't meant for him; he wasn't a similar thing to the dragon. But he could let it go. He was not mage enough to hold it, but he was sorcerer enough to unweave it and let it spill away, to unbind everything that had ever been bound to it, and pour that storm of magic into the air. It seemed a vast storm; he could hardly believe even so great a working as that harp had held so much, even here, even played with bone.

Prince Telis spun, raising the bone he held as though to throw it at Leilis. He might have thrown it; for all Taudde knew it might even have struck her through like a spear; that seemed like the sort of thing Telis might be able to do. But it was too late. With a smooth motion that seemed slow but was actually far too fast for anyone to react, the dragon reached out and plucked the dry white bone out of the serpent-prince's hand, and broke it into shards, and crushed the fragments to powder that blew away on the storm of the loosed winds and light.

And then the winds died, and the light folded gently away, and they were all left staggering out in the open, against the low slopes of Kerre Irelle, with the sky fading to an ordinary dusk above them and the town of Kedres coming slowly alight with lanterns below.

The dragon curled away into the lavender shadows, its back and part of its wing and its long tail looping into and out of the mountain's flank. Its head it brought down to rest on one taloned foot, beside Tepres and Nemienne. It no longer seemed to be made of light, nor of darkness. In a way, Taudde thought he could see both at once glimmering in its lambent eyes.

Prince Telis took one step back from the dragon, and then another.

Then the dragon said to him, **"Brittle, your heart, Sa-Telis, serpent-prince. Did I not warn you to take care?"** And before he could answer, Telis shattered like the bone, and crumbled to dust, and blew away on the ordinary evening breeze. And beyond him, jagged cracks and faults ran suddenly across the carved face of the harp and it, too, crumbled away.

Irelle and Leilis, who had been standing close by the harp, both took a startled step away, but then Leilis dropped the little knife, thrust out her hand and caught as they fell the three beads, hematite and glass and pearl, that had been set into its face.

Taudde hadn't seen any of that coming at all; not what Leilis had done to the harp, nor what the dragon had done to Prince Telis. And if it went on and did to Tepres and Geradde what it had done to Sa-Telis, he had no way to stop it. If it chose to do that to all of them, or to Kedres entire and then all the ephemeral cities of men, he had no way to prevent it. He didn't dare move, but waited to see what the dragon would do.

Then Nemienne straightened. *She* didn't look at all frightened. She and Karah were holding hands, but neither of them looked afraid. Nemienne was laughing, and Karah hugged her, but then let her go and went quickly to kneel by Tepres.

Nemienne said to the dragon, quickly and confidently, "That was *perfect*, O Ekorraodde, that was exactly right! But what about Prince Tepres? It would be terrible if he died *now,* after all this!"

The dragon did not answer, but turned its great head to regard her. Taudde, taking courage from Nemienne's evident lack of terror, put a hand down to help Geradde to his feet—the youngest prince, at least, hadn't shown any sign yet that he was going to dissolve into dust, which was perhaps reassuring. Taudde walked across the mountain's slope to Nemienne and set his hand on her shoulder, while Geradde went to kneel beside his brother, next to Karah. Geradde touched his brother's face and then looked up at the dragon, pale and steady. Then he bowed his head and said quietly, "It wasn't Tepres who bound himself to you, O Ekoraodde. That was our great-great-grandfather."

"None of you is bound to me now," said the dragon.

Taudde said, realizing as he spoke that it must be true, "You were never truly constrained, were you, O Ekorraodde? You allowed . . . all that. That conflict between the great-great-grandsons of Taliente Seriantes. You even arranged it. Because you wanted to . . . use them to dissolve the binding Taliente Seriantes set on you so long ago. Is that how it was?"

And the dragon said, **"Yes. That is how it was."**

"Blood to bind . . ."

"Blood to bind the ephemeral to the eternal and the immanent," said the dragon. **"Blood that was the blood of a man and yet my blood as well. Taliente Neredde ken Seriantes wished his descendants to have the blood of dragons in their veins. Powerful, he was, beyond doubt. But not wise."**

"And you made a way for me, for us, to walk through all your light. It might have been simpler if you had explained . . . what you meant to do." In fact, Taudde was not entirely certain even now what exactly had happened.

"You would have preferred the comfort of reassurance, perhaps. But nothing that happened would have been simpler. Nor is it possible to know what will happen before events fall out as they do."

That was probably true. Taudde touched his fingertips to his eyes, then flinched slightly and dropped his hand—his fingers were still sticky with blood. He supposed it was somewhat reassuring that the dragon had not yet destroyed them all. He said, with a glance down at Tepres and then a little gesture toward him, "Nemienne is right. None of this was any fault of Tepres. He has gone a long way along the road into silence. *Can* you restore him, O Ekorraodde? Will you?"

"You suspect me of kindness," observed the dragon. **"That is an element of the ephemeral world."**

"Oh, but it's a small thing," Nemienne pointed out. "And it's only right, after the way you used him!"

And Karah added, "Lirionne will need him. Lonne will. The

city will miss your presence, O Ekorraodde. It would not be right to leave the city bereft."

This sounded perilously like an accusation, one which the dragon might not choose to find amusing. Taudde said smoothly, "Besides, it's in the nature of men to be kind, O Ekorraodde, for are we not part of the ephemeral world? In all that you caused to happen, and encouraged to happen, did you not depend upon the nature of the ephemeral world? And it *is* a small thing to you, is it not?"

There was a pause. The dragon tilted its head to one side, regarding them all, unreadable. It might have been considering what they had said, or it might have been considering how best to destroy them all with the least trouble to itself; Taudde couldn't tell. He thought of saying something else, but did not know what he could say—and suspected the bardic arts of persuasion were not likely to be highly useful when speaking to a dragon.

Perhaps he should have let Nemienne and Karah argue. They might have done better than he after all.

Leilis and Irelle joined them, Irelle holding her flute not like a weapon now, but as though for comfort. Leilis touched Nemienne's arm and offered her the pearl and the beads, saying in a low voice, "I don't think anything else is left of it but these."

"Oh!" said Nemienne, sounding uncomplicatedly pleased. "I expect one was for the winds—glass, of course, for the ephemeral—and pearl for the tides, of course. And iron for the eternal darkness below the mountains." She looked up at the dragon. "Or for light?" she asked.

"Darkness and light are each eternal," said the dragon. It lowered its head toward Tepres—Geradde leaned back a little, but did not retreat from his brother's side. But the dragon only breathed on Tepres. Its breath was neither darkness nor light, but something like each. When it lifted its head, Tepres opened his eyes and drew a deep breath, the color coming back into his face.

"Speak for me to your father," the dragon said to him. **"He is wiser than Taliente Neredde ken Seriantes. Bid him be wise again. Sometimes an age should end. Not all that has been broken should be restored."**

Prince Tepres came up on one elbow. He could hardly have

had any idea of what had passed, or that the dragon had in some way orchestrated the whole affair. But he didn't stare around at them all or ask any questions. Instead, he only gathered himself up to a more dignified position, though he did not yet try to stand, and answered the dragon with admirable calm, "O Ekorraodde, should I have the opportunity, I will tell him just that."

-25-

The dragon poured itself away into the sky or the earth or the long shadows of the dusk, and the world was surely far more comfortable for its going. Though less splendid. Leilis tucked her hands into the sleeves of her keiso robes, gazed around at the perfectly ordinary mountain slopes, at the town below and the towering peaks above, and tried to understand what had happened, and how.

Why it had happened . . . that she thought she grasped rather clearly. The dragon had . . . written the stage directions, so one might perhaps express the idea. As a playwright managed the players of his company, the dragon had managed Prince Telis. The rest of them . . . she did not quite believe the dragon had directed *every* detail. But that the dragon had made certain they all came together here . . . she thought it likely. She didn't believe she imagined the structured order to that, or mistook the architect of that pattern. She didn't think so at all.

And, of course, the dragon had made her simple knife, the ordinary knife Gerenes Brenededd had given her into . . . the sort of knife that could cut the winds and the tides. The dragon had breathed on it when Prince Telis had been distracted, and had changed it from ordinary metal to . . . a kind of condensed light. It had not needed to tell her what to do with the knife after that. She had known exactly what she needed to do.

Even after the dragon had given her the right kind of knife, Leilis had needed Taudde's cousin to make a way for her through the music of the harp. And lo! There Irelle had been, with her silver flute and her audacity, exactly where she needed to be, exactly where she could guide someone's steps right to the harp. And so Leilis had crossed all the barriers Prince Telis had made and cut right across the complicated array of harpstrings, and had found at the end that both harpstrings and knife had burned away, or melted into the air, or something of the kind. The strings that had seemed to be simple wire had left only the lingering scent of summer storms and a tense kind of vibration that lingered for a little while after the sound itself was gone. And all that was left of the knife was a misshapen bit of ivory and a scattering of tiny sapphires that had cracked and shattered and turned to blue dust.

Leilis did not believe for a moment that any of that had been chance.

So among them all they had freed the dragon from all the bindings any Seriantes had ever put on it. She only wondered why the dragon hadn't arranged all this to happen earlier, or more conveniently. Perhaps the dragon had needed a Seriantes prince who possessed the mage gift. Or the heart of a serpent.

And now the dragon was not only awake, not only unbound, but gone. Gone about its own business, and who knew what that might entail?

Still, for all it claimed not to be kind, it had restored Prince Tepres before it had gone. And it had not torn down the mountains upon that Kalchesene town below.

At least, not yet.

One could go quite mad, worrying over what the dragon might eventually choose to do. It was hardly practical to dwell on such matters. Especially when they all had the ordinary concerns of ephemeral folk to concern them.

Taudde and Irelle stood close together, Taudde with his arm around his cousin, Irelle leaning against him. They were not speaking, not yet, but simply taking comfort from each other. Leilis might have felt jealous, if she were a fool, if she had not remembered that Taudde had for a long time been apart from all his family. Leilis could imagine how Taudde would have felt if his younger cousin had taken harm from any of this—she knew he must be feeling all that fear and shock now, because now at last there was time for it. She knew how Taudde must feel, because she felt so herself when she considered Karah and Nemienne. Nemienne was not one of the deisa of Cloisonné House, but . . . in a way Leilis felt that she was. She was Karah's sister, anyway, and so the sister of a sister of the house, and Leilis' responsibility. She tried not to imagine the grief of all the other sisters if anything had happened to the two girls. She truly did not want to imagine that.

Both sisters had joined Prince Geradde and Prince Tepres. Nemienne was explaining something, gesturing with both hands. Prince Geradde was saying very little. Prince Tepres had seated himself on a cracked bit of stone, his back against the sharply rising slope of the mountain—Leilis suspected that he might not yet be able to stand, and that he did not care to allow the rest of them to see this. But he looked well; very well indeed for a man who had so recently seemed so deathly. Karah had tucked herself down beside him. Her hand rested on his arm, and he had covered it with one of his own. But his mouth was tight set, and his expression forbidding. He was listening to Nemienne, but his gaze strayed now and then to Taudde. Or perhaps to Irelle.

Leilis began to make her way in that direction. So, seeing her move, did Taudde and his cousin.

Nemienne turned to Leilis as she approached. "I was just explaining how Geradde and I, *Prince* Geradde, I mean, how Telis took us both prisoner and held us in the tomb on Kerre Taum, so we don't know exactly what was happening in Lonne all that time."

Karah added with quiet trust, "We know *you* must know everything, Leilis."

Leilis pretended not to notice Nemienne's rather startling familiarity with Prince Geradde. Still, though Nemienne's father had been merely a tradesman, Prince Geradde was merely a left-hand prince. A friendship there might not be entirely out of the question, though Leilis could not quite see Geriodde Nerenne ken Seriantes countenancing more. She should warn Nemienne against possible expectations in that direction.

But that was a concern that could be left for the future. She turned to smile at Taudde as he and his cousin came up. She was so grateful that he was alive—that they were both alive—that they all lived and were not harmed. Not too badly harmed.

But what Taudde said to her, wry and regretful, was, "I lost Gerenes Brenedde's pipes." He spread his hands helplessly. "I have to wonder what he may make for me to replace them."

"Oh!" said Nemienne, and turned to Prince Geradde, who had stiffened as well. There was a tiny silence. Then Prince

Geradde said, "I am sorry to be the first to inform you. But Gerenes Brenedde is dead. He died to save Nemienne and me."

There was another small space of silence. Taudde looked nearly as stricken as Leilis felt. She started to say something, but found no words and only bowed her head. Taudde, seeing her grief if not her guilt for the old man's death, touched her arm and then her cheek. He said to Geradde, "I am sorry for that. I should have made a chance to repay the debt I owed him. That now I cannot will be a thing I regret for the rest of my life."

Leilis, finding her voice, said quietly, "You did repay him, Taudde. He wished you to hold to your friendship with Prince Tepres and with Lirionne, and so you did. So you have."

"Perhaps," Taudde said, studiedly neutral. "Perhaps."

"Can there be doubt of it?" Tepres asked him. "We are all in your debt; or perhaps I should say that we are all in one another's debt and may cease counting." He paused, and then said stiffly to Leilis, "I believe I am correct in understanding that . . . reports of my father's death were . . . a little beforehand?"

Leilis inclined her head to Prince Tepres. "As it happens, I *am* able to assure you that these reports were false. The king was injured. But his injuries were nothing that should not heal with proper care. As the king needed time to recover, Neriodd and I agreed that it would be better if Sehonnes did not search for him. We thought it best if a body were found instead." She glanced at Taudde. "Benne thought of it, in fact."

"Benne!" said Taudde, plainly startled. "I haven't—did he—was he—"

"I fear I do not know and cannot guess. He put himself to some trouble to protect the king and then to protect me, but I fear we became separated and I do not know what might have happened to him. These past days have been confused and confusing, and everyone has been wary of sharing what little they might know. Cloisonné House was under some suspicion, of course; that, among other reasons, was why I thought it best to set myself out of reach of any who might wish to question me."

She met Prince Tepres' eyes. "I set the king in Karah's sisters' home—" she acknowledged Karah's and Nemienne's exclamations with a slight smile, but simply went on, "So that no one could possibly know where he had gone, Benne and I took him by the way Nemienne knows, through the dark caverns. I trusted my blood and Karah's kitten, though now . . . now I suspect perhaps Ekorraodde guided my steps as well. But that is where we carried him. Only I knew, and Benne. We did not send to and fro, you understand, eminence. It would not have been safe. But Karah's sisters knew where to send word should anything of moment befall the king. Surely I would have heard if anything untoward had happened to your father."

Prince Tepres, his expression unreadable, said merely, "Very well. I am certain he was well cared for in that house. I shall hope he is well, then. And Sehonnes?"

It was surprisingly simple to reduce all of the disorder and confusion to a few simple phrases. Leilis explained, "Eminence, once Prince Sehonnes was made to believe that your father had died, naturally he immediately laid his hand on the throne. All of Lonne also believed the king had died, and you were not there. Few opposed Sehonnes when he declared he would claim the throne and the crown on the solstice." She was distantly amazed to realize that they had not yet even come to the solstice. Not even yet. Or she thought not. She found she could not quite count off the days, anymore.

"I see," said Prince Tepres. His expression had not changed, but he leaned his head back against the stone flank of the mountain and let his breath out in a long, slow exhalation. Then he folded his hands in his lap, straightened his back, and said to Taudde, in a flat, decisive tone, "I must return to Lonne, of course. Immediately. If my father lives, that is well. But we do not know his condition with any certainty, save that he was injured. What we know with certainty is that, if he believed our father dead, Sehonnes will have moved quickly to secure his position. However, if he discovered he lived, very likely the same. Whatever that might entail."

He meant, clearly, that if Prince Sehonnes had discovered that their father lived, he would have moved immediately to remedy that situation, if he could find a way to do it quietly. Leilis, remembering the big, short-tempered, angry man she had met so briefly, suspected that he might very well have even struck openly against the king, if he'd felt himself backed into a corner.

He would certainly not have counted on help from Prince Telis. Or perhaps he *had* counted on Prince Telis, and been disappointed. That might well explain some of his bitterness. And his readiness to put all the blame on Telis for the uglier acts of the usurpation. Leilis herself was certainly willing to put much of the blame on Telis herself. Though if Telis had used Sehonnes, it must also be acknowledged that Sehonnes had let himself be so used.

"Sehonnes must not be allowed to lay formal claim to the throne," Tepres concluded, his tone very flat. "Though I am naturally grateful for King Berente's courtesy, I would prefer not to be forced in this exigency to apply to him for permission or assistance in the matter." His gaze went to Irelle. "Should King Berente prove not to be fully recovered, or should his health fail under the repeated alarms of these days, then assuredly I would not wish to . . . allow myself to become an object of contention between Prince Heronn and Prince Manaskes." He turned to Taudde. "It occurs to me that perhaps there may be enough lingering power here to open Iasodde's door into Ankennes' house? I believe this may be the ideal moment to step from these northern mountains back into Lonne."

"Tepres—" Prince Geradde began, looking worriedly at his brother.

Prince Tepres only lifted a finger, but Geradde stilled as if he had shouted.

Taudde, too, was frowning. "It may be possible to open that door. You are certainly correct that the air here is filled with the remnants of power. But . . ." He looked around, with the air of a man searching for something he knew he wouldn't find. "The door—" he began.

With a loud, rather harsh mew, a heavy black cat leaped up on a stone a few feet away, regarded them all for a moment with a supercilious expression, then sat down and began grooming his tail. While they were all still staring, Karah's kitten Moonglow leaped up on the rock beside the black cat, leaped down again in a streak of silver fur, and dashed across to Karah, who, startled, put her hands out quickly to catch her as the kitten leaped to her knee. Moonglow stretched up, butted her head against Karah's chin, and began to purr.

"Yours, I gather?" Irelle said to Karah after a moment. "That's a beautiful kitten, and the male is impressive. They say odd eyes make for clear vision."

Karah smiled at her, stroking Moonglow. "Tepres gave her to me. That—" she nodded to the heavy black male—"is King Geriodde's cat, Dark Of The Moon."

"A rather definite sign," Prince Tepres said mildly. "Pinenne Cloud Cats always know their way. So it is said." He raised an eyebrow at Taudde.

"Yes," Taudde agreed. "We say that, too. Very well, suppose we can find the door after all, as I suspect we can, now; and suppose there is indeed enough magic lingering in this place to open it . . . do you have anything to discuss with my cousin, first, perhaps, before you make any plans for dramatic reappearances in Lonne?" He raised his eyebrows at Irelle.

"But—" said Karah, a beat before Leilis would have spoken. "About reappearing in Lonne, Tepres, if your father lives, then—"

Prince Tepres patted Karah's hand, but he was looking at Irelle. He said quietly, "Even so, the matter might still be settled exactly as . . . we discussed. I believe my father would recognize that a debt is owed to Taudde, and to all your family; even to King Berente. Or he could be persuaded to recognize the debt. As I do." Tepres hesitated, his expression remote, and added, "If you care to consider that we came to such an agreement." He tilted his head in query.

"I wouldn't call it an *agreement*, precisely," said Irelle. She had drifted over to stroke Dark Of The Moon. The big cat stood up, arched his back under her hand, and firmly thumped against her leg to demand more attention. Irelle smiled down at him briefly and went on, "I wouldn't care to overstate the case. We might say that we both acknowledged that an understanding might be forthcoming if . . . events fell out a certain way."

Her manner was too forthright to be entirely courteous. Or perhaps, Leilis thought, that might be the manner one expected of a high-born Kalchesene woman. Or a granddaughter of King Berente.

"What agreement?" Nemienne asked, sounding faintly suspicious. "Are *you* going marry Prince Tepres?" She looked worriedly at Karah.

"It will be well," Karah told her sister. "We shall all be friends. You'll see."

Nemienne frowned, clearly not entirely believing this.

"Nemienne, isn't it?" Irelle said to the younger girl. "Karah's told me about you, and after seeing the dragon for myself, I'm even more amazed. How could you dare speak to it?"

"Oh . . ." Nemienne couldn't help but smile. "I *didn't* dare, but after all, Ekorraodde spoke to *me*."

"I look forward to hearing the tale as it seemed to you," Irelle told her. "Maybe you can explain what happened today, too; I'm not sure I understand it even though I was here. Very strange and beautiful and frightening!"

Nemienne looked shy, and Karah smiled at Irelle.

Prince Tepres did not seem to be offended at this digression. He merely inclined his head and said to Irelle, "Given the manner in which the . . . events here have resolved themselves, I believe that such an understanding might cause events in Lonne to fall out in an acceptable pattern." He glanced around at them all. "It is my intention to be certain that my brother Sehonnes does not rule. This is my fixed intention. However, I will not raise my hand against my father, if he lives. Let us be clear on this point." Then, turning back to Irelle, he asked, "This being so, would you prefer to wait to see what occurs in Lonne? I assure you, under the circumstances, I would not resent such a delay."

There was a pause. Then Taudde said to Irelle, his tone wry, "Grandfather was quite clear about whose judgment he trusts. This is your decision, cousin, and however you choose, he'll accept it. He can hardly go back on his word now."

Irelle nodded. She glanced around at all of them. "This does seem a moment to seize. It's hard to imagine another moment quite so apt offering itself. I think . . . I *do* think it might be better to present all of our . . . more difficult relations with an agreement that's already sealed and settled. Grandfather won't want a war. No one will, not even Uncle Manaskes and his lot, not now that they've actually seen your dragon."

"Ekorraodde isn't bound to the Seriantes anymore,"

Nemienne said, diffidently but firmly.

Irelle lifted her hands. "Well, that's worse, isn't it? No one sensible would want a war when we can't begin to guess what the dragon might do. That's the last thing anyone should want. What if we all spend our strength fighting each other and then discover that Ekorraodde has come back? I trust *your* intentions more than the dragon's."

Taudde said, "I think all of us here may trust one another's intentions. That's not an inconsiderable point, either."

No one seemed inclined to argue. Leilis bowed her head a little to draw their attention and pointed out softly, "One person might go ahead. One person might step from this place into Lonne and discover how events there have indeed fallen out, if indeed matters have been settled; or if not, then we should know at least that. This might take only a little time. And if any other understanding might yet benefit from civilized and leisurely consultation with the king of Kalches, there would be time for such discussions."

"No," said Prince Tepres. "It is impossible for me to speak to King Berente *now*. No. We will go at once. Or I will." He looked around at them all, ending with his half-brother. "Geradde, if Sehonnes has seized the throne after all, or if he has brought Lonne to support him, then everything is different and there will be no safety for you there—"

"I will not possibly allow you to return to Lonne while I shelter in Kalches," Prince Geradde said shortly. "Not possibly. Do not ask it."

Prince Tepres inclined his head, resigned. "Very well. But Nemienne—"

"No!" the girl said immediately. "I want to know what's been happening. I want to be sure my sisters are all right. *Anything* might have happened, or be happening now, and I'm not even there! No, I want to go back to Lonne, too!"

"Well," Prince Tepres murmured. "Very well, I do not forbid it." He glanced around again. "Irelle Heronn ken Lariodde, if you will take the agreement between us as indeed settled and binding, I give you my word that I will hold to it. I think I can promise that my father will also agree to it, if he has reclaimed his throne." He paused, and then went on steadily,

"Taudde, if your cousin does me the honor to trust my word, I must ask you to accompany her. I believe I, or my father, will be able to deal with Sehonnes, but if I am mistaken, then you must protect your cousin. However, you and she together will be quite enough. Kalchesene soldiers, or worse, an entire company of bardic sorcerers . . . such a company is out of the question now. Meaning no disrespect to your people," he added to Taudde, remembering to add a small nod toward Irelle.

"No one could possibly take offense, under the circumstances," Taudde assured him, and looked at his cousin. "Irelle—first, are you certain of this course? And second, if you are, do you think you can help me . . . catch the other end of Iasodde's door? I don't believe there is enough lingering power here to forge another, but if Dark Of The Moon and Moonglow are willing to lead the way, I think we'll find we can still hear an . . . echo of the darkness below the mountains of Lonne."

Irelle stroked Dark one more time, then drew her flute out of her belt and turned it over in her fingers, and nodded. "I think you're right. I'm fairly certain I can hear some kind of echo even now. Of the dragon, a trace of its . . . presence? It seems . . . not quite the same."

"Akin, perhaps. The caverns were there before the dragon." Taudde paused and added, "I think."

"Oh, well, if *you* think so." But Leilis thought that Irelle's tone, though deliberately light, did not actually sound disbelieving. Taudde's cousin added, "I don't recognize it . . . but if you do, well. If you can bring that echo out clearly, Taudde, I think I can help you make it fast. Not for long. But for long enough." But then she hesitated, glancing down the mountain slopes toward the town below. "But we should at least send word—think what my mother would say if we went off without explaining anything—"

"I hardly care to imagine what Aunt Ines would say. *Someone* could stay here," Taudde suggested, and looked at Leilis, his eyebrows lifting in a kind of wry inquiry. "You *would* make a splendid emissary for Lonne, you know."

Leilis found herself smiling. Not the deliberate, elegant smile of a keiso. Just . . . a smile. She couldn't help it. Somehow when Taudde looked at her that way, as though he already knew exactly what she would say and was glad of it . . . somehow she simply felt like smiling. Even under these rather fraught circumstances, with nothing actually settled in either Lonne or below, in the Kalchesene town.

Or, well, *some* things were settled, of course. After the dragon, and Sa-Telis, surely they could all manage their various family difficulties. However complicated those might be.

And she had played some small role in persuading Geriodde Nerenne ken Seriantes toward generosity before, after all.

She said, though it hardly seemed necessary, "No. I, too, wish to return to Lonne." She smiled then with a keiso's deliberate elegance, inclining her head to Prince Tepres, "Perhaps I may find some small way to be useful."

"I don't doubt it," Taudde agreed, unsurprised and, she thought, not displeased with her answer.

And Prince Tepres added, "The flowers of Lonne may bow before every wind, but all men know that sometimes the flowers also shape the direction of the winds. I will be glad of your company, especially if I must take the city back from Sehonnes after all."

No one wondered aloud whether Prince Tepres was quite recovered, or yet possessed the strength to do as he had declared and return this moment to Lonne. Everyone, no doubt, knew as well as Leilis that the prince would not regard any argument.

Irelle, tapping her flute against her palm, said, her tone rather dry, "So we seem to have made a decision. Our unanimity is admirable, no doubt, and yet we must still leave a message of some sort for my mother. And for Father, and Grandfather, of course."

"So we must. We will. We can put it . . ." Taudde looked around thoughtfully and then smiled at Leilis and held up the pipes, which he had evidently reclaimed. "We can put a message in these—after breaking the magecrafting on them so that it'll carry a message and not fold silence around the one who plays it." He glanced soberly at Leilis. "If you think Gerenes Brenededd wouldn't . . . have minded my breaking his magecrafting?"

Leilis, startled by the sharpness of grief that came to her now that she was reminded of the king's cousin, hardly knew what answer to make. But Prince Geradde lifted his hand a little, like a polite child, and said soberly, "I think Gerenes Brenededd would be well pleased to know how his pipes have been put to use, and pleased as well that they should now prove apt for another need."

"I think he would acknowledge that the debt to him has been paid," Leilis said finally. "We may hope so, I think."

Taudde bowed his head. After a moment, he lifted the pipes, and sounded a little run of notes, from the lowest to the highest. With the first note, silence folded out of the instrument and wrapped around them. But before Taudde had gone a third of the way through the pipes' range, he must have done something to open up the magecrafted silence—Leilis could well believe he had studied that particular kind of magic, while he was in Lonne—for the notes began to fall into the silence, lightly at first and then with more resonance, and the magecrafted quiet washed away on the rippling scale of the notes.

Lowering the pipes, Taudde said to his cousin, "You see these pipes plainly have more than sufficient range to set a primary message in the major key and a secondary in the minor. If you will assist me, I'm certain we can drop the pipes directly into Aunt Ines' hands. Then we can see about opening one of Iasodde's doors and stepping away from Kalches before your mother . . . or our Grandfather . . . has the opportunity to let us all know how ridiculously we are behaving."

Irelle laughed a little. "Mother may be quicker than you expect," she warned Taudde.

He winced slightly. "Well, I'd rather hear from her than Grandfather, I think, but possibly it would be better to let the pipes fall into your father's hands? Either way, you do know how to set a message into an instrument?"

Irelle did not precisely roll her eyes, but somehow with the merest tilt of her head, she gave the impression that she had. "I'll compose a message for my mother," she said decisively. "And one for our grandfather. I'm quite certain that would be better than if you did it. You consider these magecrafted doors that open into darkness and light, and how to coax a cat to do as we wish instead of just what he wishes, and let me see these pipes." She took the pipes and moved a little away from the rest of the group, holding the instrument up, studying the three matched pairs of pipes thoughtfully.

Leilis decided, rather to her own surprise, that she might like the younger woman. She had not expected to find much in common with a Kalchesene princess. But she thought now that Irelle might manage rather well, even faced with the Dragon of Lirionne. Certainly she could not fault her courage. But then they all, whether of Kalches or Lirionne, had very little choice now but to go forward and . . . see what they would find in Lonne.

Irelle did whatever sorcerers do to set her message into the pipes—to Leilis, it seemed simply like yet more intricate melody work, pretty enough but in no way special—and then tossed the pipes up into the air. Leilis couldn't help but wince to see the instrument treated so, but the pipes did not describe any reasonable path through the empty air and then clatter down on the stony slopes of the mountain. Leilis didn't see the instant at which the pipes vanished; simply, they did not fall. It seemed to her the delicate piping lingered in the air a moment longer before fading, but Irelle had already turned briskly back to join Taudde in trying to coax Dark Of The Moon to show them the door that would lead back into Lonne. Dark did not seem impressed with their efforts, but stared down the mountain with his eyes slitted and his ears tilted back, ignoring them.

"Let me," suggested Karah, rising with her kitten on her shoulder. "I think Moonglow is not quite as willful."

"I could try to call Enkea," Nemienne offered. "But I don't think she'd come. She belongs too much to that house."

"It's just a bit difficult, without one of them to show the way," Taudde said, mildly exasperated. "Because there's plenty of magic in the air, I'm sure we can easily make the door manifest, but it's getting a view of it at just the right angle, that's what we need one or the other of them to show us—" he stopped short, turning quickly, but Leilis saw that his expression was resigned, not in the least fearful. And his cousin sighed and cast her eyes upward. Leilis was therefore not altogether surprised to hear, when she listened carefully, a faint but increasingly clear melody, warm and smooth and clearly played by an instrumentalist of considerable skill. Leilis didn't expect anyone would need to fight or run or do battle with any dragons, but she nevertheless made certain her robes draped elegantly and lifted a hand to her hair, wishing she had a mirror and a comb.

Geradde, without seeming to think about it, put his hand down to Tepres, helping his half-brother clamber stiffly to his feet; Karah took his other arm, murmuring something that made him smile wryly. Nemienne actually laughed, and so that was how Lady Ines ser Dariadd ken Lariodde found them, laughing on the slopes above Kedres.

Lady Ines lowered her simple wooden flute and smiled blandly around at them all. "Irelle, dear, how clever of you," she said warmly. "I mean, disposing of the dragon and then stepping away through the air to Lonne to clarify all these complicated matters with the King of Lirionne—whoever that may prove to be—and all in one afternoon! So very efficient. But it *will* leave everyone in rather a furor at home, don't you think? So I thought I had better just slip away and find you before you go off on your little adventure. That way I can sound a trifle more sincere when I explain things to your father, you know. Not to mention your grandfather." She considered the whole gathering. Then her gaze settled on Tepres, and she added, "One does presume honorable intentions. Whoever should lay final claim to the throne of Lirionne."

Prince Tepres inclined his head and said, a little stiffly, "I assure you, Lady Ines."

Irelle cast her eyes upward. "Yes, Mother, I actually thought I made that clear."

"Well, one does just like to be *quite sure,*" Lady Ines said politely. "After all, I am rather scant of daughters; I would hate to lose you to no purpose." She added to Taudde, "*What* a lot of magic you have let clutter up our mountains, Nephew! I gather you have dealt with the more difficult Seriantes prince? I'm afraid Irelle's message was a little sparing of detail . . ."

Taudde was smiling at his aunt, Leilis was pleased to see. The Kalchesene lady was formidable, clearly so, but anyone could see the fondness between the lady and her kin. That was reassuring. And Leilis guessed that Lady Ines must also prefer to avoid arguments, as she seemed to have made her way up the mountain quite by herself.

"The dragon dealt with Prince Telis," Taudde explained, leaving out nearly everything. "I'm quite sure that Irelle mentioned that much, Aunt. And how *is* Grandfather? Better, may one hope?"

"Refusing to retire to his chambers, the stubborn old man, and quite irate, so you had better begin composing your apology now, Nephew, and this time I trust you won't wait five years to deliver it!"

"No, Aunt, I hope not."

"Good, good. I will assure Berente of that, so please don't delay overlong." Lady Ines tapped her flute idly against her palm. "You young people plan to settle everything among yourselves, and afterward present Kalches with a settled agreement, I gather. Sometimes the direct course is indeed best. I do recommend you bring the beribboned scroll to Berente yourself, Tepres ken Seriantes, and offer it to him with your own hand. I *do* think you will find that serves best. Such niceties are so important. Irelle would have suggested such a courtesy, I'm sure, but one does like to make sure. You would, of course, be quite safe to come and go. I will venture to lay my own word on that."

"I would never doubt it," murmured Tepres. "I will endeavor to do so, if possible."

"Well, then," said Lady Ines in a brisk tone. She smiled at Karah and added without the faintest sign of discomfort, "My dear, your visit was such a pleasure. Speaking broadly. I do hope you and Irelle will be friends. You would be most welcome to return, if you like. I imagine it might be useful for our peoples to become a little more familiar with each other."

Karah smiled shyly and nodded, if not with quite the grace Leilis and the other keiso had been at pains to teach her, but with a simple charm of her own that Leilis supposed would serve.

"Well, then," Lady Ines repeated. "You are endeavoring to open . . . or perhaps discover? . . . one of those impressive magecrafted doorways, I think, Taudde? If I can assist . . ."

"I think you can always assist, Aunt," Taudde said gravely. "I'm sure Dark Of The Moon will accommodate *you*."

The big cat stood up and stretched lazily, his white undercoat showing in ripples through the black. He yawned, blinked his green eye and then his gold eye, leaped off his rock, wound twice around Lady Ines' ankles, accepted her admiration as his due, and then turned and trotted purposefully away toward the cliff edge. And vanished.

"Oh, yes, there it is," Aunt Ines exclaimed, sounded pleased.

Taudde rolled his eyes and lifted his flute, ready to hold onto the door and not let it vanish again, Leilis supposed. She said to Karah, "Don't let Moonglow follow just yet. If we lose it again, we'll need her." Karah nodded, though Leilis suspected—but didn't say—that more than likely if the kitten was determined to follow Dark, Karah would simply find her arms empty and the kitten gone. She murmured, "But it wouldn't matter anyway. Taudde would find a way."

"We all would, if we had to," Karah agreed gently.

-26-

In the end, it was the same door. Taudde had not expected that. He had expected to find a door that opened onto the darkness below Kerre Maraddras. Instead, it was the door that led from Ankennes' house of shadows to this mountain and now, apparently, back again.

Taudde stepped back and nodded to Tepres, who gave a single nod in return and stepped forward to lay his hand on the smooth granite knob. The door swung back, not silently, but with a quiet sound of stiff hinges, and thumped against an unseen wall within the house.

Taudde recognized the wooden paneling of the hallway, and anyone would have recognized the window across the hall, for the sky through that window ignored the deepening dusk to lay a bar of warm afternoon sunlight across the polished floor.

For a moment, no one moved. Taudde was remembering the sharp, deadly battle that had thrust them through this door at the beginning of everything. He could tell, from his quickened breathing and the grim set of his mouth, that Prince Tepres remembered that as well. His man Jeres Geliadde had died in this house, of course. Or at least, out on its porch. From her slow indrawn breath, Leilis, too, had difficult memories of this house. Karah had reached out to Nemienne and held her sister's hand. Nemienne had gone rather pale—even Prince Geradde had tensed.

Even if everything settled so that he stayed in Lonne—and he could hardly guess whether that might happen, far less whether he wished it to—but if he did settle again in Lonne, Taudde thought perhaps he would find a different house. One that was comfortable, and comfortably ordinary. This one had too much history and far, far too much magic layered through its puzzle-box rooms and whimsical hallways.

"Well?" said Irelle. "Shall we go through or stand here to see whether Grandfather or the dragon comes first to inquire what we're about?"

Prince Tepres tilted an eyebrow at this, and stepped through the door with no sign of discomfiture.

Nothing happened. Everything was perfectly quiet, on both sides of the door.

Taudde lifted an inviting hand, meaning for the others to go before him. Irelle passed through, her flute warily half raised, ready to play a sharp, angry defense if such should prove necessary after all. Once she was in Lonne, her head went back a little in surprise at something she heard or saw or felt. But though she frowned, she did not seem greatly alarmed.

Karah stepped across the threshold after Irelle, and then Prince Geradde and Nemienne, Nemienne cautiously but the young prince with every appearance of confidence. Taudde did not entirely believe in that confidence, although . . . perhaps that was unjust. Tepres had moved a little aside and stood now with his arms crossed, not precisely tapping his foot but clearly impatient. But he did not appear in the least alarmed. Taudde certainly found that reassuring.

He said to Leilis, who had waited for him, "Well, shall we forsake this chill shore for the warmth of candlelight?" It was a line from a play he had seen last winter in, of course, the candlelight district of Lonne. He had gone to see it with Leilis, in fact, and remembered it now. It had been a light, amusing play. Nothing like anything that had actually happened. He didn't know why he should think of it at this moment.

But Leilis smiled, and laid her hand in his as though he were escorting her to a play or a supper or something light and amusing, and they stepped forward together.

Then his foot came down on polished wood, and the air was suddenly warmer and heavier, and the sounds that came to him were the small, mysterious sounds that a house made when it spoke to itself and, distant and barely audible, the clatter of hooves on cobbles. Taudde closed the door gently behind him, shutting it on the sharp evening of the Kalchesene heights.

He turned to face the others. Irelle was gazing in fascination at the odd windows and the carved doors farther down the hallway, and Nemienne had gone, warily, with Karah holding her hand and Prince Geradde protectively at their backs, to peer through the music room door. But Prince Tepres had gone the other way, the few steps down the hall to the outside door, and flung it open. He stood there in the doorway looking out at the not-quite-even stone porch and the Lane of Shadows beyond. There was tension in the set of his shoulders, but still no alarm.

That anyone, Sa-Telis or Sehonnes or anyone at all, would leave this house unguarded and, to all appearances, unwatched, seemed . . . a trifle peculiar, certainly. Even now, Taudde suspected some sort of trick or trap, but then Nemienne let out a small cry of relief and unmistakable pleasure, and he turned again, sharply, only to find Enkea strolling toward them from the shadowy depths of the house, her tail swaying upright. But when Nemienne called out to her, the slender gray cat paused and sat down in the bar of sunlight that came in the window, her tail curled neatly around her forefeet, the gray one and the white, and began to purr.

Enkea was an unpredictable creature, but Taudde hardly thought she would behave so if enemies hid elsewhere in the house. Though he knew perfectly well that the day was far from over, he nevertheless found himself relaxing a little.

Nemienne, clearly even more pleased than Taudde, hurried across and lifted the cat to her shoulder, and Enkea purred more loudly as she wound herself about Nemienne's shoulders.

"I believe I'll take that for a sign of good fortune," Geradde remarked. "And better fortune if she will accompany us."

"She may not. She belongs to the house," Taudde warned him. He asked Tepres, "Does the city seem . . . quiet? From what you can see." Though it seemed to him that the Lane of Shadows was not likely to be subject to riots or barricades or an excess of soldierly zeal. He wouldn't be surprised to find one or several mages out there, however. In fact, he couldn't understand why no such presence seemed to be here. "No one is about? Neighbors, soldiers . . . mages?"

But Prince Tepres shook his head. He had already turned his attention outward again, toward the city. He said, "We shall go to the Laodd."

There was a small pause, as everyone looked at Tepres and no one said anything. Even Prince Geradde, who drew a breath as though he would speak, let it out again without a word. So it was Taudde who said, rather tentatively, "Do you not consider it would be wiser to find your father, first, before facing Sehonnes?"

"Yes," Tepres said shortly. "He has gone to the Laodd. Can you not tell it, bardic sorcerer? Listen to the city." Beckoning, he stepped out onto the porch.

The others moved uneasily to join him. Taudde glanced involuntarily at the place where Jeres Geliadde had fallen, but either it had rained or someone had washed the blood away. There was no trace of any stain now.

Prince Tepres did not look down. His attention was all outward, toward the silent city.

For it was silent. Taudde realized that now. It was not like the soundless prison in which he had once spent a handful of extremely unpleasant days, but . . . it wasn't like a normal city evening, either. No street vendors called their wares—well, they might not, perhaps, if they were sufficiently wary of trouble. But the quiet went beyond that. He was certain he had heard riders earlier, but no one rode through the streets now, so far as he could hear. Or walked, so far as he could see. The nearby houses all seemed deserted. All he could hear, listen as carefully as he might, was the distant roar of Nijiadde Falls, where the cataract poured over the cliffs close by the Laodd.

Then he realized that, no, he could hear something else after all. A different kind of murmur, beneath the ever-present thunder of the falls. A susurrus like the waves against the broken shore, but . . . not that, either.

"That is where the people of Lonne have gone," Tepres said abruptly. "They have gone to the Laodd. That is where my father will be." He strode away without waiting for any answer, down the uneven steps and away toward the King's District and the Falls and the cliffs, and the Laodd.

Taudde exchanged a glance with Leilis. Could that be right? Leilis opened one hand in a graceful little gesture like a shrug, then changed it to an equally graceful gesture that invited Taudde to go ahead of her, after Tepres.

"Possibly," Prince Geradde murmured, starting down the steps after his brother before Taudde had quite made up his mind to move. "Possibly. He would have gone there, maybe, if he felt himself able to set down Sehonnes." He glanced over his shoulder at Leilis. "I thought he was worse injured than that."

"He was badly injured," Leilis said, her tone calm and neutral. "But he would have felt the dragon rise, I think."

"Ah!" said Taudde, and then wasn't certain that possibility explained anything after all. Although perhaps the dragon, freed from all ties to the Seriantes line, had nevertheless reached out to restore the king, as it had restored Tepres. Or perhaps—this was Geriodde Seriantes, after all—the king had simply risen from his sickbed despite his injuries and gone to the Laodd, driven by sheer ruthless will. That . . . would be perfectly in character.

But he offered one arm to Leilis, and the other to Irelle, to help her down the uncertain footing of the steps. His cousin was very silent, though she looked this way and that as she descended the steps, considering this unfamiliar city.

And Prince Tepres proved to be correct. They found that out before they had quite made their way to the bridge that led up to the Laodd, for they began to encounter the people of Lonne before they had gone more than halfway through the King's District. Not soldiers or King's Own guardsmen; hardly any men in military red or King's Own black could be seen. And few of the high court nobility, though Taudde saw here and there the muted jewel colors of the low court. But most of the people in the streets wore the plainer garb of tradesmen and merchants, craftspeople and boat-crew, servants and bondsmen. In the distance he saw one graceful company of elegant women in the elaborate blues and pastels of keiso—Leilis looked that way, too, one glance of concern and longing, before firmly turning her face forward again.

"Cloisonné House?" Taudde asked, though he thought the keiso must be too far away for even Leilis to recognize them.

But she said, "Maple Leaf House. They will be greatly concerned, of course. These are Skyblue's sons, after all. Some of those keiso will be their aunts or cousins."

Taudde had not thought of this. He found it fairly

remarkable to think of it now, but he could see that the flower world must know the left-hand princes fairly well. On his other side, Irelle had frowned, quick and appalled, but then she looked at Karah and her expression became more thoughtful.

Everyone, whether tradesman or servant or keiso, merchant or aika or boat-crew, was surprisingly orderly. At least, the good order surprised Taudde, who could imagine his own folk in such a crowd. They would be jostling to see; climbing onto rooftops and calling out to one another; passing along rumors and trying to find out which rumors were true. Here, everyone might be doing the same, but they spoke in low murmurs. Only they were so many, their voices blended together into a sound like the sea. Yes. Very like the sea. He touched his flute, but one would not use flutes or pipes to capture the sound. A kinsana, perhaps. The burring notes of a large kinsana might have expressed something of the nature of this quiet, tense, orderly crowd.

"Or feather drums, perhaps," he murmured, and Irelle looked at him with raised eyebrows and suggested, "Or a big, resonant harp?"

Taudde found a smile pulling at his mouth. He had not realized until this moment how he has missed his own people while he lived in this foreign city. Or perhaps he had missed his cousin's wry humor. He said, "Not a harp. Definitely not," and Irelle smiled.

But they had to walk quickly to come up with Prince Tepres. He did not call out his name, and of course he wasn't mounted and had no troop of soldiers or King's Own guardsmen to show his consequence or press the common people out of his way. At first it was difficult for Tepres to make his way through the increasing crowds, more difficult as they approached the smooth arch of the bridge that crossed from the King's District to the Laodd. But as they came closer to the bridge, low court nobles began to outnumber the common folk, and the occasional vivid jewel tones of high court, and, for the first time, little knots of military red-and-grey appeared.

Then at last someone among the nobility or the soldiers must have recognized Tepres, for although Taudde could not tell who first spoke the heir's name; he discovered that suddenly Tepres' name was in the air, passing from one to another even through the increasing thunder of Nijiadde Falls. Then at last passage became easier, as men and women began to press away from their path, opening a way for the prince to approach the bridge. Tepres did not question this, but began to walk more swiftly, so that Taudde had to lengthen his stride to stay with him, and Nemienne, shortest among them, had almost to run.

"The king has certainly come here before us," Leilis remarked, slightly breathless beside him.

Taudde nodded. That was abundantly clear, now. It was a bit reassuring that he could hear no sounds of battle from the Laodd, no shouting or ring of swords. On the other hand, the bridge was long and the cataract of Nijiadde Falls loudest from this approach, so for all he knew a thousand men might be fighting there before him. But he thought not. He did think not. He thought he *would* hear that, despite the Falls and the murmur of the crowd and the more distant murmur of the sea. Besides, the people would surely know, if there were a great deal of fighting. So he thought that could not be the case.

Tepres reached the foot of the bridge, and there met a close knot of sailors—not the ordinary crew from the fishing fleet or the other close-shore boats, but deep-sea men straight from the deck of one of Lirionne's white-sailed ships. Or more than one: there were a good many of those sailors holding the bridge, with every appearance of determination to keep control of that access to the Laodd. Taudde was thoroughly startled to see them there; he would have expected soldiers or King's Own, not deep-sea sailors. But there was no mistaking their plain undyed clothing, or the boathooks and short-stocked crossbows they carried— sailor's weapons, intended for discouraging pirates rather than ordinary battle.

It was impossible to tell whether Tepres was surprised, but he drew to a sharp halt, his mouth set, looking over the men blocking his way. Taudde came up beside him, his flute in his hand, but he hesitated, uncertain whether the prince would wish to have his path cleared by bardic sorcery.

Then Geradde stepped up beside them both, nudged his brother's arm, and said quietly, "Meiredde's men, I think. But on whose side? Or is Meiredde himself making a claim after all?" Taudde knew nothing of Prince Meiredde, but the undertones of

Geradde's voice were all of disbelief on that last.

Tepres gave his younger half-brother a dark look. "He came in to find *you*, of course. He never liked Sehonnes, and he knows Telis hated you, and he was always fonder of you than of any of us. Assuredly he put into harbor for *your* sake."

Geradde stared at him for a heartbeat. Then he gave a moderately embarrassed shrug. "Well, if that's the case, perhaps those men will make way if I put the request to them—"

But at that moment there was a sharp stir at the other end of the bridge, and Prince Meiredde himself strode out, with a dozen more sailors. He wasn't in any way accoutered as a prince, but it was unmistakable in the way he strode straight forward as though he couldn't imagine anyone daring to balk him. No one did, certainly, though there were soldiers and King's Own as well as sailors holding that end of the bridge. They all, no matter whether they wore red or black or undyed linen, scattered out of Meiredde's way like lesser birds scattering before a sea-eagle. The prince strode straight across the arch of the bridge, waving an impatient hand to clear his own sailors out of his path as well, though they were already moving, almost as smartly as soldiers.

So Prince Meiredde, oldest of the king's left-hand sons, came face to face with his youngest brothers—full and half, Tepres half a step in the fore. Taudde found he had backed away a step or two without having been aware of moving; that was the force in Prince Meiredde. He looked nothing like Tepres and only a little like Geradde, but the impatience and temper in him was very like what Taudde had come to expect from all the Seriantes line. So was the quick, half-angry generosity with which Meiredde clapped Tepres on the arm. "Well!" he said, not quite a shipboard roar, but not far off it. "He'll be glad to see *you*. And you, boy!" This, with a harder buffet, was for Geradde, and Taudde saw the truth of what Tepres had said: those two were friends, more than he had yet seen for any other two princes. "Where have *you* been?" Meiredde demanded. "Everyone said some sorcerer had snatched Tepres off to Kalches, but *no one* said *anything* about *you*. You had me worried, I admit it!"

Geradde blinked, staggering from Meiredde's blow, but grinning, too. "We've been touring the mountains, and very beautiful they are this time of year, but we thought we had better come back and deal with Sehonnes! But I gather you've seen to that for us."

"Nothing like it, nothing like it," boomed Meiredde. "*He* had it all settled before ever I took a hand, as I suppose we should all have expected. So you've been *touring the mountains*, have you?" He gave Taudde and Irelle a sharp glance, but said only, "Well, well. So there's just Telis unaccounted for, eh?"

"Ah!" answered Geradde. "No, in fact. Telis is definitely accounted for. Definitely."

"Well, then! And here you both are, so it's all well, it seems," said Meiredde, and turned a harder look on Tepres. "You left it cursedly late."

Tepres, not in the least taken aback by his older half-brother's manner, turned a hand palm up in a gesture that might have been a concession of the point or a dismissal, but did not suggest temper. He said only, "Not by my choice." Then he glanced up the curve of the bridge. "He had it settled, did he?"

"Well, well, more or less. More or less. He was in the way of it, at least. A bit sharp-set, it seemed to me, and riding the edge of his temper. But then, we don't often agree. The one he wants to see is you, I'll warrant."

Tepres made another slight, ambiguous gesture. "I would like to believe so."

"Ah! Like that, is it?" said Meiredde, more gently than he had yet spoken. "I'll go back up with your lot, I think, and just watch the last winds of the storm blow out."

"Not necessary," said Tepres. Then he added, "Though I thank you for the thought."

"It may not be *necessary*, but even so, I'll go up with you." The eldest prince stood still for a moment, his head on one side, his dark eyes glinting with thought or temper or both. He added, "I'd wish you luck, but it's hardly a matter for luck. But if it comes to that, you've a place on any ship of mine." He glanced at Geradde. "Either of you. Though I may hope you, at least, have been above reproach, boy. Good that one of us has managed as much."

Geradde smiled, a weary smile, but a real one, and gripped Meiredde's arm for a moment. "I'll likely stay close-drawn to shore a while, but I'll hold that thought in mind, brother."

Meiredde shrugged. "The offer stands. Supposing you change your mind. Either of you." Then he stepped aside and waved impatiently for Tepres to go ahead of him, and all his men moved one way or the other, clearing the bridge.

Tepres nodded to his brother, a scant nod, and strode forward, up the arch of the bridge. Geradde followed, and Leilis and Karah and Nemienne all together, and Taudde moved to take the rear position just in case anyone less well intentioned than Meiredde, should come up behind them. But Irelle stopped him with a touch, lifting her eyebrows questioningly. He offered her his arm, guiding her forward, and explained in a low voice, "Obviously the king is indeed within. Evidently he's only just dealt with Sehonnes."

"Yes. And?"

"Well, cousin, you know of course that Geriodde Seriantes had three of his sons put to death over the past year or two, for attempting usurpation."

"Of course," Irelle agreed impatiently. "It was a terrible tale, he must be heartless, but we knew that already. But if he's dealt similarly with Sehonnes, that's well enough, surely."

Taudde cleared his throat. "Attempted usurpation," he repeated. "Even for Sehonnes, it was *attempted* usurpation, or so I gather, as Sehonnes never actually claimed to be king. Unlike Tepres, who quite obviously did, openly, before a foreign king, in a foreign court."

Irelle did not actually miss a step, but she hesitated. Just for a heartbeat. "Oh."

Tepres, nearing the crest of the bridge, swung around, and Taudde realized he had heard them. "*Whatever* happens," he said forcefully, "once we face my father, you will both kindly remember that *he is the king.* You will *under no circumstances* use sorcery against my father. Is that *clearly* understood?"

"But—" Irelle began.

"Under *absolutely no circumstances*," Prince Tepres snapped. "Or, let us be clear, I will hold to *no* understanding regarding borders or boundaries in the north, and let the dragon do as it will. I did *not* bring bardic sorcerers into Lonne for their assistance in usurping the throne from my father, and I absolutely will not have it. Let us be *perfectly clear* on this point." Then, relenting a little, perhaps because of Irelle's appalled expression, he said more gently, "My father will regard our agreement, Irelle Heronn ken Lariodde. Or you may assuredly return to Ankennes' house and to Kalches. Your cousin would escort you, I am certain, and your grandfather would no doubt approve of that decision."

Irelle, rallying, said crisply, "Do you think he would? I'm not so sure of it, Prince Tepres."

Refusing to be diverted, Tepres only insisted, "I assure you, our agreement *will* hold. Yet I will have your vow on this one matter, Irelle Lariodde."

Taudde set a hand on his cousin's arm to stop an intemperate answer. "It won't come to that," he said quietly. "But we shall make that vow, and keep to it. Both of us, Tepres." He layered certainty through the undertones of his voice, compelling belief. "I shall see to it."

Prince Tepres considered him for a long moment. He inclined his head, provisionally accepting this assurance. Then he turned on his heel and went on.

Taudde exchanged a glance with his cousin.

"He knows his own mind," Irelle commented. It was difficult to tell from her tone whether she approved.

Taudde lifted one shoulder. "He has had to look into his own heart over the past year or two."

"I imagine that's true." She hesitated one scant moment and then repeated, "Yes, I can see that must be so."

She didn't ask whether Taudde had been sincere in his vow, or truly believed he could make such a vow on her behalf. But she could hardly mistake the sincerity of the heir's demand. She hesitated only that moment and then went on, after Tepres, toward the massive open doors of the Laodd. She did not take Taudde's arm, but left him to follow her with the others.

Karah had fallen back to join Taudde, and now murmured in his ear, "Your cousin knows her own mind, too, I think."

"She always has," Taudde agreed, and lengthened his stride.

The doors of the Laodd were standing open. Prince Tepres did not hesitate at all, but strode straight through them, the sound of his boot heels changing to a sharper ring as he stepped from the plain stone of the bridge to the marble within. There was a considerable crowd within, mostly high and low court nobles and a good many soldiers, but there was no guard on the doors and certainly no one tried to bar their way.

"The formal throne room," Prince Meiredde told them curtly. Tepres gave him an equally curt nod and turned in that direction, with around them all the startled throng pressing out of their way. Tepres' name ran through the crowd, a surprisingly quiet murmur, but, Taudde thought, in tones of gratifying relief. It seemed to him that most—nearly all—of the people gathered in this outer part of the Laodd closed in behind them and followed. It was fortunate that Tepres had never had any intention of coming secretly to the Laodd, because he surely could not have arranged a more public return if he'd planned it out for a year beforehand.

Taudde had not previously had occasion to enter the formal throne room, and found it grander and more daunting than he had expected: all sweeping black marble below and vaulted white ceiling above, with red porphyry columns in rows. The lines of columns and the huge, dramatic paintings on the walls both served to lead the eye along the length of the hall until one's attention was focused at last on the massive grey throne at the far end.

The throne room was crowded as well, more so than the outer parts of the Laodd had been, even before they came in, trailing all their onlookers. In the main the gathering here seemed to consist of high court and soldiers; by this time he was not surprised. All along their path through the city, the throngs of people had become higher and higher ranked. But when he cast a look over his shoulder, he saw that more than a few of the low-court nobles and even the common people had followed Tepres as well. A low murmur rose on all sides as men—and women, for here there were more than a few court ladies as well—turned to whisper to their neighbors. Yet it was a subdued murmur. No one called out or cried Tepres' name. No one called out at all.

But everyone pressed to the sides of the hall, leaving a clear path that stretched from the entryway and along the rows of pillars straight to the foot of the throne.

Off to one side, not far from the entryway, lay the sprawled body of Prince Sehonnes. Taudde had not, to the best of his knowledge, ever laid eyes on Sehonnes. Save once, briefly, of course, outside Ankennes' house, when the prince had lost his hand. The prince had lost more than a hand now. A massive weapon like a giant arrow jutted from his chest—a shipboard harpoon, in fact—making it obvious that Meiredde must have had more to do with his brother's death than he had implied. A pair of the soldiers might have been about to move his body, but they, too, had moved away from the path that lay from the entryway to the throne, so that the prince's body lay abandoned and alone in the midst of the cleared space, as though arranged there solely to catch the eye of anyone who entered.

The king himself, however, drew attention from even such a spectacle. Geriodde Nerenne ken Seriantes occupied the great throne as though he always had and always would; as though, Sehonnes' body or no, everyone had merely dreamed the past weeks and the battles of princes and dragons. Even from a distance, even without moving at all, the king owned this vast room completely. But, beside Taudde, Nemienne's swift indrawn breath made him glance down at her and then follow the direction of her gaze, so that he saw that actually there were a few people close by the throne and that one of them was a girl he had met.

Then he realized that this was Nemienne's sister Enelle. He looked at her in startlement. She looked . . . ordinary. Tense, but not frightened; sturdy more than graceful; but she stood closer to the throne than anybody and, so far from overwhelmed by her nearness to power, she looked like she was thinking hard. But she had seen them—of course everyone had seen them come in, and he saw her gaze snag on Karah and then on Nemienne. Some of the tension went out of her all at once, and her sudden smile made her pretty. Beside Taudde, Karah murmured to Nemienne, but his attention was caught mostly by Prince Tepres and he did not listen.

Tepres, too, had halted just inside the entryway. His gaze was steady on his father. Beside him and a step back, Geradde began to say something, and Meiredde at the same time, but Tepres did not listen to them. His shoulders rose and fell with a quick, forceful breath. Then he strode forward without looking back, as though he were entirely alone in the hall—as though no one was present at all save for himself and his father.

By one of those unspoken moments of common accord, the others all held back a little—not only Taudde and Leilis, but also Karah and Irelle, Geradde and Nemienne and even Prince Meiredde, who hardly seemed the kind to retire from public attention. They all followed, but a little behind, so that Prince Tepres traversed the entire length of the hall alone.

It seemed to take an impossibly long time to walk that whole distance. It seemed to take an hour, or an age. But Tepres never faltered or turned his gaze aside. He walked steadily forward until he came near the throne, near enough to be able to speak to his father without raising his voice. Then he stopped, and stood still, and the rest of them trailed to a halt as well, leaving a little distance still between themselves and the prince.

Except that Geriodde Seriantes was not entirely impassive, after all. He did not smile, precisely. But the look in his eyes and the subtle tuck at corners of his mouth was somehow more expressive than a smile.

Already spare, the king had lost flesh, Taudde saw. The bones of his face were stark and severe, and there was a disturbing pallor to his skin, and the rhythm of his breathing was quick and shallow His right hand was wrapped in fine dark linen, and one could see from the shape of the bandages that he must have lost fingers. But one hardly saw any of these signs of recent injury or illness for the sheer weight of the king's attention.

Geriodde Seriantes set his uninjured hand on the smooth-carved arm of his throne, and rose to his feet, with a smoothness that seemed practiced rather than easy. He said, quietly but with a wealth of feeling, "My son—"

Then Tepres went heavily to his knees; and not only to his knees, but down all the way, with his face against the shining black marble of the floor.

There was a brief, terrible silence.

The king asked him, expressionless, "Tepres, my son. What have you done?"

Tepres straightened, although he did not get to his feet. He held up his right hand, palm inward, so that the ring showed—the iron ring, the dragon ring, its ruby eyes glittering in the light of the hall.

The king did not move or speak.

Tepres said, his voice clear and steady, "With this I have claimed the title of the Dragon of Lirionne. With this I have made agreements with foreign kings; not in your name, but in my own."

King Geriodde slowly sank back into his throne, moving carefully.

Tepres made a movement of his left hand to his right, clearly intending to take off the ring. But the king lifted a finger, halting that motion—halting all movement everywhere, by what Taudde could tell. It hardly seemed that anyone in the entire throne room even breathed.

"My son," said the king. "What agreements have you made?"

Tepres did not gesture toward Irelle, nor even nod toward her. They valued subtlety in Lonne, and so he only glanced her way. It was enough. Geriodde Seriantes looked at her. He did not frown, but the stillness of his expression deepened. He turned his gaze back to his son and lifted one eyebrow, minutely.

"My wife-to-be," stated Tepres. "Irelle Heronn ken Lariodde, eldest daughter and heir of Heronn Tamones ken Lariodde, eldest son and heir of Chontas Berente ser Omientes ken Lariodde. Affianced and agreed. The wedding gift is to be the grant of the town of Anharadde; the grant of all the lands east and south of Anharadde and north of Teleddes, including even Brenedde. All these lands, Lirionne will return to Kalches as a gift on the day of my wedding to Irelle Heronn ken Lariodde."

There was a stark pause. Taudde was vividly aware of Karah, her eyes wide, gazing from the king to Tepres and back again, sparing an occasional glance for Enelle. Irelle ran her thumb along the length of her silver flute and gazed at the king, frowning. Tepres did not look at anyone but his father.

But Geriodde Seriantes said merely, "I see."

"In the rising of the dragon of Lonne, in the breaking of the tie between the dragon and the Seriantes line, of which I am certain you must be aware . . . it seemed best to ensure a generation of peace." Tepres held up his hand again, so that the ruby eyes of the dragon ring caught the light and flared like tiny drops of blood. "So I have bound Lirionne and the throne of Lirionne. That agreement will stand, if you will permit it. I have assured my wife-to-be that you are wise and that this agreement will stand. Let all else wait for this marriage. That is what I ask of you. That is all I ask."

"It is a considerable request," said Geriodde Seriantes. But though Taudde listened carefully, he heard no anger in the king's voice, but rather something that might almost have been a kind of amusement, though very dry. The king said, this time to Irelle, "Princess Irelle Heronn ken Lariodde. You came here from your own country in this expectation?"

Irelle moved a small step forward. "I saw your dragon rise, O king of Lirionne. But I had thought of it before that moment. It seemed a way to settle matters between Lirionne and Kalches. When there is a child of Kalchesene blood on the Dragon's throne, my people will be content. When the king of Lirionne is cousin to the king of Kalches, perhaps then our two lands will find a gentler means of settling disputes about borders."

"Shared blood is hardly a guarantee of amity," the king observed, his tone biting. But then he said more gently, "But perhaps it may prove so in this instance. So you agreed to affiance yourself to my son. Giving up your claim to your grandfather's throne. And you hold to that resolution even now."

Irelle turned her hands palm up. "My grandfather will rule for some years yet, I think, and my father for many years after that. And he has a son. And . . ." she slid a sideways look at Taudde. "I have found myself dreaming of the sea, in recent years." At last she glanced at Tepres. "Also, I have found much to admire in the heir of the Dragon."

The king smiled, a barely perceptible curve of the lips that might or might not have warmed his eyes. "Have you?" he said. "So have I. Very well. That agreement may stand, if you will have it so."

A murmur went through the gathering, like wind across the sea. The king stilled it with the lift of a finger and turned his head, regarding his son with cool reserve. Tepres met his eyes for a long moment and then, with a swift movement, took the dragon ring off his finger, held it out to his father flat on his palm, and bowed his head.

The king drew a slow breath.

Taudde, who had been waiting for the precise moment and saw no likelihood of a better, said without moving, "He did not claim that ring until he believed your death confirmed. He believed it because what seemed reliable word came to us in Kalches, and we all thought it seemed certain." Lowering his voice, he layered intensity into his quiet words. "When I brought him word of your death, he wept for grief."

Tepres flinched, and the king's head came up sharply.

Leilis said softly, "When I brought him word that you lived, he wept for joy."

But the king's expressionless mask did not ease, even for that.

Then Enelle, disregarding all protocol and propriety and every possible fear of the king's temper, laid her hand on his arm, above his injured hand. Bending to his ear, she murmured—quietly, but not so softly that Taudde did not hear— "Geriodde Seriantes. You have put enough of your sons to death. You know it would be wrong to do it again. It would be wrong for Lirionne, and wrong for Tepres, and worst of all for you."

And from beside Taudde, Karah smiled at her sister as though catching her balance at last amid all these events. She came forward a graceful step, and murmured, in the same low tone, "Sometimes an age should end. Let this be the end of the age of blood and iron."

She spoke not with force, like a bard trying to persuade a king; nor cajolingly, like a woman trying to sway the father of her beloved; but with simple trust.

For a long time, the king did not move. Taudde thought of the dragon saying, *You suspect me of kindness*, and thought that the binding between the dragon and the Seriantes might be broken, but that nevertheless a great deal of the dragon lingered yet in Geriodde Seriantes.

Then at last the king stood. He moved forward slowly to stand over his son. Tepres knelt still, holding the ring out to his father in a hand that, for all his undoubted courage, trembled just perceptibly, if one observed closely.

The king took the ring, and held it up for a moment. Then he set it back in Tepres' palm, bending his son's fingers closed about it. "It will do where it is," he said.

Jerking his head up, Tepres stared at him.

"It will do very well where it is," the king repeated softly. Then he said, not loudly, but clearly, so that his words carried, "Let the ring pass to my heir. Let the crown and the throne and the title pass to my heir. Let the age of the Dragons end, and a new age begin."

This time, the murmurs that exploded through the hall were not so quiet. But Taudde clearly heard Tepres begin, bewildered, "But—Father—"

"You have claimed it. I confirm your claim. Not all that has been broken can be—or should be—repaired."

Tepres gazed at him. He said after a moment, "The dragon told me to say that to you."

Geriodde Seriantes inclined his head, seeming unsurprised. "You do not need to say it. I already know it." He smiled faintly, a startling expression on his severe face. "I am not young, my son. I am not well. I shall go south, I think. To Kennedde, perhaps. Or Komes, by the mouth of the river. I am accustomed to the voice of a river as well as the eternal sea, and Komes is warm in every season." He looked past Tepres, toward his other sons, standing now side by side in astonished stillness. "Perhaps your ship might bear me as far as Komes, Meiredde."

After a moment, Meiredde said, his deep voice for once subdued, "I would be honored to carry you wherever you wish to go, of course."

"Thank you, Meiredde." Turning once more to Tepres, Geriodde Seriantes added, "You must do better than I with your sons. Teach them to be friends to one another. Teach them that a king must be ruthless, but that power wielded without mercy is bitter to the taste, as ash is bitter on the tongue."

Tepres answered, in a low voice, "You have taught me that." He slid the ring back onto his finger, rose to his feet, and looked around. "Geradde," he said, holding out his hand. "Until I get another, you are my heir."

Geradde opened his mouth, shut it again, stepped forward, and bowed—then blurted, "A child of Kalchesene blood would be much better, Tepres!"

Tepres almost smiled. "You see," he said to his father. Then he turned to Irelle, seeming now, faced with his wife-to-be, rather uncertain.

Karah turned to smile at the other young woman. "We shall be friends," she said firmly. "We shall be almost sisters. Since you have no mother here, you must certainly stay in Cloisonné House until you are married. That *is* proper, isn't it, Leilis?"

"Not entirely," Leilis said drily, tilting an amused eyebrow at Karah. "Nor would it be proper for the princess to take rooms in the Laodd until she is married." She glanced at Enelle and added, "She could stay with your birth-sisters, however."

Enelle said, with a look from Tepres to Karah, "We would—we would be honored, if the—the Princess Irelle would allow us to show her Lonne."

"Yes!" said Nemienne, obviously pleased with this idea. "She could teach me a little about sorcery, and I could teach her a little magecraft. And if Prince Tepres can visit her, then Geradde could visit me, too! That would be perfectly proper, wouldn't it Leilis?"

"Perhaps—" Irelle began, sounding not quite certain.

"You will find all that family agreeable," Leilis assured Irelle, for the moment laying aside her keiso manners and sounding practical and brisk. "They're sensible and kind and not afraid of bardic sorcerers. To be sure, they're not even low court, or not yet, but after all, any family which shelters the king in times of trouble is likely to find its fortunes rising."

"Oh, my littlest sister, Liaska, will *love* you!" Karah promised Irelle.

Enelle said hastily, "But, but, if you are a sorceress, Princess, you must promise not to teach Liaska sorcery! She is a handful and a half already!"

Irelle laughed at this, and shrugged doubtfully, but she said to Karah, "If you think it best, I would be pleased to visit your family," which for Irelle, in Taudde's opinion, was a very good beginning.

Tepres, giving a small, relieved nod at everyone's obvious efforts to be accommodating, turned back to his father. "You are fixed on this course?"

"I am," Geriodde answered. "Nor will I turn from it."

"Well," said Tepres, and seemed somewhat at a loss.

Taudde commented, "This must surely be the first Seriantes Dragon to yield his throne while yet among the living. It will make a splendid song."

"Taudde—" said Tepres, startled. "I hardly think a *song*—"

"Filled with dragons and heroism," Taudde continued remorselessly. "A romantic song, of course. A brave young prince—a courageous young sorcerer-princess—I don't imagine it will be necessary to include trivial roles such as my own. No. A smoother plot would be better. You and Irelle, and behind you two kings, grown old in bitterness." He met Geriodde Seriantes' eyes and said steadily, "Two kings who each put bitterness aside for the sake of their children and their peoples and their countries. That is the proper ending for a song, when kings are great-hearted."

"Great-hearted, is it?" There was a wry crook to Geriodde Seriantes' mouth. "If you will have it so, Chontas Taudde ken Lariodde. You will sing this song of yours for your grandfather, will you?"

"I will, eminence," Taudde promised him.

"I regret I will not see his expression. If you should travel as far south as Komes, you may describe his reaction to me."

"I will," Taudde said again. "I have no doubt I will come eventually to Komes. I shall travel from the north to the south and back again, no doubt." He looked at Leilis.

"I shall enjoy travelling the world," Leilis said, sedately. "Until I take up my place as Mother of Cloisonné House."

"Not for years, surely," said Taudde. "But we will return to the Pearl of the West." He knew it was true. He could not quite keep from smiling, though he tried. Well, tried somewhat. Not very hard. The dragon might return, unpredictable and dangerous. Men might quarrel and threaten war. Anything might happen, and probably would. But still he could not keep from smiling. He said again, "We will always come back together to Lonne," and knew it was true.

ACKNOWLEDGMENTS

Thanks to everyone who critiqued the story, and everyone who helped catch typos before they had time to breed in the manuscript and infect the final book

And thank you to everyone who, having enjoyed this book, took the time to write a review.

ALSO BY

Black Dog Series:
BLACK DOG
BLACK DOG SHORT STORIES I (ebook)
PURE MAGIC
BLACK DOG SHORT STORIES II (ebook)
BLACK DOG SHORT STORIES I & II (paper edition)
SHADOW TWIN
BLACK DOG SHORT STORIES III (ebook)

THE CITY IN THE LAKE (Knopf)

The Griffin Mage Trilogy (Orbit):
LORD OF THE CHANGING WINDS
LAND OF THE BURNING SANDS
LAW OF THE BROKEN EARTH

THE FLOATING ISLANDS (Knopf)

HOUSE OF SHADOWS (Orbit)
DOOR INTO LIGHT

THE KEEPER OF THE MIST (Knopf)

THE MOUNTAIN OF KEPT MEMORY (Saga)

THE WHITE ROAD OF THE MOON (Knopf)

WINTER OF ICE AND IRON (Saga)

PRAISE FOR RACHEL NEUMEIER'S BOOKS

THE CITY IN THE LAKE

"It's the poetic, shimmering language and fascinating unfolding of worlds that elevates this engrossing story beyond its formula...Fans of Sharon Shinn's books will find a similar celebration of the natural world—from the dense darkness of a forest to the 'crystalline music' of the stars—in this vividly imagined debut."—Booklist, starred review.

"Oh my God, I was so not prepared for how awesome this book is. Prose, setting, story, characters, everything is top notch and I too loved this book."—Ana Grilo, the Book Smugglers.

THE FLOATING ISLANDS

An ALA Best Fiction for Young Adults selection
A Junior Library Guild selection
A Kirkus best-of-2011 selection

"Intelligent, richly detailed fantasy featuring two young cousins battered by losses, personal passions, and larger events...The author delineates complex characters, geographies and societies alike with a dab hand, deftly weaves them all— along with dragons of several sorts, mouthwatering kitchen talk, flashes of humor, and a late-blooming romance—into a suspenseful plot and delivers an outstanding tale that is self-contained but full of promise for sequels."— Kirkus Reviews, starred review.

HOUSE OF SHADOWS

"I loved *House of Shadows*. The characters, writing, and magic captivated me, but there was a lot to love in the details as well—the dragon, the cats who were characters in their own right, female characters with different situations and types of inner strength, and just a little bit of romance."—Kristen at Fantasy Book Café.

THE GRIFFIN MAGE TRILOGY

"The Griffin Mage Trilogy is recommended to anyone who enjoys a fantasy story that focuses on vivid storytelling with more emphasis on interaction instead of bold fighting."—Jasper de Joode, Fantasy Book Review.

"A theme running throughout the trilogy is the importance of trusting people with the freedom to make their own decisions, even if you may not like the result. The plot of *Lord of the Changing Winds* is full of difficult moral choices, so if you like your fantasy to be subtle and complex, this could be the trilogy for you."—Geraldine at Fantasy Reads.

THE KEEPER OF THE MIST

"Reminiscent of classic YA fantasy in the vein of *Howl's Moving Castle* and old-school Robin McKinley, *The Keeper of the Mist* is utterly, unequivocally awesome."—Thea James, The Book Smugglers.

THE WHITE ROAD OF THE MOON

"A richly rewarding stand-alone story evoking far more color than its titular tint might suggest."—Kirkus, starred review.

"An imaginative, slow-building YA fantasy… Neumeier [chooses to focus on] bonds of friendship and respect between the characters rather than romance. It's a refreshing change of pace from the pervasive romance-oriented young adult fantasies. … reminded me distinctly of Robin McKinley's style."— Fantasy Literature blog.

WINTER OF ICE AND IRON

"Neumeier's writing has a spare, haunting quality...Best of all are her characters … they work together beautifully, and their romance has a number of interesting and unconventional complications. The character's hook; the writing holds. It's comfort food, but more satisfying than most."—NK Jemisin, NYT book review.

"There's very little I can say that can even do any sort of justice to the wonderfully intricate story, the characters that get under your skin, and the intrigue seeping through the pages. … You need to take your time with this, to become immersed, in this slow-burning fantasy that will reward you if you devote your time to it." —Utopia State of Mind blog.

Rachel Neumeier

Made in the USA
San Bernardino, CA
09 July 2019